TORTURE OF THE
MOUNTAIN MAN

Look for these exciting Western series from
bestselling authors
WILLIAM W. JOHNSTONE
and **J. A. JOHNSTONE**

The Mountain Man

Preacher: The First Mountain Man

Luke Jensen, Bounty Hunter

Those Jensen Boys!

The Jensen Brand

MacCallister

Flintlock

Perley Gates

The Kerrigans: A Texas Dynasty

Sixkiller, U.S. Marshal

Texas John Slaughter

Will Tanner, U.S. Deputy Marshal

The Frontiersman

Savage Texas

The Trail West

The Chuckwagon Trail

Rattlesnake Wells, Wyoming

AVAILABLE FROM PINNACLE BOOKS

TORTURE OF THE MOUNTAIN MAN

WILLIAM W. JOHNSTONE
with J. A. Johnstone

PINNACLE BOOKS
Kensington Publishing Corp.
www.kensingtonbooks.com

PINNACLE BOOKS are published by

Kensington Publishing Corp.
119 West 40th Street
New York, NY 10018

PUBLISHER'S NOTE
Following the death of William W. Johnstone, the Johnstone family
is working with a carefully selected writer to organize and complete
Mr. Johnstone's outlines and many unfinished manuscripts to create additional novels in all of his series like The Last Gunfighter, Mountain Man,
and Eagles, among others. This novel was inspired by Mr. Johnstone's
superb storytelling.

All Kensington titles, imprints, and distributed lines are available at special
quantity discounts for bulk purchases for sales promotions, premiums,
fund-raising, educational, or institutional use. Special book excerpts or
customized printings can also be created to fit specific needs. For details,
write or phone the office of the Kensington sales manager: Kensington
Publishing Corp., 119 West 40th Street, New York, NY 10018, attn: Sales
Department; phone 1-800-221-2647.

ISBN-13: 978-0-7860-3553-3
ISBN-10: 0-7860-3553-6

First printing: December 2018

10 9 8 7 6 5 4 3 2 1

Printed in the United States of America

First electronic edition: December 2018

ISBN-13: 978-0-7860-3554-0
ISBN-10: 0-7860-3554-4

THE JENSEN FAMILY
FIRST FAMILY OF THE AMERICAN FRONTIER

Smoke Jensen—*The Mountain Man*

The youngest of three children and orphaned as a young boy, Smoke Jensen is considered one of the fastest draws in the West. His quest to tame the lawless West has become the stuff of legend. Smoke owns the Sugarloaf Ranch in Colorado. Married to Sally Jensen, father to Denise ("Denny") and Louis.

Preacher—*The First Mountain Man*

Though not a blood relative, grizzled frontiersman Preacher became a father figure to the young Smoke Jensen, teaching him how to survive in the brutal, often deadly Rocky Mountains. Fought the battles that forged his destiny. Armed with a long gun, Preacher is as fierce as the land itself.

Matt Jensen—*The Last Mountain Man*

Orphaned but taken in by Smoke Jensen, Matt Jensen has become like a younger brother to Smoke and even took the Jensen name. And like Smoke, Matt has carved out his destiny on the American frontier. He lives by the gun and surrenders to no man.

Luke Jensen—*Bounty Hunter*
Mountain Man Smoke Jensen's long-lost brother Luke Jensen is scarred by war and a dead shot—the right qualities to be a bounty hunter. And he's cunning, and fierce enough, to bring down the deadliest outlaws of his day.

Ace Jensen and Chance Jensen—*Those Jensen Boys!*
Smoke Jensen's long-lost nephews, Ace and Chance, are a pair of young-gun twins as reckless and wild as the frontier itself . . . Their father is Luke Jensen, thought killed in the Civil War. Their uncle Smoke Jensen is one of the fiercest gunfighters the West has ever known. It's no surprise that the inseparable Ace and Chance Jensen have a knack for taking risks—even if they have to blast their way out of them.

PROLOGUE

From the *Fort Worth Democrat:*

TERRIBLE CRIME !

When the sexton of St. Luke's Episcopal Church arrived to carry out his assigned duties on Monday most recent, he made a most appalling discovery. Seeing that the rector was not in his office, and knowing that to be unusual, Bill Donohue went to the parsonage to inquire as to why the priest had not arrived at his usual time and place.

He had no idea of the gruesome scene he would behold when he looked through the window. There, he saw a sight that would make the blood run cold on even the most insentient person.

Hurrying inside he discovered the bodies of Fr. Damon Grayson, his wife Millicent, and their two small children, Jerome and Marie. It is believed that the motive for the murder was the theft of the previous Sunday's collection of $117.37.

So heinous is the crime that a five thousand dollar reward has been offered for any information leading to the capture of the unknown perpetrator.

Tyrone Greene was the blacksmith, machinist, and all-round handyman for Live Oaks Ranch, a 120,000-acre spread that lay just north of Ft. Worth. His position was second only to that of Clay Ramsey, the ranch foreman. He had been very disturbed by the murder of Father Grayson, particularly since Tyrone was not only a parishioner, but a vestryman.

It was three weeks after the murder when Tyrone was moving the saddles of the cowboys so he could do some repairs to the wall. When he moved the saddle belonging to Cutter MacMurtry, one of the cowboys, a silver cup fell from the saddlebag. Tyrone picked it up and gasped. He examined the inscription.

In honor of the
First Communion
Of my daughter

TAMARA GREENE

Tyrone had given this very cup to St. Luke's Church ten years earlier for the christening of his daughter, Tamara. He knew there was only one way Cutter MacMurtry could have it, and that was to have stolen it. Going into his quarters, Tyrone got his pistol belt down from the hook where it hung and belted it around his waist.

One month later, after Cutter MacMurtry was tried and convicted for the murder of Father Grayson and his family, Tyrone Greene was presented with a check for five thousand dollars. He had not taken Cutter MacMurtry in to the sheriff for the money. He had done it because he wanted justice for Father Grayson.

But the money promised a bright future for him and his family.

When Mel Saddler, jailer for the Tarrant County jail, looked up, he saw a man with rough, blunt features and eyes as gray as a dreary winter day. This was Hatchett MacMurtry.

"I'm here to see my brother."

"You've been here before, MacMurtry, so you know the routine," Saddler said. "Take off your gun belt."

Hatchett MacMurtry did so.

"Now, hold your arms out while I search you for any weapons."

Hatchett MacMurtry complied, and Saddler made a thorough check for any hidden guns or knives. Finding none, he stepped back.

"All right, you can go back there to tell your brother good-bye," Saddler said with a little chuckle.

"What do you mean, good-bye? I just got here."

"We'll be hangin' 'im tomorrow, 'n there will be a crowd gathered around for the show," Saddler said.

"When I said you could tell 'im good-bye, that's 'cause I figured you'd want to do it alone, when there was just the two of you."

"Yeah," Hatchett said.

Saddler led Hatchett back to Cutter MacMurtry's cell.

"Hello, brother," Hatchett said.

"I wasn't sure you'd come to see me," Cutter replied.

Hatchett turned toward Saddler. "I thought you said this would be a private meeting."

"I'm supposed to stay here to keep an eye on all the visitors," Saddler replied.

"Why? You done searched me pretty good, you know I ain't got no gun to give 'im."

Saddler sighed, then looked around. "All right, seein' as your brother's goin' to get hung tomorrow anyhow, I can't see as it be any way wrong to let you talk amongst yourselves. I'm goin' to close 'n lock this outer door, call me when you're ready to leave."

"All right," Hatchett agreed.

"You goin' to watch me hang tomorrow?" Cutter asked, after the deputy closed and locked the outer door.

"No."

"Why not? It might be good to have a friendly face in the crowd."

"I ain't goin' to watch you, 'cause you ain't goin' to hang.'

"You got some way to get me out of it?"

Hatchett smiled. "Go back there 'n look at the bars on your window."

"What for?"

"Just do it, Cutter," Hatchett said, the tone of his voice reflecting his irritation.

Cutter walked to the back of his cell to examine the bars that were on the back window.

"Do you see a piece of rawhide tied around one of the bars?"

"Yeah."

"Pull it up, but be careful, you don't want to lose what's on the other side."

Cutter did as he was instructed, and when the other end of the string drew even with the window, he saw a Colt .44 suspended by the rawhide string tied around the trigger guard.

"Damn!" Cutter said with a broad smile. He pulled the gun in, then untied the cord.

"Now, pass it through to me," Hatchett ordered.

Cutter did so, and as soon as he had the gun back in hand, he called out for the jailer.

"Damn," Saddler said as he returned and unlocked the outer door. "That wasn't a long visit.'

"It don't take long to say good-bye," Hatchett said.

As soon as Slater stepped inside, Hatchett put the barrel of the pistol against Saddler's head.

"Where did you . . ."

That was as far as he got with the question before Hatchett pulled the trigger and blew the jailer's brains out.

Moving quickly, Hatchett got the jailer's keys and unlocked the cell door.

"What do we do now?" Cutter asked.

"We get out of here. I borrowed some money and a couple of horses from Live Oaks," Hatchett said,

"Colonel Conyers loaned us some money and horses?" Cutter asked, surprised by the news.

Hatchett chuckled. "Yeah, only he don't know it. 'N this here ain't the kind of loan that's ever goin' to be paid back."

CHAPTER ONE

Four years later, Sugarloaf Ranch

Smoke Jensen, the owner of Sugarloaf Ranch, stood out on the front porch, one hand leaning against one of the porch rails, and the other hand holding a cup of coffee. Smoke was a big man, over six feet tall, and with a spread of shoulders that could just about cover an axe handle. He had hair the color of ripened wheat, though not much of it could seen at the moment since it was covered with a low-crowned, brown hat.

To the east, the sun had not yet crested Casteel Ridge, but it had pushed the early morning darkness away. Pearlie, Smoke's ranch foreman, came toward him.

"Good mornin', Pearlie."

"Mornin', Smoke. We picked up six cows overnight."

"What?"

"Herefords, they were easy enough to pick out.

According to the brand, they belong to Mr. Greene. I'll get one of the hands to take the cows back."

"I thought you had a full day planned for all the hands," Smoke said.

"Yeah I do, we're re-fencing some of the south quarter. There's gaps all along the fence. More 'n likely that's how these cows got through.

"You keep the men working," Smoke said. "I'll take the cows back."

"You sure you want to do that? It'll take up half your mornin', over there and back," Pearlie said,

"I don't mind. Sally has some books she wants to take over to Tyrone's daughter, so this will give me a chance to do it.

"I'll get the cows gathered up for you," Pearlie offered.

Diamond T Ranch

"Tamara, go out to the barn and tell your father to come to breakfast," Edna said.

"Yes, Mama," Tamara replied. Tamara was a very pretty fourteen-year-old girl, a good student who had it in mind to be a schoolteacher.

"What on earth would make you want to be a schoolteacher?" one of her classmates had asked. "Why, schoolteachers can never get married."

"Yes, they can," Tamara had answered. "Miz Sally used to be a schoolteacher, and now she is married to Mr. Smoke Jensen. I want to be just like her . . . she's the smartest person I've ever met."

That conversation had taken place on the last day of school. Now, even though school was out for the summer, Tamara continued to study, reading books that their neighbor Sally Jensen had provided.

"Papa? Papa, are you out here?" Tamara called, carrying out her mother's bidding.

"I'm in the barn, darlin'," a man's voice answered. Tamara's father, Tyrone Greene, appeared in the barn door.

"Mama says to wash up, and come to breakfast."

"Your mother told me to wash up?" Tyrone asked, a grin spreading across his face.

"No, Papa, I'm saying that. You've been working in the barn where there are all kinds of dirty things. Wouldn't you want to clean up?"

Tyrone laughed. "For you, I'll clean up."

As father and daughter walked back to the house, they saw a strange horse out front.

"Who's here?" Tyrone asked. "Whose horse is that?"

"I don't know," Tamara replied. "It wasn't there when I came to get you."

"It looks like we may have company for breakfast. I hope your mama made enough."

"She always makes enough biscuits and bacon, you know that. All she'll have to do is fry a couple more eggs," Tamara said.

"Well, let's go see who it is, shall we?"

Tyrone and Tamara stepped up onto the porch, then Tyrone opened the door.

"Tell me, Mrs. Greene, what vagabond have you agreed to feed this morning? I hope you have enough . . ."

The smile left Tyrone's face to be replaced by an expression of fear and horror. There was a man standing next to his wife, with an evil grin on his face and a pistol in his hand. He was holding the pistol to Edna's temple. The uninvited visitor was a big man with a bald head, a protruding brow, and practically no neck. It was someone that Tyrone knew well.

"Hello, Greene," the man said.

"Cutter MacMurtry, what are doing here? I thought you . . ."

"You thought I'd been hung? Well, they was plannin' on doin' that, but me 'n my brother thought it might be a good idea to leave Texas, before it was that they could ever actual get around to a-doin' it," MacMurtry said.

Tyrone looked around. "Is Hatchett here with you?"

"I don't rightly know where he is now. We sort of separated oncet we come to Colorado." MacMurtry grinned again. "I see that you have yourself a nice little ranch. How'd you get it?"

"I bought it."

"You was one of Colonel Conyers' top hands, 'n I've heard he paid some of you a lot better 'n he paid me 'n a lot of the other workin' hands. But I don't figure that even the Colonel paid enough for you to buy a ranch like this. Where'd you get the money?"

Tyrone didn't answer.

"How much of a reward did you collect for turning me in? Five thousand dollars, is what I heard. Yes, sir, five thousand dollars would be enough money to buy yourself a real nice little ranch. So, you come up here from Texas 'n used that five thousand dollars of blood money to do just that, didn't you?"

Tyrone still didn't answer.

"Fact is, I wouldn't be surprised if you didn't still have some o' that money here, in the house."

"I don't keep money in the house," Tyrone said. "I have very little money anyway, as I have everything invested in this ranch."

"Well then, in that case I'll have to find some other way of gettin' back at you, won't I?"

MacMurtry turned his pistol toward the rancher and pulled the trigger. Tyrone grunted once, put his hand over the bullet hole, then collapsed

"Tyrone!" Edna yelled in horror. "You have killed him!"

"Don't worry, I'll send you to join him," MacMurtry said, and putting the pistol back up to her temple again, he pulled the trigger a second time. Blood, brain tissue, and skull fragments blew out of the exit wound in Edna's head as she went down.

Tamara had watched the whole thing in a state of shock. She had wanted to beg him not to shoot her mother or father, but she was totally unable to make a sound.

"Well, now, you warn't much more 'n a little girl the last time I seen you. You've growed up some, 'n ain't you a purty thing, though?" MacMurtry said. He put his pistol back in his holster and started toward her. "You been made a woman yet?" he asked.

Tamara's eyes got wider in terror.

"You know what I think? I think you ain't never had no man before. This is your lucky day, girlie. I'm goin' to show you what it's all about."

MacMurtry reached up to put his hand on the collar of her dress, then jerked it down. The dress parted, exposing more of her.

"Yes, ma'am, you're goin' to enjoy this," MacMurtry said. "Though prob'ly not as much as I am."

* * *

Just over an hour later Smoke Jensen was driving six Hereford cows in the direction of Tyrone Greene's ranch. Smoke was a rancher and it wasn't unusual to see him driving cattle, but it was unusual to see him driving Herefords, since he was now running only Angus cattle on Sugarloaf Ranch.

The cows he was pushing all had the Diamond T brand, indicating that they had, somehow, strayed over onto Smoke's ranch from his neighbor, Tyrone Greene. Greene had only lived in the area for a little over a year, having come up from Texas to buy the ranch when it came available. Greene had worked for Big Ben Conyers, one of the largest and most successful ranchers in Texas. And it was through Colonel Conyers' connection with Smoke that Greene was able to locate a ranch that he could afford. Tyrone and his wife Edna had become very good friends of Smoke and Sally, and Sally had all but adopted their precocious fourteen-year-old daughter.

When Smoke reached the Diamond T, he saw a gathering of cattle, and he shouted at the cows he was herding.

"Here now, go join your friends!" he called out to them, and with shouts, whistles, and vigorous waving of his hat, he pushed the wayward cows back toward the others.

Having come this far, Smoke decided to drop in and visit with Tyrone for a few minutes. He didn't want to stay too long, because if he did, Edna would insist that he remain for lunch, and he didn't want to impose, because he knew they were still on a tight budget until he got his ranch fully operational.

He also didn't want to take too much of Tyone's time, since he had no hands, and had to run the ranch all by himself. He was a good rancher, though. He knew cattle and horses, and because he had been a blacksmith, mechanic, and all around handyman for the Colonel, so he knew what it took to be successful. He also knew the value of hard work, and Smoke knew that if success depended upon hard work, Tyrone would succeed.

As he approached the house, though, he heard a cow bawling from the barn, and it was a bawl he recognized. The cow needed to be milked. That was odd. It wasn't like Edna or even Tamara to go this late into the day without milking the cow.

Now, what had been the pleasant anticipation of a visit with good friends changed to apprehension. Smoke had a very powerful feeling that something was amiss, and, dismounting, he pulled his pistol, stepped quietly up onto the porch, then, deciding against knocking, he pushed the door open and stepped into the house.

Had he gone a step farther, he would have tripped over Tyrone's body. Across the room, near the table, still set for breakfast, he saw Edna; she, too, was lying on the floor with her head in a pool of blood.

Then he saw Tamara. Tamara was sitting on the floor, leaning back against the wall. She was staring at Smoke through eyes that were open wide, but she made no sound. There were bruises on her face and her shoulders. Smoke could see the bruises on her shoulders, because they were bare. And the shoulders were bare, because Tamara was naked, preserving what modesty she had by holding what was left of her torn dress over her.

"Tamara, who did this?" Smoke asked.

Tamara didn't respond.

Smoke, realizing that he was still holding his gun, slipped it back in its holster.

"It's all right, sweetheart, nobody is going to hurt you again."

Tamara gave no sign that she had even heard him speak.

"I'm going to take you home," Smoke said.

Just over half an hour later, Sally was standing out on the porch when she saw Smoke riding up the long approach from Eagle Road to the compound of houses and ancillary buildings that made up Sugarloaf Ranch headquarters. Her smile changed to confusion, then to concern as she saw that he was cradling someone in front of him.

"Smoke! Who is that? What has happened?"

"It's Tamara, Sally. Tyrone and Edna have been murdered. Tamara has been raped. I . . . uh . . . didn't think it would be right for me to dress her, so I just wrapped her in a bedsheet."

"Oh, bless her heart!" Sally said. "Bring that child into the house!"

"I'm going in town to see Sheriff Carson, and I'll get Tyrone and Edna . . ." Smoke started to say "bodies" but thinking of Tamara, he changed his comment to "taken care of."

"I'm going to get this child cleaned up," Sally said.

"Don't worry, Smoke, I'll send some people out there to pick up Mr. and Mrs. Greene," the undertaker said. "And I'll take care of them. The little girl need not worry about that."

"Oh, and Gene, there's quite a bit of blood out there, could you . . ."

"I'll get that taken care of as well," Gene promised.

"Does the girl know who did it?" Sheriff Carson asked, as the undertaker left the sheriff's office to take care of the situation. "Has she given you any hints?"

Smoke shook his head. "So far she hasn't said a word."

"Was she . . . uh . . . what I mean is, do you think she was?" Sheriff Carson paused in mid-question, unable to go any further.

"If you are asking if she was raped, I'm sure she was," Smoke replied.

Sheriff Carson shook his head, sadly. "We've got to find out who did this, Smoke. Any son of a bitch who would do something like kill her mama and papa right in front of her eyes, then rape a young girl like that, doesn't deserve to live. I'm going to take an intense, personal pleasure in seeing that rope put around his neck. In fact, I'll do it myself."

Another person came into the sheriff's office then, and looking up, Smoke saw his foreman, Pearlie.

"Pearlie?"

"Sally wants you to come home, Smoke," Pearlie said. "Tamara is talking now."

* * *

"How is she?" Smoke asked half an hour later when he stepped into the foyer of his house. He looked through the door into the living room. There, he saw Tamara sitting on the sofa wearing one of Sally's dresses. The expression on her face had changed from a blank stare to great sadness.

"She has come out of her shock," Sally said, having met him in the foyer.

"Has she said anything?"

"We've talked a little, nothing substantive, but she is coherent. And of course, she is aware of what happened, not only to her parents, but the ordeal she went through as well."

"Does she know who did it?"

"She says that she does, but she didn't tell me. She wants to talk to you."

Because the conversation between Smoke and Sally had taken place in the entry foyer, and was quiet, Tamara couldn't overhear it. Smoke nodded at Sally, then stepped into the living room. When Tamara looked up at him, he could see that her eyes were brimming with tears, and there were tear tracks down her cheeks.

"Hello, Tamara," Smoke said quietly.

"Cutter MacMurtry," Tamara said.

"Cutter MacMurtry is the name of the man who did this?"

"Yes."

"How do you know that was his name?"

"Because I remember Mr. MacMurtry. He used to work for Colonel Conyers, same as Papa. But he killed some people and Papa found out about it, and Papa took him to the sheriff. Papa got a reward for it, and that's how he had enough money to buy the ranch."

"So, you knew him in Texas. Have you seen him up here? Before this morning, I mean."

"No sir. This morning is the first time I've seen him since we moved."

Smoke reached out to put his hand on Tamara's cheek.

"Thank you, sweetheart. You have been a big help."

CHAPTER TWO

The funerals of Tyrone and Edna Greene were held two days later. The event was referred to as "funerals" though in fact it was one joint remembrance for both of them, with the closed caskets of both decedents in the chancel of the church. The funeral was conducted by Father William Sharkey of the Holy Spirit Episcopal Church, and with every pew filled; extra chairs were put in the transepts and along the walls on both sides of the nave. The back doors were open so that the overflow could stand in the narthex.

Except for the Denver and Pacific Railroad Depot, the Rocky Mountain stagecoach office, the Big Rock Hotel, and the post office, every other building in town was closed for the service.

When the church service was over, both coffins were placed in the hearse, then taken down Center Street for interment in the Garden of Memories Cemetery.

The canopy that was erected for the "family" next to

the side-by-side graves, had only one actual family member, and that was Tamara. There were, however, four other people under the canopy with her, they being Smoke and Sally, and, at Tamara's invitation, Pearlie and Cal.

Tamara sat there, wearing a black dress and a black veil, clutching her hands together, feeling upon her finger the wedding ring that was her mother's.

Father Sharkey intoned the graveside prayers, then invited Tamara to drop a handful of dirt onto each casket, but she declined. When the service was completed, a funeral reception was held in Lamberts' Restaurant. Because Lamberts' advertised themselves as the home of the "throwed rolls" the normal atmosphere was one of fun and gaiety. Today, though, it was a very respectful event, and everyone came up to Tamara to pass on their condolences.

"Thank you for standing in the receiving line with me today," Tamara said to Sally that afternoon as they returned to Sugarloaf Ranch in the surrey.

Tamara had been with Smoke and Sally for three weeks now, and though the vivaciousness that was once such a part of her had not yet returned, she was communicative and helpful, insisting on "paying for her keep" by helping with the house chores.

In the meantime Smoke found a buyer for the Diamond T ranch, including all livestock. He got a good price for it, and was able to deposit a little over twelve thousand dollars into Tamara's account.

"When you are old enough, you'll have that money to pay for your education so you can become a school-teacher," Sally told her.

"If I still have the money then," Tamara replied. "I'll have to have something to live on between now and then."

"Oh, I think that won't be a problem," Sally said.

"Smoke, what are we going to do with Tamara?" Sally asked one afternoon when Tamara had gone for a ride. "She has no relatives; she is all alone in the world.

"We could always take her in, and let her live with us," Smoke replied. "Permanently, I mean."

"Yes, that is a possibility, and I have considered it," Sally said. "And if we can't come up with something else, that would be the solution. But it wouldn't be the best solution."

"Why not?"

"Smoke, she saw her parents killed right in front of her. The life you lead? The enemies you have made? Would you really want to put her through that again?"

"No, I guess I see what you mean. But I won't send her to an orphanage, as much as I respect the Holy Spirit home."

"I have another suggestion," Sally said. "You've just sold a thousand head of cattle to Big Ben Conyers, and you are going to deliver them, right?"

"Yes."

"Tamara has been talking about Texas, and particularly about Live Oaks Ranch. Until Tyrone moved

Tamara and her mother up here, Live Oaks was the only home she had ever known. What if . . ."

Smoke smiled. "You don't have to say another word. I know exactly what you are talking about, and I think it's great idea. I'll ask Ben."

The subject of their conversation was Big Ben Conyers, who was aptly named, for he was six feet, seven inches tall and weighed 330 pounds. Big Ben, who was often called Colonel because of his service during the civil war, was the owner of Live Oaks Ranch, near Ft. Worth. Live Oaks was one of the largest ranches in Texas, a state known for big ranches. One Christmas a few years ago, Smoke and his friends Matt Jensen and Duff MacCallister delivered some of the first Angus cattle ever to come into Texas when they took a starter herd to Conyers. Now Big Ben was increasing his Black Angus herd by one thousand head, having bought the cows from Smoke for eighteen dollars a head.

The deal included delivery of the cattle, which Smoke had agreed to do.

"I'll write Ben a letter," Smoke offered

"I don't think we should say anything to Tamara about it until we get an answer back from Ben," Sally said.

"I agree."

It was three weeks later when Pearlie returned from town bearing a letter from Live Oaks Ranch, Ft. Worth, Texas.

BENJAMIN CONYERS
Live Oaks Ranch
Ft. Worth, Texas

Mr. Kirby Jensen
Sugarloaf Ranch
Big Rock, Colorado

Dear Smoke,

Julia and I are very much looking forward to your visit to Live Oaks Ranch. I know that this is a business trip; however you said that Sally will be with you; therefore I see no reason why your business visit can't be social as well.

Of course there will be a shadow hanging over the visit because the news of the murder of Tyrone and Edna Greene has devastated not only Julia and me, but my foreman, Clay, his wife, Maria, and indeed, every other hand on Live Oaks who knew Tyrone, and counted him as a friend.

You ask if Julia and I would be willing to take into our care Tamara Greene. Of course, such a thing would have to be done with Tamara's willingness to return to Texas and live with us, but should she agree to do so, we would be more than happy to make a home for her, providing her with love and support.

Julia and I remember well the day she was born, we watched her through her childhood years, and we both know her for the delightful young lady that she is.

We sincerely hope that Tamara will agree to come and live with us, but even if she does not, please

extend to her our love and our most sincere
condolences.

Sincerely
Ben Conyers

Sally brought up the subject over dinner that night. "Tamara, you have heard Smoke and me talking about his having to deliver a herd of cows that we recently sold, haven't you?"

"Yes, ma'am," Tamara said. "I think he is taking them to Texas, isn't he?"

"We are taking them to Texas," Sally said.

"Oh, you are going with him?"

"When I say we, I mean all of us," Sally said. "We want you to come with us as well. That is, if you are willing to make the trip."

Tamara's eyes lit up in excitement. "Oh, yes, ma'am, I would be glad to go with you. It would be ever so nice to see Texas again."

"You have spoken about Texas often," Sally said. "Do you miss it?"

"Yes, ma'am. I miss Texas."

"Is it Texas you miss?" Smoke asked. "Or do you miss Live Oaks Ranch?"

"You know me too well," Tamara said. "Yes, I very much miss Live Oaks."

"Good," Sally said, with a broad smile. "Because that is where we are going!"

"Oh!" Tamara said happily. She clapped her hands. "Oh, how wonderful!"

* * *

One week later Smoke Jensen was sitting in the freight business office of the Denver and Pacific Depot at Big Rock, making arrangements for the delivery of the cattle to Fort Worth.

"You can get twenty-five head into each car without undue stress on the animals," Amos Poindexter said. "That means you shall require forty cars, and at one hundred and twenty-five dollars per car, that comes to five thousand dollars."

"I'm also going to need a private car attached . . . one that can accommodate five people.

"Yes sir, we can take care of that for you," the dispatcher said.

"Wow! A private car, all for ourselves?" Tamara said. "Doesn't this cost a lot of money?"

"Yes, but it's all right. Smoke told me that he just used the money you got from the sale of the Diamond T," Cal teased.

Tamara laughed. "Cal, I've been around you long enough now to believe only about one half of what you say."

"And that's twice as much as you should believe," Pearlie said. "I told you, Cal. This young lady is way too smart for you."

"She's too smart for both of you," Sally said with a chuckle.

Five days later they arrived in Ft. Worth, and while Sally and Tamara decided to take a walk through town, Pearlie and Cal made arrangements to have the cars shunted off onto a sidetrack so they could begin unloading them.

Smoke went into the freight dispatcher's office.

"I'm sure that you made payment when you secured the cars. Have you a receipt for your payment?" the dispatcher asked. "If not, I can telegraph back to the point of origin and get a validation of your payment."

"That won't be necessary, I have the receipt," Smoke replied, producing the document.

"Yes, very good. Let me just put my stamp on it, and you can begin unloading."

Smoke walked over to the counter and waited as Brewer affixed his stamp to the receipt.

Brewer handed the stamped receipt to Smoke. "There you go, Mr. Jensen, the cattle are yours."

"How long will I be able to keep them in your holding pens before I have to pay an additional fee?" Smoke asked.

"You have twenty-four hours, which is included in the fee you paid for the cattle cars," Brewer said. "After that, you will be charged two hundred dollars a day."

"Oh, well then, there will be no problem, because we plan to have them out of here this very afternoon, as soon as we get them all off the cars," Smoke said.

"We appreciate your patronage, Mr. Jensen, and hope you will choose to do business with us again," Brewer said.

"I'm sure I will," Smoke said.

Smoke left the dispatcher's office and started out to the holding pen.

CHAPTER THREE

As Smoke was arranging to off-load his one thousand head of cattle, seventy-five miles north of Ft. Worth, four riders stopped on a small rise and looked down at the little town of Pella, Texas. Having grown up to serve the cotton farmers of the area, the small town of Pella was hot, dry, and dusty, and it sat baking in the sun like a lizard. One of the riders had a scar that started above his right eyebrow and cut through the eye, squeezing it down to a permanent squint. The purple welt continued on down to his mouth, where the end of his lips had been cut away, leaving only an ugly puff of scar tissue.

This was Clete Lanagan, who was the recognized leader of the group. Lanagan raised the canteen to his mouth and took a drink. The water was tepid, but his tongue was dry and swollen. He wiped the back of his hand across his mouth, then recorked the canteen and hung it back on his saddle.

"There's a creek down at the bottom of this hill. Before we take care of our business, maybe we ought to refill our canteens," Lanagan told the others. "We won't have time to stop . . . after. And this water's beginnin' to taste like horse piss."

"Ha," a rider named Varney said with a chuckle. "You know what horse piss tastes like, do you, Clete?"

"It tastes like the water in this canteen," Lanagan replied.

"We take the time to fill up our canteens, someone's liable to see us, then the next thing you know everyone's goin' to have a good description of us," one of the other riders said.

"Hell, Loomis, you think they ain't goin to have a good description of us anyway, the moment we rob that there bank of their'n?" The speaker, whose name was Claymore, hawked up a spit. "Look there," he added. "I ain't ain't hardly got enough wet to spit. 'N Clete's right, when we leave town, we ain't goin' to be able to take the time to fill our canteens. We need to do it now."

"What we ought to do is get us a proper drink, over to the saloon," Varney suggested.

"Good idea, Varney," Claymore replied. "Only, why don't we rob the bank first, then go over to the saloon for a nice drink?"

"Damn, Claymore, that don't make no sense a'tall," Varney said.

"Neither does going into the saloon before we hit the bank. Look, if we do this like we talked about, we'll walk into that bank, take the money, then be out of here again afore anyone in this town knows what hit 'em. Then when we reach the next town, why, we can ride in in style. We'll have enough money to swim in beer if we want to, with enough left over for women, hotels, restaurants, and even some gamblin' money. Hell, we can do anything we want."

"How you goin' to spend your money, Varney?" Loomis asked.

"I don't know. On women I guess. Say, have any of you ever knowed anyone to get hisself two whores at the same time?"

"Ha! What do you think about that, Claymore? Varney wants two whores at the same time," Loomis said.

Claymore laughed. "Two whores? Hell, Varney, you ain't never had one yet, have you?"

"Why, sure I have, lots of times," Varney said. "Whenever I got the money, that is, which, most of the time, I don't have."

"Well, you fellas do what I tell you to do today and you'll have all the money you need . . . even enough for two whores at the same time if you think you can handle that," Lanagan said. "Now, fill up your canteens, 'n let's get on with it."

The four riders dismounted and dipped their canteens into the creek. Once all the canteens were filled and corked, they remounted.

"You boys check your pistols," Lanagan ordered.

All four pulled their pistols and checked the cylinders to see that all the chambers were properly charged. Then they slipped their guns back into their holsters.

"Ready?" Lanagan asked.

"Ready," the others replied.

"All right, let's go get us some money."

The four men rode into town, then pulled up in front of the small bank. Lanagan, Claymore, and Varney dismounted and handed their reins to Loomis.

Loomis remained in the saddle and kept his eyes open on the street out front. Lanagan and the other two looked up and down the street once, then they pulled their kerchiefs up over the bottom half of their faces and, with their guns drawn, pushed open the door.

There were three men and two women inside the bank. One of the men was the teller behind the counter; the other two men, and the woman, were customers. One of the men customers saw Lanagan, Claymore, and Varney coming in, masked, and holding guns, and knew immediately what was happening.

"It's a bank holdup!" the customer shouted.

"Ain't he the smart one though?" Lanagan said. "You," he said to the man behind the counter. He handed him a bag. "Start fillin' up this bag."

The teller began scooping money up from the drawer, then, suddenly, a gun appeared in his hand.

"Damn you!" Lanagan shouted, and he pulled the trigger. The teller, with a bullet hole between his eyes, fell back, the money bag in one hand and the unfired pistol in the other.

Lanagan leapt over the counter and grabbed the bag, then he finished emptying the cash drawer.

Across the street from the bank, Russel Jeeves, who owned a gun store, had seen the four men approach the bank. When he saw three of them dismount and hand the reins to a fourth man, rather than loop them around the hitching rail, he became curious, and he continued to stare at the bank.

Then he heard the gunshot, and his suspicion was confirmed.

Grabbing a gun, Jeeves ran outside. "Damn! The bank is being robbed," he shouted to some men who were on the boardwalk in front of his store. "Get your guns, boys! They're robbing the bank!"

Loomis, who was waiting in front of the bank, heard the shout and, pulling his pistol, fired at Jeeves but missed. One of the townspeople fired back, and Loomis took a slug through the shoulder.

The exchange of gunfire grew more intense, and of the three horses Loomis was holding, one was shot and he went down.

"Lanagan, get out here now!" Loomis shouted, returning fire. Not sure he had been heard, he ran to the bank door again and yelled inside. "The whole damn town has turned out. Come on, Lanagan, we have to go!"

As they were leaving the bank, Lanagan saw that one of the bank customers had pulled a pistol and was aiming it at Varney.

The customer pulled the trigger, and blood, brains, and bone detritus exploded from the side of Varney's head. Lanagan shot the armed bank customer.

"We've got to get out of here!" Lanagan shouted.

"What about Varney?" Claymore asked.

"He's dead! What about 'im?"

The two emerged from the bank.

"My horse!" Claymore shouted, seeing his mount lying dead.

"Take Varney's. He sure as hell won't be a-needin' it!" Lanagan said. "Let's go!"

As Lanagan and Claymore mounted, Loomis, who

had remounted, was shot from the saddle, and he fell hard to the ground.

"Wait, don't leave me!" Loomis shouted. "Help me onto my horse!"

"Sorry, we ain't got time to wait on you, 'n we can't leave you," Lanagan said. He aimed his pistol at Loomis's head.

"What? No! Lanagan, what are you do . . ." That was as far as he got before his shout was cut off by a bullet.

At that moment, someone from across the street fired at Lanagan and Claymore with a heavy-gauge shotgun. The charge of double-aught buckshot missed the robbers, but it did hit the front window of the bank, bringing it down with a loud crash.

Claymore shot back and though he missed the man with the shotgun, he at least drove him back inside. He and Lanagan started, at a gallop, down the street.

There had been several citizens out on the street and the sidewalks when the shooting erupted, and now they stood there watching in openmouthed shock as the men who had just robbed their bank were getting away.

One of the bank customers came outside then.

"They kilt Boyce 'n Woodward!" the bank customer shouted. "Woodward kilt one of them before he was kilt."

"Who was they? Did anyone recognize 'em?"

"That one there," Jeeves said, pointing to the dead outlaw in front of the bank, "I don't know who he is, but he called one of the others Lanagan."

"Clete Lanagan!" the city marshal said.

"You know this Lanagan, do you, Jim?" Jeeves asked.

"I don't know 'im, but I know of 'im. I've got paper on 'im in my office."

"Did they get any money?"

"Looks like they got just what was in Boyce's drawer," the bank customer said. "I don't know how much that was."

"Fifteen hunnert 'n forty-seven dollars," Lanagan said. "I was hopin' for more." He smiled at Claymore. "But, seein' as there is only the two of us that'll be dividin' it up, it ain't turnin' out all that bad."

"Yeah, I was hopin' for more too," Claymore said. "But, seven hunnert 'n what? Seventy-five? Dollars ain't too bad."

"Seven hunnert 'n seventy three dollars," Lanagan said after he counted out the money. "With a dollar left over."

"We'll find a place to drink up that dollar," Claymore said with a chuckle. "Tell me, Clete, what's the most money you ever got?"

"Me 'n the MacMurtry brothers, Cutter 'n Hatchett, held up a stagecoach 'n got near two thousand dollars oncet." Lanagan chuckled. "Cutter lost near ever' penny of it by gamblin'. He didn't keep the money no more 'n a week, 'n he went back to cowboyin'."

"Is he doin' that now?"

"No, they was a reward of five thousand dollars out on 'im, 'n some feller that was workin' at the same ranch seen a reward poster on 'im, 'n he turned 'im in."

"Five thousand dollars? Damn, that's a big reward just for holdin' up a stagecoach, ain't it?"

"Yeah, well, after we held up the stagecoach, ole Cutter, he kilt a preacher 'n his whole family. That's what the reward was for, 'cause it got folks pretty riled."

"What about his brother?"

"They say that Cutter escaped just before they was a-fixin' to hang 'im. 'N though there don't no one know for sure, ever' body seems to think that it was Hatchett that broke 'im out. Don't nobody know where neither one of 'em is now."

CHAPTER FOUR

Back in Ft. Worth and totally unmindful of the events that had just happened in the small town of Pella, Smoke stood at the fence that surrounded the holding pen with his right foot on the bottom rail and his arms folded across the top rail. Resting his chin on his forearms, he watched the cattle being off-loaded from the cattle cars.

"I'll bet ya, that it was lot easier bringin' 'em here by railroad, than when we druv them cows down from Dodge City, warn't it, Mr. Jensen?"

The man who spoke was a stockyard hand. He was medium height, with white hair and a bushy, sweeping mustache, and he had been part of the initial drive when Smoke and Matt Jensen, as well as Duff MacAllister, brought down the first herd of Angus to ever be in Tarrant County.

"You miss the drives, do you, Sam?"

"Yes sir, I have to confess that I do. Oh, the time out on the trail was hard enough . . . but the trail towns . . . Dodge . . . Abilene . . . ahh . . . them was some of the finest times I ever had in my life."

"The relief of the drive being over was as welcome as what the town had to offer though, wasn't it?" Smoke asked.

Sam chuckled. "You know, bein' as you are an owner, 'n I never was naught but a drover, it could be that maybe, me 'n you has different memories o' them days."

"Could be," Smoke said, chuckling in agreement.

"These cows is for Live Oaks Ranch, are they?" Sam asked.

"Yes."

"I thought they must be. I seen Clay Ramsey talkin' with your two men, Pearlie and Cal. 'N Ramsey, why, he was workin' for the colonel 'a fore I ever come to work at Live Oaks, 'n he's still workin' there. He's been there for a long time, now."

Smoke saw Clay Ramsey coming toward him. The foreman of Live Oaks Ranch was forty years old, with brown hair, a well-trimmed mustache, and blue eyes. About five feet ten, he was wiry and, according to one of the cowboys who worked for him, as tough as a piece of rawhide.

"You have brought us a good-looking bunch of cows," Clay said.

Smoke laughed. "That's not what you said the first time you saw Angus cattle. I believe you said that they looked like a herd of milk cows."

"Yes sir, well I was pretty much used to Longhorns, so you can't rightly hold that against me now."

"I suppose not. How's Big Ben doing?"

"You know the colonel, he don't never change. He's fit as a fiddle," Clay replied.

"Good. And Dalton?"

"Dalton? Well sir, he's left the ranch."

"Oh? Why? Is there bad blood between Dalton and Big Ben? I know Dalton started out a bit troublesome, but I thought he and his dad had pretty much gotten things straight between them."

"Oh, no sir, there ain't no bad blood between them. It's just that Dalton has taken on the job of deputy sheriff for Sheriff Peabody up in Audubon."

"Dalton is working as a sheriff's deputy?"

"Yes, sir, I know it sounds a mite strange, bein' as how Dalton's pa is one of the richest men in Texas 'n all. But Dalton figured he ought to go out on his own for a while 'n do some, 'growin' up.' And by the way, growin' up? Well, those are Dalton's own words."

"How did Big Ben take that?"

"Well sir, he took it just fine. I heard 'im tell Mrs. Conyers that he was proud of Dalton, and you know yourself, that hasn't always been the way the Colonel has spoke of Dalton."

"That's true," Smoke agreed. "By the way, how are Maria and Emanuel?"

"We're callin' 'im Manny," Clay said. "Wait until you see him."

Smoke felt a close connection to Clay, Maria, and their child, Manny. The boy had been born at the stroke of midnight on Christmas Eve, during the cattle drive down from Dodge City when Smoke brought Big Ben his first herd of Black Angus cattle. It had been a very difficult birth, and the mother and baby would have died, had it not been for Tom Whitman, who, at the time, Smoke had thought was just one of the trail cowboys. As it turned out, though, Tom Whitman was harboring a secret. He was actually a well-known and very skilled surgeon who had become a cowboy in an attempt to escape the personal demons that were plaguing him.

Pearlie approached Smoke.

"No need for you to hang around, Smoke, we've only got about five more cars to unload, and Cal and I can handle that. Then we can move them on out to Live Oaks."

"All right," Smoke said. "I guess I'll go find Sally and Tamara."

Pearlie chuckled. "I heard Sally say that she and Tamara were goin' to do some shopping. You'd better go find them before they spend all your money."

"Well, thanks to the Colonel, she'll have quite a bit of money to spend," Smoke said.

Five minutes later Smoke found Sally in Falkoff's Dry Goods Store. Tamara was looking down at the shoes she was wearing. Sally looked up and smiled when she saw Smoke.

"Smoke, what do you think of these shoes for Tamara?"

"I think she has chosen a fine-looking pair of shoes," Smoke said.

"Why in heaven's name would you think she has chosen these shoes?" Sally asked.

"I don't know, maybe because she is wearing them?"

"But these are only the second pair she has tried. Why on earth would she want to choose only the second pair of shoes that she has tried on?"

"Why indeed?" Smoke replied with a chuckle. "Pearlie tells me we've about got the cattle unloaded, so we'll be taking them out to Live Oaks soon."

"When you're ready, you know where to find us,"

Sally said as Tamara took off the shoes and reached for another pair.

"I think I'll go have a beer," Smoke replied.

When Smoke pushed through the batwing doors of the Purple Crackle Saloon a few minutes later, he stepped to one side of the door and put his back to the wall as he looked out across the room, studying the occupants. He wasn't looking for anyone in particular; this was just his routine way of entering any saloon.

Perceiving a lot of curiosity but no immediate danger, Smoke crossed over to the bar. Earlier, he had made a wire transfer of most of the money to the Bank of Big Rock, but kept back one thousand dollars for travel and expenses.

"I'd like a beer, please," Smoke said.

"With, or without the head?" the bartender replied.

"Without."

"Yes, sir."

"Tell me, Clinton, ain't that Smoke Jensen that just stepped up to the bar?" someone at the far end of the bar said. Smoke heard the words clearly, as the speaker made no attempt to lower his voice. In fact, he had raised his voice, clearly indicating that he wanted Smoke to overhear him. And, in the increased volume, there was an implied threat.

Smoke had been through this many times before, and it was easy for him to ignore the speaker. His experience, though, told him that he would not be able to ignore this challenge indefinitely.

"Yes, that's Jensen," Clinton answered.

"Would that be the 'great' Smoke Jensen, do you suppose?" His comment was dripping with sarcasm.

"Like I said, it's Smoke Jensen."

"What's he a-doin' here in Ft. Worth?"

"I heard he brought a bunch of cows down for the Conyers Ranch."

"Hell, ain't Conyers got enough cows?"

"He's got a big ranch, lots of room for lots of cows."

"I've heard of Smoke Jensen. He's s'posed to be some famous gunfighter is what I've heard."

"So they say," Clinton replied.

"You know what I'm thinkin'? I'm thinkin' that he don't look like all that much to me."

"Is that a fact? Well, I tell you what, Joad, there's been a whole lot of men that's said that before, 'n for some of 'em as said that, why them was the last words they ever said."

"Seems to me like he just might be a feller that's gettin' by on his reputation," Joad replied.

"That may be so, but if it is, it's a reputation he's earned."

"You a-scared of 'im, are you, Clinton?"

"I have no reason to be afraid of 'im, because I have no intention of antagonizing him," Clinton replied.

"Why don't we just see if he can live up to this reputation of being so dangerous?" Joad suggested.

"What do you have in mind?"

"Why don't you just watch, 'n maybe you'll learn somethin'."

"Joad, don't you go bitin' off more 'n you can chew," Clinton cautioned.

Joad held his hand out toward Clinton, as if telling him to watch.

"Hey, Mr. Jensen. Mr. Smoke Jensen. That is your name, ain't it? You the famous Smoke Jensen?" Joad asked, calling down to Smoke from the far end of the bar.

Smoke ignored the call, as he had ignored the earlier comments.

"What kind of a name is 'Smoke' anyhow? Did your mama actually think that Smoke is a name?"

The bartender, with a nervous glance toward Joad, handed the beer to Smoke.

"Good job of drawing the beer. It's without a head, just like I like it," Smoke said, complimenting the bartender. He lifted the mug to take a drink.

"Thank you, sir," the bartender replied.

"Tell me, Mr. Smoke Jensen, is it really true that you can walk on water? Or is that just one o' the tall tales people tells about you?"

Smoke lifted the mug to take a drink of his beer.

"Ahh, that did cut through the dust," Smoke said with a smile.

"Hey, Jensen! How come it is that you ain't payin' no attention to me?" Joad called.

"Leave 'im be, Joad. He ain't botherin' nobody," Clinton said.

"Yeah? Well he's botherin' me," Joad replied. "I don't figure he's got 'ny right comin' in here to the Purple Crackle Saloon, 'n breathin' our air. Hey, Jensen! What are you doin', breathin' our air?"

"I told you to leave 'im be."

"I'll leave 'im be when he answers my question," Joad said. "Hey Jensen, I asked you what are you doin' breathin' our air? Ain't you got air of your own to breathe? I hear you got yourself a big ranch some'ers."

"I think you should listen to your friend, Mr. Joad," Smoke said. He was leaning forward with his elbows on the bar, and both hands cupped around the mug of beer. He had not yet looked at Joad, nor did he do so now.

"You know what, Jensen? I told my friend here that I think you are the kind of a feller that sort 'a trades on your reputation. You got a lot 'o men buffaloed, but not me. I don't think you're near as fast as ever' one thinks you are, 'n I aim to prove it."

"You're dying to prove it, are you?" Smoke asked.

"Yeah, you might say that."

"Damn, Joad, did you listen to what he asked? He said are you *dyin'* to prove it!" Clinton said.

"I ain't goin' to be the one doin' the dyin'," Joad said as he started his draw.

Although Smoke had both his hands wrapped around his beer, and was seemingly paying no attention to Joad, he had his pistol out pointing at his antagonist, even before Joad's pistol cleared the holster.

"No, no! Wait!" Joad shouted. He let his pistol slide back in the holster as he stuck his hands up. "I ain't drawin' on you, Jensen, I was just funnin' you is all."

"That's a dangerous way to have fun," Smoke said.

"I didn't mean nothin' by it," Joad said, his hands still raised over his head.

"Take your pistol out of your holster," Smoke ordered.

"No, sir, now, I ain't a-goin' to do that. You'd shoot me soon as you seen my hand on the gun."

"You," Smoke said to the friend who had cautioned Joad. "Clinton, is it?"

"Yes, sir, Clinton it is, Mr. Jensen. Roy J. Clinton," the friend replied nervously.

"Well, Roy J, you seem like a sensible man. I want you to take Mr. Joad's pistol out of his holster."

Clinton did so, using only his thumb and forefinger, all the while keeping a cautious eye on Smoke.

"Take the cylinder out of the gun and hand it to me," Smoke ordered.

Clinton removed the cylinder and handed it to Smoke, who put the cylinder in his pocket.

"Now, Mr. Joad," Smoke said. "Suppose we all go back to enjoying our drinks without any more talk of shooting."

"When do I get the cylinder back for my pistol?"

"When I leave, I'll drop it in the watering trough out front. It shouldn't be that hard for you to recover it."

"The hell you will!" Joad shouted, rushing toward Smoke. He took a wild swing that Smoke ducked under. When Smoke came back up, it was with a left to Joad's chin. The uppercut snapped Joad's head back, and he backpedaled to get away from him. Then, seeing a whiskey bottle on the bar, he picked it up and threw it at Smoke.

A pistol roared and the bottle was shattered in midair. Looking around, Smoke saw Pearlie standing just inside the door, holding a smoking gun in his hand.

"Now, if you're goin' to fight my boss, who also happens to be my very good friend, I intend to see to it that you do it fair and square," Pearlie said with a broad smile.

"Hello, Pearlie," Smoke said. "It was good of you to stop by."

"I come to tell you all the cows is off-loaded," Pearlie replied.

"Barkeep, how much do I owe you for the bottle of whiskey my friend just broke?" Smoke asked.

"Uh, it was only half full, about a dollar and a half I reckon."

Smoke put a ten-dollar bill on the bar. "This will pay for the whiskey, and give free drinks to everyone else until the money runs out."

"Joad too?"

Smoke glanced over at Joad, who had a defeated look about him. "I don't know," Smoke said. "Mr. Joad, are you through trying to kill me, or beat me up?"

"Yes, sir, Mr. Jensen. I won't be tryin' nothin' no more."

Smoke put the cylinder from Joad's gun on the bar, then slid it down toward him.

"Give my new friend Mr. Joad the very first drink," Smoke said.

The others in the saloon cheered Smoke as he and Pearlie left the Purple Crackle Saloon.

CHAPTER FIVE

"There it is, just like I told you," Lanagan said, pointing to a small cabin on Turkey Creek. "I seen it for the first time 'bout a year ago. There ain't nobody that lives there, 'n it'll make a good place for us to hole up."

As Clete Lanagan and Dingus Claymore approached the little cabin, they were startled to see someone standing by the edge of the creek, in front of the cabin.

"What the hell?" Claymore said. "I thought you said there didn't nobody live here."

"It was plumb empty last time I was here."

The man standing by the creek had neither seen nor heard Lanagan and Claymore approach.

"Howdy," Lanagan called out, making his call as friendly and non-threatening as he could.

Lanagan's hail visibly startled the man, who turned toward them with a look of nervousness on his face. He looked to be in his late sixties or seventies, with a full head of white hair, and a long white beard. He was unarmed, though there was a rifle leaned up against a tree about ten feet away from him.

"Who are you?" the man asked, apprehensively.

"Oh, just a couple of hunters, scouting the area," Lanagan replied, still maintaining a friendly tone in voice and demeanor. He nodded toward the cabin. "I was surprised to see you here. I rode through here a year or so ago, and the cabin was empty."

"Yes, sir, it was empty when I come upon it back last winter, so I figured I'd just move in," the old man said. He chuckled. "I have to tell you, you two is the first human people to come by since I got here, 'n that's been at least eight months. I got some coffee, a mess 'o fish, 'n some taters from m' garden, 'n some fresh cattail that boils up just real tasty. If you'd take a meal with me, why, I'd purely love the company. The name is McCall."

"Why, thank you, Mr. McCall, we'd be pleased to join you," Lanagan said as he and Claymore dismounted.

"You said that we are the first people you have seen since you moved in. Does anyone know that you live out here, Mr. McCall?" Lanagan asked, half an hour later, as the three of them ate the meal McCall had prepared for them.

"As far as I know, there don't nobody know that I'm out here," McCall replied. "I left Ohio more 'n forty years ago, 'n don't reckon they's anyone anywhere what knows, or even cares, whether I'm dead or alive." He laughed, a high-pitched cackle. "I'll tell you the truth, I'm the kind of feller that don't particular get along all that good with people, so I don't hardly never see no one anyhow. 'N I got me enough coffee 'n flour to last at least another two, maybe three months," he laughed again. "That is, if I don't get me no more company. Then I'll have to go into town some'ers 'n get me some more. But until then, why, me'n Rhoda will just stay out here."

"Rhoda?"

"Rhoda's m' mule. You didn' see her, on account of I got 'er tied up over there in the stable."

"How do you live?" Claymore asked. "What do you do for money?"

"Oh, sonny, I don't need no money to live out here, that's what's good about it. I got game, 'n fish, 'n my garden's come along real good. 'N when I do need somethin', like maybe coffee, or flour or maybe some more bullets for m' rifle, why, I can generally sell some venison, or a mess o' mushrooms. I don't hardly need no money at all to get by."

"We need to ride on," Lanagan said after they finished their meal. "We appreciate the meal."

"I'll walk you out to your horses," McCall said.

The three men walked out to the horses Lanagan and Claymore had left ground tethered.

"I 'spect I'd best go check up on m' mule," McCall said. "It was just real fine to have you two stop by."

Lanagan waited until McCall turned away, then he drew his pistol and shot McCall in the back of his head.

"We'll make this our hideout. It was real nice of him to plant a garden for us," Lanagan said.

"Where do you think we should bury him?" Claymore asked.

"I don't care where we plant him, as long as the ground is soft so's we don't have to work so hard to get 'im planted."

The 120,000 acres of gently rolling grassland and scores of year-round streams and creeks made Live Oaks Ranch ideal for raising cattle. With two dozen cowboys who were full-time employees, some with families, and another two dozen who were part-time employees, it was almost the size of a small town. And, indeed, it was listed on several maps of Tarrant County, and even some maps of the state, as if it were a town.

The part-time and full-time employees who weren't married, lived in a couple of long, low, bunkhouses, white, with red roofs. In addition, there were at least ten permanent employees who were married, and they all lived in small houses, all of them painted green, with red roofs. These were adjacent to the bunkhouses. There was also a cookhouse that was large enough to feed all the single men, a barn, a machine shed, a granary, and a large corral. The most dominating feature of the ranch was what the cowboys called "The Big House." The Big House was a stucco-sided example of Spanish Colonial Revival, with an arcaded portico on the southeast corner, stained glass windows, and an elaborate arched entryway.

Inside the parlor of the Big House, Big Ben Conyers was pouring bourbon and branch for Smoke, Pearlie, and Cal. Earlier, he had poured white wine for Sally and his wife, Julia.

"I appreciate you bringing me another thousand

head," Big Ben said. "And for making me a good price. I know they are worth twenty dollars a head on the market."

"Yes, but these are all young cattle, and won't bring that kind of money for another couple of years," Smoke said. "I'm quite content with the deal we made." He held his glass up, and Big Ben, Pearlie, and Cal did the same.

"To fine cattle, good horses, and great friends," he said.

"Hear, hear," Big Ben replied, and the four men drank to the toast.

"Tony Peters was in the Purple Crackle today," Big Ben said. "He told me about your run-in with Hiram Joad."

"Tony Peters? I thought he was off looking for gold, somewhere," Cal said.

"He didn't find any, so he came back," Big Ben said.

"Ha!" Cal said. "Then he's smarter than I thought he was."

"What about this man, Joad?" Smoke asked. "He seemed awfully intent on starting something with me."

"I've no doubt but that he did. He used to be a pretty good hand, but he got into an argument and a shoot-out with another man last year. Turns out that the other man was wanted for murder, and Joad collected a seven-hundred-and-fifty-dollar reward, so he quit his job and lived off the reward money for a while.

"Now, he fancies himself as being good with a gun, and feels he has to prove it. You and Pearlie here probably saved his life by showing him that he could be beaten. Maybe he won't be so quick to try something now."

"Anyone can be beaten," Smoke said.

"You?" Big Ben asked.

"Anyone," Smoke replied, topping off his comment with another swallow of his drink.

Big Ben nodded. "That's probably a good attitude to have."

"It's the kind of attitude that can keep you alive," Pearlie added. Pearlie, whose real name was Wes Fontaine, was nearly as good with a gun as Smoke.

"When did you last hear from Becca?" Sally asked, wanting to change the subject away from gunfighting.

"Oh, we get at least one letter per week from Becca," Julia said. "She's in Boston now, and loves it. Tom is chief of surgeons at Massachusetts General Hospital there."

"I sure never took Tom for a doctor when I first met him," Cal said. "I mean, he doesn't look like any doctor I ever knew."

"I know," Ben said. "He doesn't have that sense of . . . oh, call it superiority that so many doctors have. But from all I've been able to find out, Tom Whitman is one of the finest doctors in the entire country."

"And how is Dalton doing?" Smoke asked. "I heard he was a deputy?"

"Yes, over in Audubon," Ben answered. "I had suggested that he learn a little more about ranching since he will be taking this place over someday, but he said he thought his first priority was to learn a little more about being a man. He thought it would do him good to get out on his own and get a little of the real world under his belt. And you know what? I agree with him. I not only agree with him, I'm proud of him."

"What kind of sheriff is he working for?" Pearlie asked.

"The sheriff he's working for is a real good man. I've known Andrew Peabody for a long time. In fact, he was my sergeant major during the war."

"You might also tell Smoke that Sheriff Peabody has a very pretty daughter," Julia added with a smile.

Ben laughed. "Yes, he does at that. And I'm certain that Martha Jane does add a degree of appeal for Dalton."

"I'm sure you miss Rebecca," Smoke said.

Big Ben smiled. "Indeed we do, but I'm happy to say that she is doing very well and seems to be quite happy there. I do wish she and Tom had stayed here in Texas, but Tom is Chief of Surgery at Massachusetts General Hospital, and by train, we are only a little over a week apart. It's not like it was in the old days when it could take months to cover such a distance."

"And by telegram, we can hear from her almost instantly," Julia said.

"The world has certainly changed, just within our lifetime," Pearlie said.

"Indeed it has," Big Ben agreed.

"By the way, I haven't seen Tamara since we got here," Smoke said. "I wonder where she's gotten off to."

"No need to be wondering," Julia said with a knowing smile. "All you have to do is find Billy Lewis."

"Billy Lewis?" Sally replied.

"He's Neil Lewis's son, maybe six months older than Tamara. Once Tyrone left, Neil became my blacksmith and machinist. It took him a while to catch on, but now he's as good as Tyrone ever was, and the truth is, I don't think I could run the ranch without him. Tamara and Neil's boy, Billy, were inseparable when they were growing up, and it looks to me as if they have taken up right where they left off," Ben said.

Julia laughed. "Not exactly where they left off. They were only ten years old then. Now that they are a little older, I expect she's aware that he's a boy, and Billy is aware that Tamara is a girl."

"Billy is a real fine boy," Big Ben said. "Does real well in school, and he's already a good hand around cattle. He's going to grow up to be a fine young man."

Big Ben and Julia exchanged an obvious look, then Ben said, "I think now would be the time to bring it up."

"You would be talking about Tamara coming here?" Sally asked.

"Yes, I am most anxious to ask Tamara if she would like to come live with us," Julia said. "But I'm not sure how best to do it."

"Suppose we ask her tonight, over dinner?" Sally suggested.

"Yes, I think that would be a good time," Julia replied.

Several people at the ranch welcomed Tamara back, but nobody was more pleased to see her than young Billy Lewis. Having just turned fifteen, Billy and Tamara were very close to the same age. Billy was tall for a fifteen-year-old, and because he had been active on the ranch, he was well proportioned.

Billy invited Tamara to go for a ride with him, and

he saddled two horses, and was about to help her mount, when she protested.

"Billy Lewis, I have been riding a horse as long as you have. I need no help in mounting," she protested.

"You don't understand, Tamara. We were kids then, but now I'm a young man and you're a young lady," Billy said. "A gentleman always helps a lady."

Tamara flashed a beautiful smile. "You're right," she said. "Please forgive me, Mr. Lewis, sir, for my outburst. I would love to have your assistance in mounting."

They left the paddock at a rapid trot, and fifteen minutes later, they dismounted on the bank of the Trinity River.

"This is the best place on the whole ranch to catch fish," Billy said. "You can 'most always come up with a mess o' fish."

"I had almost forgotten what it was like here," Tamara said, hugging herself. "Have you ever seen anything more beautiful?"

"Never." Billy was staring pointedly at Tamara when he said the word.

Tamara felt herself blushing, but it was a warm and pleasant feeling, not a blush of embarrassment.

"Why are you wearing that ring?" Billy asked, pointing to the ring on Tamara's left hand.

"It was my mother's ring," Tamara said, defensively.

"You should wear it on your other hand," Billy said. "If people see it on your left hand, they will think you are married."

"I'm too young to be married."

"Yes, but you don't look like a little girl anymore," Billy said. "Wait, maybe you should wear it on your left hand, that way if people think you are already married, nobody will try and marry you before I'm old enough."

Tamara laughed. "You are just being silly," she said.

Billy reached down to take her left hand in his. "Keep it on this hand, for me," he said.

"All right, I will," she promised.

"Oh, peach cobbler!" Tamara said with enthusiasm when desert was served after dinner that evening.

"I seem to remember that you liked that," Julia said.

"Tell me, Tamara, have you enjoyed your visit here?" Sally asked.

"Yes, ma'am!" Tamara said. "I'd almost forgotten how much I loved this place, how Papa used to put me in the saddle with him and . . ." She stopped in mid-sentence as her eyes brimmed with tears. "I'm sorry," she said, using a handkerchief supplied by Cal to wipe away the tears.

"Don't be sorry, child," Julia said. "Memories are precious, even the sad ones. And I believe that your papa is in heaven, right now, sharing that same memory with you."

"Is he remembering when you and Billy decided to play hooky from school, and wound up hiding out in a poison ivy patch?" Big Ben asked, smiling to lighten the mood.

"Oh, I hope not," Tamara said, laughing at the memory.

"Did you enjoy your visit with Billy?"

"Oh, yes, very much!" Tamara said, and as she had when she caught Billy looking at her down by the river, she felt that same warm blush of pleasure pass over her.

"Tamara, would you like to come back here to live?" Julia asked.

"Yes, and when I've grown up and can support myself, I fully intend to come back down here."

"Not when you have grown up. She means now, child," Big Ben said. "Would you like to come down here now? We have plenty of room in this house, Becca's old room, Dalton's, and we even have two guest rooms, either of which you could make into your own."

"You mean, come down here and live with you?" Tamara asked, the words so hesitantly spoken that they could barely be heard.

"Yes. We would love to have you live with us," Julia said. "We know we can never take the place of your parents, but I swear to you, we would love you, and look after you as if you were our own child."

"Oh!" Tamara said. She looked over at Sally. "Miz Sally?"

"Do you want to do it?" Sally asked, the smile on her face showing Tamara that she was agreeable to the suggestion.

"Yes!" Tamara said. "I think I would rather come back down here more than just about anything in the world. Oh, but, don't get me wrong, I am ever so grateful to you and Mr. Jensen for taking me in like you did but, yes, I want to do it."

"Then I think you should do it."

Again Tamara's eyes brimmed with tears, but this time they were tears of happiness. Getting up from her chair, she went to Sally and hugged her, before going to Julia, and then Big Ben.

"Oh, thank you," she said. "I can't thank you enough!'

"So, now that that is all taken care of, when are you going back to Colorado?" Julia asked.

"Tomorrow," Sally said. "The women of Big Rock are having a bake sale for the orphanage next week, and I intend to take part."

"Miss Sally sells her bear sign and they're always the first thing to go," Cal said.

"Yes, because you keep pilfering them," Pearlie charged.

"Oh, I think you manage to keep even with him," Smoke said, and the others laughed.

"Colonel Conyers, dinner is ready, sir," the cook said.

"Ah, good, good. Well, ladies and gentlemen, what do you say we repair to the dining room?" Big Ben invited.

CHAPTER SIX

"I'm glad Ben and Julia were willing to take Tamara in. I think she is going to be very happy there," Smoke said as he, Sally, Pearlie and Cal were on the train on their way back home.

"Oh they were more than just willing," Sally said. "It was obvious that they very much wanted to have Tamara come live with them."

"Yes," Smoke agreed.

"It's too bad you didn't get a chance to see your niece while we were there," Sally said.

"It's good enough just to know that she and Tom are happily married, and she is doing well," Smoke said. "Who would have thought that that big cowboy we met during that cattle drive from Dodge City to Live Oaks was actually a skilled surgeon? What a surprise he turned out to be."

"Well, I can't say that I knew from the beginning that he was a surgeon," Sally said. "But I knew, almost from the moment we first met him, that he was much more than a cowboy."

"How did you know that, Miss Sally?" Cal asked.

"There was an air about him," Sally said. "Not of superiority or arrogance, but certainly one of sophistication; the way he talked, the music and poetry he appreciated, the classics he had read. Despite his appearances, I knew he was an educated man."

"Makes you wonder why a man like that was workin' as a cowboy," Cal said.

"Don't you remember?" Sally asked. "He was running away from a personal tragedy."

"Oh, yes, the woman he was married to died while he was operating on her, and he felt guilty about it," Cal said.

"I can understand how the sorrow might have given him a sense of guilt, but in fact he had no reason to feel guilty," Sally said. "I'm glad he recovered. He is much too good of a man to carry such a burden."

Massachusetts General Hospital, Boston

Dr. Tom Whitman, the very person that Sally was talking about was, at that moment, getting a briefing on one of the patients in the hospital.

"The patient is a forty-three-year-old woman, Mrs. Margaret Allen. You may have heard of her. Her husband, Joe Allen, owns North Atlantic Maritime Shipping, with more ships than the entire navy of some countries," Dr. Parrish said.

"How is she presenting?" Dr. Whitman asked. Tom Whitman was six feet three inches tall, and just under two hundred and twenty-five pounds of all muscle. He was an exceptionally powerful man and he looked much more like a dockworker, than the skilled surgeon he was.

"Her symptoms are excruciating pain, a lack of

appetite, and frequent vomiting," Dr. Parrish said, reading from the admission paper.

"Have you examined her, Doctor?" Tom asked.

"I have."

"Your diagnosis?"

"She has a tumor in her stomach. I'm afraid there is nothing we can do about it."

"Maybe I can remove the tumor," Tom suggested.

"What? No, that is impossible! You can't do abdominal surgery, it is too dangerous. Why, nobody has ever removed a stomach tumor except during autopsy," Dr. Parris said.

"Not true. Dr. Theodor Billroth did so a couple of years ago at the Surgical University Clinic of the Allgemeine Krankenhaus in Vienna," Tom said.

"And the patient lived?"

"She did indeed, and had a rapid recovery. So if it has been done once, it can be done again. And what other choice do we have?"

"Tom, you are as skilled a surgeon as I have ever met, so if this guy in Vienna could do it, I've no doubt but that you can too."

"Will you assist?" Tom asked.

"I would be honored to."

When Tom stepped into the room to see Mrs. Allen a few minutes later, her husband, Joe, a tall, dignified-looking man, was sitting at her bedside. Her face reflected the pain she was experiencing.

"Mr. Allen, Mrs. Allen, I'm Dr. Tom Whitman. I would like to talk to you about a procedure I want to do."

"Will it make the pain go away?" Joe Allen asked.

"It will, if I am successful."

"Then try it."

"I have to warn you, however, that if I am not successful, the results could be fatal."

"You mean I might die," Mrs. Allen said. It wasn't a question, it was a statement, and there was no anxiety in her voice,

"Yes."

"Try it, Doctor, by all means try it," Mrs. Allen said. "If I die during the operation, I would still be better off than I am now."

Half an hour later, Tom and Dr. Parish were in the operating room with Mrs. Allen. She was on the table, unconscious now from the administration of chloroform.

The operation was being conducted in the amphitheater with other doctors and student doctors observing. The tumor, about the size of an apple, was removed from her stomach, the incisions were sewn back together, and the patient was taken to a special room set aside for recovery.

"Amazing," Dr. Parrish said as he and Tom were washing up after the operation. "How were you able to do that, knowing that the slightest slip of the scalpel could have killed her?"

"It was simple," Tom said.

"Simple? Are you crazy? What do you mean it was simple?"

"Well, you said it yourself, Harry. The slightest slip of the scalpel could have killed her, so I just made certain that the scalpel didn't slip."

Harry Parrish laughed out loud. "I suppose that is as good an explanation of how to perform a difficult surgical procedure as anything I ever heard in medical school. You're a fine doctor, Tom, and Mass General is lucky to have you."

Big Rock, Colorado

When the train carrying Smoke and the others back home pulled into the station at Big Rock three days later, Kenny Prosser, one of Smoke's hands, was standing on the depot platform to greet them.

"It's really great to see you back!" Kenny said enthusiastically.

"Wow, Kenny, I didn't think you would miss me that much," Pearlie said.

"Nah, I didn't miss you at all," Kenny said. "But it's time for the bake sale, 'n that means Miss Sally will be makin' her bear sign. Whenever she does that, why, she always makes enough for the hands to have a few."

"As soon as she gets them cooked, I'll be sure to bring a couple of them out to the bunkhouse so you and the others will have them to share," Pearlie teased.

"What? Two? For all of us to share?"

Sally laughed. "Oh, I think we can do better than that."

"Better not let Pearlie take them out there Miss Sally, or it's more than likely two to share is all they will get," Cal said.

"Ha! Like you would do any better," Pearlie challenged.

"Listen, I didn't bring your horses, seein' as I knew you would have luggage, so I brought a buckboard," Kenny said. "I hope that's all right."

"Too lazy to saddle four horses, huh?" Pearlie teased.

"What? No, I . . ."

"Did exactly the right thing," Smoke said, easing the young man's concern.

Kenny looked around. "Where's the girl? Where's Tamara?"

"She chose to stay with some old friends of hers," Sally said.

"Will she be comin' back up here?"

"No, I don't think so. She seems fairly pleased with the arrangement."

"Well, if she's happy with it. But she was a nice girl, and me 'n Lou is for sure goin' to miss her."

"They're unloadin' the luggage now," Pearlie said, glancing at the little depot cart near the baggage car. "Come on, Cal, Kenny, let's go get it."

Smoke's ranch was seven miles west of Big Rock, and the team pulling the buckboard kept up a steady trot so that they reached the ranch in just over half an hour. When they left Eagle Road, they turned under a sign that spanned the driveway, with the name Sugarloaf worked in wrought-iron letters across the arch. Driving up the long drive, they approached a big, two-story house, a large barn, a long bunkhouse, and a few other buildings. Every building was well kept and had a fresh paint job.

"Oh, it is good to be home," Sally said.

"Not as grand as Live Oaks," Smoke pointed out.

"Oh, but that is where you are wrong, sir," Sally said with a contented smile. "I would never want to live anywhere else but Sugarloaf, and that makes it as grand as any ranch, plantation, or estate."

Smoke reached over to take Sally's hand. "You're

right at that, Sally. There is nothing more grand than Sugarloaf."

When Kenny pulled the buckboard to a stop in front of the house, Smoke and Sally stepped down, and Smoke, almost without thought, put his arm around her.

"Seein' as you 'n Miss Sally are goin' to be huggin' 'n all, I'll take your luggage in," Pearlie said, grabbing Smoke and Sally's bags.

"I'll help Kenny put away the team and buckboard," Cal added.

After the other three left, Sally kissed Smoke.

"Wow, you really are happy to be back home, aren't you?" Smoke asked.

Sally smiled. "Yes, well, being back home is fine, but what I like most is the eighteen thousand dollars we made from the trip."

"Only thirteen, after paying for the cars. But it's good to know that it's my money you love, and not me. What if I go broke? Will you still love me?" Smoke teased.

"Always, my love, always," Sally replied, kissing him.

CHAPTER SEVEN

When Smoke went to town the next morning, he encountered Sheriff Monty Carson at Longmont's Saloon.

"Smoke, it's good to see you back, and you got here just in time," Sheriff Carson said.

"I got back just in time for what?"

"I got this telegram this morning," Sheriff Carson said, showing a little yellow sheet of paper to Smoke. "I think it's something that you might find very interesting.

SHERIFF I JUST SAW CUTTER MACMURTRY
IN FULFORD STOP HE IS WALKING
AROUND AS BIG AS LIFE STOP
ANGUS POTTER

"Fulford is just across the county line, so it's out of my territory. But you hold a commission from the governor, so the fact that he is across the county line won't mean anything to you."

"What about the sheriff in Fulford?" Smoke asked.

"Sheriff Burleson is death on drunks in the street, but I'll be honest with you, I don't think he wants anything to do with a man like Cutter MacMurtry. If you ask me, that's exactly why MacMurtry is there."

Smoke took another look at the telegram. "Tell me, Monty, how much faith do you put in this telegram?" he asked.

"Angus Potter was one of the first deputies I had after I was elected sheriff," Carson said. "He was a good man until he lost the use of one arm in an accident. If he says MacMurtry is there, then I'd be willing to bet the farm on it."

"All right," Smoke said. "I'll take a trip over to Fulford and check it out. But do me a favor, would you? Send one of your deputies out to tell Sally where I am."

"I won't send a deputy," Sheriff Carson said. "I will personally go out to your place and tell her myself."

"Thanks. I appreciate that."

Sally was drawing a bucket of water from the pump on the back porch when she saw Sheriff Carson riding up. At first she smiled at the visit because the sheriff was a good friend.

But why was he here, while Smoke was in town? She felt a twinge of fear and put her hand to her mouth.

"Has something happened?" Sally asked, fear in her voice.

"What? Oh, no, Sally, no! I'm sorry, I didn't mean

to frighten you. Smoke asked me to come see you to tell you he would be away for a little while."

"Away?"

"We know where Cutter MacMurtry is, and Smoke is going after him."

Sally nodded. She knew it could be dangerous, but she also had faith in him and in his ability to deal with people like MacMurtry.

"Good," she said. "After what MacMurtry did, he needs to be brought to justice."

Sheriff Carson shook his head. "Sally, it's very unlikely that someone like Cutter MacMurtry is going to let himself be taken alive."

"Well, Sheriff, there is justice, and then, there is justice," Sally said with a grim smile.

Smoke had gotten Angus Potter's address from Sheriff Carson and when he rode into the little town of Fulford, the very first place he visited was Angus Potter's house. There was a woman out in the front yard rubbing clothes against a washboard in a tub of soapy water. A line was hung with clothes, and a tub adjacent to the washtub contained clear water that was filled with even more clothes. There were many more clothes than a man and his wife would have, and Smoke realized that Mrs. Potter must be taking in wash to make ends meet.

"Mrs. Potter?"

"Yes?"

"My name is Smoke Jensen, I'm a friend of Sheriff Carson and . . ."

"Come on in, Mr. Jensen," Angus Potter said, stepping out onto the porch. He was holding a pistol in his right hand, having been ready to deal with the visitor should he have proven to be unfriendly. Potter's left arm hung, uselessly, by his side. "Monty must have gotten my telegram."

"Yes, that's why I'm here."

Smoke followed Potter into the house. It was quite small, three rooms only consisting of a living room, bedroom, and kitchen.

"I apologize for my wife not comin' in to be a hostess, but with this useless arm, there's not much I can do to make a livin'. Truth is, she supports me, and I don't know what I would do without her."

After a little more exchange of small talk, they got down to details.

"I've been keepin' an eye on MacMurtry ever since I first seen 'im," Potter said.

"You're sure it is Cutter MacMurtry."

"MacMurtry's not only wanted here, he's an escaped prisoner from Texas. There are some real good descriptions out on him; big man, bald headed, and no neck. Yeah, I'm sure it's him."

"Do you have any idea where he might be now?"

"I know exactly where he is now," Potter replied. "He's down at the Pick 'n Shovel Saloon."

Smoke nodded. "Thanks, Mr. Potter, you've been a big help."

"Watch yourself with 'im, Mr. Jensen. He's a tricky son of a bitch."

"I'll be careful."

* * *

After turning down an invitation to stay for lunch—
he didn't want to be a burden on what he knew was a
tight budget—Smoke rode on into town. Although
Fulford was in a different county, it wasn't really that
far from Big Rock, and Smoke had been there several
times. Because of that, he knew the town fairly well.
He had been here during all seasons, when the single
street was covered with snow and ice, and in the
spring, when it was a muddy mire, worked by the
horses' hooves, and mixed with their droppings so
that it became a stinking, sucking, pool of ooze. He
had also been here in the summer when it was baked
hard as a rock. It was summer now, and the sun was
yellow and hot.

The Pick 'n Shovel Saloon wasn't hard to find,
because it was the only saloon in town.

Loosening his pistol in the holster, Smoke walked
inside. Because of the shadows, there was an illusion
of coolness inside the saloon, but it was an illusion
only. It was still hot, and the dozen and a half customers who were drinking had to keep their bandannas
handy to wipe the sweat from their faces.

From what he could tell of the customers, there
were only cowboys and a few men who worked in the
Fulford Mine. Less than half were even wearing guns.

The bartender stood at the end of the bar, wiping
the used glasses with his stained apron, then setting
them among the unused glasses. When he saw Smoke
step up to the bar, he moved down toward him.

"What'll it be?"

"Beer," Smoke said.

"I know you, don't I?" the bartender asked.

"Could be," Smoke said.

The bartender grinned. "Yes, you're Smoke Jensen from over Big Rock way. What brings you to Fulford?"

"I'm looking for someone," Smoke said.

"Oh?"

"I wonder if you might have seen him," Smoke said. "He's a big man with a bald head that sits right on his shoulders like a cannonball."

"What are you lookin' for him, for?"

"He killed a friend of mine, and his wife, then he beat and raped their daughter. She is only fourteen years old."

The bartender nodded. "I heard about that case. And you think it was Joe Jones that done it?"

"Joe Jones?"

"That's what he's tellin' ever' one is what his name is, but I never believed it, not for a minute."

"So, you have seen him. Do you know where he is? I was told that he was in here," Smoke said. He took a drink and eyed the bartender coolly. "But I don't see him."

The bartender raised his head and looked toward the stairs at the back of the room. "That may be 'cause you just ain't lookin' in the right place," he said.

Smoke followed the bartender's eyes, then finishing his beer, he started upstairs.

"That's Smoke Jensen," one of the saloon patrons said, quietly.

"Smoke Jensen? Are you sure?"

"Yeah, I'm sure. His ranch is over near Big Rock, but he's been here lots of times before."

"What's he doin' here do you . . . what the hell? He's holdin' a gun in his hand!"

"He must be after somebody."

"Yeah, 'n I bet I know who," one of the other patrons said.

Muffled sounds from the room at the head of the stairs, which normally went unheard because of the flow of conversation, could clearly be heard now that all conversation had stopped. The attention of everyone was riveted on the man who was climbing the stairs, with a gun in his hand.

When Smoke reached the top of the stairs he tried to open the door, but it was locked. He knocked on it.

"We're busy in here," a gruff voice replied.

"Cutter MacMurtry, I've come for you!" Smoke called. As soon as said the words, he stepped to one side.

Just as he expected, a shot was fired, and a bullet hole the size of a man's thumb and the height of a man's chest, appeared in the door as the heavy .44 caliber slug tore through the wood.

Almost immediately after the shot, Smoke heard the crash of glass, and, kicking the door open, he rushed inside. A woman, with an expression of terror on her face lay on the bed, covering her nakedness with a blanket. The floor was covered by long shards of glass, and Smoke ran over to look outside. He saw MacMurtry running up the alley, and lifting the window, he climbed out ono the mansard ledge then dropped to the ground below.

As soon as he hit the ground there was a shot, and the bullet was so close that Smoke could not only hear the pop, he could also feel the concussion. Smoke was unable to return fire because the shot had come from around the corner of the building, and MacMurtry was not in sight.

Moving cautiously to the end of the alley, Smoke paused for a moment to look around. There was another shot and this time the bullet hit the ground beside him, then ricocheted off with a loud whine. The shot had come from the loft of the livery across the street and looking toward the opening, Smoke saw a wisp of gun smoke drifting away.

Smoke ran across the street and dived behind a watering trough, just as MacMurtry fired a third time. Smoke heard the loud thump of the bullet as it hit the side of the trough. That was followed by the sound of water as it began dripping through the hole.

Getting up, Smoke darted into the barn itself. The horses in the stalls had been made nervous by the shooting and were now quite restless. A few of the horses were actually kicking at the sides of their stalls.

Smoke smiled, because he knew that the noises the horses were making in their agitation would be enough to cover any sound he might make as he maneuvered for position against MacMurtry.

"Who are you, you son of a bitch?" MacMurtry called from the loft.

Smoke remained quiet.

"Who are you?" MacMurtry asked again, the tone and expression of his voice showing his fear and agitation. "What for are you after me?"

One of the horses whinnied, and another kicked at the side of his stall. Using that diversion, Smoke started climbing up to the hayloft, not by the ladder as would be expected, but by the cross bracings that were on the inside wall of the barn. It took him but a moment, then he was able to lift his head up above the floor of the attic and take a look out. He saw MacMurtry squatting behind a stack of hay, pointing his gun at the top of the ladder where he thought Smoke would appear.

"Drop the gun, MacMurtry," Smoke said.

MacMurtry whipped his gun around and shot at Smoke. Again, Smoke could hear the snap of the bullet as it passed close by his ear. MacMurtry missed, and before he could shoot again Smoke returned fire. Smoke didn't miss.

MacMurtry put his hand over his chest, as if attempting to stop the bleeding, but the blood flowed freely between his fingers. He looked up at Smoke with a grotesque smile on his face.

"Is this on account of I kilt Tyrone Greene?" MacMurtry asked.

"Good guess," Smoke replied.

"How'd you know I was the one that done it?"

"From an eyewitness."

"You talkin' 'bout the little girl?"

Smoke didn't reply.

"Damn, I shoulda kilt . . ." that was as far as MacMurtry got before a couple of pained gasps closed out the conversation, and his life. He fell to the loft floor, his blood staining the straw.

One week later Smoke was in the sheriff's office in Big Rock. Monty Carson was pouring coffee into two cups.

"It's all taken care of," Sheriff Carson said. "Angus Potter is getting the reward."

"Good," Smoke said. "From what I could tell, he can use it."

"It was good of you to do that."

"Like you said, I hold a state commission from the governor, so I wasn't eligible for the reward, and we wouldn't have known where to find him, had it not been for Mr. Potter. And I would hate to see the reward go to waste."

The cups full, Monty handed one of them to Smoke.

"Here's to Angus, and to justice being done," Monty said, holding his cup out.

"And to Tyrone and Mary Greene, may they rest in peace," Smoke said, touching his cup to the sheriff's.

CHAPTER EIGHT

Audubon, Texas

Aaron Dawson, who was a purchase manager for the Texas Pacific Railroad, was, at the moment, not on a train, but on a stagecoach. He was in a stagecoach because it was, currently, the only means of public transportation between Weatherford, Texas, and Audubon.

Dawson, who was an overweight man with dark and slickly combed-back hair, was wearing a three-piece brown suit. The suit was causing him to sweat quite profusely, and because of that, he clutched a handkerchief with which he was constantly wiping his face.

For the first part of the trip Dawson had been reading the newspaper, but he lay it down now and looked at the other two passengers. One of the passengers was an attractive young woman, and the other was her young son. She had told him her name, earlier, along with the information that she was going to join her husband. Her husband, Lieutenant William D. Kirby, was currently posted at Ft. Richardson.

"Have you come far, Mrs. Kirby?" Dawson asked.

"Yes, I've come all the way from Philadelphia. Of course, most of the trip was by train, so it was quick and comfortable. It has only been these last few miles that we've had to endure the ordeal of such primitive travel."

"Well, I've no doubt but that when you and Lieutenant Kirby leave Ft. Richardson for your next assignment, you will be able to do so by railroad."

"I would certainly like to think that," Mrs. Kirby said, "But I don't know if it will ever happen or not."

"Oh, it will happen all right, for I intend to see to it that it happens."

"I beg your pardon, you intend to see that it happens?" Mrs. Kirby asked. "How so?"

"I am in the preliminary stages of building it now."

"You are building a railroad?" Mrs. Kirby asked, impressed by the information.

"In a manner of speaking I am. I am the project manager, and I am making all the arrangements."

"Oh, what a marvelous thing that must be, to be able to build something as wonderful as railroad."

"I'm going to drive a train when I grow up," the boy said.

"That's quite a noble ambition, young man."

"My name is Albert."

"Well, Albert, the day will come, probably within my lifetime, but certainly within your lifetime, when every city in America will be connected by railroad. Why, I've no doubt but that it will one day be possible to travel between any two points in America, regardless of how remote, or how far apart they may be, within two weeks."

"Oh, think of that!" the young woman said. "Who would have ever thought that any two places on this vast continent would be separated by but two weeks or less?"

"We are living in a wonderful age," Dawson said. "Travel by train, and messages sent as rapidly as a streak of lightning. Why, I have even read of a device that is like the telegraph, except that it will allow a person to speak into one end of a wire and have the very words he has spoken heard by someone at the other end."

"Oh, yes!" the woman answered excitedly. "It is called a telephone. There are many who have them in Philadelphia. Why, by the time Albert is grown I've no doubt that he will have one in his house, and with it, be able to have conversations with distant friends."

"I will talk to you and Papa," Albert said.

"I'm sure you will," Mrs. Kirby replied, smiling at her son.

"Audubon!" the driver called down from his seat. "We're comin' in to Audubon!"

A few minutes later the stagecoach came to a halt in front of the depot in Audubon, and Dawson stepped down.

"Well, this is where I must leave you," Dawson said. "But I do hope the rest of your travel is comfortable."

"Hurry up and build the train so that when we leave we can ride on it," Albert said

"You can count on it, young man. I mean, Albert," Dawson replied with a smile.

He supervised the off-loading of his luggage, then

arranged for it to be taken to the Del Rey Hotel. That taken care of, he walked two blocks down to the Bank of Audubon, as the stagecoach continued on its journey.

Audubon was a bustling little town, with three churches, a school, two cotton gins, four saloons, several mercantile stores, two blacksmiths, a lawyer, Jason Pell, and one physician, Dr. E. B. Palmer.

"May I help you sir?" a rather thin, officious-looking young man asked as Dawson entered the bank building.

"Yes, you may. I am Aaron Dawson, and I would like to speak with Mr. Charles Montgomery."

"I'm Drury Metzger, the vice president of the bank. I'm certain that I can help you with any business you may have with the bank."

"No, I must speak with Mr. Montgomery."

"Really, Mr. Dawson, this is not a convenient time for the presi—"

"It's all right, Drury, I'll speak with him," a tall, silver-haired, very dignified-looking man said.

"Very well, sir. This gentleman has introduced himself as Aaron Dawson."

"Yes, Mr. Dawson, I received your letter and I have been expecting you," Montgomery said. "Please, come into my office."

Drury stepped into Montgomery's office, along with Dawson, but Montgomery held out his hand to stop him.

"That's all right, Drury, I'll handle this. If you don't mind, please see to the bank's business while I am engaged with Mr. Dawson."

Drury stopped just inside the door. He was being

dismissed. He didn't like that; he was the vice president of the bank. Dawson had no right to dismiss him.

"And please, close the door," Montgomery said. Montgomery waited until the door was closed before he turned his attention back to his visitor.

"Now, Mr. Dawson," Montgomery said. "How may I help you?"

"I'm sure that you are aware, are you not, that the Texas Pacific Railroad has laid plans to build a railroad from Weatherford to Fort Richardson. That will, of course, bring the railroad right through Audubon."

"Yes, I have heard that," Montgomery said, with a big smile on his face. "It has been the talk of the town, but we have received no official word that it is actually to be done."

"Oh, it will be done, sir. As I represent the Texas Pacific, you may regard this as official word. And, because Audubon is almost exactly halfway between Weatherford and Fort Richardson, it is our intention to use Audubon as the headquarters for this expansion project."

"What a wonderful thing that will be for our community," Montgomery said. "Now, sir, you have come to see me for a specific purpose. What can I do to help bring this about?"

"Our anticipated cost, at least for the preliminary construction, will be one hundred thousand dollars. You can be our banker for this project," Dawson said.

Montgomery gasped. "Oh," he said. "As much as I would like to, it would not be possible for this bank to make a loan that large. I'm afraid that the amount you just mentioned exceeds our total deposits."

Dawson chuckled. "You misunderstand me, sir. We

aren't asking for a loan—we have sufficient funds to carry out the building. What I meant to say is that we will soon be depositing one hundred thousand dollars in your bank."

"One hundred thousand dollars? You want to deposit one hundred thousand dollars in our bank? Oh, my, that is a great deal of money."

"Yes, it is a great deal of money. Mr. Montgomery, are you saying that you are unable to handle a deposit that large?"

"No, no, we are quite capable of handling it! And we would be happy to be your banker. Will that be in the form of a single deposit?"

"No. Our first deposit will be for ten thousand dollars. That money will be used to build our office here and to start our initial surveys. Once everything is established, we'll bring the rest of the money here."

"Very good, sir, we'll be ready for it," Montgomery said.

"Mr. Montgomery, I'm sure I don't have to stress for you the need of secrecy. Oh, not that the railroad will be coming through, that will be common knowledge soon enough. What I'm talking about is secrecy with regard to the transfer of the money."

"Oh, yes, I quite agree," Montgomery said. "We must keep the transfer of funds absolutely secret."

"Not that secret," Metzger said quietly.

After having been told to leave Montgomery's office, Metzger had gone into his own office. His office was separated from Montgomery's office by a thin wall, and he was sitting there, very quietly, listening to the discussion taking place in the next room.

Now, he thought, I need some way to take advantage of this knowledge.

Recalling an article he had read in the *Audubon Eagle*, earlier in the day, he walked over to the desk and picked it up to read again.

Bank Robbers Still At Large.

The two bank robbers who survived the shoot-out in Pella are still at large. One has been identified as Clete Lanagan, though the identity of the other robber is still not known. Readers of the Audubon Eagle will remember the recent post which described the bank robbery in vivid detail, so it is not necessary to re-examine the particulars at this point, though the courage of those brave towns people who fought so nobly to defend their bank, does bear further mention.

A reward of one thousand and five hundred dollars has been posted for the bandit Lanagan, said money to be paid when Lanagan is brought to justice, whether he be dead or alive.

What made this article particularly interesting to him was that it was about Clete Lanagan. Clete Lanagan's mother had died and his father had deserted him when he was very young. Lanagan's mother had been the older sister to Metzger's mother, so his parents had taken the young boy in. As a result, Drury Metzger and Clete Lanagan had been raised exactly as if they were brothers.

There was a reward of one thousand five hundred dollars for Clete, and Metzger thought about going to the sheriff with the information that could lead to his capture. He quickly dismissed the thought, though, not because of any familial connection, but because he believed he could use Clete to make even more money.

Metzger lay the paper down and smiled. He had recently gotten a letter from his cousin, and he knew exactly how to get a message back to him.

Opening the middle drawer of his desk, he took out the letter and reread it.

Dear Drury—

    I take pen in hand to tell you that your cuzin is doing gud. It cud be that you has herd about me seein as I just done some things that the papers has wrote about.

    You may mind that when we was boys together you was always the smart one and I was always the one what got into trubel. If you would want to rite to me send it to Orrin Morley in Post Oak Texas.

Orrin Morley had been a neighbor with the two boys were growing up, and since Morley had died a long time ago, there was no doubt in Metzger's mind that this letter was from Clete.

Metzger wrote a letter to his cousin that very day.

Douglas Wilkerson was the postmaster in Post Oak, Texas. One week earlier he had received a letter addressed to Orrin Morley at general delivery. Wilkerson had been the postmaster for two years, and because the population of Post Oak had never exceeded three hundred in all the time he had been here, he knew every resident. But he had no idea who Orrin Morley might be.

Wilkerson held the letter for nearly a week, and had just decided that he would give it but one more week before he returned it as undeliverable. As it turned out, he didn't have to wait one more week, nor even one more day. That very afternoon someone he had never seen before came into the post office. His visitor had a very disfiguring scar that gave him a misshapen eye and an ugly puff of scar tissue to one end of his mouth.

"Yes, sir, may I help you?" Wilkerson asked.

"You got 'ny mail for Orrin Morley?"

"Indeed I do, sir!" Wilkerson replied with a broad smile. "It is most fortuitous that you arrived when you did. The letter has been here for one week, and as your name is not one with which I was familiar, I'm afraid I would not have kept it for much longer before I would have been required to send it back as undeliverable. Are you a new resident, sir? Shall I look for more mail for you?"

"Quit your gabbin' 'n give me my letter."

The smile left Wilkerson's face.

"Just a moment, sir," he said in a flat and expressionless tone.

CHAPTER NINE

Audubon, Texas

Colonel Conyers' son, Dalton, was the deputy sheriff of Audubon. He was twenty-four years old with bright blue eyes, and though the freckles of his youth were gone, his hair was still a reddish blond. The young deputy was having breakfast at the Palace Café, and sharing the table with him was Sheriff Peabody's daughter, Martha Jane.

She was a very pretty girl, twenty-one years old, tall and slender, though certainly rounded enough that no one would doubt her sex, even from a distance. Auburn haired and brown eyed, her skin was fair and her cheekbones were high.

"I appreciate you having breakfast with me this morning, Marjane," Dalton said, using the name that Martha Jane's family and friends used.

"I'm always happy to take a meal with you, Dalton, though I must admit that breakfast seems a rather odd meal for courting."

"Not at all," Dalton said. "Breakfast is the most intimate meal of the day."

"Breakfast is an intimate meal? What do you mean by that?"

"Well, think about it, Marjane. Breakfast is the first meal one has after getting out of bed, and it is a meal that one generally eats alone, or with family. That makes it something very exclusive, don't you see?"

Marjane laughed. "You're funny. Maybe that's why I like you."

"You like me, huh?"

"Well, I don't dislike you," Marjane teased. "Tell me, what do you hear from your folks?"

"Oh, I have a new sister!" Dalton replied.

"What? A new sister? But . . . how is that possible?" Marjane asked. "How old are your parents?"

Dalton laughed.

"Well, she isn't really my sister. But Mom and Pop have taken her in. Her name is Tamara, and she is fourteen years old."

"How did a fourteen-year-old girl come to live with your parents?

"She lived on the ranch when she was a little girl because her pa worked for Pop. But then her ma and pa were murdered, up in Colorado, and she needed someplace to go."

"Oh, how awful for her!" Marjane said.

"I remember her from when she was a little girl. She had a way about her so that everyone on the ranch liked her. Under the circumstances, I think coming back to live on the ranch with Mom and Pop may be just what she needs to get over this tragic thing that happened," Dalton said.

"I hope so," Marjane said.

"Oh, oh, here comes your father," Dalton said, noticing the big man with gray hair and a bushy, gray mustache who had just stepped into the restaurant. Sheriff Peabody was wearing a gray shirt, which, like the shirt Dalton was wearing, sported a five-pointed star over the left breast pocket.

Sheriff Peabody removed his hat and held it as he looked around the dining room. When he saw his daughter and his deputy, he came over to the table.

"Won't you join us for a cup of coffee, Papa?" Marjane asked.

"I just had a cup, thank you, darlin'. Dalton, I'm going to need you for a job, but not this minute. You and Marjane can go ahead and finish your breakfast, then if you would, come on over to the office."

"All right, I'll be right there as soon as I can," Dalton said.

"Like I said, there's no rush. Enjoy your breakfast."

Despite Sheriff Peabody's assurance that there was no need to come right away, Dalton began to hurry through his breakfast.

"Why are you hurrying so, Dalton? Papa said you could take your time," Marjane said.

"I know, but don't you see that it was a test?" Dalton replied.

"A test?"

"Yes, of course. Your pa wants to see what kind of man is courting his daughter. If I delay he will think me lazy and inefficient. If I respond quickly, he will think me dedicated and dependable." Dalton smiled across the table at Marjane. "And *that's* the kind of man he would want for his daughter."

Marjane returned his smile. "Then you go on, don't let me detain you."

Dalton finished his coffee, then grabbing a half-eaten

biscuit to take with him, hurried down the street to the sheriff's office.

"You didn't make me an ogre in my daughter's eyes by abandoning her, did you?" Sheriff Peabody asked.

"Marjane understands," Dalton said.

"Yes, she's been a sheriff's daughter long enough that I suppose she does at that."

"What do you have for me, Sheriff?"

"It has to do with the man we have in jail."

"You mean Steve Magee, the one we picked up day before yesterday for getting drunk and breaking out a window in the Brown Dirt Cowboy Saloon?"

"That's the one," Sheriff Peabody said. "Only it turns out his real name isn't Steve Magee. I got a letter from Sheriff Wallace over in Jack County. Someone identified our prisoner as Seth McCoy, so I want you to take him over to Antelope where you can turn him over to the sheriff there."

"All right," Dalton replied.

"And Dalton, I need to tell you that McCoy is wanted for a lot more than breaking out a window. In Jack County he has already been tried and convicted for murder. He escaped the day before he was to be hanged, which makes him a very desperate man. So please, be very careful with him. I wouldn't want anything to happen to you. The Colonel would never forgive me, to say nothing of my daughter."

"I will be extremely careful," Dalton promised.

Sheriff Peabody smiled. "You should be back in time for dinner tonight, and I'm supposed to ask you out to the house, because Marjane has it in mind that you might like her fried chicken."

"Marjane is right, I *will* like her fried chicken."

"Uh, huh. But the truth is, you would probably eat boiled skunk, if Marjane cooked it for you."

"You're probably right," Dalton answered with a grin.

"Well, I can't think of a better young man for her to be interested in," Sheriff Peabody said. Opening a drawer in his desk, he pulled out a pair of wrist shackles and handed them to Dalton. "Come on to the back with me and we'll get McCoy ready to go."

There were two cells in the back of the sheriff's office, and though each cell would accommodate four prisoners, at the moment Seth McCoy was the only one in custody. He was sitting on one of the four bunks that were in his cell, and he looked up as Dalton and Sheriff Peabody came to the door. McCoy had dark, narrow eyes and a shock of coal-black hair.

"What is it?" he asked. "What do you want? What are you doin' with them wrist irons? You already got me in jail for breakin' out a winder light. There ain't no need for you to have to be puttin' me in irons."

"You're about to take a trip, McCoy," Sheriff Peabody said.

"McCoy? What are you talkin' about? My name ain't McCoy, it's Magee."

"According to Sheriff Wallace over in Jack County, your name is Seth McCoy, and you escaped jail there."

"I ain't McCoy, I tell you." There was a degree of desperation in his voice, when tended to belie his denial.

"There's lots of folks in Antelope that know Seth McCoy, because they were at the trial that convicted

McCoy and sentenced him to hang. So if we get you over there, 'n you aren't Seth McCoy, they will no doubt correct the mistake," Sheriff Peabody said. "And if that isn't who you are, why, we'll just bring you back here, let you serve out the rest of the thirty days, then let you go."

"You're sendin' this boy with me?" McCoy asked with a disdainful sneer. "Tell me this, boy, just what makes you think you'll get me there?"

"Oh, I'll get you there, McCoy," Dalton replied. "You may be lying belly down across your horse before this trip is done, and Sheriff Wallace may have to grab you by the hair and lift your head to get a good enough look so he can identify your body, but I will get you there."

"Did you hear that, Sheriff? Your deputy just threatened to kill me."

"Don't worry about it, McCoy. If Deputy Conyers is forced to kill you, the county will pay for your burial. Now, hold your hands out so we can cuff you."

While Sheriff Peabody kept his gun trained on McCoy, Dalton shackled the prisoner's hands together.

"All right, let's go," Dalton said. "I've got your horse saddled outside."

Shortly after they mounted, Dalton dropped a hangman's noose around McCoy's neck.

"Here, what is this? What are you doing? What's this for? Are you crazy? I could break my neck with this thing!"

"Yes, if you're not careful, you could indeed, break your neck," Dalton said. "So I would suggest that you make no effort to get away from me."

As the two riders left town, McCoy was in front, with

Dalton right behind him. A rope stretched from McCoy's neck to Dalton's hand, and their departure drew a lot of attention from those who were out on the street.

Less than half an hour after Dalton left with his prisoner, Lanagan and Claymore came riding into Audubon. The two men observed everything about them, the riders and wagons on the street, the pedestrians on the sidewalks, and even the gaps between the buildings.

"This don't seem like much of a town," Claymore said. "What'd we come in here, for?"

"I told you, I got a letter from someone that told me there was a chancet to make a lot o' money here."

"From a town no bigger 'n this? How?"

"I don't know yet."

"You trust the feller that sent you the letter?"

"Yeah, I trust 'im," Lanagan said without any additional comment.

"While we're here, we're goin' to spend some o' this here money we got, ain't we?" Claymore asked.

"Good idea," Lanagan replied. "I wouldn't mind havin' a drink or two."

"'N maybe a woman?" Claymore suggested.

"I ain't so sure 'bout gettin' no woman," Lanagan said.

"Why not?"

"They's been many a man betrayed by a good woman."

Claymore laughed. "Well, there you go, Clete, who said anythin' about a *good* woman?"

Lanagan laughed as well. "You got a point there. Tell me, Dingus, you ever been to Audubon?"

"Audubon?"

"That's what this town is called."

"No, I ain't never been here. Hell, I ain't never even heard of it."

"Good. I ain't never been here neither, so they's not much chance of either one of us gettin' recognized."

There were four saloons in town.

"Which one do you fancy, Clete?" Claymore asked, referencing the saloons.

"That there 'n, the Saddle 'n Blanket, looks 'bout as good as any of them," Lanagan replied. "'N it's toward the edge of town so 's if somethin' comes up 'n we have to on the run, we'll be halfway gone afore we even leave."

Tying off their horses, the two men went inside the saloon, where they were met, almost immediately, by a bar girl. She was heavily made up, and the clothes she wore left little to the imagination. The dissipation of her profession had begun to set in, so it was difficult to determine how old she was; she could have been anywhere from twenty-five to forty-five years old.

"Well now, I haven't seen you two handsome boys before," she said, putting a seductive purr into her voice.

"What's your name, honey?" Claymore asked.

"It's Candy. Candy Good," the girl said.

"Candy Good? That's quite a name."

"You like it? I made it up my ownself," Candy said with a broad smile.

Claymore looked at Lanagan. "You think you can get along without me for a while?"

"You go ahead," Lanagan said. "What I want more than anything else right now is a whiskey. That old fool McCall didn't have one drop of liquor in that cabin. Then, soon as I take care o' gettin' me the drink I need, I got someone I need to see."

Lanagan stepped up to the bar as Claymore followed Candy upstairs.

"Well, sir, I haven't seen you before," the bartender said with a friendly smile. "Are you settling here, or just passing through?"

"I'm drinkin'. That is if you'll shut up the gab, and serve me a drink."

"Yes, sir, what will it be?" the bartender asked, the friendly smile gone.

"Whiskey," he said.

The bartender poured him a shot, and Lanagan took it down in one swallow.

"You sure drank that fast," the bartender said.

"Well now, this here ain't exactly what you would call sippin' whiskey, now is it?"

"No, I don't reckon it is. I got some o' that, but it'll cost you more 'n fifteen cents. You want to try some of it? Or another from this bottle?"

"I don't want nothin' more yet," Lanagan said. "I got me some business to take care of, then I'll more 'n likely be back."

"Very good, sir," the bartender said, taking both the glass and the bottle from the bar.

The bartender watched Lanagan push through the batwing doors. "You don't have to hurry back," he said, too quietly for anyone else to hear.

The bank was only one block away from the Blanket and Saddle Saloon, and as soon as Lanagan stepped into the bank, he saw Metzger talking to the bank teller. Metzger looked toward him, but gave no sign of recognition.

"Yes, sir, can I help you?" Metzger asked as he came to him.

"I'm thinkin' 'bout puttin' some money in the bank here, 'n I want to talk to someone about it," Lanagan said, using the opening Metzger had suggested in the letter."

"Well, step into my office and we'll discuss it," Metzger said.

Fifteen minutes later, the two men came back out of the office. "Mr. Morley, I do hope you see fit to use our bank for your business," Metzger said.

"Well, I'll sure give it some thinkin' on," Lanagan replied. "I'll let you know."

Metzger followed his cousin to the door, then started back toward his office.

"Mr. Metzger, you don't really expect that man to deposit any money with us, do you?" the teller asked.

"I don't know. Why do you ask, Mr. Dunaway? Do you know him?" There was some disquiet in Metzger's question, though Dunaway didn't pick up on it.

"No, sir, I've never seen him before in my life. But he doesn't seem to me like a potential customer."

Metzger's chuckle was one of relief. "You may be right, Sid, but I can't turn someone away just based on his looks now, can I?"

Dunaway chuckled. "No, sir, I don't suppose you can."

Their conversation was interrupted by a woman customer who came into the bank then.

"Mrs. Sidwell," Dunaway said. "How good to see you this morning."

Metzger returned to his office, then sat at his desk and thought of the agreement he and Lanagan had made. Metzger would be getting ten percent of the money, which would come to ten thousand dollars.

He would go to Paris.

CHAPTER TEN

Ernest Dean Fawcett had just stepped into the saloon less than a minute before Lanagan returned from his business with the bank. The visitor from Pella was standing at the bar when Lanagan came back to the saloon. Shocked to see him, Fawcett studied Lanagan in the mirror, because he didn't want to look directly at him. The last time Fawcett had seen him, he had been looking down the barrel of a gun as Lanagan was leaving the Bank of Pella amidst a shower of bullets.

Fawcett tossed down his drink.

"Another?" the bartender asked.

"No, I gotta go," Fawcett said. He turned his head as he passed Lanagan. He didn't think Lanagan would recognize him. After all, the last time he had seen him, Lanagan had been rather busy.

Fawcett hurried down to the sheriff's office.

Sheriff Andrew Peabody was sitting at the desk in his office when Fawcett came in. Because Fawcett wasn't a resident of the town, Sheriff Peabody didn't recognize him. There was a look on the man's face that could only be described as anxious.

"Yes, sir?" the sheriff said, by way of greeting.

"Sheriff, my name is Fawcett. Ernest Dean Fawcett."

"What can I do for you, Mr. Fawcett?"

"I'm down here from Pella, I come down to buy me a team o' mules from R. D. Clayton."

"Yes, sir, I can understand that. R.D. has the best mules in the state," Sheriff Peabody said. "But I know Mr. Clayton to be an honest man. Are you having some problem with R.D.?"

"No, no, I ain't even talked to him yet. This here is somethin' else. You know how it is that you law fellas is always a-tellin' us to keep our eyes open all the time, 'n to tell you if we see somethin' that ain't right, or somethin' that maybe you should know?"

"Yes, I'm quite aware of that, Mr. Fawcett. Do you have some information I should know?"

"Yes sir, I do. There's a feller over in the Blanket and Saddle Saloon that maybe you should know about."

"Who would that be?"

"His name is Clete Lanagan. 'N I know he's a wanted man 'cause what he done is, he robbed the bank up in Pella. You have heard about that, haven't you?"

"Yes, indeed, I have heard about it. But how do you know this man in the saloon is Clete Lanagan?"

"'Cause the last time I seen 'im, me 'n him was a-shootin' at one another. That's 'cause he come runnin' out of the bank with a gun in one hand, 'n the money bag in the other. I commenced a-shootin' at 'em, just like most ever 'one else in Pella. We kilt two of 'm, but Lanagan 'n one other man got away.

I don't have no idee where that other man is, on account of I didn't see him, but I can tell you right now for sure 'n certain that Lanagan is here in your town, 'n you're the sheriff."

"You are quite right about that, Mr. Fawcett, I am the sheriff," Sheriff Peabody said, standing up, and loosening his pistol in his holster.

"There's a reward out for Lanagan, ain't there?"

"I believe there is. One thousand and five hundred dollars for robbery and murder," Sheriff Peabody replied.

"'N I'll get the reward for tellin' you about it, won't I? What I mean is, I don't have to actual go capture 'im myself or nothin' like that to get the money, do I?" Fawcett asked.

Sheriff Peabody chuckled. "So you're after the reward, are you? And here I thought you were a good citizen just doin' your job."

"Well, I am doin' my job," Fawcett insisted. "I told you about him, didn't I?"

"I reckon you did at that."

"You goin' to bring 'im in by your own self?"

"It looks like I'm going to have to. My deputy is out delivering a prisoner to the jail over in Antelope."

"Yeah, well, you better watch out, they say Lanagan is a mean 'un."

"So I hear. But, I can deputize you if you'd like to come help me," Sheriff Peabody said.

"What? Uh, no, I ain't none prepared for nothin' like that. What I mean is, well, it's your job, ain't it?"

Sheriff Peabody sighed. "Yes, it's my job. You can wait here if you like. When I get back I'll validate your claim that you're the one who pointed him out to me. That way, you can put in for the reward that's being offered."

"Yeah, all right, I'll stay here," Fawcett said, obviously relieved that he would not have to take part in confronting the known outlaw.

Fawcett watched the sheriff leave, thinking about the reward money. It would more than pay for the mules he had come over here to buy. He smiled. This was goin' to turn into a pretty profitable trip.

Lanagan had spent a quarter for a glass of whiskey from the "good" bottle, and though it was a little better, he couldn't tell that it was any better than the fifteen-cent whiskey had been.

"I just heard me some o' the damndest news ever," one of the other drinkers in the bar said.

"What's that?"

"You know the feller Sheriff Peabody's got 'n the jail here, the one that broke out the winder over at the Brown Dirt Cowboy?"

"Yeah, what about 'im?"

"Turns out his real name is Seth McCoy, 'n they was fixin' to hang 'im over in Antelope, afore he escaped."

"So, what's Sheriff Peabody goin' to do with 'im?"

"I don' know, I guess he'll hang on to 'im, 'til they send somebody over to fetch him."

"Hell, he's already gone, Deputy Conyers took 'im back to Antelope this mornin'."

"That ain't hardly likely. I mean, Conyers ain't hardly wet behind his ears yet. Could you see Peabody trustin' him to take a prisoner like Seth McCoy?"

The others laughed. "More 'n likely, what you seen

Conyers takin' was some drunk somewhere. No, sir, my bet is that Seth McCoy is still a-sittin' in our jail."

"Wouldn't it be somethin' if they was to hang 'im here? It's been a while since I seen me a hangin'."

"I ain't ever seen one, 'n I don't want to see one."

Lanagan listened to the conversation with interest. He and Seth McCoy had done a few jobs together. If he was going to steal this hundred thousand dollars Drury had told him about, he was going to have to start rounding up some good men, and Seth McCoy would be one he would like to have.

Sheriff Peabody had never seen Clete Lanagan before, but he did have a description of him. Lanagan had been a wanted man long before the bank robbery up in Pella. He stepped into the Blanket and Saddle Saloon, and after a quick glance around, saw someone standing at the bar. The man was tall and husky, with pale gray eyes and, most noticeably, a very prominent scar on his left cheek that disfigured both his eye and the corner of his mouth. This fit the description he had of the wanted man, Clete Lanagan.

The irony was that though Sheriff Peabody was the one who would have to confront Lanagan and actually make the arrest, the reward money would be paid to Fawcett. That was because Peabody, being an officer of the law, would not be able to collect a reward for bringing a fugitive in.

That didn't really bother him; he wasn't after the reward. Sheriff Peabody was an honest sheriff and a man as dedicated to his profession of being a lawman, as he had been when, as a sergeant major in Conyers' legion, he had been cited for bravery at the Battle of Seven Pines. Peabody wanted Lanagan simply because it was his job to bring him in.

"Mr. Lanagan?" Sheriff Peabody called from the opposite end of the bar.

Lanagan did not react to the call.

"You, standing there at the bar. Your name is Clete Lanagan, isn't it?"

The other drinkers moved quickly away from the bar, and even the bartender ducked down out of sight.

Lanagan had still not moved, which was evidence enough that he was the man Sheriff Peabody thought he was.

"You talkin' to me?" the solitary figure at the bar asked in a low, guttural voice.

"I am, sir. I am Sheriff Andrew Peabody, and I am putting you under arrest for bank robbery and murder. Will you come peaceably? Or, do you intend to give me trouble?"

Lanagan saw something in the mirror, just before he turned to face Sheriff Peabody. Peabody was holding a gun, pointing it at the man he had just placed under arrest.

"Well now, Sheriff, I ain't never done nothin' peaceable in my whole life," Lanagan replied with what could best be described as a mordant laugh. "You plannin' on shootin' me, are you?"

"I would rather not shoot you, Lanagan, I would rather give you the opportunity to stand trial. But as you can see, I am holding a gun on you and I must warn you that I am perfectly prepared to shoot you if it should come to that. I hope that it does not."

Lanagan let his hand hang just over the handle of his pistol.

"Well, it's goin' to come to that," Lanagan said with a confident smirk.

"Don't be a fool, Lanagan. I've got the drop on you, and I told you, I will shoot if I have . . ."

The sheriff's admonition was interrupted in mid-sentence by a gunshot, and Peabody went down with a bullet in his upper chest.

"Did that fool really plan on arrestin' you?" a thin-faced, beady-eyed man asked, as he stood on the bottom step of the stairs, holding a smoking pistol in his hand.

"Damn, Claymore, I seen you in the mirror just a standin' there. You sure took your own sweet time in shootin' 'im," Lanagan complained. "You almost waited too long."

Candy Good had started down the stairs with Claymore, but now, having witnessed the unexpected shooting, she stood behind him with a look of horror on her face.

"You might say I was . . . occupied," Claymore replied with a ribald smile, jerking his thumb back toward the girl. He looked back toward the sheriff's body which was lying still, on the floor. "Did I kill 'im?"

Lanagan stepped over to look down at the man Claymore had just shot. "No, you didn't kill 'im."

"Too bad. Maybe I had better finish him off," Claymore replied, heading toward the supine form.

Though Sheriff Peabody was flat on his back, he was conscious, and at the moment, staring up at the man, aware that he was about to breathe his last.

Claymore pulled the hammer back.

"No, wait!" Lanagan said, holding up his hand. "Don't kill 'im."

"Why not?"

"It might be more useful for us to keep 'im alive," Lanagan said.

"How would that be?"

"If he ain't dead they'll be more worryied about takin' care of him than they will be about comin' after us."

"All right," Claymore replied, lowering his pistol. "I don't know why, but if you say so, I'll let 'im live."

Except for the conversation between the two men, there was absolute silence in the saloon as everyone stared at them.

"Anybody here got 'ny plans to do somethin' 'bout what just happened?" Lanagan asked. Now he, like Claymore, was holding a pistol in his hand.

The bartender looked out over the room at all the remaining customers. Nobody said a word.

"We have no such plans," the bartender said.

"That's smart of you. It's a good way to stay alive," Lanagan said. "By the way, that bottle of the quarter whiskey? Give it to me."

"Sure thing, Mr. Lanagan," the bartender said, turning to get the bottle off the shelf behind him. "There won't be no charge." He held the bottle out across the bar.

"No charge," Lanagan said with a little laugh. "Well now, barkeep, that's a good one. It really is."

With Lanagan and Claymore holding pistols in their hands, and Lanagan clasping the bottle of whisky in his other hand, the two men pushed through the doors and hurried out front.

"Before we leave town we've got to take care of a little business," Lanagan said as he and Claymore hurried out of the saloon.

"What kind of business?"

"I just learned that they're holdin' Seth McCoy in jail here. He's a good man, 'n we're goin' to need some more men for what I got in mind now."

"We're goin' to break him out?"

"Yeah, who's goin' to stop us? The sheriff?" Lanagan asked with a little laugh.

"All right, if you say so. But considerin' I just shot the sheriff, I don't think it would be a good idea for us to hang around here much longer."

"The sheriff ain't in no condition to be doin' nothin' about it, 'n like I told you, as long as he's still alive, why ever' one will be worryin' so about him, that they won't be payin' no attention to us. 'N we're goin' to need more men, a lot more men, to do this job I'm plannin'."

"What job?"

"One that'll make us a lot of money. I'll tell you later, Right now, let's get McCoy 'n get out of here."

With their guns still in hand, the two men pushed the door open and rushed into the sheriff's office. The only person there was Ernest Dean Fawcett, who was waiting for the return of the sheriff so he could collect the reward.

"What? What are you doing here?" Fawcett asked, the tone of his voice betraying his fear.

"You the jailer?" Lanagan asked.

"What? No."

"Then, what the hell are you doing here?"

"I . . . I'm just waiting to see the sheriff."

"Yeah? Well, I got a feelin' he ain't goin' to be around for a while," Lanagan said with an evil laugh. "Keep this here feller covered, Claymore, while I go after McCoy."

Lanagan hurried into the back of the jail, but was surprised to see that both cells were empty. He came back out front.

"Where's McCoy?" he demanded.

"Who is McCoy?" Fawcett asid.

"The feller that was in jail. Where is he?"

"I . . . I don't know. Like I say, I'm just waitin' to see the sheriff. The office was empty when I got here."

"You seen the deputy?"

"No, sir, I ain't seen him."

"They said the deputy was takin' somebody somewhere, it must have been McCoy after all," Lanagan said, his words little more than a growl. "Come on, let's go."

As Lanagan and Claymore started for the door, Fawcett, in a bold and foolish move, drew his pistol.

"You're worth fifteen hunnert dollars, 'n you ain't gettin' away!" Fawcett shouted.

Lanagan and Claymore both whirled around, and both men fired. Fawcett was thrown back against the wall by the heavy impact of the two bullets. He slid down to the floor where he remained, held up in a sitting position by the wall against his back.

"Fifteen hunnert dollars," he said, the words barely audible.

CHAPTER ELEVEN

"They're gone, they've rode out of town!" Someone called back into the saloon. He was standing at the batwing doors, and had seen Lanagan and Claymore go into the jail, then come back out no more than a minute later, and ride away.

"Quick, somebody get Doc Palmer," the bartender said.

"What for? The sheriff is more 'n likely goin' to die."

"Well, he isn't dead yet, so do what I said, and get the doctor!" the bartender repeated, this time putting it in the form of an order.

Barely five minutes later Dr. Palmer hurried in, carrying a little black bag. He knelt beside the sheriff. Bar towels had been used to stop the bleeding, and Dr. Palmer removed them, cleaned the wound with carbolic acid, then stuffed some gauze into the bullet hole. That done, he ordered a couple of the bystanders to get the sheriff down to his office.

"Someone ought to get the sheriff's daughter," one of the saloon patrons said.

* * *

Marjane Peabody was employed as a clerk in Miss Suzie's Dress Emporium, and she was dealing with a customer at the moment.

"This dress will be just perfect for you, Mrs. Dungey. Why, whoever picked out the blue dye for the dress must have been thinking of your eyes."

"Oh, Marjane," Roxanne Dungey said with a self-conscious laugh. "I must say, you are the perfect salesperson."

Marjane had just finished making a package of the dress when she looked up to see Jason Pell coming into the store. Pell was a lawyer and a good friend of her father's.

"Mr. Pell, did you come to buy something for Mrs. Pell?" Marjane asked with a warm, welcoming smile. "We've got some new . . ."

"No," Pell said, interrupting her in mid-sentence.

There was something in the tone of Pell's voice, something in the expression on his face, that Marjane found frightening. She took a deep breath as she felt her stomach grow light.

"What is it, Mr. Pell? What's wrong?" Marjane asked.

"It's your father, Marjane. Sheriff Peabody has been shot."

"Oh, God in Heaven no!" Marjane said, lifting her hand to her mouth. "Has he been . . ." she stopped in midsentence, unable to say the word "killed."

"No, dear, he's still alive, but he is badly hurt. He's down at Dr. Palmer's office now."

Suzie York, who owned Miss Suzie's Dress Emporium, had come to the front of the store when she heard the jingle of the doorbell announcing Lawyer Pell's entrance. Because she had done so, she had also overheard the conversation.

Marjane looked toward her employer.

"Go, Marjane, by all means, go to your father!" Suzie said.

With a nod of her head, and tear-filled eyes, Marjane left the store with the lawyer. That was when she saw Ponder leaving the sheriff's office with a covered body lying in the back of his funeral wagon.

"No! No!"

"That's not your father!" Pell said quickly, when he saw where Marjane was looking. "We don't know who he is, but we believe he may be the man who identified Lanagan, the man your father was trying to arrest when he was shot. The sheriff is down at Dr. Palmer's office."

Marjane ran down the street to Dr. Palmer's office.

"Where is he? Where is my father?" she shouted, as she ran inside.

"He's back here, child," Dr. Palmer's disembodied voice called from the back room of the office.

Marjane went into the back of the office, where she saw her father, lying on his back on a small operating table.

"Is he . . ."

"He's still alive," Dr. Palmer said.

"Papa! Oh, Papa!" Tears were streaming down her face.

Sheriff Peabody opened his eyes, then opened and closed his hand, as a signal for her to take it. She did so, and he tried to squeeze it, but didn't have the strength to do so.

"You are going to have to be brave for him," Dr. Palmer said. "He is going to need your strength."

"Where is Dalton?" Marjane asked. "Why isn't he here?"

"I . . . sent . . . him . . . to . . . Antelope," Sheriff Peabody said, gasping out the words.

Just as the sight of one man holding a rope looped around another man's neck had drawn attention when Dalton and McCoy had left Audubon, so too did it as they rode into Antelope.

"McCoy!" someone said. "That's Seth McCoy!"

"I didn't think they would ever catch that murderin' son of a bitch!" another said.

Paying no attention to the gathering excitement their arrival had caused, Dalton directed McCoy to the jailhouse.

"Get down off your horse," Dalton said once they reached their destination.

When McCoy refused to dismount, Dalton gave the rope a little jerk.

"Careful with that, careful!" McCoy said. "I'm gettin' down."

McCoy dismounted and, with the rope still attached to McCoy's neck, the two men went inside.

"Sheriff Wallace?"

"Yes, that's me," Wallace said.

"I'm Deputy Conyers from over in Audubon. I have a prisoner for you."

"Seth McCoy," Sheriff Wallace said. He smiled. "Well now, I must say that the folks here in Antelope are going to be awful happy to see you."

"Sheriff, I wonder if you would sign a receipt for the prisoner so Sheriff Peabody can get it cleared off our books," Dalton asked.

"I'll be glad to. By the way, McCoy had already been tried, found guilty, and condemned before he escaped. I expect we'll get the gallows built and hang him rather quickly so he doesn't get away from us again. We'll be hangin' 'im real soon, just in case you'd like to come back over and see the results of your work."

"Uh, thank you, no," Dalton said. "I wouldn't care to see anyone hang."

"It's not a pretty sight, I'll give you that," Sheriff Wallace said as he finished writing out the receipt. "Here you are, my good man, and, do give Andy my best, will you?"

"Yes, sir, I will," Dalton replied.

"Good for you, mister, for bringin' that killer back so's we could hang him!" someone shouted to Dalton as he rode out of town.

When Dalton dismounted in front of the Audubon sheriff's office much later that afternoon, he was carrying both the receipt for the prisoner and a letter of thanks to Sheriff Peabody from Sheriff Wallace in Antelope. He was trying to decide whether to give the thank-you letter to him right away, or give it to him over the chicken dinner.

"Hey, Deputy, where've you been?" C. G. Marvin asked. Marvin was the editor of the *Audubon Eagle*.

"I was delivering Seth McCoy to the sheriff in

Antelope," Dalton replied. He smiled. "He was just real pleased to get him too."

"Then you don't know about Sheriff Peabody, do you?"

Dalton's smile was replaced by a look of concern. "Know about Sheriff Peabody? What are you talking about? What is there I should know about him?"

"Then you don't know. I'm afraid the sheriff has been shot."

"What? Oh, no! Was he killed?"

"No, he's still alive, but barely. Doc Palmer has him in his office now."

Dalton glanced toward the doctor's office.

"Go on down there, if you want to," Marvin said. "I'll take the saddle off your horse and take him to the stable for you."

"Thanks, C.G., I appreciate that," Dalton said, handing over the reins absently, his mind already on the sheriff.

The first person Dalton saw when he stepped into the doctor's office was Marjane. She was sitting in a chair clutching a tear-stained handkerchief.

"Marjane, I just heard! How is your father?"

"Oh, Dalton!" She said, getting up and hurrying over to him. Dalton took her in his arms.

"Is he . . . ?" Dalton asked, anxiously, unable to complete the sentence.

"He's still alive," she said in a weak voice. "Oh, Dalton, what will I do if he dies?"

Dalton embraced her, and while still holding her

in his embrace, looked up as Dr. Palmer came into the room.

"You two can come on back now, if you would like," Dr. Palmer invited.

Stepping into the back room, they saw Sheriff Andrew Peabody stretched out on the operating table.

"Is he going to make it, Doc?" Dalton asked.

"I'll be honest with you, Dalton, I don't know," Dr. Palmer said. "There is no more internal bleeding, and I've managed to keep him from going into hemorrhagic shock. But that bullet is going to have to come out, or it's going to get much worse."

"Why haven't you taken it out?" Marjane asked.

"Sweetheart, I'm just a country doctor, I can get most bullets out, but this one is too close to the heart, and I'm afraid if I make an effort I might well wind up killing him. Only a skilled surgeon would even try."

"You said yourself that he was going to die if that bullet doesn't come out," Marjane said. "So at least try."

"Wait a minute, Marjane," Dalton said, laying his hand on her arm. "Dr. Palmer, have you ever heard of Dr. Thomas Whitman?"

"Thomas Whitman?" Dr. Palmer replied. "Yes, of course I have. What doctor hasn't? As a matter of fact, he has an article on enteric paraplegia in a recent issue of the *New England Journal of Medicine*."

"Do you think he could get the bullet out?"

"Look, I'm very flattered, but I hope you aren't comparing me to him."

"No, I'm talking about Dr. Whitman. Do you think he could get the bullet out?"

"Oh, I'm sure he could, but Dr. Whitman is chief surgeon at Mass General Hospital in Boston, and to be honest with you, Dalton, I don't think Sheriff Peabody could stand the trip."

"I wasn't planning on sending the sheriff to Boston, I was planning on asking the doctor to come here."

Dr. Palmer chuckled. "You are going to ask one of the most renowned surgeons in America to come to Audubon, Texas, to operate on the sheriff?"

"Yes."

"I admire your loyalty to the sheriff, Dalton, and your desire to do what is best for him. But just what makes you think a noted surgeon like Dr. Whitman would come here?"

"I'll ask him to come," Dalton replied, innocently.

"And you think Dr. Whitman is just going to drop everything and come running to Audubon, Texas. Is that what you're telling me?"

"Yes."

"Oh, Dalton, please don't tease about a thing like that," Marjane said. "This is my father we're talking about."

"I'm not teasing, Marjane. I'm going to ask him."

"I must say, I admire your confidence, Deputy. But just what makes you think he would even read your letter?"

A huge smile spread across Dalton's face. "It won't be a letter, it'll be a telegram, and I won't be sending it to him, I'll be sending it to my sister."

"I don't understand. Why would you send a telegram to your sister?"

"Because my sister is married to Tom Whitman."

"You . . . you mean you actually know him?" Marjane asked, the concern in her face replaced by a hopeful smile.

"Yes, Tom is my brother-in-law."

"Oh, Dalton!" Marjane said, excitedly. "Do you really think he will come?"

"I know he will come," Dalton said.

Dr. Palmer stared at Dalton for a long moment. "Well, Dalton, if you know him, and you really think he might come, I suggest you get in touch with him, right away, because if that bullet doesn't come out within a matter of a few weeks, Sheriff Peabody is certain to die. In the meantime I'll keep Andy stabilized and aseptic, which is the best I can do. But your brother-in-law must get here as quickly as he can."

"Come, Marjane, walk down to the telegraph office with me," Dalton invited.

"Yes, I will. Oh, Dalton, thank you, thank you, thank you."

CHAPTER TWELVE

At Massachusetts General Hospital in Boston Dr. Tom Whitman and Dr. Gene Parrish visited Mrs. Allen, who was now recovering nicely in her own, private room. Her husband, Joe Allen, was in the room with her

"Well, Mrs. Allen, you're going to be released tomorrow, so how do you feel?" Tom asked.

Mrs. Allen smiled, broadly. "I haven't felt this well since I was a young woman," she said.

"Ha! That's not saying much. You are still a young woman," Tom said.

"Doc, they tell me that what you did with my wife is something just real special," Mr. Allen said. "And to show you how much I appreciate it, I just gave the hospital a gift of one hundred thousand dollars, and I did it in your name."

"Why, thank you, Mr. Allen, I appreciate that, and I know that the hospital appreciates it as well."

"To have my Maggie back, healthy again? Believe me, Doc, I'm the one that is appreciative."

When Tom returned to his office, he found his wife, Rebecca, waiting for him.

"Hello, Becca. What a happy surprise to see you here."

"Tom, you've been saying you wanted to take some time off, haven't you?"

"Yes, I have. Why do you ask? Do you have someplace in mind you would like to go?"

"Audubon, Texas."

Tom chuckled. "Audubon, Texas? Oh, I don't know if we can manage that or not. I mean, a place like Audubon? Why, there must be thousands of people wanting to go there," he teased.

"I'm serious, Tom. I got this telegram from Dalton."

SIS DO YOU THINK YOU AND TOM COULD
COME TO AUDUBON STOP SHERIFF
PEABODY SHOT DOC SAYS BULLET
TOO CLOSE TO HEART TO REMOVE STOP
WOULD TAKE SOMEONE LIKE TOM STOP
PEABODY IS GOOD MAN DON'T WANT
HIM TO DIE STOP PLEASE COME QUICKLY
LOVE DALTON

The hospital administrator of Massachusetts General had just heard Tom's request to take leave of the hospital.

"I don't know, it took me forever to get you to leave Texas in the first place, and now you want to go back?"

"Dalton needs me."

"If the bullet is all that close to the heart, what makes you think you could remove it?"

"I may wind up killing him," Tom said. "But if I don't try, he'll be dead within another month, anyway."

The hospital administrator nodded. "You're right about that. How long do you plan to be gone?"

"About a hundred thousand dollars' worth."

The administrator laughed. "You do have a point there. All right, go ahead, Tom, and stay as long as you need. You have my blessing."

"Thanks, Dad," Tom replied with a broad smile.

Hatchett MacMurtry pushed his hat back and stroked the week-old stubble on his chin. "You sure he's in there?" MacMurtry asked.

"Yeah, it's Smoke Jensen, all right. I seen 'im go into Longmont's saloon not more 'n ten minutes ago, 'n he ain't come back out yet," Poke Gilley said. Poke was one of two men that Hatchett MacMurtry had with him. The other man was Frank Ethan."

"The son of a bitch kilt my brother," MacMurtry said. "So I aim to kill him."

"From ever' thing I've heard about Smoke Jensen, he's goin' to take a heap o' killin'," Frank Ethan said.

"You don't want the hunnert dollars?" MacMurtry asked.

"Yeah, I want it. I was just commentin' is all. I mean, hell, who ain't heard o' Smoke Jensen?"

"After today, folks will be sayin', who ain't heard o' Frank Ethan," MacMurtry said. "You'll have the hunnert dollars 'n you'll be famous."

"Yeah!" Ethan said as a broad smile spread across

his face. "I'll be known as the man who kilt Smoke Jensen."

"Where are we goin' to do it?" Gilley asked.

"His ranch is out on Eagle Road, some east of here. Way I figure it is, we'll wait 'til he starts back home, 'n we'll be ridin' toward him like as if we was just comin' into town, mindin' our own business and such. Then when we get into range, why, we'll just open up on the son of a bitch."

"Yeah," Ethan said. "He won't be suspectin' nothin' like that. More 'n likely we'll put three or four bullets in 'im afore he even knows what's goin' on."

MacMurtry, Gilley, and Ethan rode out of town on Front Street until it turned to Eagle Road. When they were about a mile west of Big Rock, MacMurtry held up his hand.

"We'll wait here," he said. "You two fellers, make sure your guns is loaded, 'n take 'em out 'n hold 'em on the saddle in front of you. That way he won't know that you already got 'em out, 'n when you're close enough, you can just raise 'em up 'n start shootin' without givin' him no warnin' or nothin'. You'll both be shootin' while his gun is still in the holster."

"Yeah, that's a good idea," Gilley said.

"I got me another idea too," MacMurtry said.

"What's that?"

"I ain't goin' to be down here on the road with you."

"What? You ain't? Why not?"

"'Cause I'm goin' to be up there on that rock with a rifle." MacMurtry laughed. "Like as not, before you all start in a-shootin', I'll have already kilt the son of a bitch."

"Wait, if you're the one what kills him, we'll still get the hunnert dollars, won't we?" Ethan asked.

"Yeah, you'll still get it."

"All right, only don't start shootin' too quick, 'cause I want to get famous for bein' the one that kilt 'im," Ethan insisted.

"If we're both a-shootin' at 'im, how will we know which one of us done it?" Gilley asked.

Ethan chuckled. "It won't make no never mind which one of us it is what actually kills 'em. With us both shootin', more 'n likely both of us will be the one that done it."

"Unless it's MacMurtry," Gilley said.

"MacMurtry, don't you go shootin' 'til after we start shootin' first," Ethan said.

"All right, all right. Quit you palaverin' about it 'n just be ready when you see 'im comin'," MacMurtry said.

After leaving Longmont's, Smoke stopped at Murchison's Leather Goods shop to pick up a pair of leather chaps Kenny Prosser had asked him to get for him.

"Ha, I see you burned Kenny's name on the chaps," Smoke said.

"Yes, sir, just like he wanted."

"Well, I'm sure he'll be pleased with them."

"Say, Smoke, I don't know if anyone else has told you, but speakin' for myself, I'm damn glad you got MacMurtry. He was one mean bastard, killin' Tyrone Green 'n his wife like that. 'N what he done to that little girl, well, sir, I just want to tell you I'm glad you got 'im."

"Thank you, Tim. But I just wish it hadn't happened at all. The Greenes hadn't been here all that long, but they were mighty good neighbors while they were."

"Where's the little girl now?" Tim asked.

"Oh, she's down in Texas with some people who have known her since she was born. They're giving her a real good home."

"I'm glad for her, bless her little heart. Nobody should have to go through what she did."

Leaving the leather goods shop, Smoke mounted Seven, then rode past Delmonico Restaurant, Nancy's Bakery, White's Apothecary, then past the Denver and Pacific Depot where Front Street became Eagle Road, which led to his ranch, Sugarloaf, seven miles west of town.

"Here he comes," Ethan said. "We'll start ridin' toward him just real natural like we're goin' into town 'n when we get in range, just lift up your gun 'n commence a-shootin'."

"I'm ready," Gilley said. "Let's make sure we start in to shootin' before MacMurtry does."

The two men started down the road, riding slowly and deliberately.

It may have been the slow and deliberate pace the two men were setting as they were approaching that caught Smoke's attention first. Also the way the two men were holding the reins, both of them using only their left hand, while their right hand was folded across the saddle in front of them.

Then he saw a flash of sunlight from the saddle just in front of one of the men . . . it was a brief flash of light, and nothing more, but it did heighten Smoke's awareness.

Reaching down to his own gun, he loosened it in his holster, just in case. He continued to close the distance between them, but did so with a heightened degree of caution.

On top of the little hill behind Gilley and Ethan, MacMurtry watched the two men approach Smoke Jensen. He sighted down his rifle and waited, then, suddenly and unexpectedly, he saw both Gilley and Ethan raise their pistols. He was about to shoot, to time his shot with their two shots, but there weren't two shots! There were four shots! And as the gun smoke drifted across the road, MacMurtry saw Smoke Jensen still mounted on his horse, holding a pistol in his hand. Both Gilly and Ethan were lying on the road.

Now there was just him, and he aimed at Jensen, but held his fire. A moment earlier he had enjoyed the advantage of three to one. Now, the odds were even, and MacMurtry didn't like even odds when it meant one-on-one with someone like Smoke Jensen.

MacMurtry watched as Jensen checked on each of the two men, then lifted them up and draped them across the saddles. That done, he stood in the middle of the road, his pistol still in his hand, observing all around him.

Damn! He's looking right at me! MacMurtry thought.

Still on his stomach, MacMurtry slithered down the back side of the hill. He waited there, scarcely daring to breathe, until he heard the hoofbeats of more than one horse. Crawling, carefully, back to the top of the hill, he saw Smoke Jensen going back into town, leading Gilley and Ethan's horses, with their bodies draped belly down over the saddles.

Once more MacMurtry raised the rifle to his shoulder and sighted down the barrel at Smoke Jensen's back as he rode away. His finger began to slowly tighten on the trigger.

"No," he said, speaking the word aloud, though too quietly for Jensen to hear him. "He's too far away now, for me to be certain I can hit him. 'N if I miss, he'll for sure come back after me. There ain't no way I'll be a-goin' after than son of a bitch all by myself."

MacMurtry walked back to his horse, angry that he wasn't able to kill Jensen.

"I tried, Cutter, I truly did. But here's the thing. You're dead, 'n I ain't. 'N I ain't goin' to get myself kilt tryin' to get revenge for you, be you my brother or not."

Mounting his horse, MacMurtry started south. He had had enough of Colorado. He was going back to Texas.

CHAPTER THIRTEEN

It was the middle of the night and the little town of Antelope, Texas, was dark except for six gas street lamps, spread out along Sharp Road. They were positioned one on either side of the street, at the south end of the town limits, one on either side in the middle of the town, and one on either side of the street at the north end of the town limits. This created three golden bubbles of light, separated by larger spaces of darkness.

Two riders and three horses approached from the south. They were illuminated for just a moment, then passed back into the darkness, their presence marked only by the hollow, clopping sound of hoofbeats. Then they reappeared under the lamps that lit the middle of town. Here, a hangman's scaffold had been constructed, and a printed sign attached to the front. Because the scaffold was illuminated, the sign could be read.

Lanagan and Claymore, the two riders who had just

come into town, stopped in front of the scaffold to study the sign:

SETH M^cCOY
To be <u>legally</u>
HANGED
HERE

On Friday Next

"They ain't wastin' no time gettin' around to it, are they?" Claymore said.

"There are goin' to be a lot of pissed-off people when they find out their little necktie party has been canceled," Lanagan replied with a little chuckle.

"You got a dime?" a slurred voice asked.

"Who the hell is that?" Claymore asked, startled by the voice.

"You got a dime?"

It was then that they saw the man who was asking the question. He was a derelict, lying in the open space between the gallows and the porch. He got up from the ground and came toward Lanagan, reaching out toward him.

"You got a dime for a poor man? A nickel will do."

"Get away!" Lanagan said, lifting his foot from the stirrup and using it to shove him down.

"Come on, let's go," Lanagan said as the vagrant moved quickly, to avoid being stepped on by the horse.

The two men rode on down Commercial Street, then stopped just in front of the sheriff's office where both dismounted and tied the three horses off at the hitching rail. The third horse, though riderless, was already saddled.

With guns drawn, the two men opened the front door and stepped inside. They could hear loud snoring coming from the side of the room.

"I can't see a damn thing," Claymore complained.

Lanagan struck a match and in the flickering flame, saw a lantern. He lit it, then looked over toward the sound of the snoring. He saw a rather portly man sitting in the chair with his feet up on the desk before him. His head was tipped back and his mouth was open, the source of the snoring.

Lanagan pulled a knife from a sheath on his belt then, moving quietly, got around behind the man. In the next second, he brought the knife across the deputy's throat, cutting through his jugular and his windpipe.

The deputy's eyes came open in surprise, then, feeling pain and a wetness on his neck, he put his hand to his throat, pulled it away, and saw that it was covered with blood. The look of surprise turned to one of horror, and he tried to call out, but the severance of his windpipe had left him mute. Within a few seconds all life and animation left, as he died.

Picking up the lantern, Lanagan and Claymore moved into the cell area at the back of the jailhouse. Seth McCoy was the only prisoner, and he was sound asleep.

"McCoy," Lanagan called.

"What the hell you want? Can't a man sleep?" McCoy called back, his voice groggy.

"Well, you can sleep if you want to," Lanagan said. "Or, you can come with us, and miss your necktie party."

"What?" McCoy said. Sitting up he looked into the lantern, but couldn't see beyond the light. "Who are you? What are you talking about?"

Lanagan lowered the lantern so that the light shined onto his face. He was grinning.

"Lanagan!" McCoy called excitedly. "What are you doing here?"

"Why, me 'n my pal here have come to take you with us," Lanagan replied. "That is, unless you had rather stay here 'n hang."

"What? No! No! I want to come with you! But what about the guard?"

"He's sleeping," Lanagan said. "And he ain't likely to ever wake up," he added, as he fit the key into the lock of the cell door.

As they passed through the front office, McCoy stopped.

"Wait a minute," he said, and he walked around to the back of the jailer's desk and jerked open a drawer.

"What are you doing?" Lanagan asked.

"This fat son of a bitch keeps a sack of horehound candy, and he never would give me a piece," McCoy said.

McCoy took out the sack of candy, then stuck a piece in the jailer's mouth. "There you go," he said with a little chuckle. "Don't say I never gave you anything."

"Wait, I got an idea," Lanagan said. "The folks in this town are wantin' to see a hangin', aren't they?"

"Sure looks like to me, the way they got the gallows 'n sign up 'n all," Claymore said.

"Let's give 'em one," Lanagan said with a smile.

The three men rode back down to the gallows

where the old homeless man had moved back to his position near the porch of the feedstore.

"Hey, you," Lanagan called. "If you still want that dime, come over here."

The man got to his feet, but he hesitated for a moment, not sure whether or not the offer was genuine.

"Come over here," Lanagan said, stretching his hand out. He was holding a dime between his thumb and forefinger.

With a smile, the bum moved toward him, and when he got there and reached out for the coin, Lanagan brought his pistol down, hard, on the man's head.

When Lanagan, Claymore, and McCoy rode out of town five minutes later, the old derelict was hanging by his neck from the recently constructed gallows.

"Hey, McCoy, who was that feller we hung back there?" Lanagan asked. "When you was here before you went to jail, did you ever see 'im?"

"Only when he would come around beggin'," McCoy said. "Somebody said that he used to be a soldier oncet, but I don't know if that's true or not."

Convicted Criminal Escapes.

Leaves Behind Two Murdered Men.

Seth McCoy, a man who had been convicted of a brutal murder and was, until recently, waiting in a jail cell that was in the very shadow of what was to be the instrument of his demise, has cheated the hangman. It is not known how McCoy made good his escape, though it is an absolute certainty that he had assistance.

Before leaving, McCoy added two more murders to his gruesome tally. His first victim was Martin Coker, the jailer, who was 49 years old. Coker was a widower, his wife having died two years previous. He had one son who lives in St. Louis.

When the sun rose this morning, its beams fell upon the pathetic figure of Carmine Teodoro, who, by his neck, hung suspended from the same gallows that had been constructed for the special purpose of hurling into eternity the most foul and perfidious Seth McCoy.

Most citizens of Antelope knew Teodoro only as a derelict who, of late, has been roaming the streets of our fair town begging for coins from those who pass by. But there is much more to know about this gentleman, and had we known the full story, our citizens would have looked on him with more kindness and, yes, perhaps even some admiration.

Sergeant Major Teodoro served with the Seventh Cavalry under the gallant George A. Custer and was with him on the august general's last ride to Glory. Of course Teodoro wasn't with Custer himself, for all the troopers with him perished. Sergeant Major Teodoro was actually with Major Marcus Reno and so great were his personal actions in the fight against the Sioux that he was awarded the coveted Medal of Honor. It is believed that the horrors he witnessed on that fateful day contributed to his becoming the drunk that we knew.

Weatherford, Texas

After three days of travel, Rebecca was in the waiting room of the Texas and Pacific Depot in Weatherford, Texas while Tom was making arrangements to hire a surrey to take them the fifteen miles north, to Audubon.

"Hello, little lady, you're sure a purty thang, though. You come to work for Lulu, did you?"

Rebecca turned to see a scruffy-looking man, a week since his last shave, a month since his last bath, and at least three months since any attempt at a haircut. He was grinning at her with what could only be described as a ribald smile.

She looked away from him without answering.

"Don't look away from me when I'm talkin' to you," the man said. "Why, I'm one of Lulu's best customers. Like as not, oncet you become one of her whores, why me 'n you's goin' to get to know each other just real good."

"I have not come to work at Lulu's," Rebecca said without looking back toward him.

"Goin' inter business for yourself, are you?"

"Please, sir, leave me alone."

"Well now, I'm just tryin' to be friendly, is all." He reached out for her, and she turned to avoid him.

"Now that ain't very friendly," he said. He reached out again, and again Rebecca was able to avoid him.

"Playin' hard to get, are ye? Well, I like them little games," the man said.

"Sir, I do believe my wife has shown you, by word and action, that she would prefer that you leave her alone," Tom said, coming back into the depot then. The one who had been pestering Rebecca looked around to see a rather large man. His size was offset by what he was wearing. He had on a three-piece suit, a four-in-hand tie, and a bowler hat.

Rebecca's tormentor laughed.

"Well now, ain't you the fancy lookin' one, though? This here is your wife, is it?"

"She is."

"You look to me like an Eastern dude. Is that what ye are? Some Eastern dude?"

"I am from Massachusetts."

The expression on the man's face showed, clearly, that he had no idea where, or even what, Massachusetts was.

"Yes, I am from the East."

Now the man smiled again, a diagonal slash of mouth that displayed missing, crooked, yellow teeth.

"Yeah, that's what I thought. So, tell me, how'd some Eastern dude like you ever manage to get yourself such a purty whore for a wife? You ever been in Texas before?"

"Becca, I have rented a surrey and have it loaded," Tom said, ignoring the question of the irritating man. "We can go, now."

"Hey, Eastern dude, it ain't very nice, you not answerin' me 'n all, so I'm goin' to forgive you this one time on account of you not bein' from here. It's more 'n likely that you ain't never heard of me before, but my name is Emile Gates. And they don't nobody be uppity aroun' me 'n stay healthy, if you know what I mean."

"If we get started now, we can be there before dark," Tom said, putting his hand on Rebecca's elbow and starting toward the door.

Gates hurried over to stand in the door to prevent them from leaving.

"I ain't through with you yet," Gates said.

"Perhaps not, but we are through with you," Tom said. "I would appreciate it if you would step aside."

"'N I'd appreciate it if you showed me a little respect," Gates said. He pulled his pistol and pointed it at Tom. "Now you may be a big feller 'n all, but out here in Texas that don't make no never mind." Once again, a twisted smile appeared on Gates' face. "'Cause you see, here's the thing. It don't much matter none how big 'n strong you are, 'cause you sure as hell ain't bigger'n a .44 caliber bullet. Now, this is what we're goin' to do. You're goin' to have that purty little lady of your'n give me a kiss, right here on the cheek. If she does that, I'll let the two of you get on about your business." Gates put his finger to his cheek and again showed his yellowed teeth in a crooked smile.

"Oh, I don't think she would want to do that," Tom said.

"Then I reckon I'll just shoot you."

By now everyone else in the waiting room had been drawn into the drama playing out before them, and they watched to see how the Eastern dude would handle it.

"Oh, I hardly think you would shoot me in front of these witnesses," Tom said, confidently.

"I wouldn't count on that, mister," one of the others in the depot said. "It's pretty clear that you ain't never heard nothin' about 'im, or else you'd know better. But the truth is, if Gates wants to shoot you here in front of ever' one else, he's likely to do it."

"That's the truth," another said.

"All right, go ahead and shoot," Tom said, calmly.

The smirking smile left Gates' face and he glared at Tom.

"What did you say?"

"I said, go ahead and shoot me, if you think you can." Tom's words were quiet and calm, so calm that Gates became agitated.

"What do you mean, if I think I can?" Gates asked.

"I'll tell you what I'll do. I'll make it real easy for you. I'll move closer so that it is impossible for you to miss." Tom stepped right up to him.

"Mister, don't say I didn't warn you," Gates muttered, cocking the pistol.

Tom reached down and wrapped his left hand around the pistol, putting his thumb against the hammer so it couldn't fall, and preventing the cylinder from turning. Then, reaching up with his right hand, he applied pressure to the area of Gate's neck that joined his right shoulder.

"Ow, ow, ow!" Gates cried. He sank to his knees and released his grip on the pistol so that Tom pulled it away from him. Tom continued the pressure and Gates' cries of pain grew louder, to the complete shock of everyone else in the depot.

Tom released the pressure, but Gates remained on his knees. "What was that?" Gates asked, his voice laced with pain. "What was that you done?"

"I applied pressure to the levator scapulae. That can be quite painful, can't it?" Tom said easily.

"I . . . I can't move my right arm!" Gates said.

"Oh, that's right, you can't, can you? Well, I'm afraid your right arm will be paralyzed for a while, but there's no need for you to worry, it's only a temporary condition. By tomorrow you'll regain use of it. Oh, it'll still hurt, and it will continue to do so for two or three more days, but at least the paralysis won't be permanent."

Tom put his thumb and forefinger back to the same sensitive spot. "I think you should know that I could, quite easily, paralyze this arm for the rest of your life. And should you desire to continue your rude comments, I shall do that very thing."

"No, no!" Gates begged. "Please, don't! I beg of you, please don't! I didn't mean nothin', I was just funnin' you is all. Sort of welcomin' you to Texas, if you know what I mean. Let me go, please, let me go!"

Tom held his thumb and finger on the tender spot for no more than a second longer, then he let go and stepped back. After emptying the shells, Tom took the pistol over and dropped it into the cold stove.

"That should hold you until my wife and I are safely away," he said. "Come, dear."

The others in the depot stared in shocked silence as the well-dressed Eastern dude and his equally well dressed, beautiful wife left the depot and climbed into the surrey Tom had hired.

"Damn, I ain't never seen nothin' like that," someone said.

"Gates, if I was you, I would be gettin' out of town now," another said. This was the same man who had warned Tom. "You've made yourself a lot of enemies and as soon as they learn you have a arm crippled up so as you can't use it no more, one of them is quite likely to pay you a visit."

Still wincing in pain, Gates walked over to the stove. He tried to lift his right hand to open the door, but, as the big stranger from the East had warned him, he was unable to move his arm.

"Would somebody get my gun for me?"

Nobody offered to help, leaving Gates to fish down into the stove with his left hand.

"I don't know who that son of a bitch is, but I'll find him someday and when I do, I'll kill 'im," Gates said, speaking aloud.

"If I was you, Gates, I wouldn't be wantin' to run in to that feller again. It don't matter none whether he's a Eastern dude or not. I got me a idee that he could handle just about anythin' that he's likely to run into, from a grizzly bear to a Injun warrior."

CHAPTER FOURTEEN

When the hired surrey came to a stop in front of the sheriff's office in Audubon, Dalton came hurrying out to meet Tom and Rebecca even before they climbed down.

"Thank God you got here in time," Dalton said. "He's still alive."

"Where is the doctor's office?" Tom asked.

"Right there," Dalton replied, pointing to a building across the street and about half a block down. "Why don't you go have a look at him? I'll get you 'n Becca checked in to the hotel."

"Thank you, driver," Tom said, giving the driver a dollar tip.

"Thank you, sir," the driver said with a broad appreciative smile.

Climbing down, Tom grabbed his medical bag and started down Franklin Street to Dr. Palmer's office.

"Why, aren't you going to greet me, little brother?" Rebecca asked with a warm smile.

"Thanks, Becca, thanks for coming," Dalton said, helping his sister down, then embracing her.

"Dr. Palmer?" Tom said as he stepped inside. "I'm Dr. Whitman."

"Dr. Whitman! What an honor it is to meet you, sir!"

Tom took the doctor's extended hand. "The patient?"

"He's back here. His daughter is with him."

"Is he conscious?"

"Yes."

Tom followed Dr. Palmer to the back of his office, where he saw someone lying in bed. A very pretty young woman was sitting by his side.

"Marjane, this is Dr. Whitman," Dr. Palmer said.

"You are Dalton's brother-in-law, aren't you?" Marjane said.

"Yes."

"According to Dalton, you can do miracles. I certainly hope you can work a miracle with my father."

"Well, I'm surely going to try," Tom said, without questioning the "miracle" accolade.

"Sheriff, how are you feeling?" Tom asked.

"Well, I don't think I'm up to breakin' any broncos," Sheriff Peabody replied with a strained chuckle.

Tom laughed. "It's good that you still have a sense of humor. That means you have a good attitude, and in a procedure like this, having a good attitude is at least half of the fight."

"When do you want to do it?" Dr. Palmer asked.

"I see no reason to waste any time, let's do it right now, as soon as we can get him up on the operating table and sedated."

* * *

"He's under," Dr. Palmer said about ten minutes later.

"You monitor his pulse rate while I do this," Tom said, as he cut into the sheriff's chest.

Dr. Palmer put his finger on the inside of Sheriff Peabody's wrist, keeping it there all the time Tom was searching for the bullet. He gave continuous reports.

"His pulse is still steady, Doctor."

"Here it is," Tom said a moment later. "You were quite right in your assessment; the bullet is quite close to the heart."

"Do you think you can get it, Doctor?" Dr. Palmer asked.

"Hand me the retractors," Tom said.

Dr. Palmer responded, Tom held open the wound. "Forceps."

Using the forceps, Tom very carefully grasped the bullet, pulled it out, then dropped it into the pan of water that sat on a bedside table. The bullet made a clanking sound as it hit the bottom of the pan, and little swirls of blood curled up to the top of the water.

"How's his pulse?"

"Strong, still strong," Dr. Palmer said.

Tom smiled, then removed the retractor.

"You did it," Dr. Palmer said a moment later

"Now, all we have to do is cleanse the wound," Tom said and, opening a little tin box, he poured several white things onto the wound.

"Maggots? You are putting maggots into the wound?" Dr. Palmer asked.

"Yes, they are an excellent way of debridement, that is to say cleaning out the necrotic tissue within a wound. It isn't enough just to remove the bullet, we also have to prevent infection," Tom said.

"And maggots will do that?"

"Indeed they will."

"Damn, I wish I had known about that durin' the war," Dr. Palmer said. "I used to clean all the maggots out of the soldiers' wounds when I saw them."

"That is a natural reaction," Tom replied. "But it was actually during the war that maggot therapy was discovered."

Dr. Palmer stepped into the front of his office, where Marjane was waiting, nervously.

"Marjane, we got the bullet out," Dr. Palmer said. "That is, Dr. Whitman got the bullet out."

"Oh! How is he?"

"He came through the operation well," Tom said. "I think that, barring anything unforeseen, he should have a full recovery."

"Oh! Thank God!" Marjane said, getting up from her chair and hurrying to Tom to give him a hug. "Thank you, thank you."

"I don't deserve all the thanks," Tom said. "If Dr. Palmer hadn't controlled the bleeding and the shock, and kept him stable immediately after your father was shot, he wouldn't have been here for me to operate on."

Marjane smiled through her tears. "I thank both of you," she said.

* * *

When Tom stepped into the sheriff's office a few minutes later, he saw Becca sitting across the table from Dalton. The two were playing chess.

"How is Andy?" Dalton asked, anxiously.

"I think he's going to have a full recovery," Tom replied.

"I knew you could do it," Dalton said. "Thank you, Tom.

Tom chuckled, and pointed to the chessboard. "Why do I get the idea that this is something the two of you have done quite often in your lives?"

"It was a way of keeping our mind off what was going on down in the doctor's office," Dalton said. "When we were growing up, she used to beat me mercilessly," Dalton complained. "Can you imagine having a big sister as cruel as that?"

"It made you a good chess player, didn't it?" Tom asked.

"Best in this town," Dalton said with a confident nod. "And, I'm pretty sure I'm about to beat my sister this time."

"You're going to have to do it without a queen," Becca said as she picked the piece up from the board.

"Damn! How did you do that?"

"It's called concentration," Becca replied.

No more than six moves later, she put Dalton in check, and when he was unable to save his king, the game ended.

"Tell me, Dalton, how did Sheriff Peabody get shot? Do you know who did it?"

"I know exactly who did it," Dalton replied. "Andy

was trying to arrest Clete Lanagan, when Dingus Claymore shot him."

"They both got away?"

"I was delivering a prisoner to the sheriff in Antelope," Dalton said. "By the time I got back, Andy was in the doctor's office, half dead, and Lanagan and Claymore were gone."

"Do you have any idea where they are now?"

"I have no idea where they are now, but I expect we'll be hearing from them soon," Dalton said. "Lanagan isn't the kind not to take advantage of the situation. And with Andy down and me here, by myself, I've got a feeling Lanagan has some devilment in mind. And McCoy may be with them."

"McCoy?" Tom asked.

"The prisoner I delivered to Antelope was Seth McCoy. There was notice, by telegram, that went out to sheriffs all over northern Colorado and southern Wyoming. According to the notice I received, the jailer over in Antelope was killed, and McCoy escaped."

"And you are suggesting that there is some connection between McCoy and the man who shot Sheriff Peabody?"

"I'm doing more than just suggesting. McCoy and Lanagan used to ride together. There is absolutely no doubt in my mind but that Lanagan is the one who busted McCoy out of jail."

"You think McCoy will be joining him?"

"Yes, I do. And that would make three of them. Lanagan, Claymore, and McCoy together would be quite a formidable group. I just hope they don't get anyone else."

* * *

Three weeks after the aborted ambush of Smoke Jensen, Hatchett MacMurtry was the little town of Rowland, Texas. He had fourteen dollars, which was enough to sustain him for a short while, but he was going to have to find some way to make a little more money, and he hoped to do that here.

Going into the Ox Bow Saloon, he stepped up to the bar and ordered a whiskey. He was just starting on his second whiskey when he saw a familiar face.

"Slater? Ed Slater?"

The man at the far end of the bar turned toward him with a look of irritation on his face. But the irritation turned to recognition and a smile.

"Hatchett MacMurtry," he said. "Damn if I ain't seen you in a coon's age. Where you been off to?"

"I was in Colorado some."

"So you decided to come back to Texas, did you? What about your brother? Where's Cutter at?"

"Cutter got hisself kilt up there."

"Oh, I'm sorry to hear that. What brings you back to Texas?"

"Lookin' for work, I guess. You know any ranchers that's lookin' for hands?"

"They's prob'ly some at's lookin', but I got a line on somethin' that's just a hell of a lot better," Slater said. "That is, if you're interested."

"Yeah, I'm interested."

"Bring your drink over to the table, 'n let's talk a bit about it," Slater said.

"Hi, hon," one of the girls said to MacMurtry. "I

don't think I ain't never seen you in here, before. Are you lookin' for a little fun?"

"Leave 'im be, Trudy," Slater said. "Me 'n him has got some business to take care of. After we're done, he's all yours."

"What is this job you're talkin' about that's a lot better 'n punchin' cows?" MacMurtry asked when they sat down at a table.

Slater laughed. "Hell, MacMurtry, what ain't better 'n punchin' cows?"

Hatchett laughed as well.

Dingus Claymore and Vernon Joad dismounted in front of the cabin that sat just back from Rock Creek.

"What's this place?" Joad asked.

"You said you was lookin' to get on somewhere, didn't you?" Claymore asked.

"Well, yeah, but I was figurin' on doin' somethin' that could maybe make a little money. I mean if it's trappin' or somethin' like that, I ain't interested."

Claymore laughed. "It ain't nothin' like that. Come on in, I'll introduce you."

When Claymore and Joad stepped into the cabin he saw two men. One was sitting at the table playing solitaire, and the other was standing at the stove, cooking bacon.

"Put on a little more bacon, McCoy," Claymore said. "I've got us another soldier."

Claymore introduced Joad to both McCoy and Lanagan. "Lanagan is the one you got to listen to," Claymore said. "He's the boss."

"Boss of what?" Joad asked.

"Why, he's the boss of our group," Claymore said.

"I think what Joad is wanting to know, is what is it we plan to do with this little group," Lanagan said. "Is that it?"

"Yeah," Joad said. "That's sort of what I had in mind."

"I can tell you in two words. Make money."

Joad smiled. "Well, sir, I do like to make money."

"Are you particular about how you make it?" Lanagan asked. "What I'm askin' is, you got 'ny thing against stealin'?"

"It don't matter none to me how we get it, long as I get my share."

"Well, Joad, what we do is, we steal money. 'N if somebody gets in our way, it may be that we'll have to kill 'im."

"Is this all we got?" Joad asked. "Just the four of us?"

"It ain't four, yet," Lanagan answered. "Right now there's just the three of us. There won't be four, 'til you decide to come in. Are you in, or out?"

Joad looked at the other three, and saw, by the way they were looking at him that he really had no choice. It was too late now to tell them he didn't want to join them. Lanagan had already told him that they wouldn't hesitate to kill, which meant that if he left them, he would represent a threat to them. And he knew they wouldn't tolerate a threat.

"Hell, I'm in," he said

CHAPTER FIFTEEN

The stagecoach was two and a half hours into its trip from Weatherford to Audubon. There were three passengers inside: a young, newlywed couple and a man in his midfifties.

"I have never seen so much country with so few people," the young woman said. "Why, we haven't seen a town for the last two hours. We would never travel so far in Virginia without seeing some form of life."

"You folks are from Virginia, are you?" the older man asked.

"Yes, sir." The young man put his arm around his wife. "My name is Gary Sinclair, and this is my wife, Bobbi Lee. We were married as soon as I graduated from William and Mary, and now we are going to Audubon, where I am to be an apprentice lawyer with Jason Pell."

"Well, you couldn't pick a better man to start out with," the older man said. "Jason Pell is very well thought of throughout the whole state." He stuck his hand across the gap between the seats.

"I'm Josh Tanner, I own the Audubon Mercantile."

He smiled. "I expect you'll be seeing me whenever you set up your house."

"Yes, sir, I expect we will," Gary replied.

"I wish we would see someone," Bobbi Lee said. "All this open space seems so desolate."

Less than one mile ahead, Clete Lanagan, Dingus Claymore, Seth McCoy, and Vernon Joad were waiting on the Weatherford Road, about to carry out the robbery of the stagecoach.

"You sure this here stagecoach is carryin' money?" McCoy asked.

"No, I ain't exactly sure, but it more 'n likely is," Lanagan said. "Anyway we're in the need of some operatin' money right now, so we're goin' to have to take whatever it has."

McCoy smiled. "You got that right. I ain't got two nickels to my name. I'd kind 'a like to have me a little spendin' money."

Claymore pointed to a rooster tail of dust, which was at a considerable distance down the road.

"Coach is a-comin'," Claymore said.

"Yeah, I see it," Lanagan replied.

"How far away is it, do you think?" McCoy asked.

"I don't know. I'd make it half a mile, maybe," Claymore said.

"All right boys, get ready," Lanagan said. "It'll be here just real soon."

The horses of the four outlaws were staked out about twenty yards off the road, behind a stand of trees. Lanagan went over to his own horse and snaked the Winchester .44-.40 from the saddle sheath. Returning to the road, he got behind a rock, levered a shell into the chamber, and waited.

McCoy had been looking at the approaching coach through a telescope. He slid the scope shut. "I'll be damned."

"What is it?"

"That's Hank Waters, ridin' shotgun," McCoy said.

"You know him?" Lanagan asked.

"Yeah, I know the son of a bitch. He was in the posse that catched me 'n got me put 'n jail. They didn't nobody know who I was then, but that's how I wound up over in Antelope near 'bout to be hung."

"Well, you got nothin' to worry about, 'cause I'm about to take care of him," Lanagan said.

"This dust is just terrible," Bobbi Lee Sinclair said of the dust that was rolling in through the window of the stagecoach. She was using a fan in a losing effort to brush it away.

"I know, dear," Gary replied. "But it won't be much longer."

"The railroad will be coming soon. By this time next year, we'll be able to make this trip by train," Josh said. "Why, then, the trip from Weatherford to Audubon will take little more than an hour, quite different from the half day it requires now."

"Oh, how wonderful that will be," Bobbi Lee said.

"Yes, it will be. Everyone in town is quite excited by it. Why, I expect our population will just about double, in no time."

* * *

Up on the high seat, the driver fought the "ribbons," as the six reins were called.

"They say Sheriff Peabody is gettin' along just real fine," Sam Parsons said. Sam was driving the coach. Hank Waters, his shotgun guard, was riding alongside him. "It was that Eastern doc who done it. He's the brother-in-law to Deputy Conyers, 'n the deputy, he wrote 'im a letter, or sent 'im a telegram, one or the other, don't know which it was."

"More 'n likely it was a telegram," Hank said. "That's what you'd send in case of it bein' an emergency 'n all."

"Yeah, well I'm glad he done it, 'cause the sheriff now, he's a real good man," Sam said.

"Ha, did you see the sheriff dancin' at the cattleman's dance last month, cuttin' up 'n prancin' around somethin' grand?"

"Well, sir, the sheriff is a widow man now, seein' as his wife died a few years ago. 'N ever widow woman in the whole county sees him as someone they could maybe possible marry up with. Once women gets to a certain age, it ain't good for 'em to be alone. Fact is, they nearly 'bout, almost can't stand it, so they go on the prowl for someone like the sheriff." Sam's long dissertation nearly left him breathless.

"Yes, sir, I reckon that might be why they's so many womenfolk that's after the sheriff now. It sure don't seem right to think about him layin' there in the doc's office all shot up now," the shotgun guard said.

"Speakin' of that dance, Hank, I sure as hell don't know how it is that you managed to get Dolly Murphy to dance with you at that selfsame dance. I mean she's as purty as little pair of red shoes, 'n you, why, you're uglier 'n a horny toad," the driver said, teasing the man who was riding beside him.

"What are you talkin' about, Sam? Why, I been told I was right handsome!" Hank replied.

"Yeah? Who would tell you a thing like that?"

"My mama told me," Hank replied, and he began to laugh. His laugh was cut off by the sound of a gunshot. "Uhh!"

"Hank!" Sam shouted as he saw the front of Hank's shirt begin to turn red from blood flowing from a chest wound.

Looking back up, Sam saw four men blocking the road in front of him. All four men were armed. Three of the men were pointing pistols at him, and the fourth had a rifle. Sam was certain that it was a rifle shot that had hit Hank.

He considered trying to run on through them, but realized that such a thing would be foolish. Reluctantly, he pulled the coach to a halt.

"Well now, looks to me like as if you was a-thinkin' 'bout tryin' to run us down. Was you thinkin' that?" the man with the rifle asked.

"I give it a thought," Sam agreed. "But I seen I couldn't do it."

"Uh huh. Well, mayhaps you ain't as dumb as you look. Let's see if you're smart enough to follow orders. Tell your passengers to climb down from the coach."

"You folks inside," Sam called back to his passengers. "Climb out."

Three people exited the coach, two men and a woman.

"It's Lanagan!" the older of the two men said.

"Yeah," Lanagan said. "And now that you know who

I am, you know that you'd better do what I say. You," he added, pointing at the woman. "Get over here."

"What do you want with my wife?" the younger man shouted, putting his hands protectively around the woman.

"You done shot Hank," Sam said. "Don't you be doin' no harm to none o' my passengers."

"Now, driver, you ain't really got nothin' to say about that, seein' as we got you good 'n covered. But, she ain't goin' to be hurt none if you do what I tell you. 'Matter of fact, there won't nobody be hurt if you cooperate."

"You say there won't nobody be hurt, but you done kilt Hank."

"Well, let's just say there won't nobody else be hurt," Lanagan said.

"What do you want?"

Lanagan pulled his pistol, pointed it at the woman's head, and cocked it. "You know what I want," he said.

"Gary?" the woman cried out in fear.

"Don't do anything, Bobbi Lee," Gary said. "The man said he won't hurt you, and at this point we have no option but to take him at his word."

"It depends on whether the driver does what I tell 'im to do," Lanagan said.

Joad had not realized they were going to kill the shotgun guard as they had, and he didn't like it. He liked even less the idea of perhaps shooting a woman, but he thought it best not to say anything.

"Lower your pistol 'n I'll toss the money pouch to you," Sam said.

Lanagan smiled, an evil smile. "Well now, driver,

you really ain't in no position to be a-tellin' us nothin."
He eased the hammer back down and lowered his
pistol. "But to show you what a nice guy I can be, I'll
do it." The smile left his face. "Now throw down the
money pouch," he ordered.

Sam reached under the seat and pulled out a
canvas bag, then tossed it down.

"That's more like it," he said. "All right, you folks
get back on the coach 'n get on out of here. You too,
Bobbi Lee." Lanagan added, with a smile. He let the
woman go, and she hurried over to let her husband
help her climb back in to the coach.

"All right, driver, your passengers are back in the
coach, you can go now."

Without the slightest hesitation, Sam snapped the
whip over the team.

"Heeyah!" he shouted, and the six-horse team
leaped ahead, jerking the coach into motion.

Lanagan watched the coach until it was well down
the road, then he turned to Claymore. "Open it up,"
he ordered.

The top of the pouch was locked, but Claymore was
able to cut through the heavy canvas with his bowie
knife.

"How much is there?" Lanagan asked, once the
money was removed.

"Damn," Claymore said.

"What is it?"

"There ain't no more 'n five hunnert dollars here,"
Claymore said.

"Five hundred?" McCoy said. "You got five stacks of bills there, man!"

"Yeah, but look at 'em. They're all one-dollar bills."

"Damn, why would they make a money shipment o' nothin' but one-dollar bills?" McCoy asked.

"Banks do that sometimes when they need money to make change and such," Lanagan said.

"That's only a hunnert 'n twenty five dollars apiece," McCoy complained.

"It's five hundred dollars, 'n it ain't goin' to be divided."

"What do you mean, it ain't goin to be divided?" McCoy asked.

"I told you what we're goin' to do with it," Lanagan said. "Think of it as seed."

"Seed?"

"Yeah, if you was a farmer, 'n you got some seed corn, you wouldn't eat it, would you?"

"No, that would be dumb," McCoy said.

Claymore laughed. "Clete's right. This is like seed corn. You don't eat your seed, 'cause you can plant it 'n get a lot more."

"Yeah," McCoy said. "Yeah, I understand now."

"We need somethin' that pays a little better," Lanagan said.

"There's a bank over in Salcedo," McCoy suggested.

"No, no banks," Claymore said. "We already did that 'n it didn't turn out so good."

Lanagan raised his hand. "No, now, let's not be too quick," he said. "True, we lost a couple of men, but we came away with some money. What do you know about the bank in Salcedo?" Lanagan asked McCoy.

"I've give some thought to hittin' it my ownself," McCoy said. "It prob'ly don't have more 'n five thousand dollars, but there ain't but one lawman in Salcedo, him bein' an old man that more 'n likely won't be able to do nothin' to stop us."

Lanagan smiled. "All right, we'll hold up the bank in Salcedo."

"Holdup!" Sam shouted as he brought the stagecoach into Audubon, with the horses lathered from their gallop. "We been robbed, Hank got kilt! Holdup!"

By the time the coach reached the station, more than three dozen people, attracted by the driver's shouts, had gathered to meet it.

"It was Clete Lanagan!" Sam said. "He stoled the money 'n kilt Hank."

"What are you goin' to do about this, Deputy?" someone asked Dalton who, like the others, had come to meet the coach.

"I'll go after them as soon as I can raise a posse," Dalton replied. "What about you, Garland? Will you be part of the posse?" Garland Castleberry was the man who had questioned Dalton.

"I wish I could, Dalton. But I got a wife 'n kids to look after."

For two hours Dalton tried to raise a posse, but he could get no one.

"You're the one that's gettin' paid," McKinley said. Abner McKinley was a clerk in the feedstore.

"Sam said there were four of them," Dalton replied.

"Surely people aren't expecting me to go after those four men by myself?"

"Like I said, you're the one we're payin'," McKinley said,

"Sheriff Peabody is counting on me," Dalton said to Tom and Rebecca when he returned to the sheriff's office. "He is counting on me, and I'm failing him." He made a movement with his hands to show his frustration. "Lanagan, Claymore, most likely, Seth McCoy, and a fourth man I don't know anything about held up the stagecoach and I can't even raise a posse. That means I'm going to have to go after him myself."

"You'll have to raise a posse, Dalton. You certainly can't go after them by yourself!" Rebecca said.

"I have no choice, I have to go by myself. I've tried to raise a posse, sis, I really have. If Sheriff Peabody hadn't been shot, then I've no doubt but the two of us could get a few more to help, but seeing as I'm by myself, I'm not able to get anyone."

"I'll go with you," Tom volunteered.

"You will not!" Dalton said. "You're a doctor, you're not a lawman."

"I will be if you deputize me."

"No," Rebecca said. "Dalton's right. He can't go after them himself, and you would be no help going with him."

"I'll try again to raise a posse," Dalton said. "Maybe now that word has gotten around as to what is going on, I'll find someone courageous enough to let me deputize him."

A few minutes later, Dalton stepped into the Blanket and Saddle Saloon.

"People!" he shouted, loudly holding up his hands to get everyone's attention. "People!" he called again.

All conversation stopped and everyone looked over at him.

"First of all, I have good news to report. By now most of you have heard that Dr. Whitman operated on Sheriff Peabody, and he managed to get the bullet out. Now he and Dr. Palmer both tell me that Sheriff Peabody is coming along fine, and they expect the sheriff to make a full recovery."

"Here now, that's damn good news, deputy!" someone said, and several others agreed.

"The bad news, which many of you already know, is that Hank Waters was killed by the same people who shot Sheriff Peabody. According to Sam, the driver, there were four men who held up the stage, Lanagan and Claymore being two of them. I've no doubt but that one of the other two was Seth McCoy, but have no idea who the fourth one was."

"McCoy? Ain't he the one that murdered that store clerk 'n his wife up in Antelope, a couple months ago?" someone asked.

"Yes," Dalton said. "And I'm sure you can see that nothing good can come from having those men running free. So the reason I'm here is, I'm raising a posse, and I'm asking for volunteers."

Several of the patrons who had been paying close attention to Dalton up until now turned away from him, as if purposely avoiding his eyes. Nobody volunteered.

"What about you, Ross? You went with Andy and me three months ago when we tracked down Zeke Muldoon. Will you join me?"

"Well, I . . . uh . . . I'd like to, Deputy, but m' wife, she . . ." Ross paused in midsentence.

"Muley? You were with us on the last posse," Dalton said, turning to one of the others.

"I'm sorry, Deputy," Muley mumbled, staring into his beer.

The Brown Dirt Cowboy, the Ace High, and the Watering Hole, the other three saloons in Audubon, proved just as unproductive as far as recruiting a posse was concerned. Dalton also tried to get volunteers from the freight company, but he was unsuccessful. When he returned to the sheriff's office, Marjane was there with Rebecca. Tom was absent.

"Where's Tom?" he asked.

"He's with Papa," Marjane replied.

"Is Andy all right?" Dalton asked, anxiously.

"Yes, he's doing well," Marjane said. "Dr. Whitman just wanted to check on him."

"What about the posse, Dalton?" Rebecca asked.

Dalton shook his head. "I didn't get a single man. I know Andy could raise a posse," Dalton said. "But nobody wants to trust their life to me."

"I've been thinking about it," Rebecca said. She smiled. "And I've come up with an idea."

"You have? Well, I hope it's a good one, because I'll be honest with you, Becca, I don't know where to turn next."

"Uncle Kirby," Becca said. "If we ask him, he'll help. I know he will."

Dalton shook his head. "Why would Smoke Jensen help?"

"He'll help, because he's my uncle," Rebecca said. "If I ask him to come, I know that he will."

"Smoke Jensen?" Marjane said. "I've heard of him. Dalton, I didn't know you were kin to Smoke Jensen. Why, he's famous!"

"I'm not related to him, Becca is," Dalton said.

"He's my uncle, and you are my brother, and that makes all of us part of the same family," Rebecca insisted.

"He's your uncle, but not Dalton's uncle?" Marjane asked, confused.

"Becca and I have the same father, but not the same mother," Dalton explained.

"Dalton Conyers, we certainly do have the same mother. I was raised from the time I was a baby by the same woman who raised you. Julia Conyers is every bit my mother. She just isn't my biological mother," Rebecca said.

CHAPTER SIXTEEN

Rebecca began an account of her personal history and Marjane, fascinated by the story, hung on every word.

"I was an adult before I learned that Dalton's mother and my mother were not the same. The woman who raised me was the only mother I had ever known until a few years ago, when I met my real mother. Her name was Janie Davenport, and she lived in Dodge City, Kansas. That was when I learned that I also had an uncle. I had been with her almost a month before she told me, and I asked her why she hadn't told me before.

"'I thought it best not to, but as I think more about it, you have the right to know about him. Kirby thinks I'm dead,' she told me. 'He thinks I died a long time ago. I'm afraid I was quite a disappointment to him. No man wants a whore for a sister, so I let him think that.'

"I told her not to talk like that, but she explained why she did.

"'It's true, honey, as much as I hate to admit it,' she

said. 'During the war, I ran off with a man named Paul Garner. I was young then, much younger than you are now. Paul was a gambling man, and he promised me a life of fun and excitement. At the time, anything seemed better than living on a dirt farm in Missouri. Paul and I went to Fort Worth and stayed there until the war was over. Then after my gambling man got himself killed, I got a job as bargirl working in one of the saloons in Hell's Half Acre. That was when I met Big Ben Conyers, your papa. The Colonel was fresh back from the war, a wounded hero. Oh, he made quite a presence, Becca. He was a magnificent and kingly looking man. I fell head over heels in love with him, and one thing led to another, until I became pregnant. I feared that he might run away then, but he didn't. As soon as he learned I was pregnant, he moved me out to his ranch and I stayed there until you were born.'

"That was when I asked her if she and Papa had ever gotten married. Mama said that Papa had asked her to marry him, but she couldn't do it. And when I asked her why, she explained.

"'Honey, your papa was one of richest men in Texas. Before I met him I was a gambler's widow, and a part-time soiled dove. Can you imagine what his enemies could have made of that? Someone would have said something and your father would have challenged him. He would have either killed someone, or gotten killed himself. I would not have been able to accept either outcome.

"I didn't fit in his society, Becca. I was a mule in horse harness. So one morning I just left. I know that sounds harsh, but believe me, it was much better for both of you. And I found out that within a couple of months after I left, your papa had married a decent and respectable woman.'

"Of course, she was talking about Julia, Dalton's mama, and the woman who had raised me," Rebecca continued. "She wanted to know if Julia had been good to me, and when I answered that Julia had been a mother to me, the only mother I had ever known, I felt a little guilty about it, but she told me not to.

"'You can say it, honey. She has been a mother to you. And judging from the way you turned out, she has been a much better mother to you than I could have ever been.'

"'But you are my mother,' I told her, not exactly knowing where to go with this.

"'Yes, I am your mother,' she replied, almost as if apologizing. She was quiet for a long moment. 'After I left your father I went farther west, where I whored for quite a number of years, then I met Oscar. Oscar didn't care that I used to be on the line. But I want you to know, Becca, that I have reformed. And you know what they say. No one is more righteous than a reformed whore.'

"She told me that when she learned that her brother thought she was dead, that she thought it best not to ever tell him any different."

Tom stepped into the sheriff's office then, his arrival interrupting Rebecca's story.

"How's Papa?" Marjane asked, anxiously.

"He's complaining about the food," Tom said with a little chuckle. "That means he's doing very well."

"Oh, thank God," Marjane said with relief.

"Have you been able to raise a posse?" Tom asked.

Dalton shook his head. "I'm afraid not."

"I want him to ask Uncle Kirby to come help him," Becca said.

"Yes, I think that would be a great idea," Tom said, enthusiastically.

"Becca is telling us a story about him."

"A story?" Tom asked.

"I'm telling Marjane how I'm related to him, and a little about him as well."

"Go ahead, don't let me interrupt you," Tom said, stepping over to the coffee pot to pour himself a cup.

"I asked Mama what Uncle Kirby was like," Rebecca said, continuing her narrative.

"That's when she told me that he was a man of legendary accomplishments, and that books and even a play had been written about him."

"I know about the books that have been written about him," Dalton said, interrupting Becca's account. "And I admit that if you can talk him into coming he would be a big, big help. But I have to confess that coming here wouldn't be the smartest thing he had ever done. It might even be the dumbest thing he has ever done."

Becca laughed. "No, he's done something dumber. Mama told me a story about him that I've never told you. Mama said that Uncle Kirby did something way back before the war when they were both kids.

"They lived on a farm, and she and Uncle Kirby had the job of milking the cows. Well, the two cows were kept in the same stall, and one morning Uncle Kirby got it in mind to tie their tails together."

"Wait a minute," Dalton interrupted. "You can't tie cows' tails together."

"Well of course, you can't tie the tails themselves, but what Mama told me was that he took the hairy tufts at the end of their tails and tied them together. Then, when the cows were turned out into the pasture, one wanted to go one way, and the other wanted go in the opposite direction, so they pulled against each other, and the harder they pulled, the tighter the knot got in their tails.

"Well, those two cows just kept pulling, and bawling, and pulling and bawling, until finally Uncle Kirby's pa . . ."

"Your grandpa," Dalton said.

"Yes, funny, I hadn't thought of it that way, but yes, he was. Anyway, Grandpa came out to see what they were bawling about. When he saw those two tails tied together he had conniptions. Uncle Kirby had tied so many of the hairs together that Grandpa couldn't get them untied, so he finally gave up trying and just cut them apart. Then he asked Uncle Kirby what he knew about it.

"'Well, Pa, the flies were real bad,' Uncle Kirby said, "and those two cows were being tormented something awful by them, so they started sweeping their tails back and forth, trying to keep the flies away. Now I didn't exactly see it happen, but if you were to ask me, I'd say that those cows tied their own tails together while they were trying to swish away those flies."

Becca, Dalton, and Tom were laughing hard by the time she finished the story.

"Dalton," Tom said. "If anyone can help you, Smoke can."

"I agree. But I just don't know if he will come."

"He'll come," Tom said. "Smoke Jensen is as good a man as I've ever met in my life, and if he thinks someone in his family needs him, he will come."

"That's just it," Dalton said. "I'm not really part of his family."

"I'll ask him myself," Becca said.

"You're the brother of his niece," Tom added. "For someone like Smoke, that's family enough."

CHAPTER SEVENTEEN

"There's the bank over there," McCoy pointed out as the four men rode into the little town of Salcedo.

The bank was a rather flimsy looking building, thrown together from rip-sawed lumber and leaning so that it looked as if a good stiff wind would knock it over. Claymore chuckled when he saw it.

"Hell, we don't have to rob this bank, boys. We can just kick it down," he said.

"Let's do it and be gone," McCoy suggested.

"Wait a minute, wait a minute," Lanagan said, holding up his hand. "Dingus, you remember what happened to us up in Pella, don't you? How it was that the whole damn town turned out after us?"

"Yeah, I remember," McCoy said.

"I don't want that to happen here, so I tell you what we will do. First thing, before anyone sets one foot into the building, let's take us a ride up and down the street, just to get our bearings."

"Yeah, seein' as what happened to you boys in Pella, I think that's a good idea," McCoy said.

"Joad, you take the left side. Count everybody you

see carryin' a gun. McCoy, you take the right. Me 'n
Claymore will just ride on through, normal like, but
we'll sort of take a look around, too."

As Joad and McCoy rode slowly down the street,
making a thorough observation of everyone outside at
the moment, Lanagan and McCoy rode on through
at a normal pace.

"We shoulda done this in Pella before we hit the
bank," Claymore said.

"Yeah, well, we can't go back 'n undo what we already done," Lanagan said. "So we'll just be extra
careful this time."

The two men rode the entire length of the town,
then they turned their horses and waited for the reports from Joad and McCoy.

"I seen three that was wearin' guns on my side 'o
the street," Joad said.

"I only seen one on my side," McCoy added.

"Any of them look like they knew how to use
them?" Lanagan asked.

"Hell, that old fart on my side looked like he didn't
even have the strength to pull his gun out of the holster, let alone use it," McCoy said.

"What about the ones you saw, Joad?"

"I don't see no problem," Joad answered. "They
didn't any of 'em look like they knew much more'n
which end of the gun the bullet come out."

"Remember, when we come out of the bank we will
huzzah the town, 'n that'll more 'n likely send ever'
one a-scurryin'." Lanagan smiled. "Well, then, boys,
what do you say we go get us a little workin' money?
Joad, you stay outside with the horses."

Lanagan, Claymore, and McCoy swung down from

their horses and handed the reins over to Joad, who stayed mounted. He held the reins of all three horses with his left hand, while in his right he held his own reins, as well as his pistol, though he kept it low and out of sight.

As soon as Lanagan, Claymore and McCoy were inside, they pulled their pistols.

"This is a holdup!" Lanagan shouted. "You, teller, empty out your bank drawer and put all the money in a bag!"

Nervously, the teller began to comply, emptying his drawer in just a few seconds.

Lanagan took the sack, looked down inside, and smiled. "Well now, that looks pretty good. Now I want to see what you've got in the safe," he demanded.

"You can take a look if you want," the teller said, holding his hand out toward the open safe. "Only you won't find any money there, because we bring it all outside during business hours."

"You don't say," Lanagan replied with a little chuckle. "They don't seem like such a good idea, what with bank robbers 'n the like."

"We have never been robbed before," the bank teller replied. "This is the first."

"Let's go, boys," Lanagan said. "We've got what we come for."

"Lanagan, look out!" McCoy shouted.

Looking toward the danger, Lanagan saw that one of the three customers in the bank was armed, and pointing his pistol at Lanagan. Both McCoy and Clayborn fired at the customer, just as he fired. The customer's bullet hit an inkwell on one of the tables, sending up a spray of ink.

McCoy and Clayborn's bullets found their mark, and the customer went down. Lanagan fired toward the teller's window and his bullet shattered the shaded glass around the teller cage, though the teller had already ducked out of danger.

A quick perusal of the two other customers in the bank showed that they had no intention of getting involved.

"Let's get the hell out of here!" Lanagan shouted.

The three men came running from the bank, with Lanagan holding onto the bag.

"Yahoo, boys, huzzah the town!" Lanagan shouted as he leaped into the saddle.

The four men galloped out of town shooting into the storefronts on either side of the street. No one was left outside, and no one returned fire as the four rode away.

From the *Audubon Eagle:*

Young Girl Killed
in Bank Robbery

Clete Lanagan and three other outlaws struck the Bank of Salcedo in Clay County two days previous. As the robbery was being perpetrated, Rodney Gibson, a customer in the bank at the time, bravely attempted to foil their scheme, but in an exchange of gunfire, the brave young cowboy was killed.

As the robbers left town at a gallop, they engaged in the activity known as huzzahing, firing their guns indiscriminately. The balls from the pistol of one of the outlaws, thus energized, took effect with devastating results upon Kathleen Gray, an eight-year-old girl who was, at the time, with her mother in Annie's Dress Emporium, trying on a dress that was to be her birthday present. It was then that a bullet smashed through the window, ending her brief life.

The identity of the leader of the outlaws was confirmed when one of the outlaws yelled out his name, in giving alarm to the planned action of Mr. Gibson. Our readers will no doubt remember that it was Clete Lanagan and others who robbed the Bank of Pella.

This robbery netted the villainous gang three thousand and seventeen dollars, said amount to represent the total assets of the bank.

Lanagan, Claymore, and McCoy were celebrating the success of the bank robbery by passing around a bottle of whiskey they had recently purchased. They had also bought the newspaper, by which Joad learned of the death of the little girl.

Joad did not feel like celebrating.

Big Rock, Colorado

Unaware of the bank robbery down in Texas, and having just picked up the mail, Cal tied his horse off in front of the Longmont Saloon.

"Hello, Cal," Louis Longmont greeted. "Are you

alone, or did Smoke and Pearlie come into town with you?"

"They're back at the ranch," Cal said. "I just came in town for the mail."

"Really? Well, I hate to tell you this, Cal, but this is a saloon. You'll find the post office over on Center Street," Louis teased.

"Funny thing," Cal said. "The postmaster said something almost just like that, when I tried to order a beer at the post office."

Louis laughed. "It's good for you to drop by. If you don't mind the company, I'll grab a beer as well, and join you at your table," he said, and a moment later Louis came over to the table with a beer mug in each hand.

"By the way, when you go back out to the ranch, you tell Smoke that the Holy Spirit Episcopal Church was just real thankful that he donated the reward money for Poke Gilley and Frank Ethan for use in their orphanage. That seven hundred and fifty dollars was enough to buy a new set of clothes for every boy and girl in the orphanage, with quite a bit left over."

"I know Smoke was real glad to do it," Cal said.

"The irony is that Gilley and Ethan were two of the most no-account outlaws you can imagine, and they finally did something good," Louis said. "They got themselves killed, so that a number of children, living in an orphanage, could have a better life."

"Yes, it's good that something positive came out of it."

"So tell me, what's going on out at the ranch?" Louis asked, as he took a sip of his beer.

Cal chuckled. "Today they're bucking steers out of

mudholes. I didn't mind coming into town for the mail, I can tell you that for sure."

Out at Sugarloaf ranch, Smoke was mounted on his horse, Seven, looking at a steer that was struggling to get free. The animal had gotten bogged down in a mudhole that was so deep that it came halfway up to the steer's shoulders.

"There's no way he's going to get out of there by himself," Smoke said to Pearlie, as his foreman came riding up alongside.

"I know, that's why I've got Kenny and Lon coming," Pearlie said.

Turning in his saddle, Smoke saw his two riders approaching.

"Lordy, Lordy, look at him," Kenny said. "How in the world did he ever get himself in that fix?"

"How he got in isn't important," Smoke said. "What is important is getting him out." Smoke chuckled. "I take it you two men can handle that."

"Yes, sir, Mr. Jensen, you ain't goin' to have to draw us no pictures," Lon said.

"Ha! That's good," Pearlie said, "'cause if you had to depend on a picture Smoke drew, you wouldn't know whether to pick your nose or scratch your ass. I've seen him try to draw, and he couldn't draw a circle if his life depended on it. He's sure no *Mona Lisa.*"

Smoke chuckled. "I would hope not," he said. "*Mona Lisa* is the painting, not the painter. The artist was Leonardo da Vinci."

"Really?" Pearlie asked, confused by the response.

"Really."

"How come you know stuff like that?"

"'Cause he's a lot smarter 'n you," Lon said, with a laugh.

"Come on, Lon, we ain't goin' to get him out just sittin' here a-lookin' at 'im," Kenny said.

The two Sugarloaf hands climbed down into the mud alongside the steer, then managed to get a couple of ropes around him, just behind its front legs. Pearlie took one of the ropes and Smoke the other, then they wrapped the rope around their saddle horns.

"All right!" Pearlie said. "You boys push, and we'll pull."

The two horses strained against the ropes, while the two cowboys in the mud with the animal pushed. After a few minutes of pushing and pulling, a very muddy steer emerged. Cal hopped down and loosened the ropes, then the steer, aware now that it was free, trotted off.

"Kenny, Lou, don't you boys be late for supper," Pearlie said.

"Hey, wait, you aren't goin' to leave us stuck in this here mudhole, are you?" Kenny called. "We can't get out of here by ourselves!"

"Well, we would throw these ropes out to you two, but they are muddy, and you would get it on you," Pearlie said.

"Are you crazy?" Lou shouted. "We're already covered with mud!"

"Yeah, I guess you are," Pearlie said. He laughed. "You two are taking being teased far too seriously."

Smoke and Pearlie threw out their ropes and Kenny and Lou grabbed the end and held on. A moment later two very muddy cowboys emerged from the bog.

"You boys might want to wash off in the creek before you come back in," Smoke suggested. "Then you can take the rest of the day off."

"Yes, sir, thank you," Kenny said, answering for both of them.

The creek was Rock Creek, a year-round tributary from Grand River, which also ran through Sugarloaf. It was these two dependable sources of water that made Smoke's ranch one of the most productive ranches in Colorado.

When Smoke and Pearlie stepped into the house, half an hour later, Sally was sitting in the keeping room reading a newspaper. She looked up and smiled as they came in.

"How many cows did you rescue?" she asked.

"Just one, today. Cal isn't back from town yet?"

"Not yet."

"He's drinking beer at Longmont's, Smoke, you know that," Pearlie offered.

"Well, don't you, when you go in for mail?"

"How else do you think I know what he's doing?" Pearlie responded with a little laugh.

"Have you found anything interesting to read?" Smoke asked, nodding toward the newspaper in Sally's hand.

"I have indeed," Sally replied. "Did you know that they have just finished constructing a building in Chicago that is ten stories high? It's what they call a skyscraper."

"A skyscraper?" Pearlie asked. "Now, isn't that a funny name?"

"Well, if it is ten stories high, I expect it does scrape the sky," Smoke said. "But who would need a building so tall?"

"It's the Home Insurance Company building," Sally said. "It's so tall that if you're standing on the ground, looking up, you can't see the top of the building."

"What? Really?" Pearlie said. "You mean it's higher than a mountain? Oh, wait, you was just funnin' me, weren't you?"

Sally sighed. "I may have been having some fun at your expense, Pearlie, but I was not 'funnin' you.'"

"You'll never quit being a schoolteacher, will you, Sally?" Smoke asked. "How long has it been since you last taught a class?"

"It has been quite a while. But you know what they say," Sally replied. "Once a teacher, always a teacher."

"That ain't nothin' I never heard nobody say," Pearlie said.

"What? Pearlie, you clean up that statement! You know better than that!" Sally said.

"I beg your pardon, Mrs. Jensen. I was merely having a bit of fun with you. Of course I know better than that. What I should have said was 'That is not a saying with which I am familiar.'"

Sally laughed, and applauded. "Very good, Pearlie, very good indeed. And now it would appear that you were having a bit of fun at my expense."

At that moment Cal came into the house carrying a small cloth bag.

"See there, Smoke, and you said he would be passed out drunk on Front Street," Pearlie teased. "Not Cal, I said. Not our Cal."

"Smoke, did you . . ." but even before he got his question asked, Pearlie was already laughing.

"You were teasing me."

"Yeah, I was."

"That's not very nice of you, Pearlie," Sally said.

"I know, but he's just so easy to tease," Pearlie said.

"That's because Cal is an exceptionally honest man, and not subject to pulling hurtful jokes on others," Smoke said, butting into the conversation. "Let me see the mail," he added, holding his hand out toward the young man.

Smoke began looking through the mail until one letter in particular caught his attention.

"Well, this is strange."

"What do you have?" Sally asked.

"A letter from Becca."

"What's so strange about that? She is your niece," Sally said. "You get mail from her all the time."

"Yes, but she lives in Boston, and this letter is from Texas."

Dear Uncle Kirby:

You may remember that in a letter previous I made it known to you that my half-brother Dalton had left the ranch to take a position as a deputy sheriff with Sheriff Peabody of Parker County. Sheriff Peabody has been shot, and though he wasn't killed, he is too badly wounded to resume his duties.

As a result of Sheriff Peabody's incapacitation, Dalton has been elevated to fill that position until Sheriff Peabody is able to function once more as the chief law officer, not only of Audubon, but of the whole county. And that, Uncle Kirby, brings me to the purpose of this letter.

Dalton believes that the two men who are accountable for shooting Sheriff Peabody have begun to raise a gang of men to ride with him. It is said that Clete Lanagan has stated that with a gang of men of his choosing that he will soon control the entire area. They have already begun, having recently robbed a stage coach and killed the shotgun guard, as well as robbing a bank in Salcedo, a nearby town, and killing both a customer of the bank and a little 8-year-old girl as they left town. There have been several other incidents as well, but because the eye-witnesses have been killed, we have no real evidence to point to Lanagan and his gang for those particular depredations. However, there is no question in the minds of most as to their involvement in these crimes.

Dalton has made many attempts to recruit men to come to his aid, but so far has been unable to do so. And as he was Sheriff Peabody's sole deputy, he is now totally alone. The smart thing for him to do would be to resign and return to Papa's ranch, but Dalton won't do that. He says that it is a matter of honor that he carry out the task that has befallen him, and while I am very worried about him, I am also very proud of his adherence to that code of honor.

Dalton has said that he will face up to Clete

*Lanagan and his men whether he is able to find
those who will stand with him or not. You remember
Dalton from when we made the cattle drive from
Dodge City to my father's ranch, and you remember
also that if he says he is going to do something,
he will.*

*I fear what will happen if he goes up against the
Lanagan gang alone, and therefore I am begging of
you, Uncle Kirby, to please come to Audubon, Texas,
to help him. I am sure that you must be very busy
with your ranch, but I have nowhere else to turn.
I have talked Dalton into waiting at least two
more weeks so that we may hear from you before
he undertakes any action on his own.*

*Please let us know by telegraph whether it will
be your intention or not to help us, or to decline.*

> *Your niece,*
> *Rebecca Conyers Whitman*

"Well, I suppose that answers the question as to why Becca is in Texas," Sally said.

"Only partially," Smoke said. "If Dalton is in trouble, I can see Becca writing to ask me to help, but I don't know why she felt the need to go there herself."

"Don't you imagine that if this sheriff had been shot that Tom Whitman would be there?" Sally asked.

"Yes, I guess he would be," Smoke agreed.

"So, how soon are we leaving?" Sally asked.

"What do you mean, how soon are *we* leaving?" Smoke replied.

"You, me, Pearlie and Cal. Surely you weren't planning on taking on this gang all by yourself, were you?"

"Miss Sally's right," Cal said. "If this man that shot

Sheriff Peabody is actually rounding up a gang . . . what was his name?"

"Lanagan," Sally said. "Clete Lanagan."

"Yes, ma'am, Clete Lanagan. Anyhow, if he's actually starting up a gang, then the more of us there are, the better," Cal said.

"Somebody has to stay with the ranch," Smoke said.

"Lon and Kenny can run the ranch while we're gone," Pearlie said. "That is, if they can get themselves cleaned up enough that they don't scare the cows," he added with a giggle.

"Cleaned up?" Cal asked. "What do you mean, cleaned up?"

Pearlie told of the two men getting into the muddy bog to free a steer, and by the time he was finished with the story, all four were laughing.

"All right,' Smoke said. "I can't fight all three of you. Get yourself packed, we'll take the morning train."

"What about horses? Are we going to take them?" Cal asked.

Smoke shook his head. "No, we'll rent horses from the Audubon livery."

CHAPTER EIGHTEEN

"Mr. Metzger, would you step into my office for a moment?" the president of the Bank of Audubon asked.

"Yes, sir, Mr. Montgomery, I'll be right there."

When Metzger went into the office, he saw a smiling Charles Montgomery sitting behind his desk.

"It has started, Drury," Montgomery said.

"I beg your pardon, sir?"

"The transfer of railroad money. I just received a telegram informing me that ten thousand dollars will come by stagecoach as early as next week."

"Ten thousand dollars, to build a railroad? That doesn't seem like very much money, certainly not enough to build a railroad, I wouldn't think."

"Oh, but that is just the first of it," Montgomery said. "I imagine that money will be used for little more than to establish an office here. I have already been informed by Mr. Dawson that one hundred thousand dollars will be deposited soon, and I wouldn't be surprised if, over the time of the actual construction, we received many more times that amount before all is said and done."

"That's quite impressive sir," Metzger replied.

"Indeed it is. I have no doubt but that the railroad is going to stimulate a most rapid growth in our town, and that means much building. Increased building means that people will be needing to borrow money, and the fact that we will have railroad money on deposit means that we will be able to make those loans. Drury, my boy, I see a great future for this town and for our bank."

"Yes, sir," Metzger said.

Returning to his desk, Metzger wrote a letter to his cousin, describing the immediate opportunity that would be presenting itself.

On the morning Smoke and the others were to leave Big Rock for a trip that would eventually get them to Audubon, Texas, Kenny took them into town in the surrey. Pearlie and Cal were crowded in the front seat with Kenny, with Smoke and Sally in the rear. With the two-horse team proceeding at a brisk trot, it took them less than half an hour to reach the depot.

Cal brought one of the luggage carts over, and he, Pearlie and Kenny loaded the cart, then took the luggage to be checked in while Smoke and Sally went inside to buy tickets for them.

"You just got back from a trip, Mr. Jensen. Going again, so quickly? Why, a person might get the idea that you aren't happy with us," the ticket agent teased.

"I guess I was just born to roam," Smoke replied, exchanging easy banter with the ticket agent.

"You'll change trains in Denver," the agent said, stamping the four tickets. "Though, of course, having so recently made this same trip, you are well aware of that."

Pearlie and Cal joined them then. "The luggage is all checked through," Cal said.

"That's good," Sally said with a smile. "I wouldn't want to spend the next few weeks there without the opportunity of changing clothes."

"See there, Cal, I told you that some people change clothes at least once a month," Pearlie said.

"Come on, I changed clothes just last week," Cal replied, going along with the teasing.

"I guess I had better step over to the Western Union office to send a telegram," Smoke said.

The Western Union office was in the building next door to the depot.

BECCA WE ARE LEAVING THIS VERY DAY
WILL BE THERE AS SOON AS POSSIBLE
UNCLE KIRBY

Pearlie was explaining to Cal that the *Mona Lisa* was the name of the painting, and not the name of the painter.

"It was painted by a man named Leonard Vinchey, or Vichi, or something like that," Pearlie said.

Smoke and Sally just looked at each other and smiled.

Any further discussion about the painting, or any other subject, was shut off by the sound of the whistle of the approaching train.

"Here it comes," Pearlie said.

Shortly after Pearlie's announcement, the floor of the depot began to shake, and the windows rattled as the heavy locomotive rolled into the station, ribbons of steam escaping from the drive cylinders. The train rumbled, squeaked, and clanked to a halt.

"One of these days, I'd like to go somewhere on a train," Kenny said as he followed the four out onto the depot platform.

"You mean you've never been on a train?" Sally asked.

"No, ma'am."

"Well, we'll just have to take care of that little deficiency when we return," she promised.

"Board!" the conductor shouted, and with waves of good-bye, Smoke and the others boarded the train. There were no sleeper cars on this train, for its sole purpose was to connect Big Rock with Denver. It was now nine-oh-five in the morning, and they would reach Denver by one o'clock in the afternoon.

The train started with a few jerks as the slack was taken up between the couplers, then, gradually it smoothed out. Pearlie and Cal were sitting across from Smoke and Sally, so that they were riding backwards. Pearlie was nearest the window, and was able to see Kenny, who hadn't moved, until they were well underway.

"It seems like we were just there, and here we are going back," Cal said.

"We were just there," Pearlie said.

"Smoke, will we have time to drop by Live Oaks so we can see Tamara?" Sally asked.

"We're going to have to, I suppose," Smoke said

with a smile. "Otherwise you won't be able to give her that new dress you bought at the Elite Dress Shop."

"How did you know I had done that?"

Smoke laughed. "I didn't know, until now. You just gave yourself away."

"Smoke, you are awful," Sally said, but she, too, was laughing.

Clete Lanagan's gang had grown by five, and one of the new gang members, Dooley Thompson, was frying some bacon when Seth McCoy came in. There were two new people with him.

"Who are these men?" Lanagan asked.

"You said you wanted to round up some more good men," McCoy replied. "I told you I had one man in mind, so when I got in touch with him, he had another recruit for us. This here is Ed Slater, and this is Hatchett MacMurtry."

Lanagan studied the new men. "Slater 'n MacMurtry, huh? I ain't never heard of either one of you."

"Hell, that's good ain't it?" Slater replied. "When a feller is in this kind o' business, it's a good thing that there don't nobody know your name."

Lanagan chuckled. "I reckon you do have a point there. McCoy, you're willin' to vouch for them?"

"Well, I can't vouch for both of 'em, seein' as I don't know MacMurtry. But I know Slater just real good, 'cause me 'n him has done three or four little jobs together. He's a good man 'n I will vouch for him."

"I know 'im, too," Dooley Thompson said. "Ain't seen you around in a while, Slater."

"I been keepin' quiet," Slater said.

"What about MacMurtry?" Lanagan asked. "Any of you men know him?"

Nobody responded.

"I know 'im," Slater said. "'N if ya'll are goin' to take me, why, I can't hardly see why you won't take him too, bein' as I know he's all right."

Lanagan nodded. "All right, Slater, I guess you got a point, so the two of you can ride with us. You may as well meet the others. Thompson, you know. This is Dingus Claymore. These boys is Rufus Small, Pete Grogan, Emile Gates, 'n Norm Vargas."

"Me 'n Hatchett MacMurtry know each other," Small said.

"Is that a fact? You know MacMurtry, do you, Small?" Lanagan asked. "How come you didn't say nothin' a while ago? Are you sayin' you can't vouch for 'im?"

"No, I ain't exactly sayin' that," Small said. "I can't say one way or the other, 'cause the onliest place I know him from is because me n his brother was in prison together oncet, 'n from time to time this here feller would come for a visit."

"Yeah, that's right, when Cutter was in Huntsville I did come up to see him a few times," MacMurtry said. "'N when I first come in here, 'n seen you over there, I sort 'a got it in my mind that maybe I had saw you some'ers before."

"Where at is your brother Cutter? Now him, I could for sure vouch for."

"Cutter got hisself kilt up in Colorado."

"He didn't duck, huh?" Small said with a chuckle.

"I reckon not," MacMurtry replied without showing any animus over the inappropriate remark.

"Like I said, MacMurtry's a good man," Slater said.

"All right, I'll take him on," Lanagan agreed. "This here one cabin is all we've got, so you two men go find yourself a place to flop."

"What kind o' law do we have to deal with around here?" MacMurtry asked.

"Ha!" Claymore replied. "There's damn near no law a-tall, seein' as the sheriff has been shot 'n is lyin' up in the doctor's office, near 'bout dead. That don't leave nothin' but a deputy, 'n he can't even raise a posse."

"Claymore is right," Lanagan said. "Dalton Conyers ain't nobody to worry about."

"Who?" MacMurtry asked, reacting to the name. "What did you say his name was?"

"Dalton Conyers."

MacMurtry thought back to his time on the Live Oaks Ranch. It was owned by Big Ben Conyers, and he had a son named Dalton. But Live Oaks was one of the biggest ranches in the state. This couldn't possibly be the same Dalton, could it?

"And you say this Conyers feller ain't nothin' but a deputy sheriff?"

"That's right. Why do you ask? Do you know him?" Lanagan asked.

"No, I must be thinking of someone else," MacMurtry said. He was sure that was the case. There is no way that Colonel Conyers' son would be working as a deputy sheriff.

"Hey, MacMurtry, how much money you got?" Slater asked.

"Only about twelve dollars," MacMurtry replied. "Why do you ask?"

"I need the borry of about six dollars."

"Damn, that's half the money I got. What do you need the money for?"

"I know where at I can pick up some money in Ft. Worth, but I need to buy a train ticket from Weatherford to there 'n then back."

"That'll only leave me with six dollars," MacMurtry complained.

"I'll make it up to you when I get back," Slater promised. "I'll give you your six dollars back, 'n ten more to boot."

MacMurtry smiled. "All right, you got yourself a deal. But I expect you'd better be askin' Lanagan can you go, afore you start out on your own."

"Yeah, you're more 'n likely right. I'll be askin' 'im now."

"I need to go to Ft. Worth," Slater said a few minutes later.

"You just got here. What you need to go over there, for?" Lanagan asked.

"On account of I know where there's a little money that I can get my hands on, 'n I aim to get ahold of it."

"How long you plannin' on bein' gone?"

"I'll ride in to Weatherford 'n take the train from there. Three, maybe four days at most."

"The reason I ask is, I've just found out that there's some money that's goin' to be comin' by stage in a few more days, 'n I plan to go after it. If you ain't here when we do it, you won't be gettin' none o' the money. But, if you're still wantin' to ride with us, well, come on out here when you get back, 'n you'll be in on our next job."

"Thanks. I'll be back soon as I can."

"How long you 'n Slater been ridin' together?" Lanagan asked MacMurtry after Slater rode away.

MacMurtry wasn't sure how to answer the question. He had done a few jobs with Slater, but that was several months ago. When he ran into him in Rowland, that was the first time he had seen him in over a year.

"I've knowed 'im for a couple of years," MacMurtry replied. That wasn't entirely a lie. He had actually known Slater that long, he just hadn't actually ridden with him that much.

"You got 'ny paper out on you?" Lanagan asked.

"I don't know. I did have, but that's been quite a while. 'N what paper I got is most likely all forgot now."

Lanagan shook his head. "There don't ever' body forget paper, oncet it's been put out, it purt nigh stays out."

"Is that a problem? I mean, me havin' dodgers out for me?"

Lanagan laughed. "Hell no, in my business, bein' wanted is near the same as havin' someone vouch for you."

MacMurtry laughed as well. "If that's the case, I reckon I'm comin' to you with high recommendations."

"What's this money that Slater says he has?" Lanagan asked.

MacMurtry shook his head. "I don't know, he never told me. He just said it was over in Ft. Worth."

"You think he'll be comin' back? Or once he gets his money, will he strike out for some'ers else?"

"He better come back," MacMurtry said. "The son of a bitch borrowed six dollars from me."

Lanagan laughed. "He's goin' to have the chance to make a lot more 'n six dollars by ridin' with us. I figure he'll be back."

CHAPTER NINETEEN

Slater had not been entirely honest with Lanagan when he said that he had some money in Ft. Worth. What he had in Ft. Worth was a plan to get some money. While living there he had made the acquaintance of Dan Dolan, and had done most of his shopping in Dolan's Grocery Store. He had even rented a room at the back of the store, and this was his destination now. Dolan's Grocery Store occupied a small building just beyond the edge of town, north of the railroad depot.

Slater's entry into the store was announced by the jingle of a bell that was attached to the door. At the moment, Dolan seemed to be the only one in the store.

"Why, Ed Slater," Dolan said, looking up with a smile. "My oh my, it's been a month o' Sundays since you was last in here. It's good to see you back. The missus and I were talking about you just the other day. 'What happened to our good friend Ed Slater?' she asked. I told her you were just traveling around but that I was sure you would come back soon. Ma!" Dolan called. "Ma, look who has come to see us!"

"Eddie!" a short, stout, white-haired lady said coming from the back of the store. She had a broad smile on her face, and she opened her arms to pull him into an embrace. "Have you come to stay with us some more? Because if you have, your room is still in the back, just the way you left it."

"No," Slater said. "I haven't come to stay."

"You haven't? Well, that's too bad," Dolan said. "We so enjoyed having you here. I'm glad the prison warden sent you to us to work out your last six months of probation. Why, it was almost like you were part of the family. You will have dinner with us, though, won't you?" Dolan looked over at his wife. "I'll just bet that Betty Ann would be willing to make a peach pie, wouldn't you?"

"Of course I will," Betty Ann said. "I remember how much Eddie liked my peach pies."

"I won't be here for dinner," Slater said.

"Well, I am glad that you stopped by to pay us a visit. But if you haven't come to stay with us, and you can't even stay for dinner, what does bring you to Fort Worth?" Betty Ann asked.

"Money," Slater replied.

Dolan laughed. "Money? Oh, you mean you have found a job here, in Ft. Worth? Why, that's wonderful. Look, while you're getting on your feet with your new job, why not stay here, with us?"

Slater drew his pistol, cocked it, and pointed it at Mrs. Dolan.

"Like I said, money. Empty out your cash drawer if you don't want to see this old woman shot."

The smile left Dolan's face to be replaced by a look of shock and fear. "Ed, what are you doing? If this is a joke, I'm afraid I don't find it very funny."

Slater shot Betty Ann Dolan in the leg, and she screamed.

"Does that look like it's a joke? The money, Dolan, give me the money!" Slater demanded.

"All right, all right, here it is!" Dolan said, emptying the cash drawer. "I don't understand this. I thought we were friends! You were like a son to us!"

"I had one old man that I couldn't stand, I sure as hell don't need another one," Slater said. He raised the pistol and pulled the trigger, shooting Dolan right between the eyes.

Betty Ann Dolan's cries of pain turned to screams of horror when she saw her husband shot.

"Dan! Dan!" she shouted at the lifeless form of her husband. "Eddie, what have you done?"

The next shot ended her cries as she, too, took a bullet to the head. Slater counted the money, forty-seven dollars and eighty-one cents, and stuck it in his pocket as he left the store. There was no one in sight, and no one who had seen, or had even heard, the shooting.

It was no more than half a mile from Dolan's store to the depot.

"I'd like a ticket to Weatherford," Slater said, stepping up to the ticket counter.

"Yes, sir, that'll be two dollars and fifty cents," the ticket agent said.

"Is the train on time?"

"Oh, indeed, it is, sir," the ticket agent replied, proudly. "We just got a message that it departed Dallas on time. It should be here within half an hour."

Slater took a seat in the waiting room, confident that even if the bodies were discovered within the next half hour, he would be gone before the city police began looking for the killer.

Having reached Ft. Worth the day before, Smoke, Sally, Pearlie, and Cal spent the night at the Live Oaks Ranch. Big Ben's foreman, Clay Ramsey, brought them back to the depot in the big barouche. Tamara had come with them, and she was riding between Pearlie and Cal.

"My goodness, Tamara, it looks to me like you have two beaus after you," Sally teased.

"Yes, and you're going to have to choose one of us, but be careful when you make your choice, because I'm the kind that gets very jealous," Pearlie said.

"Oh, but how can I choose between two such handsome men?" Tamara replied, going along with the banter.

Smoke laughed. "Artfully dodged. I'd say that Tamara is already learning the wiles of being a young woman."

"So it would appear," Sally agreed.

"From what I remember, and what I have seen since she came back, I would say that Tamara is going to choose Billy Lewis," Clay said, and Tamara blushed.

"Ah ha! Now I really am jealous," Pearlie said.

"Are you enjoying your time here with the Conyers family?" Sally asked.

"Oh, yes, ma'am, I'm enjoying it very much. They are such nice people, and they are treating me ever so well."

"Good, I thought that would be the case. But please know, Tamara, that whatever you might need, at any point in your life, Smoke and I will always be here for you."

"You have already been there for me," Tamara said, reaching over to take Sally's hand.

The train was pulling into the station just as Smoke and the others arrived. They were already ticketed through to Weatherford, and their luggage had shipped ahead the day before. Because of that, it wasn't even necessary for them to go into the depot, so, bidding good-bye to Tamara and Clay, they stepped down from the carriage and onto the train.

As they boarded the train, they saw a very pretty and unaccompanied young woman sitting in the first seat. Pearlie smiled at her and, showing a flash of embarrassment, the young woman returned the smile.

The four moved halfway back in the car, then Pearlie and Cal took the backward facing seats just across from Smoke and Sally. This position afforded Pearlie and Cal a clear view of the attractive young woman.

"Oh, my, Pearlie, I think she likes you," Cal teased, once they took their seats.

"How can she not like me? She was just taken by my irresistible charm," Pearlie replied. "Also, I'm a lot better looking than you are."

"To say nothing of your humble demeanor," Sally teased.

Pearlie was still looking at the young woman when the last passenger boarded. He didn't have a beard, as such, but he did have what looked like about a ten-day stubble. His hair was disheveled, and he looked as if he hadn't bathed or changed clothes in a while. He took a seat right across the aisle from the young woman.

"Look at that," Pearlie said. "There are empty seats all through the car, and he chose to sit right across from her."

"Well, can you blame him? She's a pretty girl," Cal said.

"Yes, she is," Pearlie agreed

Shortly after the train got underway, Pearlie saw that the man was talking to the woman, though because he was halfway back in the car, he was unable to hear what the man was saying.

"Say, darlin', why don't you come over here 'n sit with me? As long as we're together on this train, why, we may as well get to know each other. My name is Ed Slater. What's your name?"

"Thank you, no, I'm quite comfortable where I am."

"What's your name?"

The young woman didn't answer.

"I give you my name, it's only decent that you give me your name. How are we goin' to become friends, iffen you don't tell me your name?"

"Please, sir . . ."

"It's Slater. But you can call me Ed."

"Please, Mr. Slater, I would rather not make friends with strangers on the train."

"Well see there, that's what I'm gettin' at. I done told you my name and iffen you was to tell me your name, why, we wouldn't be strangers no more."

"Excuse me, I think it would be better if I moved up to the next car," the young woman said as she stood.

Slater reached out for her, but she pulled her arm away from him.

Pearlie was not close enough to overhear the conversation between the two, but he could tell from the way the young woman was reacting to the man, that she had neither solicited the interest nor appreciated it. Then she stood up and Pearlie saw her move her arm, sharply, to avoid his reach. The young woman stepped through the front door of the car, and the man went after her.

Pearlie stood.

"Where are you goin'?" Cal asked.

"Maybe to save a damsel in distress," Pearlie replied, heading quickly toward the rear door of the car.

When Pearlie stepped out onto the connecting platform he could feel the vibration of the car through his feet. Out here, the noise of the train was much louder because it was not muted by the walls of the passenger car. Here, too, he could see the track ballast flashing by, quickly.

Pearlie had thought to follow them into the next car to see if the man was still bothering the young woman, but he didn't have to go any farther than the connection between the cars. The man had pushed the young woman up against the railing.

"Please, let me be!" the woman cried out, her voice high-pitched with fear.

"One little kiss," the man said. "One little kiss and I'll let you go."

The young woman saw Pearlie and, with her eyes, pleaded for help. The sound of the train was loud enough so that Slater had not heard Pearlie step out from the car, and because his back was to him, he hadn't seen him.

Pearlie reached up, and grabbing Slater by his shoulder, jerked him away from the girl and spun him around.

"What? Who the hell are you?"

"I'm the trash collector," Pearlie said.

Grabbing him by his belt and the top of his shirt, Pearlie tossed the man off the train. The man fell, then rolled away from the track, and Pearlie watched as he got up then held up his fist in anger. Pearlie could tell that he was yelling something, but he couldn't hear it.

"Oh! Did you kill him?" the young woman asked.

"No, come over here and take a look," Pearlie invited.

The young woman accepted the invitation, then when she saw that Slater wasn't injured, she laughed.

"I know it is awful of me to laugh about it," she said. "But it is funny."

"If you're all right, I'll rejoin my friends," Pearlie said.

"Would you like to . . . that is, if . . . well, I would feel a lot safer if you would sit with me for a while."

"Where are you going?" Pearlie asked.

"I'm going to Santa Fe."

Pearlie smiled. "I'm only going as far as Weatherford, but I would be happy to sit with you until then. My name is Pearlie."

"Pearlie?"

"That's what all my friends call me."

"Well, after what you just did for me, I consider you my friend, Pearlie. My name is Jill. Jill Castle."

Pearlie smiled, and dipped his head, slightly. "It's very nice to meet you, Miss Castle."

"My friends call me Jill," she said.

Returning to the car Pearlie stepped to one side so Jill could regain her seat. Once she was seated, he took his seat beside her.

Cal laughed.

"What is it?" Sally asked.

"Pearlie said he was going to rescue a damsel in destress, and doggone if if doesn't look like he did just that."

Because Smoke and Sally were facing the front of the car, neither of them had noticed the exchange between the girl and the man who had been in the seat across the aisle from her. Sally turned now to see what Cal was talking about.

"Oh, my," Sally said. "What a pretty young lady. Pearlie does seem to be doing all right for himself, doesn't he?"

"Yes, ma'am, he does at that," Cal said. "The lucky so-and-so."

"It looks to me like Pearlie may have made his own luck," Smoke said.

"Well, never let it be said that Pearlie is one to spurn an opportunity," Sally added.

CHAPTER TWENTY

With a few bruises and superficial cuts, Slater dusted himself off, then left the tracks and stepped out onto the dirt road that ran parallel with the railroad. He began walking west, toward the town of Weatherford, continuing on foot the trip that he had started by train.

"I'll kill that son of a bitch if I ever see him again," he muttered. But even as he spoke the words, he realized that he wouldn't even recognize the person if he ever saw him again. It had all happened so fast that he was not able to get a good look at whoever it was that threw him from the train.

Before Slater took the train to Ft. Worth the day before, he had boarded his horse in Weatherford. Now he was afoot, with at least twenty miles to go.

"I'll kill him," he said again. "I'll kill him the moment I see him."

Slater had a moment of concern. Had he lost his gun when he was thrown from the train? He reached down to his holster and wrapped his hand carefully around the handle. Good, it was still there.

"I'll kill the son of a bitch," he repeated, pulling the pistol up, slightly, and letting it fall back into the holster. "The moment I see him."

"So, you're going to Santa Fe to be a schoolteacher, are you?" Pearlie asked the young lady he was sitting beside. "Miss Sally is a schoolteacher."

"Miss Sally?" Jill asked.

"She's married to Smoke Jensen, and Smoke is my boss. That's them up there."

He pointed, and Cal, who was watching intently, smiled and waved.

Jill waved back. "And who is that?"

"Oh, that's a sad story," Pearlie said. "I'm glad you waved at him. He's a pitiful case. He was kicked in the head by a mule about a year ago and he hasn't been the same since." Pearlie made a circle with his finger at his temple. "He's a little slow, now."

"Oh, the poor thing," Jill said, and she looked at Cal again, this time with an expression of pity on her face.

Cal frowned, surprised by the look on her face.

"Why did he frown?"

"Pay him no mind," Pearlie said. "Remember, he's not quite right in the head."

"Oh, bless his heart."

"Let's not talk about him anymore," Pearlie said. "Cal is my friend, and I don't want to embarrass him."

"How sweet of you," Jill said. "You said you worked for the gentleman who is married to the schoolteacher. What sort of work do you do?"

"Smoke owns a big ranch in Colorado, one of the biggest, in fact. And I'm his foreman."

"Oh, what a responsible job. And I'm sure you are very good at it," she added, the broad smile showing her dimples.

For the next hour Pearlie enjoyed his conversation with the attractive young woman, who, he learned, was from Austin, Texas, the daughter of a lawyer. Their visit was interrupted when the conductor came through the car.

"Weatherford!" the conductor called as he passed through the car. "Folks, this is Weatherford. Don't leave the train unless you are supposed to be getting off here, because we won't be standing in the station for no longer than five minutes."

Pearlie turned to the young woman with her. "This is where I get off," he said.

Pearlie stood, then as Smoke, Sally, and Cal passed by, he introduced them. "Smoke, Miss Sally, this is Jill Castle. She's going to be a schoolteacher in Santa Fe."

"Oh, how delightful," Sally said.

"Pearlie said you were a schoolteacher," Jill said.

"I was. It is a wonderful and most rewarding profession."

"I'm Cal," Cal said with a smile.

Jill took Cal's hand in hers, then put her other hand on top. "You have a very good friend in Pearlie," she said. "You don't have a thing to worry about. I'm sure that, in time, everything will be just fine."

Cal got a very confused look on his face. "Everything will be fine?"

"Yes, I just know it will," Jill said enthusiastically.

"Come on, Cal, the conductor said we were only

going to be here for about five minutes," Pearlie said, hurrying him out of the car. Looking back at Jill, he shook his head sadly, and Jill nodded, to show that she understood.

"Pearlie, what did she mean when she said that I didn't have anything to worry about, that everything would be fine?" Cal asked.

"Oh, she was just a very nice young lady who wanted to make you feel better."

"Feel better?"

"Yes, you know, after you were made a little daft by being kicked in the head by a mule," Pearlie added with a chuckle.

"What? What did you tell her?"

"I told her you were my friend, and I promised that I would look out for you," Pearlie said.

Cal looked back at the train, which was just now leaving the station. "Hey!" he shouted. "Jill! I'm not crazy!"

"For heaven's sake, Cal, don't you think standing here, shouting at a moving train that you aren't crazy, is little crazy?" Sally asked with a laugh.

"I'll get even," Cal promised.

"Let's see about the stagecoach to Audubon," Smoke suggested, after they retrieved their luggage.

Right across the street from the depot was the depot for the Risher and Hall Stage Coach Lines. Smoke learned, upon inquiring, that they had a daily coach that ran to Audubon. He bought four tickets.

"You'll be the only passengers," the ticket agent said. "So you should have quite a comfortable ride. And, you'll be there just in time for supper."

"Hey, Pearlie, it's too bad Jill didn't leave the train

here," Cal said. "We could take her in the coach with us, and you could have taken her to dinner tonight. You and Jill could have gotten a table all by yourselves. Pearlie and Jill, all alone. Jill and Pearlie, Pearlie and Jill," Cal said in a teasing, singsong voice.

"I should have never told you her name," Pearlie said. "Damn, Cal, you are being insufferable."

Sally smiled, and applauded, lightly. "Insufferable is it? My, Pearlie, that's a great word! 'Damn,' not so good a word, but I applaud you for the proper use of 'insufferable,' for indeed, on this subject at least," Sally cast a disapproving look toward Cal, "I agree with you. Cal is being most insufferable."

"Gee, Miss Sally, you really know how to hurt a guy," Cal said, though the smile on his face and the way in which he spoke let it be known that he was not really offended by Sally's remark.

As they waited for the coach to leave, Smoke stepped outside for a moment. That was when he saw, and heard, the exchange between the driver and another man.

"There's ten thousand dollars in the pouch," the man said. "You'll be met at the Audubon stage depot by Mister Charles Montgomery from the Bank of Audubon. Do you know him on sight?"

"Yes, I've taken money shipments to him before," the driver replied

"We have very strict instructions in regard to handling this money. Don't give the pouch to anyone but Charles Montgomery."

"I won't," the driver said.

Still unnoticed, Smoke watched the banker walk

away as the driver climbed up onto the coach to stick the pouch under the seat.

"You got Harry on this trip, Mr. Parsons," one of the hostlers called up to the driver.

"Where did you put 'im?"

"He is in the first row offside, just like you said."

"Good. Ole Harry's got it in mind that he's a lead horse, 'n that's about the only place you can handle 'im."

"Have a good trip," the hostler said as he headed for the barn.

The driver climbed down then walked around the coach, grabbing hold of each wheel and trying to move it back and forth, checking the security of their attachment. Then he checked the doubletree, as well as the attachment of each of the horses.

Smoke felt a sense of appreciation for the driver's professionalism as he watched Mr. Parsons make a thorough pre-trip inspection of team and coach. Finally, satisfied that all was in order, Parsons stepped back to the depot itself.

"You folks inside!" Parsons shouted. "If you're goin' with me you better get out here now, 'cause I don't have no intention of a-waitin' on you."

At the driver's call, Sally and the others came out of the depot and boarded the coach. Because the coach could carry six, twelve when the center seats were used, and there were only the four of them, there was enough room for them to ride without being crowded.

"Hey, do we stop anywhere between here and Audubon?" Cal asked.

"No, why?" Smoke replied.

"'Cause if we don't, than that'll mean we won't be taking on any more passengers. And look at this," Cal said, turning so he could spread his legs out on the seat between him and Pearlie. "A fella could really get comfortable in here."

"Cal, you really are puerile," Pearlie said.

"Puerile," Sally said. "Another good word. I'm quite impressed."

"He's just showing off," Cal said. "You might say that he's being a bit supercilious."

"Sally, you should never have given them that thesaurus, I'm afraid we'll never hear the end of their attempts to impress us with big words," Smoke said with a little chuckle.

"Well, I, for one, am proud of them," Sally said.

"By the way, just so you know, I think we should keep a sharp eye open, during this trip," Smoke added.

"Oh? Why? Keep a sharp eye open for what?" Pearlie asked.

Smoke told the others what he had overheard about the money shipment.

"That's a lot of money to be sending by stage-coach," Pearlie said.

"Other than by a special courier, stagecoach is the only way to send money to a place like Weatherford," Smoke said. "And couriers attract more attention than a stagecoach."

"That might be so," Pearlie agreed. "But it seems to me like ten thousand dollars is enough to make a very tempting prize, no matter how it is being shipped."

"Smoke is right," Cal said. "We had better keep a sharp eye out, until we get there."

CHAPTER TWENTY-ONE

Ed Slater was afoot on the Ft. Worth road, still some distance from Weatherford. He had no idea how far he had come, but his feet were sore from the long walk, and he was hurting from the bruises he had sustained when he was thrown from the train. He didn't even hear the lone rider until he was right upon him.

"Mister, what are you doin' afoot out here, a long way from nowhere?" the rider asked.

"I fell off the train," Slater said.

"How in the world did you fall from a train?"

"I stepped out onto the platform to have a smoke because I didn't want to bother any of the ladies in the car. The train hit a bump, and I was thrown off."

"You were fortunate that the car didn't run over you, but it was very gentlemanly of you to look out for the ladies as you did."

"What's the next town?" Slater asked.

"Parker, it's about three miles down the road."

"I'll give you ten dollars to carry me double into town."

"Are you serious? Ten dollars, just to carry you three miles?"

"It may as well be three hundred miles," Slater replied. "I'm about wore out."

"Yes, sir, bless your soul, I can see that you are. I tell you what, Mister, I can't take ten dollars from you for just carryin' you three miles. The Christian thing of me to do would be to take you for nothing. But, if you would make it a dollar, I could buy some candy for my kids. They don't get a lot of nice things, and this would be a happy surprise for them. I've got three of 'em now, 'n a fourth one on the way," he said, proudly.

"All right, here's a dollar," Slater said as he produced the bill.

The rider took the dollar and smiled. "Ha! I can not only buy the kids some candy, I can even buy the wife something without her feeling guilty about it. By the way, my name is Morgan. Brother Morgan some call me, because I'm a part-time preacher at the Brotherhood Assembly Church. What would your name be?"

"Slater."

"Well, Mr. Slater, climb up here and take a load off your feet," he suggested as he reached his hand down toward Slater.

With the assistance offered by Morgan, Slater climbed up behind him. As soon as he was astraddle of the horse he pulled his pistol and stuck it in the preacher's back.

"What? What are you doing?" Morgan asked, the break in his voice showing his fear.

Slater pulled the trigger.

Morgan fell from the horse and lay facedown on the ground, moaning.

Slater dismounted and looked down at him.

'"Why? Why did you shoot me?" Morgan asked.

"I don't like to ride double," Slater said. He fired again, this time shooting the wounded man in the head. Then he retrieved his dollar bill and searched the body for more money, finding another two dollars.

"Two dollars? Damn, you really was a poor sumbitch. You must not of been all that good of a preachin' man."

Slater pulled the body off the road and pushed it over into a depression so that it wouldn't be seen unless someone was actually standing over it.

Morgan had told him that the town of Parker was only three miles away, but Slater figured why stop in Parker, when he could ride all the way to Weatherford?

Through his recruiting effort, Clete Lanagan had managed to gather twelve men for his gang. There was a negative side to having so many men to be responsible for, for he had to find ways to support such a large number. On the other hand he now had enough men to allow him to do just about anything he wanted to do in Parker County, or even the adjoining counties such as Pinto, Wise, Jack, and Denton.

In order to keep the men happy he had to maintain a steady source of income and so far he had managed to do that, by robbing a store here, or rustling a few cattle there. Except for robbing the bank in Salcedo, which he had done when there were only four of them, he had not yet made a significant score. But a few days ago he had received a letter from his cousin telling him about an opportunity that seemed promising. Lanagan had kept the information to himself until the day the money was scheduled to be transferred. Not until today did he share it with the others.

"Ten thousand dollars," Lanagan said.

"How do you know the coach is carryin' that much?" Chaney asked.

"Somebody told me."

"Who told you?"

"You don't need to know. Let's just say that it's somebody who knows what he is talking about."

"How do you know you can trust him?" Chaney asked.

"He's somebody that I have knowed for a long time. If he tells me there's ten thousand dollars comin' in on this stage, then you can take it to the bank."

Lanagan laughed. "Take it to the bank. That's funny, seein' as this money is goin' to the bank, 'n we'll be stoppin' it from goin'."

"This feller that told you about the money, will he be gettin' anythin' from it?"

"He gets a thousand dollars, once we get the money."

"A thousand dollars?" Chaney said. "Ain't that a awful lot of money for someone that ain't takin' the same chance as the rest of us?"

"He's a good source of information," Lanagan said. "He knows ever' thing that's goin' on, 'n there don't nobody suspect him of doin' nothin' wrong. I expect that, over time, he'll be a-bringin' us a lot of tips like this."

"All right, you're the boss. How are we going to do this?" Chaney asked.

"To begin with, for this job, I don't intend to use no more 'n six men."

"Why six?" Claymore asked.

"Any more than six men would make it difficult to handle, but with as many as six, it's likely that once we kill the shotgun guard, there won't be nobody who happens to be on the stage that'll get any notions to do anything about it. And as long as we have the edge in any confrontation, we'll come out ahead."

Lanagan chose the men he wanted to ride with him, purposely choosing only the newer men.

"Hold it, Lanagan, that ain't right," Chaney said. "We ain't pulled a good job yet, 'n now that we finally get one, you're only goin' to use six men? Why are you usin' these here new fellers to do the job instead of the ones of us that's been here the longest? This way all the money's goin' to wind up with just you 'n them six, 'n that'll leave the rest of us plumb out of it."

Lanagan shook his head. "No it won't. From now on no matter who it is that actually pulls the job, the rest of us is goin' to share 'n share alike, just like as if we was all there when the job is done. Besides which, just look at it this a-way. You 'n the others won't be goin' out this time, which means that those of you who don't go, ain't a-goin' to be in no danger with this job. But that won't matter none, on account of you'll be gettin' your share of the money anyway, just like as if you'd stood up the stagecoach with us."

"Yeah, well, what about Slater? I mean, bein' as he

ain't even back from Ft. Worth yet, it don't look to me like he ought to get a share."

"If we're goin' to share, 'n share alike, seems to me like Slater ought to get his share too, seein' as he's one of us now," McCoy said.

"Yeah, maybe that would be so iffen he had ever rid with us before. But the thing is, he ain't even done one job with us yet. So I don't think he ought to get nothin'," Chaney said.

"If he is one of us, he'll get his share just like the rest of us," Claymore said. "Ain't that right, Clete?"

"Yes, that is how it will be," Lanagan replied. "Put yourselves in Slater's shoes. If you was the one that was gone right now, wouldn't you want us to look out for you?"

"Yeah, well, it don't seem right to me," Chaney said.

"Them's my rules," Lanagan said. "If you don't like 'em, you can leave."

"No, no, you're the one in charge, so if it's your rules, then that's the way it'll be," Chaney said.

Lanagan nodded, then turned to the men he had chosen to ride with him. "All right, men, let's go," he said.

"Where we plannin' on hittin' 'em?" Emile Gates asked. Gates was one of the newest of Lanagan's recruits, having recently left Weatherford.

"There's a place on the road where it makes a curve, 'n right in the curve is a hill that hides the road. I'll put someone up on the hill so's he can look out for the coach as it approaches," Lanagan said.

"Hey, Smitty, what are you goin' to do with the money?" Collins asked as the men rode out to wait for the stage.

"Why, I'm goin' to spend it," Smitty replied.

"What are you goin' to spend it on?"

"I'm goin' to spend it on good whiskey 'n bad women," Smitty said, and the others laughed.

MacMurtry watched Lanagan and the six men ride off, then he stepped back inside and poured himself a cup of coffee.

"You want some sweetener with that coffee?" McCoy asked.

"I don't never put no sugar in m' coffee 'cause they's too many times when I ain't got it," MacMurtry replied.

McCoy smiled. "I ain't talkin' about sugar," he said, as he held up a bottle of whiskey.

"Yeah," MacMurtry said, with a smile. "That kind of sweetener I will take."

McCoy poured some whiskey into MacMurtry's cup, then fixed a cup for himself.

"So, tell me, McCoy, do you think Lanagan really will see to it that we all get a share of that ten thousand dollars?" MacMurtry asked as he took a swallow.

"Yeah, I do. Lanagan is a good man." McCoy chuckled. "And I ought to know. I was about to get myself hung, hell, they already had the gallows built 'n the invitations was sent out. But the day before I was scheduled to do my dance, Lanagan 'n Claymore showed up, 'n broke me out of jail."

"What kind of setup do we have goin' here? I'll tell you the truth, I ain't never seen a outlaw outfit that had this many men. They's seven of us here, 'n Slater, he'll more 'n likely be back, plus the seven that's gone out to stand up the coach that's carryin' ten thousand dollars. That means we're goin' to have to divide it by fifteen. No, wait, there will only be nine thousand for us to divide up, seein' as he said that the feller that told him about it is goin' to get a thousand dollars, all by his ownself. That's goin' to cut it down some considerable."

"Can you cipher?" McCoy asked.

"I can cipher some."

"I can cipher real good, 'n I done figured this out. This'll come to over six hunnert 'n ninety dollars for each 'n ever' one of us. Now, let me ask you this. What is it that you've had to do to earn this near 'bout seven hunnert dollars?"

MacMurtry stared at McCoy for just a second, then he broke into a wide grin. "Yeah," he said. "Yeah, you're right, I ain't had to do nothin' for it."

"You ain't done nothin' for it, but it's goin' to be put right in your hands. So, what do you think of Lanagan's outfit now?"

"I say it sounds like a pretty good outfit to ride with."

"I'll say. 'N this won't be the all of it, neither. What with the fool Dalton Conyers actin' as the sheriff in Audubon, why we can have our run of the place, 'n he won't be able to do nothin' at all about it."

"What does Conyers look like? Have you ever seen 'im?" MacMurtry asked.

"Hell yeah, I've seen 'im. He's the son of a bitch that took me over to Antelope, so's I could be hung."

"What's he look like?"

"Well, he's kind of tall and gangly lookin', got blond hair 'n a few freckles. Why do you ask? Do you think you know 'im?"

MacMurtry took another swallow of his coffee. "I don't know, I have to say that, that sounds like the Conyers I know. But the one I know is the son of a big rancher that I once rode for. I can't see him actual bein' a deputy sheriff. If he is the same man, don't sell 'im short. The Dalton Conyers I know is smart and pretty determined. The only thing is, I can't see someone as rich as Dalton Conyers bein' a sheriff's deputy, so we more 'n likely ain't got to worry none about 'im."

"Well, I don't know whether this is the feller you're thinkin' about or not," McCoy said. "All I know is that he's the one that's actin' as the sheriff now, seein' as Peabody has been shot 'n all."

"I wonder," MacMurtry said as he refilled his cup with coffee and the "sweetener."

Chapter Twenty-two

Cal, who had stretched his legs out on the seat, was sitting with his head resting in the corner of the coach. His eyes were closed.

"Ha!" Pearlie said, pointing to his friend. "I see where Cal is being extra vigilant."

"Well, after all, Pearlie, you did have a mule kick him in the head," Sally said. "So are you going to begrudge him a little nap?"

"What? I had a mule . . ." Pearlie paused in mid-comment as he realized what Sally was talking about.

"I reckon he's got a right to sleep some," he said.

The coach had come ten miles in the last hour, and was now about halfway to Audubon. Pearlie looked out the window. "No trouble so far," he said. "We may be worrying about nothing."

"It's better to be alert and have nothing happen, than to have something happen and not be alert," Smoke said.

"Well, I sure can't argue with you about that," Pearlie agreed.

About five minutes later, Cal woke up, then stretched. He was aware that the others were staring at him.

"What?"

"How does it look over there on your side, Cal?" Pearlie asked. "Everything look all right to you?"

"Uh, yeah, I haven't seen anything."

"That's very reassuring," Pearlie said.

"Yeah, well, I tell you what, I'm glad the driver said we'd be there by suppertime, because if you want to know the truth of it, I'm getting a little hungry," Cal said.

"Cal, would you mind telling us when you have not been hungry?" Sally teased. "I do believe you were born hungry, and had a relapse."

"Get the horses off the road, over there behind those trees," Lanagan ordered.

"Aren't we goin' to be mounted when we brace 'em?" Grogan asked.

"No. I've got it in mind how I'm goin' to do this," Lanagan said.

"You're the boss," Grogan replied.

"Yes, I am, 'n don't none of you never forget that. Teeter, you're the smallest of us, you can prob'ly climb the best, 'n bein' as you ain't all that big, you ain't as likely to be seen. What I want you to do now is climb up on this hill here, 'n when you get to the top, why, you should be able to see a long way down the road. Soon as you see the coach a-comin', you yell out, then come on back down so's we can all get ourselves where we need to be."

"All right," Teeter, who stood only one inch over five feet tall, replied. "Somebody give me a boost up to that first rock," he asked.

Vargas grabbed him by his pants waist, then chuckled. "Hey, Gates, you get 'im on the other side. He's such a little feller we can just throw 'im up there."

"Just give him a boost and stop tryin' to be funny," Lanagan ordered.

Teeter climbed to the top of the hill, and no sooner did he get there than he saw a plume of dust down the road. Shielding his eyes with his hand, he stared at it until the stagecoach appeared.

"Here comes the coach!" he shouted down to the others.

"Any outriders?" Lanagan called up.

"Nah, onliest thang I can see is the coach. Lanagan, you sure this coach is carryin' that money like you said? The reason I ask is, it don't look to me like it's even got no shotgun guard a-ridin' with it."

Lanagan smiled, and rubbed his hands together in anticipation.

"You know what that means, don't you, boys? That means we've caught 'em by surprise 'n this is goin' to be as easy as taking candy from a baby."

Teeter remained standing on top of the hill, looking down the road toward the coach.

"Teeter, don't just keep standin' up like that, you fool! If you can see them, they can see you," Lanagan said.

"Oh, yeah," Teeter said. He dropped back down onto his stomach, then slithered down.

"Ever' body get ready," Lanagan ordered. "This

is goin' to be the easiest money any of you has ever made."

In the coach, Smoke was looking through the window as he listened to the conversation of the others. That was when he saw someone standing on top of a hill ahead. It might have been nothing more than someone who was merely curious about the approaching coach. But any innocence in the observation was put to question when Smoke saw the observer suddenly drop down, as if purposely trying to avoid being seen. That act, happening as quickly as it did, pushed the observation beyond mere curiosity.

"It looks like our peaceful trip is about to be interrupted. I think we are going to have some unwanted company," Smoke said.

"Why do you say that? Did you see something?" Cal asked.

"Yes, I did," Smoke replied. "There's a hill a little ahead of us, where the road curves. I just saw someone climb down from that hill, only he didn't exactly climb down. What he did was drop down to keep from being seen. I do have a feeling that he's telling some others that we are coming."

"What do you think we should do?" Pearlie asked.

"For now, I suppose the only thing we can do is just be alert."

"Smoke, we should warn the driver," Sally said.

"You're right."

"You know what? Maybe one of us should get up there with the driver," Pearlie suggested.

"Good idea," Smoke agreed.

Smoke opened the door and leaned out the window.

"Driver!" he called up. "Stop the coach!"

The driver pulled the team to a stop. "What is it?" he asked. "Is something wrong? What did you want me to stop for?"

"I've got a feeling that up ahead, just around the bend, there are some men who are planning to make a try for the ten thousand dollars you're carrying."

"What are you talking about?" the driver replied sharply. "What makes you think I'm carrying ten thousand dollars?"

"I overheard you and the courier from the bank talking, just before we left Weatherford. I don't blame you for being cautious. But I am not your problem, Mr. Parsons. Whoever is waiting for us up ahead, is."

"What . . . what do you think I should do?"

"My two friends and I are armed," Smoke said. "I'll come up there with you, and they'll stay down in the coach, but they'll be ready if anything happens."

"All right," the driver said. "As far as I know, you might be tellin' me this so you can take the money, but seein' as you got no horses so as to make a getaway, I reckon I may as well trust you."

"I think that would be a good idea," Smoke replied, smiling at the driver as he climbed up to settle in the seat beside the driver. "All right, go ahead."

"Heyah!" Parsons called, snapping his whip over the heads of the team. The six horses strained into the harness and started forward.

"How many did you see?" Parsons asked.

"Just the one at the top of the hill," Smoke said. "But you can bet your bottom dollar there are more of them in wait." He chuckled, though it was without mirth. "I suppose I could say you bet your bottom ten thousand dollars, since that's what's at stake here."

"Mister, I sure hope you're the Good Samaritan you say you are, 'cause I'm puttin' ever'thing up to 'n includin' my life in your hands right now."

"Like I said, Mr. Parsons. I'm not your enemy," Smoke replied.

"All right, what do I do?"

"You just keep driving," Smoke said. "My friends and I will take care of anything that comes up."

"What's keepin' 'em?" Gates asked.

"Don't be so anxious," Lanagan replied. "It ain't like they're goin' to turn around 'n start back. They'll be here."

"Yeah. I guess I'm just anxious to get my hands on the money," Gates replied.

"All right, Cooper, you get here on the left side of the road. Teeter, you get on the right. You other four stand across the middle of the road. That way the coach won't have nowhere to go, 'n he'll have to stop. All of you, be ready, 'n have your guns in your hands."

"Where you goin' to be?" Teeter asked.

"Right back here so I can keep an eye on things 'n make sure ever' thing is goin' all right."

"Think we should start shootin' soon as he comes around the curve?" Gates asked.

"No, if you kill the driver the team might bolt 'n we'd have to chase the coach down. If he sees all of us, he'll stop."

* * *

As soon as the coach rounded the corner, Smoke saw the armed men standing spread across the road.

"Damn! You was right!" the driver said.

"Yeah, I wish I hadn't been," Smoke replied.

"Stop that coach!" The man who yelled was standing behind the six.

"What should I do?" Parsons asked.

"Stop the coach, we'll handle it from here," Smoke said.

The driver pulled the coach to a halt.

"What'll we do now, Lanagan?" one of the six men standing in the road asked, turning toward the man who was standing behind them.

"Pearlie, Cal, now!" Smoke shouted, and Pearlie and Cal jumped out of either side of the coach. Smoke stood up.

"Drop your guns!" Smoke called to the outlaws.

"What the hell!" the man standing behind the would-be robbers shouted. "Kill 'em, kill 'em all!"

The six bandits opened fire, as did Smoke, Pearlie and Cal. The six who were spread across the road went down, the seventh, the one who had shouted the order, didn't engage in the gunfight. Instead, as soon as the shooting started, he ran off the road, darting so quickly behind the cover of rocks that he took himself out of the fight.

For the next few seconds the air was filled with the flash and roar of gunfire, as a cloud of acrid, nostril-burning gun smoke drifted across the road. Then it grew quiet, with even the final echo fading away. Smoke, Pearlie and Cal stood still for a moment, holding smoking guns in their hands as they looked toward the downed men to see if any of them represented a challenge.

"It looks like one of them got away," Cal said.

"Yeah," Pearlie said.

They heard the hoof beats of what sounded like more than one horse.

"Damn, how many more were there?" Pearlie asked.

"There couldn't have been more than one or two more, or they would have joined the fight," Smoke said. "I think this was pretty much the lot of them."

"Me 'n Cal will go check on the men who are down," Pearlie said.

"Cal and I," Sally's disembodied voice came from inside the coach.

"Cal and I," Pearlie corrected, with a little chuckle.

"Be careful," Smoke said.

As Pearlie and Cal walked up to check the downed men, Smoke remained by the coach. He was alert, not only with regard to the men who were down, but also to the rock abutments that came out on both sides of the road, either of which could be harboring more men for a potential ambush.

Cal and Pearlie made a thorough examination of the downed men. They said a few words to each other, but so quietly did they speak that Smoke couldn't hear them. Then Pearlie called back.

"They're dead, Smoke," he shouted. "All six of 'em."

Sally climbed out of the coach. "What are we going to do with them, Smoke? We can't just leave them there. This is a public road."

"You're right. We'll take them in. Pearlie, do you see their horses anywhere?"

"We'll look around, but I heard more than one horse running off."

"I did too. There was at least one man who got away. I heard the others call him Lanagan. He might have run the other horses off."

After a fruitless search, Smoke concluded that that was exactly what happened. Without the horses to carry them, Smoke, Pearlie, Cal, and the driver had no choice but to lift the six outlaws onto the top of the coach.

"I heard the others call you Smoke," the driver said. "Is that your name? Smoke?"

"Yes, Smoke Jensen."

"Well, Mr. Jensen, I was damn glad . . ." the driver stopped and seeing Sally, nodded. "Beg your pardon for the language, ma'am. What I meant to say is, I'm awful glad you men was with me. 'N if you wouldn't mind, none, I'd take it kindly if you'd ride the rest of the way up here with me. There's a rifle in the boot."

"I'll be glad to," Smoke replied, climbing back up onto the driver's seat.

"Smoke Jensen," the driver said a few minutes later, after they were underway again. "Damn if I ain't never heard that name before, somewhere."

"You may have," Smoke said without further edification.

"Well, I'm mighty glad to meet you, Mr. Jensen. My name is Parsons, which you already know, 'cause I heard you call me that."

"I heard the hostler address you back at the stage depot."

"Yes, sir, well, what you might not know is my first name is Sam."

Sam Parsons was a talkative man, or perhaps he was just a man who, because he spent most of his time alone, was someone who would take advantage of having a conversation. Though, Smoke observed with a smile, most of the conversation was one-sided.

"Joined up as a boy, I did. Went off to fight for the Texas Volunteers when I was no more 'n sixteen years old. Got captured by the blue bellies at the Second Battle of Sabine Pass, 'n that ended my fightin'. I reckon you was too young for the war."

In fact, Smoke was only fourteen when, after his mother was killed, he joined the Ghost Riders, a group of Missouri Bushwhackers led by a man named Asa Briggs. But he said nothing about it, listening instead to Parsons' dissertations, which went from the war to his opinions on such things as mules or horses . . . "now mules is real good at pullin' freight wagons, fact is, they're better 'n horses, but horses is best for pullin' a stagecoach," to food, "I guess bein' from Texas it prob'ly ain't right for me to say this, but I'd much rather eat pork, than beef," to women. "The purtiest women don't need to be puttin' nothin' on their faces to look purty."

Smoke saw a town rising from the prairie in front of them.

"There it is, Mr. Jensen. That's the town of Audubon, population eight hunnert 'n twelve at last count. 'N if you ask me, it's just a real nice town, too. They say a railroad will be comin' through soon, 'n when it does, I don't know what'll happen to my job. More 'n likely the stage company will shut down, 'cause there won't be no need for it."

"Aren't there other towns around that won't be served by the railroads?" Smoke asked.

"Well, yes, sir, I reckon there are."

"The railroad will be bringing in more people than ever before," Smoke said. "And most will be coming to Audubon, just because the train will get them this far. But most will be going on to other places then, places that aren't served by the railroad. Your destination will probably change, you won't be going to Weatherford as much, but I have a feeling you'll be doing more business than ever."

A broad smile spread across Parsons' face. "Yeah," he said. "Yeah, that's right, ain't it? I hadn't thought about it like that before. I'm goin' to have to tell my wife about it. She's been some worried 'bout me maybe losin' my job when the railroad comes. This'll cheer her up. Thanks."

Smoke chuckled. "Always glad to lend a helping hand."

"Hyeah!" the driver shouted, snapping his whip over the heads of the horses, urging the team to go faster.

"I always like to come in at a gallop," Parsons said. "I think the folks in town have come to expect it."

CHAPTER TWENTY-THREE

Because the daily arrival of the stage from Weatherford meant mail and news, it was always greeted by a handful of people, but today, with six bodies lying in obvious view on top, there was a lot more interest than normal. And one of the most interested was Deputy Sheriff Dalton Conyers.

"What happened?" Dalton asked.

"I'll tell you what happened," Parsons replied as he pulled the coach to a halt. "These galoots that's a-lying dead up here on top o' the coach tried to hold us up, only they wasn't countin' on me carrying these three fellers."

"What three?" someone asked.

"This feller," Parsons said, indicating Smoke, who was sitting beside him, "'n the two others that's in the coach."

Smoke climbed down from his perch on the driver's seat, then opened the door to the coach to help Sally down. Pearlie and Cal left by the door on the opposite side.

"Smoke!" Dalton said, happily, noticing Smoke for the first time. "I wasn't sure you would come!"

"I never say no to family," Smoke replied.

"Hello, Miss Sally."

"Hello, Dalton," Sally said giving him a hug.

As Dalton was greeting Smoke and the others, Smoke overheard someone asking the driver for the bank pouch.

"No, sir," the driver replied. "I can't give it to you on account of I have been told that I was s'posed to give it only to Mr. Montgomery."

"That's nonsense, I work at the bank. Give it to me; I will give the pouch to Charles Montgomery."

"No, sir, now, Mr. Metzger, I know you work at the bank, but I can't give you this here money pouch," Parsons said. "It's like I told you, I can only give it directly to Mr. Montgomery."

"Conyers, you're the law here now, tell this damn fool driver to give me the transfer pouch,"

"Dalton, I don't mean to mess into anyone else's business, but I did hear the banker in Weatherford specifically tell Mr. Parsons to give the pouch only to Mr. Montgomery," Smoke said.

"Sorry, Drury," Dalton said. "If Mr. Parsons has his orders I'm not going to override them. You'd better tell Montgomery to come down himself to get the pouch."

"This makes absolutely no sense at all. I demand that the pouch be given to me," Metzger said, angrily.

"You demand? Who are you demanding it of?" Dalton asked.

"This fool driver," Drury said. "Do something, you're the sheriff now. Make him give the pouch to me."

"Seems to me like the only thing that has to be done with the pouch is see to it that it gets to the bank. And seeing as Montgomery is the president of the bank, putting it in his hands will meet that requirement. Now you're wasting time here, so I suggest that you go back to the bank and ask Charles to come down here."

Metzger glared at both Dalton and the driver, then he turned and started back down toward the bank.

"Here now, wouldn't you like to be stuck alone in a stagecoach with *that* man for a long trip?" Cal asked.

"He always has been a little full of himself," Dalton replied.

By now, the bodies on top of the coach had been taken down and laid out on the ground so they could be identified.

"That's Pete Grogan," someone said.

"'N them two is Emile Gates, 'n Norm Vargas," another said.

"That little feller there is Teeter, but I don't know his first name."

Nobody was able to identify the remaining two men.

"What are we goin' to do with 'em, Deputy?" Philbin asked. Philbin was the manager of the depot for the Risher and Hall Stage Coach Lines. "I don't want 'em lyin' out here in front of the depot, that wouldn't be good for business."

"Take them down to the undertaker," Dalton said. "Oh, and tell Mr. Ponder to stand these two up out front to see if anyone can identify them."

* * *

"Look who just showed up," Dalton said, leading Smoke and the others into the sheriff's office where Rebecca was. Looking up from the book she had been reading, she smiled broadly when she saw Smoke and the others.

"Uncle Kirby!" she shouted enthusiastically, and tossing the book aside she ran to him with her arms spread wide. Smoke gave her a hug, then she went to Sally. Pearlie and Cal were standing by, self-consciously.

"Pearlie and Cal, oh, I'm so glad you two came as well," Becca said, hugging them as she had the others.

"They had a little excitement on the way here," Dalton said, and he told about the attempted stage holdup.

"Lanagan was behind it," Dalton said in conclusion.

"How do you know?"

"Smoke heard one of the men call out his name."

"Is he one of the six who was killed?" Becca asked.

Dalton shook his head. "No such luck. He got away, the only one to do so."

"Ha! Maybe Uncle Kirby has taken care of your problem already," Becca said.

"I don't know," Dalton said. "I know that Claymore is a member of Lanagan's gang, and probably Seth McCoy. But neither of them were among the six killed. I expect Lanagan still has a number of men in his gang."

* * *

Ed Slater, one of the newest members of the gang, abandoned the horse he had stolen before entering Weatherford. He did that, rather than ride all the way, because he was afraid that someone might recognize the horse. Taking a hotel room in Weatherford, he used the time to recover from the bruises sustained in his fall from the train, and the long walk. The next day, he reclaimed his own horse from the livery and continued his journey to Audubon. And now, almost forty-eight hours since he boarded the train in Ft. Worth, he rode into Audubon. As he rode down the street, he saw a dozen or more people gathered in a group. Curious as to what it was that had their attention, he rode over to see.

"Damn!" he said aloud.

There, in front of Ponder's funeral home, were two open caskets standing up on their ends, exposing the bodies inside. A sign over the two caskets read Do You Know These Men?

In fact, Slater knew both of them because he had met them only a week before, when he joined Lanagan's gang. One, he remembered, was Rufus Small, and the other was Dooley Thompson. Of course, Slater didn't know if those were their real names or not, because most men who rode the outlaw trail didn't use the names they were born with. He did know, however, that they were the names the two men had been using when he met them. They were part of Lanagan's gang, but what happened to them? How did they wind up gettin' themselves killed?

The long ride had made Slater thirsty, so he decided to stop in the Blanket and Saddle for a beer.

But it wasn't just the beer that took him there. He knew that having two bodies exposed in such a way was not a normal thing; therefore it was likely to be the subject of conversation in the saloon. And if he wanted to find out what had happened, all he had to do was listen.

"Has they been anybody that says they know who them other two outlaws is, yet?" someone asked, shortly after Slater ordered his beer. "I'm talkin' 'bout the ones that's standin' up in front of Ponder's place."

"No. They got the names of the four others though, the ones that was inside."

"Six of 'em. Six of 'em try 'n hold up a stage that don't even have no shotgun guard ridin' on it, 'n all six of 'em gets shot down."

Six of Lanagan's men killed? Slater thought. That didn't seem very likely, but there was no denying that it happened. He had seen two of them himself.

Slater got his beer and drank it quietly, listening to the conversation going on around him.

"They was actually seven of 'em," one of others said.

"No, they's only six. Ponder's got four of 'em inside because they was some people that knowed who they was. It's them two that's standin' up out in the front o' his place that they don't nobody know who it is."

"They was seven of 'em, but one of 'em got away. Lanagan, it was, who's the one that got away."

"Lanagan? Clete Lanagan? Wait a minute, ain't he the one that robbed the banks up in Pella 'n Salcedo. 'N, come to think of it, ain't he also the one that shot Sheriff Peabody?"

"Well, he was there when the sheriff was shot, but

he warn't the one what actual shot the sheriff, that bein' Claymore."

"But you're sayin' that it was Lanagan that tried to hold up the stagecoach."

"Yes."

"That seems kind 'a odd to me, on account of 'cause most of the time when Lanagan sets out to do a thing, why, he generally gets it done."

"Yeah, well, that's cause he ain't never run into the feller that was ridin' shotgun before."

"Shotgun? I thought Parsons didn't have no shotgun guard with 'im."

"Yeah, well, here's the thing, It wasn't no real shotgun guard, it was one of the passengers."

"They was six of 'em killed. Are you tellin' me that it was one of the passengers that done the shootin'?"

"Actually, they was three of 'em on the stage, 'n all three of 'em was shootin', but I only know the name of one of 'em, him bein' Smoke Jensen."

"Smoke Jensen? Why, I've heard of Smoke Jensen. He's sort of a really famous feller, ain't he? 'N you're a-tellin' me that he was a passenger on the stagecoach?"

"Yep."

"Now, what do you suppose a feller like Smoke Jensen would be doin' here, in Audubon? I mean, especially what with him bein' famous 'n all. Don't he live up in Colorado or Wyoming, or some such place?"

"He lives in Colorado, but it turns out that he's some kind of kin to Deputy Conyers. He's his uncle or somethin', 'n what I heard is he's come down here to help 'im out."

"Help 'im out with what?"

"Help 'im out with Lanagan. Like you said, Lanagan most often gets done what he sets out to do, 'n he's got 'im a gang goin' now. So, what with Sheriff Peabody down, 'n Conyers not bein' able to raise a posse or nothin' . . ."

"Now wait, I woulda gone with 'im iffen he coulda got hisself anyone else, but there didn't nobody else say they would go with 'im. 'N what good will one more man have done 'im?"

"Yes, well, him not bein' able to get nobody a-tall meant he was havin' to handle things all by hisself. So what he done was, he sent off for his uncle to come help him out."

"I can't say as I blame him for lookin' for help, but the truth is I don't see how somebody like Lanagan can be handled by just two men, even if one of 'em is somebody like Smoke Jensen. And you most especial ain't goin' to be able to handle Lanagan with just the two of 'em seein' as Lanagan has more 'n likely got hisself a gang."

"Don't forget, there was two more men that come with Jensen. And besides which, Lanagan more 'n likely don't have no gang left by now anyhow, or at least not much of one. They's them six dead men that's down at Ponder's place, all of 'em kilt by Smoke Jensen. 'N like you say, Lanagan was with 'em, but he got away."

"Yeah, but Claymore ain't one o' them six men 'n like as not Lanagan has got more."

"McCoy warn't one of 'em neither."

"McCoy's in jail over in Antelope."

"No, he ain't. He escaped. Didn't you read it in the paper?"

"I don't figure it'll much matter to Jensen how many men Lanagan has with 'im. From what I've heard of him, he's the type of feller that would go into a bear's den 'n snatch a whisker off'n its face."

Slater, who had nursing his beer as he listened to the conversation, turned toward the one who seemed to be best informed.

"Who is this Jensen feller you boys is talkin' about?" Slater asked, topping off the inquiry with a swallow of his beer as if showing that the question was of idle curiosity only.

"You ain't never heard of Smoke Jensen?"

"No, I can't say as I have heard of 'im," Slater replied.

"Well, he's just about the biggest hero there ever was, is all. Wild Bill Hickok, Wyatt Earp, Bat Masterson, there ain't none of 'em can hold a candle to Smoke Jensen. Why, it's said that he can shoot the flame out of a candle, then have his pistol back in the holster before the light goes out."

"Good gunfighter, is he?"

"Why don't you ask them six dead boys down at Ponder's? They'll tell you how good he is."

"I expect he'll get this town 'n whole county cleaned up better 'n Sheriff Peabody ever coulda done," one of the others said.

CHAPTER TWENTY-FOUR

While Becca helped Sally, Pearlie, and Cal get checked in to the Del Rey Hotel, Dalton took Smoke down to Dr. Palmer's office to see Tom. When they stepped into the back of the office, they saw Dr. Palmer and Tom talking with a patient who was sitting up in bed.

"Damn, Sheriff, I thought sure I'd find you still sleeping," Dalton said.

"Dalton, m' boy, you should know by now that it's goin' to take more than one bullet to put me down," Sheriff Peabody replied, ebulliently. "Who's this feller with you?"

"Hello, Smoke, it's been a while," Tom Whitman said, extending his hand.

"Hello, Doc," Smoke replied.

"Dr. Palmer, Sheriff Peabody, this is my uncle, Kirby Jensen. Though you may have heard of him as Smoke Jensen."

"Smoke Jensen? Yes, indeed, I've heard of you.

What in the world are you doing here?" Sheriff Peabody asked.

"I sent for him," Dalton said. He smiled, then nodded toward Tom. "Just like I sent for Dr. Whitman. I wanted to get the absolute best doctor in America to help you, and the best lawman in America to help me, and by damn, that's what I did."

"Lawman?" Peabody asked.

Smoke smiled. "Well, not exactly. At least, not down here. The governor of Colorado has given me a state commission as a deputy. I'm not a regular lawmen, but it's a title I can use up there when having such a position can come in handy. I guess you might say I'm a deputy ex cathedra."

"An ex what?" Sheriff Peabody asked.

"Sally taught me that word. It means that, even though I'm not a regular deputy, I have the authority of a deputy. At least, in Colorado."

"Well, I'm glad Dalton was able to get you," Sheriff Peabody said. "There is no doubt in my mind but that this man, Lanagan, is going to cause us a lot of trouble. And the truth is, I have heard of you, but you're only one man."

"He brought two very good men with him, and he's already got a good start," Dalton said.

"What do you mean, he has a good start?"

"You know about the railroad coming through Audubon. Well, today ten thousand dollars was being transferred by the railroad to our bank. The money was on today's stagecoach from Weatherford, and Lanagan and six of his men held it up. That is, they tried to hold it up. They hadn't counted on Smoke,

Pearlie, and Cal being on the coach. The money got through and is now on deposit in our bank."

"Pearlie and Cal came down too, did they?" Tom asked.

"Yeah, they did."

"I'm glad they came as well. They are both exceptionally good men."

"You know them, do you, Doc?" Sheriff Peabody asked.

"We were once drovers together," Tom said.

"Drovers? You? Are you telling me you once worked a herd of cattle?"

"Tom was as good a drover as we had," Dalton said.

"Hmm." Sheriff Peabody looked over at Dr. Palmer. "Didn't you say this man took a bullet out that was less than an inch from my heart?"

"That he did."

"A drover operated on me?"

"Well, Andy, you have to understand that Tom was just real handy around the cows, why, I once saw him get a thistle from side of a heifer's eye without blinding her. That's why I thought he'd be good for getting the bullet out."

Dr. Palmer laughed. "Dalton is riding you a bit, Andy. Dr. Whitman is one of the finest surgeons in the country."

"But I did work as a drover for Dalton's father."

"Yes, well, The Colonel always did have a nose for picking good men." Sheriff Peabody smiled. "After all, he made me his sergeant major."

"And my father says it was the best decision he made during the whole war," Dalton said.

Sheriff Peabody turned his attention back to Smoke. "So Smoke and his men drove the robbers off?"

Dalton chuckled. "In a manner of speaking they did, although the only one they drove off was Lanagan. The other six are down at Ponder's funeral home. That stopped the robbery."

"Yes, I would think so," Sheriff Peabody agreed. "Do you know who any of the six men are?"

"We've identified Pete Grogan, Emile Gates, Norm Vegas, and one named Teeter, but nobody knew his first name."

"This Teeter, he was a small man, was he?" the sheriff asked.

"Yes, you know him?"

"If he is the one I'm thinking about, it would be Walt Teeter. And don't let the fact that he was a little man fool you. He was as cold blooded as they come, with at least six killin's to his credit, 'n two of em were women. Grogan and Miller I know too, but I don't know anything about Vargas."

"Well, like I said, those four, and the two standing up in front of Ponder's place, won't be bothering us anymore, thanks to Smoke, Pearlie, and Cal. Sheriff, I hope you don't mind that I asked Smoke, Pearlie, and Cal to come down and help me," Dalton said.

"No, not at all! Why should I mind? I think it was real smart of you to ask for help. I just wish I could be out there with you, but the doc says I'm goin' to have to stay down for a couple more days."

"I would say that a few more weeks is more like it," Tom said.

"Well, if I can't do it, at least I know it is in good

hands." Peabody looked at Dalton. "I heard how you got this part-time doc," he paused and smiled before he continued, "and part-time drover, to come take the bullet out. I owe you a lot, Dalton, and I won't forget it."

"I didn't want to lose you, Andy. You're not just my boss, you're a very good friend."

"Not to say the father of the girl you're courting, right?" Dr. Palmer added with a little chuckle.

Dalton laughed as well. "Yes, there is that," he agreed.

"Smoke?" Sheriff Peabody said.

"Yes, Sheriff?"

"Hold up your right hand. I'm about to give you cathed . . . uh . . . ex . . . uh, well, whatever the hell it is that you have up there in Colorado."

Smoke raised his hand.

"Do you swear to uphold the law of Texas, 'n do whatever you can to help Dalton bring in that son of a bitch Clete Lanagan 'n his men, so help you God?"

"I do."

"You're a deputy. Dalton, bring those other two men in sometime soon, 'n I'll swear them in as well."

"Thanks, Sheriff."

"Don't think I have any more badges."

"Dalton's badge will be enough for all of us," Smoke said. He stuck out his hand to shake hands with the sheriff. "Get well quick, Sheriff, I've got a ranch to run, and I need to get back to my cattle."

"I'll get well as fast as I can, I promise you that," Sheriff Peabody replied.

* * *

From the *Audubon Eagle:*

Attempted Stage Coach
Robbery Foiled !

Sam Parsons, stage coach driver for the Risher and Hall Stage Coach Company, was interrupted on the 10th Instant, when his Weatherford to Audubon run was stood up by a group of would-be stage coach robbers. Mr. Parsons was carrying a money pouch containing ten thousand dollars, the money to be deposited in the Bank of Audubon for use by the Texas and Pacific Railroad in construction of a line to Audubon.

There were seven armed and desperate men spread across the Weatherford Road, and the purpose of their presence was made immediately clear when they called upon Mr. Parsons to halt the coach. It is not known whether they were aware of the amount of money being transported by Mr. Parsons, or if they were merely attempting to rob the stage coach in the hopes of coming away with sufficient funds as to make their adventure profitable.

One might think that, in choosing this particular stage coach on this particular day, they might have enjoyed the opportune happenstance of intersecting their greed and ambition, with the unannounced transfer of a significant amount of money. Unfortunately for the brigands who had put their foul deed into motion, there were three passengers on board the stage coach who, at the time the robbery was attempted, offered their services for the protection of the stage coach and the money. Leaving the coach with pistols in hand, the stalwart band of heroes engaged the vandals with guns ablaze.

As a result of their ill-conceived plan, six of the outlaws are now temporary guests of Ponder's Undertaking Establishment, soon to be permanent residents of the Potter's Field corner of the Audubon Memorial Cemetery. Four of the decedents have been identified, they being Pete Grogan, Emile Gates, Norm Vegas, and Walt Teeter. Two of the outlaws have not been identified, and their grisly remains are as of this writing, standing in front of Ponder's mortuary establishment. A printed sign has been placed over the two corpses for the purpose of soliciting identification from any who may recognize their final remains.

Lanagan and Claymore were passing a bottle of whiskey back and forth when Slater returned to the outlaw camp.

"How was your trip to Ft. Worth?" Lanagan asked. "Were you able to get the money you went after?"

"Yeah," Slater replied with a smile as he thought of Frank and Betty Ann Dolan lying dead on the floor. "It wasn't much, but it was just where I left it."

Lanagan nodded. "Good, I'm glad it worked out for you." He took the bottle from Claymore and turned it up for another drink.

"I seen Small 'n Thompson," Slater said.

Lanagan looked around sharply. "What do you mean, you seen 'em? Seen 'em where?"

"They was standin' up in front of the undertaker's place in Audubon."

"Standing?"

"Yeah, sort of. They was both in pine boxes, 'n the boxes was stood up under a sign askin' if anybody knowed who they was."

"You didn't tell nobody you knew 'em, did you?" Lanagan asked.

Slater shook his head. "I got better sense 'n that," he said.

"I sure as hell would hope so. But they was six of 'em that was shot. What about the other four?"

"They was inside. From what I was able to learn at the saloon, they was some people in town that already knowed who they was. It was just Small 'n Thompson that they didn't nobody know who it was."

"Yeah, well, it's no wonder there didn't nobody know who Small and Thompson was, seein' as they just come to join up with us about two weeks ago. That was only about a week before you did, and I think both of 'em was from The Nations, or maybe Kansas, or some such place," Lanagan replied. "So all six of 'em is dead, are they?"

"Yeah."

"I figured they prob'ly was, but I didn't stay around to find out. I don't know who them three was that was in the coach, passengers they was, but they come pourin' out, shootin' like madmen. It was almost like they knowed we was plannin' on holdin' up the stage."

"I don't know all three of them, but I do know one of them," Slater said. "His name is Smoke Jensen."

"Smoke Jensen?" MacMurtry said with a sharp reaction.

"That's the name they was sayin'."

"Do you know Jensen, MacMurtry?" Lanagan asked.

"He don't know me, but I know him."

"Would you know him when you seen 'im?"

"Yeah, I would," MacMurtry said without any further explanation.

"Well, I ain't never even heard of 'im," Lanagan said.

"I have," McCoy said. "Leastwise, if this here is the same Smoke Jensen. Onliest thing, until MacMurtry spoke up as to how he knows 'im, I wouldn't of even thought he was a real person, seein' as I oncet read about him in a book."

"He's real, all right," Slater said. "'N from what I've heard of him, he's the kind of feller that someone might write a book about."

"Where is this Jensen, now?" Lanagan asked.

"I don't know, I didn't see 'im," Slater said. "But I expect he's in Audubon. They say he's some kin to the deputy sheriff."

"That would be Conyers," Lanagan said. "I figured that without Sheriff Peabody, that Audubon would be an easy town to raze, but Conyers may well turn out to be more difficult to deal with than I thought."

"Why don't we send a couple of men in to kill 'im?" Claymore suggested.

"Nah, killin' Conyers won't do anything for us,"

Lanagan said. "If we're goin' to kill somebody, it should be this Jensen person."

"Smoke Jensen ain't goin' to be that easy to kill," MacMurtry said. "And the reason I can tell you for a fact that he won't be easy to kill is 'cause I done tried to do it oncet, 'n I didn't get the job done."

"Why was it you tried to kill im?"

"On account of he is the son of a bitch that kilt my brother."

"So, that's how come you know 'im, huh? 'Cause he kilt your brother?" Claymore asked.

"Yeah."

"What happened?" Lanagan asked. "What I mean is, if you tried to kill 'im 'n you failed, how is it that you're still alive?"

"They was three of us," MacMurtry said. "The other two was kilt, but I got away." He didn't expand on his answer, and nobody questioned him further.

CHAPTER TWENTY-FIVE

"Yeah, I remember Cutter MacMurtry. I remember his brother, Hatchett, too. They both worked for Pa until Cutter got arrested for killing Father Grayson and his wife and two little children. All for just over a hundred dollars as I recall," Dalton said.

"Did that happen when Tyrone Greene was working there?" Smoke asked.

"Yes. It was Mr. Greene that discovered he was the one that did it, and it was him who took MacMurtry to jail. I never liked either one of the MacMurtrys, but I had no idea they were that evil. I can see how he would have murdered Mr. and Mrs. Greene, though."

Dalton smiled. "I got a letter from Pa, telling me about Tamara, though, and how she has come to live with them. I guess that means I have a new little sister."

"She lived with Sally and me for a while," Smoke said. "She is a most charming young lady, I'm sure that your mother and father will be very happy that they took her in."

"I can't wait to see her again. She was only ten years

old, the last time I saw her. If it weren't for the fact that Andy is lying up wounded, and I'm having to act as sheriff, I would have already gone home to do so."

"Tell me more about Hatchett MacMurtry," Smoke said.

Dalton shook his head. "He is every bit as evil as Cutter was. He's the one who broke Cutter out of prison and no more than ten miles away from the prison, a farmer and his wife and ten-year-old boy were murdered. They have never officially pinned the crime on the MacMurtry brothers, but they did find an abandoned prison uniform there. It's a lead pipe cinch Cutter and Hatchett killed them for a change of clothes, and probably some provisions. Why do you ask? Was Hatchett involved in the murder of Mr. and Mrs. Greene?"

"No," Smoke replied. "At least I don't think so. But, not long after I killed Cutter, I was ambushed on the road home from Big Rock. There were two of them, and I had no choice but to kill them before I had a chance to talk to them.

"And you think one of them might have been Hatchett?" Dalton asked.

"No, neither of them were, but I had the strongest feeling that someone else was there, someone who was watching, but didn't participate. And I think it might have been Hatchett MacMurtry, looking for revenge over me killing his brother."

"It could very well have been," Dalton agreed. "Hatchett MacMurtry is quite evil enough to do such a thing."

This discussion between Smoke and Dalton was taking place in the sheriff's office. At the moment,

Pearlie and Cal were down at the doctor's office, being sworn in as deputies by Sheriff Peabody.

"Tell me more about the sheriff," Smoke asked.

"He is as good a man as I have ever known," Dalton replied. "Honest as the day is long. Pa wanted to make him an officer, during the war, but Andy wouldn't have it. He said that as long as he stayed a sergeant, he would be able to stay closer to the men. That's why he was a sergeant major, instead of a captain.

"His wife died six years ago, leaving him with a fifteen year-old daughter. He has done a great job raising her."

"I can see why you are taken with her."

"Speaking of Marjane, I think she's planning on inviting all of you over to the house for dinner tonight. And I can tell you for a fact that she's a great cook."

Smoke chuckled. "If that invitation includes Pearlie and Cal, I hope she has some idea of what kind of appetite those two have. They eat every meal as if they aren't going to eat again for a week."

Out at the outlaw encampment, Lanagan was trying to learn what he could about Smoke Jensen.

"MacMurtry, this killin' of your brother 'n all, I mean, when Jensen done that, did it happen down here in Texas?" Lanagan asked.

"No, it was up in Colorado."

"Did you chase him down here?"

"No, I didn't even know he was here 'til you all started talkin' about it."

"All right, you've all told me how hard it's goin' to

be to kill Smoke Jensen, but that's exactly what we're goin' to have to do. We're goin' to have to kill Jensen and those two men who came with him."

"You goin' to do it?" MacMurtry asked.

"No, it can't be me, because they would more 'n likely recognize me right off," Lanagan said. "They seen me standin' out 'n the road when we stood up the stage, remember? Someone else is goin' to have to do it."

"Who?"

"I'll be needin' a volunteer."

"Who's goin' to volunteer to go up ag'in Smoke Jensen and the two who come with him?" McCoy asked.

"I will give a one-thousand-dollar bonus to whoever kills them," Lanagan said.

"Damn, Lanagan, where are you going to get a thousand dollars?" Claymore asked, surprised by the size of the offer.

Lanagan smiled. "There's somethin' I ain't told you fellers yet, but I reckon this is as good a time as any. Boys, the plan I got 'n mind, 'n what we're about to set out to do, is goin' to get us a hunnert thousand dollars."

"What?" Slater gasped. "A hunnert thousand dollars?"

"Where are we goin' to get a hunnert thousand dollars?" McCoy asked.

"From the bank in Audubon."

"Clete, me 'n you has been together a long time, but I don't mind tellin' you, you're crazy if you think that bank will have a hunnert thousand dollars," Claymore said. "Hell, I bet it don't have no more 'n fifteen thousand or so, 'n that includes the ten thousand that just got through to 'em."

"You're talking about the ten thousand dollars that got away from me 'n the others when we went after it?" Lanagan asked, the expression on his face and the tone of his voice indicating his irritation at being reminded of the failure.

"Well, yeah, but I don't mean nothin' by it," Claymore said quickly, reading Lanagan's reaction. "I mean, how would anyone know that Jensen 'n them other two would have been on that selfsame stagecoach?"

"Yeah, well, what happened, has happened," Lanagan said with a dismissive wave of his hand. "But I don't intend to let that hunnert thousand dollars get away from us."

"The hunnert thousand that you say is in the bank in Audubon," Claymore said.

"It's there. Or it will be there. And when it is there, I'll know about it."

"How?"

"I ain't never told you this before, Dingus, but they's a man in the bank in Audubon who's a cousin' of mine. 'N we're real close cousins too, seein' as how we was mostly brung up together. You want to know how it is that I knowed 'bout the ten thousand dollars that was on the stage that we tried to hold up? It was my cousin that told me that the money was bein' sent to the bank."

"Ten thousand dollars is a lot of money, all right, but it ain't a hunnert thousand," Slater said.

"It turns out that they's a railroad bein' built to come through Audubon, 'n that selfsame railroad is fixin' to put a hunnert thousand dollars in the bank there. My cousin's goin' to let me know when it gets there, 'n when it does, we're a-goin' to go get it."

"That ain't goin' to exactly be like gatherin' up eggs," Claymore said. "Are you forgettin' about Jensen?"

"No, I ain't forgettin' about 'im. That's why I say that I'll pay a thousand dollars to anyone that kills him."

"I'll do it," MacMurtry said.

"Seein' as how he knows you, what makes you think you can get close enough to him to get the job done?" Lanagan asked.

"He don't know me."

"What do you mean, he don't know you? I thought you said he kilt your brother, so you tried to kill him."

"I did try, only he don't know that it was me that was tryin', on account of he never even seen me."

"You think you can kill 'im, do you?" Lanagan asked.

"It's goin' to take some studyin', but yeah, I think I can kill 'im."

"Clete, it ain't just him that's goin' to need killin'," Claymore said. "You said yourself they was three of 'em in the coach, 'n that all three of 'em come out shootin'."

"That's right," Lanagan replied.

"Then it seems to me like all three of 'em are goin' to need killin'. And if you're goin' to give a thousand dollars for Jensen, you ought to give a thousand for the others too."

"Not a thousand," Lanagan said. "But I'll give five hunnert apiece for each one o' them other two. I don't know what their names are, though."

"One of 'em is called Pearlie 'n the other 'n is called Cal," MacMurtry said. "I heard their names spoke while I was up in Colorado. I don't know their whole names, though."

"It don't matter none what their whole names is," Slater said. "If we kill 'em, they'll be just as dead with one name as they would with two names."

The others laughed.

"All right, MacMurtry, you kill them three, 'n you'll get the first two thousand dollars right off the top, then you'll get your equal share to what's left of the money."

"I ain't interested in killin' them other two, Pearlie 'n Cal. Onliest one I'm interested in killin' is Smoke Jensen. Let someone else kill them other two."

"All right, the same deal goes," Lanagan said. "Whoever it is that kills them other two will get five hunnert dollars for each one, then they'll also get a equal share to what's left o' the hunnert thousand dollars."

"A hunnert thousand dollars," Claymore said, speaking the words in awe.

"I didn't know there was that much money in the whole state o' Texas," McCoy said.

"When does the money get put in the bank?" Slater asked.

"I don't know, on account of my cousin ain't told me yet." Lanagan glanced over at MacMurtry. "But there ain't no need for you to wait 'til the money is put there before you kill Jensen."

"I don't intend to wait," MacMurtry said. "Truth is, I wanted to kill that son of a bitch even before you said you'd pay a thousand dollars to have it done."

"You said you tried it before 'n didn't get it done,"

Claymore said. "What makes you think you'll be able to kill him this time?"

"'Cause I'm goin' to be smarter about it this time."

Smoke was riding with Dalton, doing a wide swing around the town, just to acquaint himself with the area.

"You were right about Marjane being a good cook. Chicken and dumplin's have always been a favorite of mine, and she did a great job with them," Smoke said, speaking of the dinner Marjane had prepared for them the night before.

Dalton laughed. "And you were right about Pearlie and Cal's appetite. I should have remembered how much they like to eat from the cattle drive we made.

"Not necessarily," Smoke said. "Everyone has a good appetite during a cattle drive."

They were about three miles northwest of the town and they came across a stream of water.

"What is this stream?" Smoke asked.

"This is Beans Creek," Dalton said. "It feeds into the Trinity River.

Smoke saw a cabin, sitting under some post oak and mesquite trees along the banks of the creek.

"Who lives in the cabin?" Smoke asked.

Dalton shook his head. "Nobody lives there now. It belonged to Amos Purdy. Captain Purdy, he was called, but he died about six months ago. Someone said that he has a brother back in Arkansas, so I guess it belongs to him now. Jason Pell, a lawyer in town, has been tryin' to locate Purdy's brother, but he hasn't been able to do so, yet."

"Shall we take a look?" Smoke invited.

"Sure, if you would like to, I see no reason why not," Dalton replied. "But like I said, no one lives there now."

"The outlaws we're looking for have to have someplace to be," Smoke said. "It won't hurt to check out a few places."

"Oh, yeah, I hadn't thought about that. I see what you mean."

"I notice you've got a little strap over the hammer of your pistol," Smoke said. "You might want to loosen it."

"Good idea."

Dalton turned his horse in the direction of the little cabin, but Smoke reached out to stop him.

"If there's someone in the cabin who doesn't want visitors, it would be better if we don't ride right up on him."

"Good idea," Dalton agreed.

The two men rode on by the cabin, then when they were about half a mile beyond it, they turned back around a stand of trees and rode far enough so that they would be behind the cabin when they approached it. It was almost half an hour before they rounded a small thicket and saw the cabin, now no more than a hundred yards distant.

If Smoke had been on his horse, Seven, he would have trusted his mount to take him all the way up to the cabin without being heard. But he was astride a rented horse.

"Leave the horses here," Smoke suggested.

The two men tied their horses to a tree that couldn't be seen from the cabin, then, drawing their pistols they approached quietly, all the while keeping the cabin under a very close observation. When they reached the rear of the cabin, Smoke backed up against the wall, then worked his way around to the side so he could look in through the window.

The cabin was empty.

Smoke let out a relieved sigh and holstered his pistol.

"Nobody here," he said.

The front door wasn't locked, and the two men stepped inside. The cabin was still furnished and incredibly clean, except for the expected patina of dust.

"Captain Purdy must have been a very neat person," Smoke said. "By the way, captain of what?"

"He was an old retired riverboat captain. I'm not sure why he came out here, he didn't try to ranch, or farm, or even trap or hunt. He seemed to have enough money to get by without doing any of that. I think he just liked the area."

"Where is he buried?"

Dalton pointed to a lone tree about fifty yards from the cabin. "Right over there, under that tree. It turns out that he had a bad heart, and he knew he was dying. The last time he saw the doc, he told him exactly where he wanted to be buried, so that's what we did."

"He picked a good spot," Smoke said.

CHAPTER TWENTY-SIX

Live Oaks Ranch

Tamara was in the library with Billy Lewis, viewing pictures through the stereoscope. Julia was looking on as she crocheted a scarf for Tamara.

"Look at this one," Billy invited, passing the viewer to Tamara. "This is Castle Garden, in New York."

"My, it's as if we could walk right up to it and go inside," Tamara said. "What makes it look so real? I've never seen photographs like this, before."

"It is a special type of photography that produces something called a 'three-dimensional' photograph," Julia explained. "It gives the pictures depth. I don't quite know how it works, but it is perfectly marvelous."

"Ha!" Billy said. "Here is a picture of a woman looking at pictures through the same device we are using. I wonder if she is looking at herself," he added with a chuckle.

Tamara took the viewer from her and saw a woman, sitting in a parlor between a fireplace and a bookshelf, looking, as Billy had pointed out, at pictures through a viewer.

"Why, we are right there in the room with her," Tamara said. "Yes, thank you Mrs. Saddler, I believe I would like some tea. I'll just take a seat on this sofa, until your servant brings it to me."

Billy laughed out loud.

Big Ben came into the library then. "Hello, ladies," he greeted. "Hello, Billy."

"Hello, Colonel," Billy replied.

Conyers held up an envelope. "Look here, my dear. We got a letter from Dalton, today."

"Oh, I hope the sheriff is all right," Julia said. "Dalton's last letter said that Tom had managed to get the bullet out. Has Sheriff Peabody taken a turn for the worse?"

"No, the sergeant major is doing quite well."

Julia laughed. "He may have been your sergeant major, but he is a sheriff now, and he is Dalton's boss."

"So he is. Anyway, he was just letting us know that Tom and Becca are still in Audubon. Smoke and Sally too."

"How far is Audubon from here?" Tamara asked. "Is there any chance they might come here?"

"I don't know, but I doubt that they will," Big Ben replied. "Remember, they stopped here on the way to Audubon."

"Oh," Tamara said, her response showing her obvious disappointment.

"You would like to see them again, wouldn't you?" Julia asked.

"Yes, ma'am, I would," Tamara said. "Oh, please don't think me ungrateful about living here with you and Colonel Conyers," she added quickly. "You have been wonderful, and there is no place I would rather be. But after Cutter MacMurtry killed my parents, Mr. Smoke and Miz Sally were so nice to me."

"I understand perfectly," Julia said. She smiled, and looked over at Ben. "Ben, I would like to see Dalton, Becca, and Tom. Why don't we go up to Audubon for a visit? We can take Tamara with us."

"Oh, can we?" Tamara asked, enthusiastically.

"I can't get away from the ranch right now," Ben replied. "But, I see no reason why the two of you couldn't go."

"Oh, can we?" Tamara asked.

"Yes, my dear, we can," Julia said. "Tomorrow we'll take the train to Weatherford then the stagecoach on up to Audubon."

At the outlaw hideout, Hatchett MacMurtry was outside the cabin, sitting on the front porch with his legs hanging over the edge, when Slater walked up to him.

"When are you plannin' on killin' Jensen?" Slater asked.

"I ain't in no rush," MacMurtry said. "That's why I didn't get the job done last time I tried it. I'm goin' to take my time 'til I can come up with a plan that will work."

"I've got a suggestion" Slater said.

"What is that?"

"I think me 'n you should team up. Iffen we kill all three of 'em, why, that'd be a thousand dollars apiece.

Then, with them three gone, there's no way that one deputy that's left will be able to stop us. That means we'll also be able to hold up the bank, oncet the hunnert thousand dollars is there, so it'll be even more money."

"Yeah, but there ain't really no need for us to be a-teamin' up," MacMurtry said. "You kill Pearlie 'n Cal, 'n I'll kill Jensen, 'n that'll be a thousand dollars apiece."

"It would be easier if you help me kill them other two, Pearlie and Cal, 'n then I'll help you kill Jensen."

"No, I don't want no help in killin' Jensen, I want to kill 'im myself," MacMurtry said. "And it ain't just 'cause of the money Lanagan said he would pay for the killin'. Like I said, I'd be a-wantin' to kill the son of a bitch whether I was goin' to get paid for it or not. This here is personal."

"Yeah, I know, 'cause he killed your brother," Slater said. "All right, you kill Jensen, 'n I'll kill them other two."

"I'd just as soon me 'n you not go into town at the same time, on account of if I go in by myself, I won't draw as much attention," MacMurtry said.

"Yeah, all right. I wasn't plannin' on waitin' around no more, nohow. I'm figurin' on goin' in tonight."

"Leave Jensen for me," MacMurtry said.

"I ain't goin' to exactly try 'n kill 'im, but if I see some chance to do it easy, well, I'm a-goin' to do it,' Slater replied.

MacMurtry chuckled. "I don't have to worry none, then, 'cause you ain't goin' to see no way to kill 'im that's easy."

* * *

Tom and Becca Whitman were staying on the same floor in the Del Rey Hotel as were Smoke and Sally, and Pearlie and Cal. The restaurant that was adjacent to the Del Rey hotel was the Palace Café and that evening all but Cal and Dalton were sharing a table with Marjane Peabody. At the moment, Cal was making the rounds with Dalton.

"Hold two places open for Dalton and Cal," Marjane told the waiter. "They'll be joining us here before too long."

"Yes, ma'am, Miss Marjane," the waiter replied.

"I was so happy when you and Dr. Whitman came to Audubon," Marjane said to Becca. "Dalton has spoken so lovingly of his sister, and I've been wanting to meet you, I just wish it could have been in happier circumstances."

"It looks to me like your father is going to make a complete recovery," Sally said, smiling at the young woman. "So how happy does the occasion have to be?"

Marjane laughed. "I suppose you do have a point."

"You and Dalton seem to be getting along very well," Becca said.

"Oh, yes!" Marjane's response was very enthusiastic. "Dalton is the most wonderful man. He's smart, he is very nice to everyone, and my father just thinks the world of him. He says he is the finest deputy he has ever had."

"I know that he feels the same about you and your father. I'm just glad that you are here for him."

"I'll always be here for him," Marjane said, then she

paused for a moment, and the expression on her face, and in her voice, grew pensive. "But I know he won't always be here. After all, the Colonel is a big rancher, and Dalton is his only son. I know that Dalton plans to go back some day, and he really should. After all, he does have a responsibility to his father."

"You can go with him," Becca suggested. "After all, I left home to go with my husband," she added, looking toward Tom who, at the moment, was engrossed in conversation with Smoke and Pearlie."

"Yes, but he *was* your husband, after all. There is a difference, if you are going to leave with your husband."

Becca smiled, and put her hand on Marjane's shoulder. "Who is to say that Dalton wouldn't be your husband, when you leave?"

Sally chuckled. "Watching this is like déjà vu."

"Déjà vu?" Marjane said. She shook her head in confusion. "I don't know what that means."

"It means that you feel like you have seen all this before. I recall a scene with Becca and Tom. You might even say it was the pivotal scene in their relationship."

"Tell me about it," Marjane said.

Sally looked toward Rebecca. "It's a private scene, I'll have to have Becca's permission to share it with you. It is something that happened during the cattle drive down from Dodge City, when the Indians thought that the Angus cattle were buffalo."

"Oh, I know what you are talking about," Becca said. "It was when Tom went to see them, alone, to show that we weren't taking buffalo from them."

"Yes," Sally said. "But what I am specifically talking

about is what went on between you and Tom, just before he left."

Becca smiled, and nodded. "I remember that as well. Yes, Aunt Sally, you can tell her."

Sally told the story with such detail and intensity that it was as if Rebecca were actually reliving the moment, and Marjane, as Sally had done, was an actual witness.

"Tom?" Rebecca called.

"Rebecca, I'm going to see if I can pacify the Indians. You aren't going to be able to talk me out of this," Tom said.

"I know," she said. "So I won't even try."

"Good."

"Do you love me, Tom?"

"Rebecca, this hardly seems the time or place for us to discuss something like this."

"I will ask you again, very slowly, and very distinctly. Do—you—love—me—Tom? It's not a hard question."

"Yes," Tom said. "I do love you."

"Oh!" Marjane said, when Sally finished the story. "Oh, how wonderful that was! Why, it is like reading the most wonderful tale of love."

"What did you learn from it?" Sally asked.

Both Sally and Rebecca stared at the younger woman, waiting to see her response.

Marjane smiled.

"I learned that sometimes men need to be given a little push," she said.

Rebecca opened her arms, pulling Marjane into an embrace. "I have a feeling that the time will come, and soon, when I'll have a sister-in-law," she said. "And I can't think of anyone I would rather have."

CHAPTER TWENTY-SEVEN

Since MacMurtry didn't particularly want to work as a team, and didn't even want to go into town with him, Slater decided to go into town by himself. It was just coming on dusk as he rode into Audubon, and he saw the lamplighter at the top of his ladder at one of the lamp poles. Three of the ten city street lamps had already been lit.

Slater had come into town to kill Pearlie and Cal, but he had no idea who they were, and wouldn't recognize them on sight. His best bet, he realized, would be to sort of stay quiet and just watch and listen.

Slater learned long ago that the best place to find out about anything that was going on in town, would be in a saloon. There were four saloons in town and it just so happened that Slater, as a result of his "visit" with the Dolans, had some money to spend. His first stop was at the Watering Hole Saloon. As the evening progressed, Slater moved from the Watering Hole, to the Ace High, and the Brown Dirt Cowboy. He had not heard anything helpful in any of them, so he headed toward the Blanket and Saddle Saloon. He had purposely saved this one for last, because it was the most popular, and it was here that he had gotten the information about Jensen.

As Slater was conducting his tour of the saloons, Dalton and Cal were making their rounds of the town.

"Mostly all you have to do is make a presence," Dalton said. "If someone has it in mind that they are going to sneak into a store or a home to commit a burglary, seeing a lawman moving about might well discourage them. That's because most burglars are cowards at heart. They don't risk armed confrontations, they are sneak thieves."

Cal had done this exact thing for Sheriff Carson on a few occasions, so he didn't really need instruction from Dalton, but he let the young man go through his spiel anyway.

"Also," Dalton said as he continued with his orientation, "check all the doors and make sure they're locked, and take a look through the windows to see if there's anyone in there who isn't supposed to be."

"What about a safety check?" Cal asked.

"Good question. A couple of weeks ago I saw a candle burning in the front of Fahlkoff's clothing store. I figure Mr. Fahlkoff must have been looking for something, and forgot about the candle. It could have caused a fire."

With the rounds having been made, Dalton smiled. "Now, here comes the best part. Our final stop is the Blanket and Saddle Saloon, and the best way to check it is to go inside, have a beer, and see who is there, and if any trouble is brewing."

Dalton pushed through the batwing doors with Cal right behind him.

"Hello, Deputy," the bartender said, greeting Dalton as he and Cal stepped up to the bar. "You must be through with your rounds, seein' as this is always your last stop."

"Hello, George. Yep, we've completed our rounds."

"How are the new deputies working out for you?" George asked as, without being told, he drew two beers and set them in front of Dalton and Cal. "This is one of them, isn't it?"

"Yes, though you might say that he is a temporary deputy," Dalton replied. "You've probably already heard that my Uncle Kirby has come to town to help out while Sheriff Peabody is recovering. When he came, he brought two of his friends with him, Pearlie and Cal. This is Cal . . ." Dalton paused in midsentence and looked over at Cal, "You know what, Cal? As long as I've known you, I don't think I've ever heard your last name."

"It's Wood, Calvin Wood, but I never use it," Cal said. "I'm afraid that if I started using it, why, the next thing you know folks would be calling me Mister Wood, 'n that just wouldn't set well with me."

"Your uncle is a fella by the name of Kirby?" George asked.

"Actually, he isn't really my uncle, he's my halfsister's uncle," Dalton said.

"Hmm, I heard you had an uncle that came to help you out, but I was given to believe that it was a feller by the name of Smoke Jensen."

Dalton laughed. "That's him. His real name is Kirby Jensen, but everyone calls him Smoke."

"So," George said to Cal, "if you come to town with Smoke Jensen, then that means you're one of the fellas that prevented the stagecoach robbery."

"He sure is!" Dalton said, answering for Cal. "He, Smoke, and Pearlie stopped the stagecoach robbers in their tracks."

George pushed the money Dalton had given him for the two beers back across the bar. "In that case your money is no good in here. Your beer is on the house."

"Why, I thank you, sir," Cal said, lifting his beer in salute.

"Ha!" one of the other patrons said. "Cal here, 'n them other two did more than stop 'em in their tracks. They's six outlaws that's all stretched out down at Ponder's undertakin' shop right now. It seems they bit off a mite more'n they could chew."

"You got that right," another said. He lifted his beer mug. "Here's to you, Deputy Conyers, 'n to them three men you brought here to help keep the peace."

"Hear, hear," another patron added, and all in the saloon lifted their mugs.

There was a saloon patron standing midway down the bar from Dalton and Cal, and he did not join the others in lifting his mug in salute. Instead, Ed Slater was looking at Cal in the mirror. He wasn't just looking at him, he was studying him. He knew he had never met this man before, and yet, as he continued to study him there was something familiar about him. The problem was, he just couldn't quite place it.

Then he remembered.

As if reliving the moment, he saw himself stepping onto the train in Ft. Worth for the two-hour trip to Weatherford, a trip he didn't complete by train. He remembered, now, that he had seen three men and a woman sitting together in that car, and this man, Cal, was one of the three men. And if there were three of them, and Cal was one of them, the other two had to be Smoke Jensen and the one called Pearlie.

Slater had not gotten a good look at the man who threw him off the train, but he was certain that it was either this man or one of the other two who had been with him. There were only two other men in that car, and both of those men had long white beards. The man who had tossed him from the train was clean-shaven.

Was it this man?

Slater studied him as closely as he could in the mirror, but he simply had not gotten a good enough look at the man who tossed him to know if this was the one who did it.

The truth is, at this point it didn't matter whether Cal was the one who threw him off or not. It had to be one of the three, and as far as Slater was concerned, it wouldn't make any difference to him, whether he killed the man who had actually thrown him off, or his friend. He would derive just as much personal satisfaction from it, no matter who it was.

Son of a bitch! He thought. The man who threw him off the train had to be one of the three that Lanagan wanted killed! That meant that there would be more than personal satisfaction involved in killing him, it also meant that Lanagan would pay five hundred dollars to whoever killed him.

And right now it looked as if he was the one best situated to collect the money.

What if Cal recognized him? Slater could remember making such a thing with the young woman that all the others in the car, including Cal, must have seen him.

He turned so that he was presenting three quarters of his back to Cal, enough to avoid being seen, but not so much as to make it obvious.

"Would you gentlemen like something from the kitchen?" George asked Dalton and Cal. "Like the beer, for you two, the food will be on the house."

"No, thank you, George, but we're going to join my sister and brother in law, Marjane, Uncle Kirby, and Pearlie down at the Palace Café," Dalton answered.

George chuckled. "Well, I can't say as I blame you, Deputy. Not only is the company good, but the food will be much better. I'm afraid that bacon, beans, and cornbread is about all you can get here. I eat down at the Palace myself, from time to time."

Down at the other end of the bar, Slater, even though he had turned away so that he couldn't be easily seen, had been listening carefully to the conversation. He smiled, because his strategy of visiting the four saloons had paid off. He now knew that they planned to take their meal at the Palace Café. He couldn't have learned more if they had been talking directly to him.

"Is there a privy out back?" Slater asked.

"No, it's out in the middle of the street," George replied with a laugh. "Yeah, it's back there."

Slater knew exactly where the privy was. He had asked the question for only one reason. By inquiring about the privy, he was establishing the alibi he would need for carrying out the rest of his plan. Slater set his drink down then started toward the back door as if he were going to the privy. The half-drunk beer supported the belief, by those who watched him leave, that he would be coming back.

It had gotten considerably darker since he arrived in town earlier this same evening, and because there weren't any streetlights in the alley it was dark indeed. The waste drums in the outhouse had not been emptied for a couple of days, and as a result the odor behind the saloon was quite foul.

Anxious to get away from the stench, Slater started moving north along the alley, quickly leaving the back of the saloon. If the deputy sheriff and Cal said they were going down to the Palace Café, he knew the perfect place to set up the ambush.

Leaving by the back door had not only enabled him to leave the saloon without being noticed, it also provided him with the cover of the alley. There was virtually no ambient light in the alley, so Slater was able to proceed to his destination without being seen. Shortly after leaving the saloon, he reached the opening between the Sikes Hardware store and the Buckner and Ragsdale Mercantile. This was halfway between the Blanket and Saddle Saloon and the Palace Café. There were no windows on the adjoining sides of either store and the space in between the two buildings was pitch-black dark. Slater saw that he could stand no more than a few feet back from the street and be totally invisible. He got into position and waited for the two deputies.

Slater didn't have to wait very long before he heard the two men laughing and talking as they came from the saloon.

"I hope Pearlie hasn't eaten everything in the café," Cal teased. "I don't believe I've ever known anyone else with an appetite like his."

Dalton laughed. "Well now, I recall that you seemed to hold your own with him when Marjane had us all over for dinner."

"Yeah, well, Marjane does make a real good pot of chicken and dumplin's," Cal said.

This was the man he wanted, this was Cal. Slater drew his pistol and stepped up to the front of the opening, as far as he could get without exposing himself. Slowly, so as to make it the action as quiet as he possibly could, Slater cocked the pistol.

Just a few more steps, he thought. Yes, that's it—bring the five hundred dollars to papa.

"But I sure don't eat like Pearlie. I learned a long time ago not to ever get behind him in the chow line if you want . . ."

Cal's sentence was interrupted by the loud bang of a pistol shot, and for an instant, the dark space between the two buildings was illuminated by the brilliant light of a muzzle flash.

"Uhhn!" Cal groaned and he went down.

Dalton saw the flame pattern of the muzzle flash, and he heard the sound of a gunshot. Drawing his pistol, he fired back into the darkness, even though he had no real target. He heard the sound of someone running, and he thought about giving chase, but he didn't want to leave Cal.

"Cal!" he shouted, kneeling beside him.

A few others came outside then, some from The Watering Hole, and some from Ace High, both saloons being the closest occupied buildings. They had been drawn to the scene by the sound of the gunshot, and looking up at the anxious faces, Dalton recognized one of them.

"Phil, run down to the Palace Café. Dr. Whitman and a man named Smoke Jensen are having dinner there. Tell them I asked them to come, and tell them that I said it's an emergency!"

"Is he still alive?" Phil asked, nodding toward Cal's supine form. "You know they're going to ask me that," he said to justify his curiosity.

"I don't know if he's still alive or not. But if he is, he won't be alive long unless the doctor can see to him. Now, please, hurry!"

Phil nodded, then began running toward the café as Dalton took off his own shirt, then held it over the wound to stop the bleeding.

"Cal, answer me!"

Cal's eyes were shut, and he lay where he fell, without moving and without making a sound.

CHAPTER TWENTY-EIGHT

Immediately after he saw his target go down, Slater ran back up the alley to the rear of the Blanket and Saddle saloon. Then, going back into the barroom, he began hitching up his trousers, doing so in order to complete the illusion that he was just returning from the privy. Seeing that his beer was just where he left it, he stepped up to the bar and lifted it to his lips.

"I was about to pour your beer out," the bartender said.

"Do you do that often? I mean, throw a feller's beer out when he steps out to the privy."

"No, it's just that you . . ."

"Hey!" someone called out as he stepped in through the batwing doors. His shout interrupted the bartender in mid-comment.

"Bledsoe was right! That *was* a shot we heard, and that feller Cal, the one that's helpin' the deputy, 'n the one that was just in here? Well sir, he just got hisself kilt, is what he done."

"Where's he at?" one of the saloon patrons asked.

"He's lyin' down there in front of Sikes Hardware, deader 'n all hell."

Several of the customers hurried out of the saloon then. Slater, rather casually, drained the rest of his beer, then went out front and mounted his horse. He took a look down the street and saw that a crowd was gathering quickly. The excited shout of the man who had come into the saloon but a moment earlier replayed in his mind.

"Well sir, he just got hisself kilt, is what he done."

"Five hunnert dollars now, 'n five hunnert dollars to go," Slater said with a little chuckle, as he rode away.

Pearlie had just told the story of pulling Kenny and Lou out of the quagmire, and there was laughter around the table when someone came running into the café.

"Is there a Dr. Whitman here?" the man shouted.

"I'm Dr. Whitman," Tom said, looking up at the agitated man who was calling out for him.

"You better come quick, Doc. Deputy Conyers is with a man that just got hisself shot, 'n he's askin' for you. He's askin' for a feller by the name o' Smoke Jensen too."

"Cal!" Pearlie said. "Cal has to be the one who was shot!"

"Oh, heavens!" Sally said, the expression in her voice showing her concern. "The man who was shot! Was he killed?"

"I don't know, ma'am, but it looks to me like he most likely was kilt," Phil replied. "I mean he's just lyin' there 'n he ain't sayin' nothin', 'n he ain't moving none, neither."

"Oh, Smoke!" Sally was on the verge of tears.

"Don't go jumping to conclusions yet, Sally," Smoke said. "If he had been killed, I don't think Dalton would have sent for Tom."

"Yes, yes, that's right, isn't it?" Sally replied, the tone of her voice now, more hopeful.

At Phil's summons, everyone at the table was on their feet and they all followed the messenger out of the café. He didn't have to lead them to the spot because as soon as they were outside they saw a gathering crowd, and they hurried toward it.

"Make way!" Smoke shouted. "Make way for the doctor!"

The crowd parted and Tom hurried through to kneel beside Cal.

"Cal, can you speak to me?" Tom asked.

"Hi, Tom. Look's like I'm going to need a little of your doctoring," Cal said.

"Oh, thank God!" Sally said.

Tom felt of Cal's pulse.

"How is he, Tom?" Smoke asked.

"His pulse is strong."

"I've done what I could to stop the bleeding, Tom," Dalton said.

"You did well," Tom replied. "Let's get him down to Dr. Palmer's office."

Smoke and Pearlie each took an arm, Dalton took one leg and Phil the other, and they hurried Cal down to the doctor's office. Because it was after duty hours, the office was closed, but Dr. Palmer had given Tom a key so he could check in on Sheriff Peabody and by the time they got Cal to the office, Tom had already opened the door. They were met by Dr. Palmer, who, upon hearing the commotion had lit a lantern and was now standing in his reception room.

"Sorry to break in like this, Egan, but we have a good man who has been shot," Tom said.

"Take him back into the operating room," Dr. Palmer said. "Everyone else, stay back," he added.

"I've assisted my husband as a nurse, from time to time," Becca said.

Dr. Palmer looked at Tom.

"Yes, I would like to have her with me," Tom said.

"Then by all means, go. Deputy, we don't need all these people here," Dr. Palmer added.

"The rest of you please, wait outside," Dalton said to the others.

By now there were at least fifteen townspeople who had been drawn by curiosity. "Not you, Smoke, Miss Sally, Pearlie, Marjane, you all can wait here.

"The deputy is right, there is no need for us to be crowdin' in here," Phil said, responding to a look from Dalton. "We should make room for the folks that actual knows the feller that got shot."

"Thanks, Phil," Dalton said as Phil ushered the merely curious, out.

"What happened, Dalton?" Smoke asked. "How did Cal get shot?"

Dalton told of the shot that had come from the dark.

"I don't know, maybe I should have gone after him," Dalton said. "But I was worried about Cal."

Smoke shook his head. "No, you were right to stay with him. By stopping the bleeding, you probably saved his life."

"Oh, Smoke if . . . if Cal . . ." Sally started.

"Don't be making yourself sick with worry, Sally," Smoke said. "You heard Tom say that Cal's pulse was strong."

"And I can tell you for a fact that, that boy has the constitution of an ox," Pearlie said. "He's goin' to be all right, I know he is."

"I think so too," Sally said. "But a prayer certainly can't hurt."

"Prayer helped with my father," Marjane said. "I believe it with all my heart." She looked over at Dalton and smiled. "That is, prayer, and you asking your brother-in-law to come tend to him."

"That's one thing Cal has going for him for sure, Sally. Tom Whitman is here, in Audubon, right when we need him," Smoke said.

"Yes," Sally said. "That certainly is a positive thing."

"Dalton, you got a good look at the wound. How bad do you think it is?" Pearlie asked as they waited in the front of the doctor's office. It was obvious by the expression on his face that he was very concerned about the injury to his friend.

"There was blood all over his shirt and pants," Dalton said. "All I could tell was that he was hit right about his waistline."

"Where, exactly, was that?" Smoke asked.

"Seems to me like it was right about here," Dalton said, pointing to his own upper thigh.

"That's good," Sally said. "If it's there, it's too low, and too far to one side to have hit the intestines, or any of his vital organs."

"He'll be all right, Miss Sally," Dalton said. "Look at Sheriff Peabody, he had a bullet right next to his heart and would have died if Tom hadn't of gotten it out. Tom is the best surgeon in the country."

"I know, I know," Sally said. "It's just that, well, I have a very special place in my heart for Cal."

Sally sat there with her hands drawn up into fists, waiting, patiently, for further word on Cal. And as she waited, she recalled her first meeting with him.

It was back in Big Rock. She had just come out of a store with her purchases and was putting them away in the surrey when she heard a voice, a young voice, behind her . . .

"Put your hands up, lady, don't move, and give me all your money."

Turning toward her assailant, Sally saw a young man who could not have been much over fourteen years old.

"Now, how am I supposed to give you all my money, if I also have to keep my hands up, and not move?" Sally asked.

"Oh. Uh, well, you can move."

"Thank you," Sally said, and in a lightning move she drew her pistol and pointed it at the young man.

"How did you do that so fast?" the young man asked.

"Oh, I'm quite good at this," Sally said.

"Yes, ma'am, I would say that you are."

"What are you going to do now?" Sally asked.

"I don't know. I can't shoot you. Well, the truth is, I wasn't really going to shoot you anyway, even if you didn't give me none of your money."

"Any."

"What?"

"It isn't 'give me none of your money' the correct way to say that is, 'give me any of your money.'

"I ain't never had much schoolin'."

"We can take care of that."

"Ma'am? What do you mean we can take care of that?"

"When did you eat last?"

"I had me a biscuit and a piece of bacon yesterday or else maybe it was the day before. I don't rightly recollect."

"Give me your gun," Sally said, holding out her hand.

"You goin' to take me to jail?"

"No, young man, I'm going to take you home and give you a good meal. I'll also have my husband give you a job, if you want one."

A huge smile spread across the young man's face. *"Yes, ma'am, I'd purely love a meal, and a job."*

"What is your name?"

"It's Cal, ma'am. My name is Cal Wood."

"Cal, my husband and I own the Sugarloaf Ranch, and as of now, you ride for the brand."

As Sally sat quietly, remembering that first encounter with the young man who had, for all intents and purposes, become a son to her and Smoke. Cal was, at this very moment, being attended to in the back of the office, in the little operating room. Becca stood to one side of the operating table, holding a mirror in such a way as to catch the light of a kerosene lantern, and sent a bright beam right onto the purple and red hole in the flesh that marked where the bullet had entered. The wound was on the lower abdomen, just where the leg joined the trunk, and to get to it, Cal's trousers and drawers, both very bloody, had to be removed. His modesty was preserved by means of a towel.

Using a retractor, Tom opened the wound and looked inside.

"It doesn't look like the bullet hit anything vital," he said. "But I am going to have to go in for it."

"Here are the forceps," Dr. Palmer said, handing the surgical instrument to Tom.

"Suction," Tom said, and using a small, bulb-operated suction tube, Dr. Palmer sucked out some of the blood.

"Good, good, I see the bullet," Tom said and he went in with the forceps. It took but a second, and the bloody slug was removed.

"Becca, if you would, please, clean and disinfect the wound," Tom directed.

Rebecca poured carbolic acid onto a clean towel, then used it to clean around the wound until all that could be seen was the puffy red and purple hole. She lay layers of gauze over the wound, then expertly applied a bandage and began holding it in place with adhesive tape.

"Looks to me like you're going to have to get him some new trousers," Sheriff Peabody said.

"Andy, what are you doing out of your bed?" Dr. Palmer scolded.

"I just wanted to see what was going on."

"Get back over there now," Dr. Palmer ordered. "Unless you want to wind up on this table again."

"All right, all right," Sheriff Peabody agreed. "It's just that I recognize him as one of the men I just deputized, and seein' as he was shot, I feel a little responsible is all."

"I'd better go out front and give everyone a report,"

Tom said. "I expect there are a bunch of worried people out there."

"I'll be out there as soon as I finish with the bandage," Becca said.

"You go on out there too, Mrs. Whitman," Dr. Palmer said. "I can take care of this, and I'm sure you'll want to visit with your friends."

"Thank you, Doctor."

As soon as Tom and Becca stepped out into the reception room, everyone stood in anticipation of his announcement. Sally didn't have to ask about Cal, she could tell by the smiles on Tom and Becca's faces.

"Cal is going to be just fine," Tom said.

"Oh, thank God," Sally said and she turned to get an embrace from Smoke.

As Sally was hugging Smoke, Marjane hugged Dalton.

"I'm sure glad he's going to be all right," Pearlie said. "But I'm feelin' a little left out here in the huggin' department."

"Well, I can take care of that," Sally said, as she hugged Pearlie.

"Me too," Marjane said with a happy smile, hugging Pearlie in turn.

"When can I see him?" Sally asked.

"You can step back there now if you want," Tom said. "But he won't come out from under anesthesia for several more minutes, and even when he does, he'll still be a little groggy."

"But he'll know that it is me?"

"Oh yes, he'll know that it's you."

"Then I plan to wait until he wakes up."

"I'll wait with you," Smoke said.

"We'll all wait," Pearlie said. "That is, if it is all right with you, Tom, uh, I mean, Doctor."

Tom chuckled. "For that entire cattle drive we made together, you called me Tom. I see no reason for you to change, now."

"I'll step outside, I'm sure the others will want to know how Cal is doing," Dalton offered.

When Dalton stepped out front, there were at least a dozen people waiting. Phil was the first person he saw, so it was to him, that he addressed his remarks.

"Phil, I want to thank you for getting help back to us so quickly. I'm happy to say that my deputy, Cal, is going to be just fine," he said.

Those gathered around the front of the doctor's office cheered.

Half an hour later Becca returned to the front, where Smoke, Sally, Pearlie, Dalton, and Marjane were waiting.

"Cal has come out of anesthesia and Tom says that if you would like to come back and visit for a while, you can do so now."

All five of them followed Becca to the little room at the back of the doctor's office. Cal was awake.

"Well now," Cal said, in a weak voice. "I feel like a king or something, with all of you coming to see me like this."

"How do you feel?" Sally asked, then she chuckled, nervously. "That's a silly question. You've just been shot, how do I expect you to feel?"

"It don't hurt none too much," Cal said.

"It d . . ." Sally said, starting to correct his grammar, but she held back. "Good," she said, instead, "I'm glad the pain isn't too severe."

"Wait until the laudanum wears off, then it'll hurt like the devil," Sheriff Peabody said with a little chuckle.

"Papa!" Marjane scolded. "You needn't be so negative."

"Well, it won't hurt none for him to know, so he can be ready for it," Sheriff Peabody said.

"I've been shot before, Miss Marjane," Cal said. "Your papa speaks the truth."

"Cal, did you see anything?" Smoke asked. "Do you have any idea who shot you?"

"No idea at all," Cal said. "One minute I was walking toward the Palace Café, thinking about a good meal, and the next thing I remember is lying on my back, wondering why everyone was staring down at me. I don't even remember getting shot."

Smoke glanced over at Tom.

"It's called traumatic amnesia," Tom said. "Quite common. Some think that it may be the brain's way of helping by denying the patient's memory of such things as severe injury."

"It's possible that Cal wasn't even the target," Sheriff Peabody said. "Everybody knows that Dalton is now the acting sheriff. The shooter, whoever it was, may have been after him."

"Yes," Smoke agreed with a nod. "That could be the case."

CHAPTER TWENTY-NINE

The next morning the bright sunlight that fell through the window of the Del Rey Hotel pushed away the shadows and awakened Smoke. He looked over at Sally, who was still asleep. She had had a very difficult time getting to sleep last night because she was worried about Cal.

"You heard what Tom said. He said Cal was doing well," Smoke had told her in an attempt to comfort her.

"I know he did, but that doesn't stop me from worrying about him."

"Worry if you must, but try and set it aside at least long enough for you to get some sleep."

That discussion had taken place at about one in the morning. Smoke had no idea what time it was now, but from the angle of the light, he surmised that it was at least six, and perhaps even a little later than that.

A slight morning breeze filled the muslin curtains and lifted them out over the wide-beamed planking in the floor. Moving quietly, so as not to awaken Sally, Smoke got out of bed. A moment later, standing at the window, he looked out over the town, which was beginning to awaken.

Just down the street he could hear the ring of steel on steel as the blacksmith was already at work. Water was being heated behind the laundry, and boxes were being stacked behind the grocery store. A team of four big horses pulled a fully loaded freight wagon down the main street. From somewhere Smoke could smell bacon frying, and his stomach growled, reminding him that he was hungry.

"Uhmm, I didn't hear you get up," Sally said from the bed, her voice thick with sleep.

"I didn't want you to hear me. I didn't want to wake you up."

"You didn't wake me." Sally stretched and smiled at Smoke, who was looking over at her. "What are you looking at?"

Smoke chuckled. "Sally, ending a sentence with 'at'? Haven't you spent all the years of our married life teaching me the perils of ending a sentence with a preposition?"

"I'm sorry," Sally said, her smile broadening. "At what are you looking?"

"A beautiful woman who can often be a pain in the ass," Smoke replied with a little laugh. "But I find myself hopelessly in love with her anyway."

"I meant out on the street," Sally said.

"Yes, I meant that as well," Smoke teased.

"Oh, my, I hope there isn't a beautiful woman out there who has caught your fancy."

Smoke looked out onto the street again. "Oh, she's gone now," he teased.

"You're a nut," Sally said, laughing. "I can smell bacon cooking, and it's making me hungry."

"Good, I was hoping you would say that."

As Sally was getting dressed, Smoke splashed some water in the basin, washed his face and hands, then strapped on his gun, put on his hat, and sat down to wait for Sally to get ready.

Pearlie had spent the night at the doctor's office, stretched out on a hard canvas cot, sleeping in the same room as Cal and Sheriff Peabody. When he woke up the next morning, both Cal and the sheriff were snoring.

"You'll need to keep an eye on the wound, to make certain infection doesn't set in," Tom had told him last night. "Look for swelling, redness, red streaks coming from the wound, or drainage of pus from the wound."

Pearlie examined the wound closely, and found none of the visual signs. Tom also suggested that a fever might be indicative of infection, so he lay the back of his hand on Cal's cheek.

"Damn, Pearlie, you aren't planning on kissing me too, are you?" Cal asked before he opened his eyes.

"I'd sooner kiss a mule's ass," Pearlie replied. Then he chuckled. "On second thought, that would be about the same thing."

"So, what about it? Is infection setting in?"

"Aha, so you do know what I was doing."

"I heard Tom telling you what to look for. How'm I doing?

"From all that I can tell, I'd say you're doing pretty damn well. You aren't in a great deal of pain, are you?"

"Well, it does hurt, but I don't know what you mean by a great deal of pain. I wouldn't say that."

"Good! That means I can pronounce you on the way to recovery."

Cal chuckled. "Thank you, Dr. Pearlie. Now, does the doctor have any idea as to when his patient is going to get something to eat?"

"I'll bring you some breakfast," Pearlie promised.

"While you're doin' the fetchin' 'n carryin', I would be just real grateful if you would bring me some breakfast too," Sheriff Peabody asked. "Bacon 'n a hard fried egg on a biscuit would suit me just fine."

"I reckon a couple of those would suit me as well," Cal said.

"All right, but I plan to eat my own breakfast first," Pearlie called back to them. He met Tom and Becca just as he was about to leave.

"How are the patients doing?" Tom asked.

"They're both doin' all right, I reckon. They slept quiet, that is if you call snoring like a steam-powered saw quiet. And they're both hungry. I was just goin' for breakfast my ownself. Can I get somethin' for you two?"

"What did the patients order?" Tom asked

"Bacon and egg on a biscuit."

"Sounds like it'll be fine," Tom replied. "Nurse, would you like to help me with the new dressing?"

"I'll be glad to, Doctor," Becca replied.

"Nurse? Doctor? Damn, that sounds like you two don't even know each other," Pearlie teased.

"It's better that way," Tom replied. "It keeps us professional, when we need to be."

"Pearlie, what are you doin' standin' out there gabbing?" Cal called from the back. "You could have already eaten your own breakfast and had ours back here, by now."

"Aw, quit your grumbling," Pearlie called back.

Rebecca laughed. "Doctor, I would say that the patient is doing fine."

"I do believe you are right," Tom replied, and as he and Becca started toward the back of the office, Pearlie let himself out.

By the time he reached the Palace Café, Smoke and Sally were already enjoying a breakfast of bacon, eggs, and fried potatoes.

"Pearlie, how's Cal doing?" Sally asked, anxiously.

"He says it's sore where the bullet went in, but other than that he's feeling pretty chipper. Oh, and he's hungry."

"Hungry? Oh, that's a good sign," Sally said.

"Not necessarily. From what I know of Cal, he'll still be hungry two weeks after he's dead," Smoke joked.

"Oh, Smoke, please don't joke about a thing like that," Sally said, disquieted by Smoke's joke.

"You're right. That was sort of insensitive, wasn't it? Sorry."

The waiter approached Pearlie then, holding a small tablet. "Do you wish to order, sir?"

"Yes, I'll have four eggs, four pieces of bacon, a couple of patties of sausage, a side of grits, two biscuits, and a stack of pancakes. Oh, and four bacon and egg and biscuit sandwiches."

"Would you like a table in the kitchen next to the cook range, sir? I'm sure it would be much more efficient for you," the waiter asked.

Smoke laughed. "Don't ask him that, he may take you up on the offer."

"Smoke, who do you think shot Cal?" Pearlie asked. "We don't even know anybody here, so it can't be someone who is our enemy."

"We don't know anybody, but people certainly know about us now," Smoke said, "especially since the attempted stagecoach robbery that failed. I wouldn't be surprised if this man, Lanagan, didn't have something to do with it."

"You reckon Lanagan came into town just to shoot Cal?"

"Oh, I doubt Lanagan himself came into town. I think there are too many people who would recognize him on sight. But, I'm sure he was behind the attack, perhaps directing one of his people to make the effort."

"But why Cal?"

"Oh, it wasn't Cal in particular. It could have been any of us," Smoke replied. "I'm sure that Cal just happened to be the target of the moment. Whoever did the shooting saw Cal and decided to take advantage of it."

The waiter brought Pearlie's order, then spread it out on the table in front of him.

"Oh, I didn't tell you, keep these four sausage, egg,

and biscuit sandwiches warm for me until I leave. I'll be taking them with me," Pearlie said.

"Oh, that's a very good idea, sir," the waiter replied. "You certainly wouldn't want to take a chance on getting hungry before lunch, now would you?"

Sally laughed out loud. "Pearlie, I do believe the waiter has figured you out."

After breakfast Smoke and Sally accompanied Pearlie back to the doctor's office to deliver the sausage and egg sandwiches. The two men were sitting on the edge of their beds, with a small table between them.

"What do you say, Sheriff?" Cal asked. "It's up to you now, are you goin' to call me, or fold?"

Sheriff Peabody examined the cards in his hand. He and Cal, both recuperating from gunshot wounds, were now engaged in a two-handed game of seven-card stud, the cards laid out on the small table that separated the beds.

"How are you doing, Cal?"

"I'm doing great, I'm about to bankrupt the sheriff here. I've already won fifteen cents."

Smoke chuckled. "It looks to me like you two are in a pretty high-stakes game here."

"Watch me clean him out with this hand," Cal said.

Cal had a pair of aces showing, Peabody had a pair of jacks showing, and one of his sevens showing was backed up by another seven in his hold.

"I'm goin' to raise you by a nickel," Peabody said.

"You want me to think you have those jacks backed up, do you?" Cal asked as he examined his hole cards again. The pair of aces he had showing represented his entire hand.

"All right, I call. What have you got?"

"Two pair, jacks and sevens," the sheriff said, turning up his hole card, which was also a seven.

"Damn, you did have them backed up. Beats my aces," Pearlie replied.

"If you folks are just going to sit around and play cards, you won't mind if I eat your breakfast," Pearlie said.

"Don't even try," Cal replied. "Bullet wound or no, I'll come after you."

Pearlie put the four biscuit sandwiches on the table.

"Cal, when we talked last night you couldn't remember anything about what happened to you. Has your memory returned?" Smoke asked.

"No, sir, I don't remember a damn thing," Cal replied. "Oh, sorry for the cussin', Miz Sally and Miz Whitman."

"That's all right," Sally said. "After what happened to you, I suppose you have every right to express your frustration in such a way."

"It was Clete Lanagan," Sheriff Peabody said.

"How do you know?" Smoke asked.

"Oh, he may not have been the one who actually shot Cal, but whoever it was that pulled the trigger did so because Lanagan wanted it done."

"Hmm, that's just what you were saying, Smoke," Pearlie said. "It looks like you are right."

"You saw the shooter?" Sheriff Peabody asked.

"No," Smoke said. "Like you, I just made a supposition."

* * *

"I just earned myself five hunnert dollars," Slater said when he returned to the outlaw camp the next morning.

"What do you mean, you earned yourself five hunnert dollars? What did you do?" Lanagan asked.

"You offered five hunnert dollars apiece for killin' them two men that was with Smoke Jensen whenever you tried to hold up the stagecoach, didn't you? Well, sir, I got one of 'em. I shot 'im last night."

"How do you know he was one of 'em?" Lanagan asked.

"On account of I was in the Blanket and Saddle when the deputy 'n this feller come in. MacMurtry told us that them two that runs with Smoke was called Cal 'n Pearlie, didn't he? Well sir, the feller I kilt was called Cal by them that was in the saloon. 'N also, they was talkin' about the stagecoach robbery."

"You shot 'im there, in the saloon?" Lanagan asked.

"No, I didn't shoot 'im there. Hell, I didn't even say nothin' to 'im there. Mostly what I done is, I just listened to 'em talk, 'n that's how I learnt that they was goin' to have their supper down to the Palace Café. So, I just waited halfway between the saloon 'n the café, 'n when him 'n the deputy come by, I shot 'im."

"Did you shoot the deputy too?" Lanagan asked.

"No, I just shot the Cal feller."

"You shoulda shot the deputy too."

"You didn't say nothin' 'bout shootin' the deputy too. 'N you didn't offer no reward for killin' him neither. Onliest ones you've offered the rewards for is Smoke Jensen, 'n them two fellers, Pearlie and Cal. MacMurtry says he's goin' to kill Jensen, 'n me 'n MacMurtry have it worked out that I'm goin' to kill the other two fellers, Pearlie 'n Cal. 'N I done got a start on that, cause Cal, he's the one I shot."

"Did you kill 'im?"

"Yeah, I kilt 'im."

"How do you know, for sure? Did you stay there 'n check up on 'im?"

"Nah, I didn't have to. After I shot 'im, I went back to the saloon so's that nobody would think I'm the one that done it. 'N while I was there, someone come runnin' into the saloon sayin' that Cal was kilt. So, after that, I left. Oh, 'n I got some more news for you too."

"What news would that be?"

"Well, sir, it seems that the deputy in town, the one that's actin' as the sheriff now, ain't been able to raise a posse."

"How do you know?"

"I heard 'em talkin' about it in the saloon. He's been tryin' to get a posse up, but there won't nobody go with 'im."

"Yeah, well, the way them three men that was in the stagecoach handled themselves, that's more 'n likely all the posse Conyers would need," Lanagan said.

"That might be so if they was actual three of 'em left. But they ain't three men no more, seein' as I kilt one of 'em last night," Slater said.

"Except you don't know for sure whether you kilt 'im or not, do you? I mean you said yourself that you didn't actual see him dead. All you got is that someone come into the saloon 'n said that he had been kilt, but sometimes people just get excited 'n they talk about somethin' whether they know if it's true or not."

"The way he went down when I shot 'im, I'd be willin' to bet that he's deader 'n a doornail, now."

"I would like to know for sure."

"Hey, Lanagan, maybe a couple of us ought to go to town to see if he really was kilt," Bo Higgins suggested. "They ain't nobody in town that's ever seen me before."

"Ain't nobody in town ever seen me before, neither," Jay Garland said. "Me 'n Higgins could find out for sure, for you."

"All right, you two go into town 'n see what's goin' on," Lanagan ordered.

Garland and Higgins looked at each other and smiled.

"Yes, sir!" Higgins said.

"But remember, you're going in town to find out some information, you ain't going in town to pleasure the women."

"But we can have a few drinks, can't we?" Higgins asked. "I mean, the best place to find out anything is in a saloon."

"All right, you can have a few drinks. But don't forget what you're there for," Lanagan said.

"Come on, Jay," Higgins said. "Let's go into town 'n have us a little look around."

Hatchett MacMurtry had listened in on the conversation between Slater and Lanagan, but he had not participated in it. He had heard Garland and Higgins offer to go into town, and watched them leave, but again, said nothing. Not until the two men were gone, and the remaining men of Lanagan's gang had found some way to pass the time, did MacMurtry leave.

MacMurtry had one thing in mind, and that was to kill Smoke Jensen. The one-thousand-dollar reward offered by Lanagan was a good thing, but he was determined to kill Jensen whether there was a reward for him or not. He left the encampment without saying anything to any of the others, because he didn't want anyone volunteering their help. He wanted the personal satisfaction of killing Smoke Jensen all by himself.

CHAPTER THIRTY

Jay Garland and Bo Higgins sat in the Watering Hole, nursing their beers. This was the third saloon they had been in, and so far they had learned nothing about anyone having been shot the night before.

"If you ask me, it didn't never even happen," Garland said. "On account if it had, seems to me like folks would be talkin' 'bout it all over town."

"You sayin' you think Slater lied about it? That he didn't shoot nobody?"

"He might 'a took a shot, but it was dark, 'n he said his ownself that he run soon as he shot. I'm thinkin' maybe if he did shoot, why he just plain missed."

"Yeah, I'm beginnin' to think . . ."

"Do any of you know that feller that was kilt last night?" someone asked of nobody in particular.

"Are you talkin' 'bout one o' them new men that's come in to deputy with Conyers?"

"Is that who it was? I just heard that someone was shot 'n kilt last night, but I didn't know who it was."

"Yeah, it was one o' them that's come to help the deputy, but I don't know his name."

"He ain't dead," one of the others said.

"What are you talkin' about, Travis? What do you mean he ain't dead? I was in the Blanket and Saddle last night when Tobin stuck his head in 'n said he was kilt."

"Tobin was wrong. He warn't kilt, he's down the doc's office now. The doc's got him lyin' in the back along with the sheriff," Travis said.

"How do you know he wasn't kilt?"

"I'll tell you how I know, Morris. I know, 'cause I was down there at the doc's office last night when they brought him in. He warn't actually even shot all that bad. They was able to take out the bullet 'n sew 'im up so that he's comin' along real good."

"Did you hear that?" Higgins asked, with a qualifying nod toward the men who were carrying on the conversation.

"Yeah," Garland said. "I heard it. So, it turns out Slater did shoot 'im after all, he just didn't do a very good job of it."

"Quiet, let's listen in, 'n see what we can find out."

Both Garland and Higgins stared into their beers as they listened to the ongoing discussion.

"Is it true that the feller that was shot was one o' the ones that was on the stagecoach when it was held up?" Morris asked.

"Ha! You mean when they *tried* to hold it up, don't you? The outlaws didn't get the job done 'cause they was all shot down," the bartender said, joining into the conversation between Travis and Morris.

"They wasn't all shot down," Morris said. "Least-wise, that's what Sam Parsons told me. And he ought to know, seein' as he was drivin' the coach. What he said was that one of 'em turned tail 'n run, soon as the shootin' started."

Garland and Higgins exchanged glances over that bit of information.

"Maybe so, but the rest of 'em was shot down," the bartender said, continuing his narrative. "Two of 'em is still standin' up down there in front of Ponder's undertakin' business, 'n the other four is stretched out inside."

"Damn, they must be gettin' pretty ripe, by now."

"Yeah, well, Ponder plans on buryin' 'em tomorrow, whether or not anyone claims to know them two that's standin' out front or not."

"They didn't nobody answer my question," Morris said. "Was the feller that was shot one of them men that was on the stage?"

"Yeah, the one that got shot was Cal, 'n he was one of the men that stopped the stagecoach from bein' robbed."

"We've found out what we need to know," Higgins said, speaking quietly to Garland. "What do you say we have us a drink or two, then go on back out to the camp?"

"All right. But there's one more saloon to check out first," Garland said.

"Why? Accordin' to what we just found out, the feller that Slater shot is still alive in this saloon, you think maybe he'll be dead in the other one?" Higgins asked.

"I ain't concerned about that. It's just that, as long as we're in town, seems to me like we ought to enjoy ourselves a bit, 'n visit all four of the saloons."

"Yeah," Higgins said. "Yeah, come to think of it, that's a pretty good idea after all."

The Weatherford stagecoach was moving quickly and smoothly down the Weatherford and Audubon Road. Julia Conyers and Tamara Greene were the only two passengers in the coach, and Tamara was talking in a slow, halting voice, often interrupted by quiet sobs. Julia had asked no questions to solicit such a response, but Tamara had opened up to her. Until now, Tamara had not spoken of the horrors she had witnessed when her father was killed, nor had she spoken of the indignities she had suffered.

Even as Tamara related the story it was if she were reliving it, because as she spoke, her facial expressions displayed the pain and her eyes filled with tears that flowed down her cheeks. At first Julia thought that perhaps she should stop Tamara because the memories were so painful to her, but then she realized that Tamara needed to talk about it, that this was necessary for her to get the terrible trauma out of her system.

"I don't know how long it was after Mr. MacMurtry left, before Mr. Smoke arrived. Some of Papa's cows had wandered over to Sugarloaf, and he was bringing them back. I'm sure glad that he did. I . . . I really don't have any idea what I would have done if he had not come when he did."

Julia took a silk handkerchief from her purse and handed it to the young girl.

"I am glad he came as well," Julia said. She smiled at Tamara. "And would you like to know what I am even happier about?"

"What's that?" Tamara asked as she wiped her eyes.

"I'm glad that he brought you down here to live with us. With both Dalton and Rebecca gone, it was beginning to get very lonely for Ben and me. Why, you came along at just the right time."

"I am so thankful to you for taking me in, as you did," Tamara said. "Of course, I'm thankful to Mr. Smoke and Miz Sally as well but . . ." Tamara paused in mid-sentence.

"But what, child?"

"They always seem to be so busy. And they travel a lot. Oh, not while I was with them, but I remember Papa talking about how much they traveled. I used to think what a wonderful and glamorous thing that must be, to travel all the time. But, as I have grown older, I can see the benefits of staying in one place." Tamara smiled through the tears then returned the handkerchief and reached out to hold Julia's hand as she did so. "And of course, I could not think of a more wonderful place to be than Live Oaks. It was so much a part of my youth."

"Your youth?" Julia laughed. "Heavens, child, you are still in your youth. You should enjoy it while you can."

A shadow passed across Tamara's eyes.

"No, ma'am, I have no youth, except in my memories. My youth was taken from me."

Julia felt a terrible jolt of pain as she realized that Tamara was right, her youth had been taken from her.

"AUDUBON!" The driver's shout came down into the coach, interrupting the moment. It was a welcome interruption as far as Julia was concerned.

When the coach pulled to a stop in front of the

Audubon Stage Coach Depot, Tamara saw Sally and Becca waiting for them, having been informed by a telegram Julia sent from Weatherford. One of the employees of the depot opened the door and helped them down. Tamara was warmly embraced by Sally, while Julia went into Becca's open arms.

"Well, look at you!" Becca said when she saw Tamara. "What a beautiful young lady my new sister turned out to be! This can't be the little girl who once chased me trying to put a frog down my dress, can it?"

"Oh! Did I ever do something like that?" Tamara asked, with an embarrassed gasp.

Becca laughed. "I'm afraid you did. But, what little girl hasn't done things in her past that would embarrass her now?"

"I can name several things you did," Julia charged.

"No, Mama, don't, spare me the embarrassment, please," Becca replied, joining the others in the laughter.

"Come, we have a room for the two of you at the Del Rey Hotel," Sally said. "I hope you don't mind sharing a room, it's the last one left."

"We don't mind at all," Julia said, answering for both of them.

"Mr. Bond, would you see to the luggage of my mother and sister, and have it sent over to the hotel?" Becca asked the employee of the hotel depot.

"I'd be glad to, ma'am," Mr. Bond replied.

Sister, Tamara thought. That was twice now that Becca had referred to her as her sister. It was a little thing, but it gave her the best feeling, and the greatest sense of inclusion of anything that had happened since that awful morning when her parents were murdered.

"Where is Mr. Smoke?" Tamara asked.

"He is doing something for Dalton," Sally answered. "I don't know if you have been told, but he's working as a deputy sheriff here for a little while. I do expect him to show up for dinner tonight."

"And will Pearlie and Cal be there as well?"

Sally and Becca looked at each other, and Tamara was troubled by the expression she saw on their faces as they exchanged glances.

"Pearlie will be there," Sally said. "But, you haven't heard about Cal. You couldn't have, there was no time to get word to you after it happened."

"After what happened?" Tamara asked, anxiously.

"Now, don't get too alarmed," Sally said. "Cal was shot but . . ."

"Oh, no! Cal was shot?"

"Yes, but he was not badly wounded, and he is recovering nicely. He just needs a few days of recuperation is all, so, no, he won't be coming to supper tonight."

"Where is he?" Tamara asked. "Can I see him?"

"Of course you can. He's down at the doctor's office and I know he would be very glad to see you," Sally said.

"I want to go see him."

"We'll go together," Sally said. "But, why don't we get you and Mrs. Conyers checked in first?"

The Ace High Saloon was across the street from the stage depot, and MacMurtry was just dismounting in front of the saloon when he saw the passengers step down from the stage. At first it meant nothing to him, beyond the mere greetings that occurred with the arrival of any stagecoach, but one of the women passengers caught his attention, and he stood there for a moment, staring at her.

It was Julia Conyers!

MacMurtry recognized her because he had once worked on Live Oaks Ranch, and Julia Conyers, who was Colonel Conyers' wife, was well known to everyone who worked on the ranch. She took an interest in the welfare of all the hands, so she was often seen in one capacity or another. And since she was quite attractive, she was the kind of woman one could remember.

If Julia Conyers was here, then that meant that Deputy Conyers really was the same Dalton he had known before. But why was Dalton Conyers acting as a deputy sheriff when his father was one of the wealthiest men in the state? Had there been some sort of falling-out between father and son?

That was possible. As he remembered Dalton, he was sort of a high-strung kind of person, always just on the edge of getting into trouble. Julia Conyers always put up with him better than the Colonel. It would be like her to come visit him, even if his old man had turned him out.

But who was the young girl with her?

He would have to find out. He wasn't sure exactly how he would do it, but he had a feeling that, somehow, he might be able to use one or more of these women to help him get to Smoke Jensen.

CHAPTER THIRTY-ONE

As she had promised, right after Julia and Tamara were checked in to the hotel, Sally took Tamara down to the doctor's office so she could visit with Cal.

"Just let me check in back to see if Cal and the Sheriff are ready to receive visitors," Dr. Palmer said.

"Don't tell Cal who is with me," Sally said. "We want to surprise him."

Dr. Palmer nodded, and stepped into the back. A moment later he reappeared.

"Cal is ready for visitors."

Sally went to the door, then, with a smile, indicated that Tamara should wait for a moment.

"Miss Sally, it's good of you to come see me," Cal said by way of greeting.

"I didn't come alone."

"Pearlie? You brought Pearlie with you?"

"No, the person I brought is a lot prettier than Pearlie."

"Well, Good Lord, Miss Sally, who *isn't* prettier than Pearlie?"

Sally chuckled, then turned to wave toward the

door, where Tamara had been waiting just on the other side.

"Tamara!" Cal said with genuine appreciation for her visit. "What a wonderful surprise!"

Cal introduced Tamara to Sheriff Peabody, then for the next several minutes they talked.

"How do you like Live Oaks Ranch?" Cal asked.

"Oh, it's wonderful there," Tamara said. "Mrs. Conyers and the Colonel have been just ever so nice to me."

"There's another reason you like it there, too, I'm told," Sally said, with a smile.

"Another reason?" Tamara asked.

"I'm told that you have a beau."

"Oh," Tamara replied with an embarrassed smile. "You must be talking about Billy Lewis. But he isn't my beau."

"Really? What is he then?"

"Well, he's my . . ." Tamara stopped in mid-sentence, then a huge smile spread across her face, "beau," she concluded.

"Oh, and here, I thought I was your beau," Cal teased.

As Sally and Tamara were visiting with Cal, Garland and Higgins were in the Blanket and Saddle Saloon. And it was there that Garland came up with the idea that he and Higgins could finish the job Slater had started.

"What do you mean?" Higgins asked.

"Think about it, Higgins. This feller Cal that they've been talkin' about is lyin' down there in the back of the doctor's office. We could wait 'til midnight or so, then sneak in there 'n kill 'im just real easy. That would leave only two of 'em left." He smiled. "And not only that, but we would be gettin' that five hunnert dollars that Slater is thinkin' he's a-goin' to get."

"Yeah," Higgins said returning the smile. "But it wouldn't be two left, it would be three, countin' the deputy."

"Hell, the deputy ain't nothin' a-tall. He couldn't do nothin' by hisself, which is why he had Smoke Jensen 'n them other two come down here to help 'im out in the first place."

"Maybe the deputy ain't much, but this feller Smoke Jensen is. You've heard 'em, how they are talkin' about 'im, 'n all. The way I been hearin' it told, why, they say that Jensen is the fastest man with a gun there is, or even was."

"Yeah, well, here's the thing. You put a whole bunch o' sticks together, 'n you can't hardly break 'em. But, you take 'em on at a time, 'n you can break 'em just real easy," Garland said.

Higgins looked confused. "We're goin' to break some sticks?"

"No, dumb ass, I was just tellin' you that to make a point. What I'm sayin' is, we'll kill 'em one at a time, 'n we'll be startin' tonight, with the feller that's a lyin' down there in the doctor's office."

A look of understanding replaced the confused expression on Higgins' face, and he smiled.

"Yeah!" he said. "Yeah, I see what you're talkin' about now. If we do it one at a time, why, we'll always have 'em outnumbered."

A man stepped into the saloon at that moment and stood just inside the batwing doors, surveying the bar area. Dull gray eyes were looking out from a rough, brooding face.

"There's MacMurtry," Garland said. "What's he doin' in here?"

"He said he was goin' to kill Jensen, remember?" Higgins replied.

"Yeah. Maybe we can work out somethin' so's that we work together."

"Huh, uh," Higgins said, shaking his head. "I don't mind goin' after someone who's lyin' already shot oncet, down in the doctor's office. But I don't want nothin' to do with Smoke Jensen."

"I ain't talkn' 'bout us goin' after Jensen. I'm just sayin' that maybe whilest MacMurtry is goin' after Jensen, it'll keep Jensen 'n the others busy, 'n it'll make it even easier for us to kill Cal."

"Yeah," Higgins said. "Yeah, I see what you mean."

MacMurtry, seeing Garland and Higgins sharing a table, got a beer, then walked over to join them.

"What have you found out about the man Slater shot?" MacMurtry asked.

"He warn't kilt," Garland said.

"So we're goin' to do it," Higgins added.

"Are you saying Slater didn't even shoot 'im?" MacMurtry asked.

"No, he shot 'im all right, only now, this feller Cal is down at the doctor's office lyin' there shot, but not dead," Garland said.

"And on account of he's already shot, it'll make 'im real easy to kill," Higgins said.

"But that don't mean that Slater is goin' to get any

of the five hunnert dollars, 'cause it's like Lanagan said, he wasn't payin' nobody money just for shootin' someone. The onliest way they can get the money is if they actual kill 'im, which is what me 'n Higgins is goin' to do," Garland said.

"You say he's down at the doctor's office?"

"Yeah, but don't you go gettin' no ideas about you killin' im. You want some of the money, you go find your own one to kill, either Jensen, or the other feller, Pearlie, I think he's called.

"I'm not interested in Cal or Pearlie," MacMurtry said. "Smoke Jensen is the one I want."

"You plannin' on goin' up ag'in 'im?" Garland asked. "The reason I ask is, I've heard he's most the fastest man with a gun there ever was."

"I plan to kill him," MacMurtry said, "but that don't mean I'm plannin' on havin' a contest with him."

"Yeah, well, whether you go up ag'in 'im or not, a feller like him is just real hard to kill. You got yourself a idea how you're a-goin' to do it?"

"I'm workin' on it," MacMurtry said. "When are you two plannin' on takin' care of Cal?"

"We figure on doin' it tonight, after ever' one is gone to sleep," Higgins said.

"Yeah, you do that," MacMurtry said. He saw Candy coming down the stairs with a man she had just entertained. "Just stay out of my way."

MacMurtry stood up and started toward Candy, who initially greeted him with a smile, but, as he came close enough to her for her to get a good look at him the easy smile changed to one that was obviously forced. He put a hand on her arm and started up the stairs with her.

"I don't much like him," Garland said.

"Yeah, if you ask me, they's somethin' about him that ain't quite right," Higgins agreed.

"If if warn't for the fact that killin' Jensen would help us rob the bank, I wouldn't care if Jensen kilt him."

Higgins laughed. "You know what would be good? What would be good would be iffin' they was to both kill one another."

"Yeah," Garland agreed.

Audubon was a different town at one o'clock in the morning. The saloons, which, but an hour earlier had been alive with conversation, laughter, and piano music, now sat dark and quiet. There were no signs of commerce, only the call of night insects, and the occasional bray of a mule from the freight yard.

Garland and Higgins, with guns drawn, moved as quietly as possible through the night. As they passed a house they were startled by the ribbony yap of a dog.

"What the hell?" Higgins shouted.

"Shh," Garland hissed. "Be quiet!"

In the back of the doctor's office, Cal, who had just gotten out of bed to use the chamber pot, heard Higgins' startled call. He was curious about who had called out, so he listened more attentively.

"There's the doctor's office."

The disembodied voice was quiet, though loud enough for Cal to hear it.

"How are we goin' to get in?"

"I can slide the lock back with my knife."

Cal moved over to the sheriff's bed and put his hand on the sheriff's shoulder. "Sheriff Peabody," he hissed. He shook the sheriff's shoulder, gently. "Sheriff?"

"What? What is it?" Peabody asked, groggily.

"I think we're about to have some company," Cal said. "Some unwanted company."

"What are you talking about?"

"Someone is about to try and come in here," Cal said. "And I don't think it's going to be a friendly visit."

Sheriff Peabody sat up, slowly.

"I don't think we should stay in bed. Can you get up?" Cal asked.

"Yeah. Where's my gun?"

"I think both of them are in the front of the . . ."

Right in the middle of Cal's response, they heard the front door open.

"Damn, too late now," Cal whispered.

"Whoever it is, I'm not up to fightin' them," Sheriff Peabody said.

"I'm not either," Cal said. "We need to hide."

"I've been here longer than you and, believe me, there's no place to hide."

Dalton had been on duty until ten o'clock, then Smoke took over. Smoke would be on until two, at which time Pearlie would take over. Pearlie would be on until six in the morning.

It was a little after one now and Smoke didn't have to be walking around the town, but he had found himself getting very sleepy, and he figured that some fresh air would wake him up. He had reached the end of the street and was about to cross over to come back, when he saw two men standing in front of the doctor's office. And if their presence there wasn't troubling enough, both were carrying drawn pistols.

Drawing his own pistol, Smoke ran down the street toward the doctor's office. He had no idea who the two men were, but he figured they were after the sheriff, or Cal, or both. He heard a gunshot just as he reached the front of the building.

Cal and the sheriff were backed into a corner, and in the light of the muzzle flash, Cal saw two men. One of them had fired into his bed.

"Son of a bitch! There ain't nobody in that bed!" one of them said.

"Drop the guns!" another voice called, and Cal felt a huge sense of relief when he recognized Smoke's voice.

"The hell we will!" one of the two men shouted and turning back toward the front of the office, they began shooting.

Smoke returned fire and for the next few seconds the room was filled with the roar of gunfire, intermittently illuminated by the light of the muzzle flashes, and perfumed with the acrid smell of gunfire.

Cal heard both men go down and he knew, even without a clear view, that both intruders had just been killed.

"Cal?" Smoke called, anxiously.

"We're all right, Smoke," Cal called back, relieved

to hear Smoke's voice. "Both of us are all right. What about you?"

"I'm fine, but I can't see a damn thing," Smoke said.

"Just to the right of the door as you come in, there's a desk, and there's a lantern on the desk," Cal said.

Cal heard the sound of a match being struck and a moment later a bar of golden light spilled through the door from the front office, then the light grew into an illuminating bubble as Smoke followed it into the back, carrying the lantern.

"You picked a good time to drop by," Cal said with a little chuckle.

"Well, I was in the neighborhood, and I didn't have anything else to do," Smoke said. Setting the lantern on the floor he knelt by the two men and examined them. It was immediately clear that both men were dead.

"Do you know either of them, Sheriff?" Smoke aske.

"As a matter of fact, I do," Sheriff Peabody said. "I've run across both of them a few times. That one is Jay Garland, and that one is Bo Higgins. They are a couple of no accounts. You did the world a big favor by taking them out."

"There's no doubt but that they came in here with killing on their mind," Smoke said. "The only question is, which one of you did they want to kill?"

"To tell the truth, Smoke, it didn't look to me like they were bein' all that particular," Cal said.

Smoke chuckled. "I don't think they were, either."

* * *

From the *Audubon Eagle:*

Murderous Attempt !

Foiled by a Brave Hero.

Our noble Sheriff Andrew Peabody lying in the confines of Dr. Palmer's recovery room, was joined recently by Calvin Wood, one of the heroes of the recent attempt to hold up the stage coach. As the two men were peacefully convalescing, they were set upon by two fiendish intruders who were bent upon sending both Sheriff Peabody and Deputy Wood to their graves.

Fortunately, their evil intent was thwarted when the two would-be murderers had their assassination attempt interrupted by the timely intrusion of the noted Western figure, Smoke Jensen. Mr. Jensen, acting as a deputy sheriff, was making his rounds when he happened upon the two brigands in the middle of their deed most foul. When they failed to respond to his demand that they drop their weapons, he stopped them by using his pistol. The two vandals were, themselves, killed and are now being introduced to eternal damnation in the fiery furnaces of the Devil's realm. Readers of this newspaper will recognize that Smoke Jensen, too, is one of the heroes of the thwarted attempt to rob the stage coach.

The two desperadoes have been identified as Jay Garland and Bo Higgins. It is not known, for certain, that the two men have any direct connection with the outlaw, Clete Lanagan, but that is generally believed to be the case. And if this is true, it means that Lanagan, and those evildoers in his company, are bent upon eliminating any opposition to the nefarious plans they have, not only for Audubon, but, no doubt, for all of Jack County.

That being the case, our community owes a vote of thanks to Deputy Dalton Conyers for stepping up to the task of serving as sheriff during the current incapacitation of Sheriff Peabody, and to the three men who have come, not only to assist him, but to defend our fair city in its time of peril.

CHAPTER THIRTY-TWO

"They're both dead," McCoy said. "Garland and Higgins broke in to the doctor's office and tried to kill Sheriff Peabody and this Cal feller that Slater said he kilt, 'n both of 'em wound up gettin' their own-selves kilt."

"So what you're tellin' me is that Cal ain't dead," Lanagan said.

"No, he sure ain't."

Lanagan looked over at Slater, glaring at him. "You told us you kilt 'im. Did you think you could lie 'n I wouldn't find out?"

"I thought I kilt 'im," Slater replied. "I seen 'im go down, 'n someone come into the saloon 'n said he was kilt. 'N anyhow I warn't lyin' none 'cause McCoy hisself just told you he was shot."

"Well, he wasn't shot good enough, else wise Sheriff Peabody and Cal couldn't have kilt Garland and Higgins."

"It warn't Peabody 'n Cal what killed Garland and Higgins, it was Smoke Jensen that done it."

"Damn," Lanagan swore, driving his fist into the

palm of his hand. "That means that that son of a bitch has killed eight of my men! We have got to get rid of him."

"Ain't that what MacMurtry says he's goin' to do?" Claymore asked.

"He ain't goin' to have no more luck doin' that, than Garland 'n Higgins had tryin' to kill Cal 'n the sheriff," McCoy said. "'N they was both lyin' down, most dead anyway when Garland and Higgins tried to do it."

"And it was Jensen that kilt 'em both," Claymore said. "Our only hope is that MacMurtry does kill 'im."

"Where is MacMurtry anyway?" Lanagan asked. "He went off to kill Jensen, but I ain't seen 'im in a couple of days."

"Maybe he's done been kilt too," McCoy said. "It's like ever' body is sayin', Jensen is a hard man to kill."

"I know someone who could can kill 'im," Slater said.

"Who?" Lanagan asked.

"Before I tell you, we need to talk about money," Slater said.

"We've already talked about money," Lanagan replied. "I'll give a thousand dollars to whoever kills Jensen."

"After the railroad money has been brought to the bank in Audubon, 'n we rob it, you're sayin'."

"Yes, that's the deal."

"If this feller that I'm talkin' about will do it for five hunnert dollars can I have the other five hunnert for setting it up?"

Lanagan stroked his chin and studied Slater for a long, quiet moment.

"You said yourself that we need 'im dead," Slater said. "'N this deal won't cost you 'ny more than you already said you was goin' to pay."

"All right, I'll go along with that," Lanagan agreed.

"Onliest thing is, this feller I'm talkin' about won't do it if he has to wait until we rob the bank before he gets the money. He'll be wantin' his five hunnert dollars soon as he gets the job done."

"Five hunnert dollars?" Lanagan asked.

"Yeah. I'm willin' to wait for my five hunnert, just like what you said. But I don't think this feller is goin' to be willin' to do that. He's goin' to want his money, soon as the job is done."

"How much you got left, Claymore?"

"I got about six, or maybe seven hunnert."

"How much, you got, McCoy?"

"Five hunnert."

"Joad?"

"I've got seven hunnert dollars left," Joad said.

"All right, you fellers come up with a hunnert dollars apiece, 'n I'll come up with two hundred. Slater, find this man you're talking about, 'n if he kills Jensen, we'll give 'im five hunnert dollars."

"That's a lot of money to have to be comin' up with now," Claymore complained."

"Think about it, Dingus," Lanagan said. "If we don't get rid of Jensen, we might never get the money that'll be put in the bank by the railroad. If we do get rid of him, why, stealin' that money will be like takin' candy from a baby."

"Yeah," Claymore replied, smiling in understanding. "Yeah, that's right, ain't it? All right, I'll put up my share."

"Me too," McCoy said.

"Joad?"

"Yeah," Joad said with a nod.

"Who is this man you say can kill Smoke Jensen for us?" Lanagan asked.

"His name is Proffer, Lucien Proffer."

"Lucien Proffer?" Lanagan stroked his cheek for a moment, then he nodded his head. "Yeah, he most likely could do it all right. Are you tellin' us you can get him?"

"Yeah, I can get 'im."

"All right, you get a-holt of 'im 'n tell 'im we'll give 'im five hunnert dollars as soon as Jensen is dead, but not one penny before."

"What's MacMurtry going to think about this?" McCoy asked. "He's the one you sent out to kill Jensen."

"I didn't send 'im out, he volunteered to go. 'N I ain't heard from him since. Anyway, it don't much matter none what he thinks," Lanagan said. "I want Jensen dead, 'n I don't care which one of 'em it is that kills 'im."

Longview, Texas

"Proffer? Is your name Lucien Proffer?" The question was cold, flat, and menacing.

The man being addressed as Proffer was tall with an olive-skinned face, pronounced cheekbones, dark hair, and very dark rather narrow eyes. At the moment he was standing at the bar of the Thirsty Lizard Saloon, and he didn't turn toward the speaker. Instead, he stared into his glass of beer with cold, droopy eyes.

"That's who you are, ain't it? Lucien Proffer?"

Not until then did Proffer take a look into the mirror to see who was challenging him. The speaker was a tall thin man with white hair and a white mustache. Proffer had never met him, but he had heard him described, so he knew who this was.

"Yeah, I'm Lucien Proffer. What's it to you?" Proffer finally replied.

"You want to know what it is to me, do you? There's a fifteen-hundred-dollar reward out for you, that's what it is to me."

"That's old paper, 'n it's from Kansas. There ain't no Texas paper on me."

"It might be old paper, but you ain't been caught yet, so it's still good," the white-haired man said.

"Ha! How do you expect to get me to Kansas?"

"Belly down over your saddle."

The others in the saloon had tensed up at the first challenge, and they stood transfixed by the drama that was playing out before them.

"What's an old man like you doin' still bounty hunting? You really think you're going to be able to collect that reward? How are you plannin' on collectin' that reward?"

"By killin' you."

"What's your name, bounty hunter?" Proffer asked.

"The name is Boyle. Barney Boyle," the bounty hunter replied. "I reckon you've heard of me."

Proffer had heard of the man that everyone on the run feared. It was said that he had gotten rich by bounty hunting, and he didn't actually need the reward money anymore. What he needed was the legal authority to kill people, and that he did with great relish.

"Really? You're plannin' on killin' me, are you?"

"I am. So step away from that bar and face me, you son of a bitch, 'cause I don't intend to hang for shootin' you without it bein' a fair fight."

Now the others in the saloon realized that this about to come to a deadly head, and they hurried to get out of the away. Tables and chairs made scuffing and squeaking sounds as they were scooted across the floor. Every patron in the saloon got up and moved back against the wall, out of the line of fire.

"It's four-fifteen," one of the customers said, glancing at the grandfather clock that stood against the back wall of the saloon.

"Four fifteen? What the hell does that matter?" one of the other saloon patrons asked.

"We're about to see somethin' we'll be able to tell our grandkids," the first speaker said. "I want to be able to remember ever' thing about it, even the time."

"Oh, yeah," the questioner said. "Yeah, you're right. This is goin' to be somethin' to behold."

"I told you to step away from the bar, Proffer," Boyle said, his voice showing even more irritation than before.

Proffer stepped away from the bar, then turned to look at Parker. There was an evil smile on his face. It was that, the smile, that elicited a collective gasp from the other patrons. They had expected fear, anger, but not a smile.

"Like I said, Boyle, that paper is old, 'n it's from Kansas. Hell, even if you was to kill me, you'd more 'n likely not even get to collect any reward."

"It don't matter," Boyle said.

"It don't matter? You're a bounty hunter, and you

tell me the reward don't matter? Then, if this ain't about the reward, it has to be personal with you."

"Yeah," Boyle said in a low, gravelly voice. "It's personal."

"Why? What are you tryin' to do, prove to ever' body that an old man like you can still get the job done?"

"Oh, I know I can still get the job done. No, this is somethin' else. This is about Lucy."

"Lucy? I don't know what your talkin' about. I don't know nobody named Lucy."

"How many women have you kilt, that you can't even remember their name?"

"What makes you think I've ever kilt a woman?"

"I was told you was the one that kilt her."

"You was told wrong."

"She's the one that told me."

"How could she have told you, if I had kilt her?"

"She committed suicide. Oh, you didn't pull the trigger, but you kilt her just the same. You left 'er pregnant."

"You're talkin' about Anabelle?"

"Lucy was her real name."

"So, some whore kilt herself. How should that matter to either one of us?"

"She was my wife," Boyle said.

"Is that a fact? Well, I understand now why she said she had never been with a real man before me," Proffer said.

With an anguished shout, Boyle reached for his pistol, but even as he did so, Proffer was drawing his own gun. Before Boyle even realized he was in danger, Proffer was pulling the trigger, and the bounty hunter went down with a bullet in his heart.

The others in the saloon looked on in total shock over what had just transpired in front of them.

"Is there anybody in here who didn't see him start his draw first?" Proffer asked.

Nobody disagreed, and several went over to look down at Boyle's body.

"He's dead," one of the men said, though his affirmation wasn't needed.

At that moment a boy came into the saloon, wearing a cap that said Western Union. He looked down at the body on the floor, then, frightened, stepped back.

"Boy, you got a telegram for someone in here?" the bartender asked.

"Yes, sir," the boy said.

"Well, deliver it, then get on out of here."

"It's for him," the boy said, looking toward Proffer.

Proffer held out his hand.

The boy handed him the telegram, then waited a moment for an expected tip, which didn't come.

"What are you waitin' for, boy? I told you, deliver your telegram and get on out of here," the bartender said.

"Yes, sir, but I normally get . . ."

"You normally get what?" the bartender asked, sharply.

"Uh, nothin', sir. I don't normally get nothin'."

"Then get."

The boy turned and, with one final look at the body lying on the floor, hurried out.

Proffer opened the telegram.

IF YOU ARE INTERESTED IN MAKING
SOME MONEY MEET ME IN FORT WORTH
YOUR COUSIN ED

It was nearly a month after Sheriff Peabody was shot, and two weeks after Cal had been shot, when Tom told both of them that they could go home. And in celebration of that event Marjane prepared a huge roast, inviting Tom and Becca, Dr. and Mrs. Palmer, Smoke and Sally, Pearlie and Cal, Julia and Tamara, and of course Dalton, to the sheriff's house for dinner.

Ever since her mother had died, Marjane had been acting as the woman of the house, taking on the responsibility at the young age of fifteen. And because her father had to run for reelection twice in that time, it had often been necessary to have social events for his campaign workers and supporters. Those affairs made Marjane quite proficient as a hostess, a talent that was much on display at the gathering.

After they were called to dinner and all were seated around the table, Sheriff Peabody stood, and by that action garnered the immediate attention of all present.

"I would like to propose a toast," he said, as he picked up his glass of wine. "First to you, Dr. Palmer. Dr. Whitman has assured me that if you had not done the things that needed to be done immediately after I was shot, that I wouldn't have lived long enough for him to get here." He turned his attention to Tom. "And to you, Dr. Whitman, for removing a bullet that was all but impossible to remove, and to you, Dalton, the best deputy I have ever had, for getting Dr. Whitman to come and treat me, and to you, Smoke, for saving my life when Garland and Higgins attempted to take it last week. And finally, to my daughter, for providing me with the comfort and love that has sustained me, not only through this recent ordeal, but also for the last six years, since my beloved Sara Lou died."

With the toasting completed, he held his glass out toward the others, who also lifted their glasses.

"Well said, Sheriff," Dr. Palmer replied. "Hear, hear."

CHAPTER THIRTY-THREE

When MacMurtry first saw the little cabin on Beans Creek, he knew it would be perfect for his needs. He didn't know who lived there, but he was prepared to kill whoever it was, just so he could use the cabin.

He rode right up to the cabin then dismounted, so that anyone who might be in the cabin wouldn't suspect anything. Walking up to the cabin, he knocked on the front door.

"Hello the cabin!" he called. "Hello, anyone here? I'm lost, and I need directions!" MacMurtry pulled his pistol, and held it down by his leg. What he intended to do was shoot the occupant of the house, as soon as the door was opened.

He knocked again, and when he got no reply, he tried the doorknob, surprised to find it unlocked. Pushing the door open, he stepped inside with his gun out in front of him.

The gun wasn't needed because there was no one here. Without putting his gun away, MacMurtry studied the inside of the cabin. There was no food, no coffee, no personal effects of any kind. There weren't even any clothes.

Not until MacMurtry ascertained that the cabin was empty, and had, in fact, been deserted for a long time, did he put his gun back in the holster.

The cabin would just right for the use he intended to make of it.

Now, all he had to do was go back to Audubon and keep his eyes open. He didn't want his quarry to get away before he was ready.

From the *Fort Worth Democrat:*

Murder Still Unsolved.

The fiend or fiends who perpetrated the heinous murder of Dan and Betty Ann Dolan remain at large. It is suspected that one or more itinerant cowboys, out of work for the season, may have stopped by the store, perhaps in search of a handout.

The Dolans were well known for their generosity, and no doubt word of their beneficence has traveled far and wide, inducing the destitute to call upon them to provide just enough assistance to enable them to reach their destination. It is believed that this was just such a case, where, rather than be grateful for assistance thus tendered, that magnanimity was repaid with unspeakable evil. The bodies of the husband and wife were found together in death, as so many remembered them in life, their marriage to be continued in eternal glory.

The sheriff has neither clue nor idea as to who may have committed such a horrendous deed, but asks for anyone who may have some information to turn it over to his office. In the meantime the search, fruitless though it may be, will continue.

Ed Slater folded the newspaper and put it away, smiling as he did so. Had one of the others in the depot witnessed the smile with a knowledge of the article Slater had most recently read, they would have been curious as to how such a depressing article could have brought about a reaction. What they would not know is that the smile was in recognition that, though it was he who committed murder, it was now abundantly clear that he was free of any suspicion of the foul deed.

"Mama, the train is coming!" a young boy called, rushing into the depot.

The boy's call was followed, almost immediately, by the whistle of the approaching train.

Lucien Proffer would be on this train, and Slater was here to meet him. Slater walked out onto the depot platform with the others, some to board the train and some to meet the arriving passengers. Slater was to do both. He would meet Proffer, then ride on to Weatherford with him. Two horses waited in the livery at Weatherford, one for Slater, and one for Proffer.

"Here it comes, Mama, here it comes!" the young boy shouted, excitedly.

The heavy engine rolled by with red-hot coals dripping from the firebox, leaving a glowing path between the tracks. There was screech of steel on steel as the train finally came to a stop. As the engine sat waiting on the track, its relief valves opened and closed rhythmically so that it almost took on a life of its own. The heaving sighs of escaping steam seemed to match that of those who were waiting, anxiously, for the train to depart.

Slater watched until the arriving passengers disembarked from the train, then he joined those who were boarding and, once aboard, stepped into the last daycar, moving all the way to the rear to take the last seat.

The train got away with a series of jerks, each jerk accompanied by loud clanks as the slack was taken up between cars. Quickly the train gained speed and was traveling at a smooth twenty miles an hour by the time the conductor came through, checking the tickets.

Not until all the tickets were punched, and the conductor had left the car, did a tall, dark man with a sharp-featured face come to the back of the car and take the seat beside him.

"How am I s'posed to make this money?" he asked.

"Have you ever heard of a man named Smoke Jensen?" Slater asked.

"No."

"It's worth two hunnert and fifty dollars for you to get to know him."

"You don't mean know him, do you?"

"Not exactly."

"Then two hunnert 'n fifty ain't enough."

"Three hunnert," Slater said.

"Five hunnert."

"Three fifty."

"Four hunnert, 'n I ain't goin' no lower," Proffer said.

Slater fought to hold in his smile. By getting Proffer to do the job for four hundred dollars, that left a hundred for him from the advance, and the entire five hundred, after the bank was robbed.

"You drive a hard bargain, Lucien. But you don't get any of the money 'til after the job is done."

"Tell me about this man, Jensen. Who is he, and why do you want him . . ." Proffer stopped, then looked around the car to see if anyone was close enough to overhear the conversation. Deciding that they were not, he added the last word. "Killed."

During the ride from Weatherford to Audubon, Slater started filling Proffer in on who Smoke was, and why he was to be killed.

"Maybe I'm not supposed to tell you this," Slater said, "but the group I'm ridin' with has big plans. Onliest thing is, we can't put them plans into operation until after Smoke Jensen is kilt."

"What kind of plans?"

"Hunnert-thousand-dollar plans," Slater said.

"I want in on it."

"It ain't for me to say whether you can get in on it or not. That's up to Clete Lanagan. He's the boss."

"You say this plan ain't goin' to work unless Jensen is kilt?"

"Yeah."

"If you want him kilt, then I want in."

"All right," Slaters agreed. "I reckon if you kill Jensen, you got a right to join us. I'll talk to Lanagan about it, 'n tell 'im I think we should let you join up with us."

Slater was certain that, because they had lost so many men, already, that Lanagan would jump at the chance to have Proffer join them. But he didn't say so, because he thought it would be advantageous for Proffer to think that Slater had paved the way for him.

"All right, I'll kill this feller Jensen for you."

"A beer will wash down the dust from the ride," Slater said as they rode into town. He pointed to the Blanket and Saddle Saloon. "We'll go there. If you want to find out about anythin' that's goin' on in this town, that's the place to start. Oh, but I don't think we should go in together."

"Why not?"

"I just think it would be better that way. I'll go in first 'n you wait about a minute before you come in."

"All right," Proffer agreed.

Slater stepped inside.

"Tell me, Smoke, how is Cal doing?" the bartender asked the tall man who was standing at the bar.

"He's coming along well, George, thanks for asking," Smoke said. "He's back at the hotel now, and Dr. Whitfield has let the sheriff go home, too."

"That's good news. They're both good men, I'm glad to see that they're doing so well. You know, Andy was standing just about where you are now, when was shot. Yes, sir, the cowardly bastard that shot him was standing right over there on the stairs. Candy had just been with him, 'n she still feels guilty about I, but I told her, they don't nobody blame her for it."

"Hey, Mr. Jensen, is it true that there's been books wrote about you?"

Smoke chuckled. "Unfortunately, that is true. But

I hasten to tell you that I have authorized no such books, and they are all fiction. I have done none of the heroic exploits portrayed in them."

Slater listened to the conversation. Though Smoke Jensen had become the man who stood between the Lanagan gang and one hundred thousand dollars, he had never actually seen him before. This was a stroke of luck that he not only was able, now, to identify Smoke Jensen, the opportunity had also just presented itself for Jensen to be killed.

When Proffer came into the saloon, he walked down to the far end of the bar. Slater joined him.

"Do you see that tall man standing at the other end of the bar?" Slater asked, quietly.

"How can I miss the son of a bitch? It looks like a tree growin' down there."

"That's Smoke Jensen," Slater said. "I'll just get out of your way and let you go to work."

Slater took his beer and walked over to an empty table at the back end of the room.

Although Smoke didn't know who the man was, he had seen Slater when he came into the saloon a moment earlier. And it did not escape his observation that when the second man came in, the two had a brief conversation, before the first man left, and took the farthest table from the bar. Why would he do that?

After he left, the tall, dark man with the chiseled face remained standing at the bar, and Smoke saw that the man was studying him in the mirror. When Smoke looked up to lock eyes in the mirror, the man, pointedly, looked away.

Smoke was used to people recognizing him, and

then staring at him. He was a well-known personality, and people looked at him to satisfy their curiosity. But he also knew what it was like to be measured as a target, and that was exactly what was happening now.

In many life-and-death engagements over the past several years, Smoke had prevailed because he could draw faster and shoot straighter than anyone he had faced. However, as he had told the Colonel, anyone can be beaten. But Smoke possessed another talent, one that couldn't be taught, but had become more pronounced with time and experience. Smoke had the unique sense, a gut instinct is the way he would describe it, to know when someone was about to try to kill him. And he felt that now.

Smoke studied his beer, and though Proffer might have thought that Smoke hadn't noticed him, nothing could be further from the truth. Smoke was intently aware of the man standing at the far end of the bar, and every nerve ending of his body was alert and ready.

"You want another beer, Smoke?" the bartender asked.

"No, thank you, George, I think I'll just nurse this one a little longer."

"'Yes, sir, just let me know when whenever you want another one," George said, and because at the moment, only Smoke and the man at the far end were actually standing at the bar, George busied himself by cleaning the empty glasses.

Smoke continued to monitor, in the mirror, the man at the far end of the bar, doing it in way that wasn't obvious. But the more he studied him, the more he was certain that the subject of his close observation was going to make a play.

Smoke decided to test his conjecture. He knew that if the man did intend to draw on him, he would want to do so when he perceived he had the maximum advantage. Smoke put it into motion by picking up his beer with his right hand, so that his gun hand would be occupied. However, he was keenly aware of the situation, and ready to react, instantly.

Proffer, seeing that Jensen's gun hand was occupied, and believing that Smoke was totally unaware that he was about to be challenged, took advantage of the opportunity that had just been presented.

"Draw, Jensen!" the man shouted from the other end of the bar.

The loud challenge shocked everyone else in the bar, who had no inkling that they were about to be witness to a life-and-death confrontation.

Smoke was not shocked, and reacting quickly, he dropped the beer mug, drew, and fired before the mug even hit the floor.

The man fired as well, but his pulling of the trigger was nothing but a reflexive action, muscle memory in the finger of a dead man. Lucien Proffer fell facedown on the floor.

Slater, who had witnessed the scene from the back of the bar, was shocked, not that the shooting had occurred; he had expected that, but he was shocked at the results. He had believed that in a face-off gunfight between Proffer and Jensen, even with the conditions neutral for both parties, that Proffer would prevail. But this gunfight had taken place with Proffer having all the advantages. And yet, Proffer lost.

Smoke Jensen was going to be an even bigger problem than any of them had realized.

CHAPTER THIRTY-FOUR

From the *Audubon Eagle*:

Deadly Encounter
In Blanket and Saddle

Yesterday Lucien Proffer, a person with the reputation as a gunfighter that was thought to be nulli secundus, involuntarily surrendered that accolade when Smoke Jensen proved that Proffer's "second to none" was but a hollow claim. Proffer, in front of a dozen men and two of the Blanket and Saddle's "working ladies," pulled his pistol and shouted his kill or be killed challenge.

Proffer failed that test and has now been dispatched into eternity, no doubt wondering how he got there. There is no known motive for the shooting, though it is believed that Proffer wanted only to enhance his reputation by besting a gunfighter of Smoke Jensen's level.

James Ponder has said that Proffer's body will be consigned to Potters Field ere the sun sets on the morrow. He will thus lie close to the other villains who have been so recently consigned to their eternal sleep in the ground, as a result of their ill-advised encounter with Smoke Jensen.

Hatchett MacMurtry took in stride news of the failed attempt on Smoke Jensen's life. He had already encountered Smoke Jensen once, and watched him kill two men who, for all intent and purposes, had the drop on him. As a result of that incident he knew that Jensen could not be killed in any kind of face-to-face meeting; one would have to have to wait until some unique opportunity presented itself.

And opportunity did just that, three days later.

Sally had rented two horses, and she and Tamara went riding along Beans Creek. It was a swiftly flowing stream with wild flowers growing in colorful profusion along its banks.

"He is a nice boy, and we have been friends for as long as I can remember," Tamara said. She laughed, and held up her hand. "You know what he said? He said he wanted me to keep wearing Mama's ring on my left hand, so that people would think I'm married and not take me away from him."

"How do you feel about that? Is he somebody you think you would like to marry some day?"

"I don't know," Tamara said. "He might be, but now I think I'm too young to really . . ."

Tamara's sentence was interrupted by a gunshot, and the horse she was riding went down.

"Tamara!" Sally shouted, leaping down from her own horse and hurrying to Tamara, who, thankfully, had fallen clear of the horse. "Are you hurt?"

"No ma'am. Somebody shot my horse. Who would do such a thing?"

"I did it," Hatchett MacMurtry said, stepping out from behind a very close tree. He was still holding the gun in his hand.

"Who are you?" Sally asked, angrily.

"This is Mr. MacMurtry," Tamara said in a quiet, frightened voice.

"MacMurtry?"

"The other MacMurtry," Tamara said.

"I'm Cutter's brother," MacMurtry said. "And I have a bone to pick with your husband."

MacMurtry put a gun to Tamara's head. "Now, if you don't want to see me blow this little girl's brains out, you'll do exactly as I say."

"What kind of man are you, that you would threaten a little girl?" Sally asked.

"I'm the kind of man that is going do what I set out to do. I'm going to get my horse now, and I'm taking her with me. You wait right here until I get back. If you are gone, I'll kill her."

"Miss Sally?"

"I'm not going anywhere, honey," Sally said.

Sally watched as MacMurtry and Tamara stepped out of sight behind some trees. Though she normally wore a pistol, she had not done so this morning, and as she sat on the horse waiting for MacMurtry and Tamara to reappear, she cursed herself for her negligence.

Smoke was sitting in the sheriff's office talking to Dalton when Julia Conyers came in.

"Hello, Julia, what brings you by?" Smoke asked.

"I'm a little worried about Sally and Tamara," Julia said.

"Oh? Why?"

"Sally and Tamara rented horses this morning so they could go riding. Sally said they would be back by ten o'clock, but it's after eleven now, and they haven't returned."

Smoke's face registered his concern. "Hmm, it's not like Sally to be that late for anything. She's the biggest stickler on punctuality of anyone I know. Where did they go, do you know?"

"Tamara wanted to explore the creek, I don't know the name of it."

"Beans Creek," Dalton said.

Smoke smiled. "Well, if they stayed on the creek, it should be pretty easy to find them. I'll go look for them."

Smoke had followed their trail for about two miles. It was an easy enough trail to follow, two horses lightly loaded and moving at an easy pace. So far he had seen nothing to cause him any worry. Then, Smoke saw several buzzards circling ahead . . . too many for them to have found some small dead game. With a feeling of dread, he urged the horse into a gallop, then he saw what was attracting them.

The buzzards were circling over a dead horse.

The saddle was still on the horse, and Smoke dismounted to have a closer look. That was when he saw them . . . two rings attached to the bridle. He recognized both of them . . . one of them immediately, because he had bought that very ring for Sally. The other ring, he knew, was the one that Tamara had been wearing.

Why were the rings left here like this? It was obvious that they were here as a message of some sort, but why would Sally have done that? Why wouldn't they have just ridden double and come back home?

Then Smoke saw it . . . a little blood under the horse's head. He lifted the horse's head, and felt a flush of anger and concern. The horse had been shot.

Smoke stood up and looked around and saw then, that two horses had ridden away from this site. One of the horses was familiar, it was one of the ones he had been following. The other horse was new, and it was carrying a heavier load.

Whoever it was that shot the horse had taken Sally and Tamara, and because they were heading away from town, and Smoke was certain that whoever took them did not have good intentions.

But why the rings? Sally wouldn't have done that, more than likely she couldn't have done it, because Smoke was certain that she was a prisoner.

"You wanted me to find them, didn't you, you son of a bitch?" Smoke muttered, aloud. "That means you want me to come after you. Well, mister, whoever the hell you are, you are about to get your wish."

Smoke remounted, and began to follow the tracks.

* * *

Sally and Tamara were tied to chairs in the cabin that had once belonged to Captain Amos Purdy.

"There, now," MacMurtry said. "That ought to hold you two."

"Do you think Smoke isn't going to come looking for us?" Sally asked.

"Oh, I intend for him to come looking for you," MacMurtry said. "That's why I left your rings on the horse. I just hope he is smart enough to find them, is all."

"Why are you doing this?" Sally asked.

"Jensen killed my brother."

"I'm glad he killed him," Tamara said. "Mr. MacMurtry was a mean man."

"Evil best describes it," Sally said. "If ever there was anyone who deserved to die, it was Cutter MacMurtry."

"He killed my mama and papa."

"Yeah, well, it was your papa that got Cutter put in jail, 'n they was goin' to hang 'im. They would have done it, too, iffen I hadn't got him out of jail."

"It would have been better for everyone if the execution had been carried out," Sally said.

"Execution," MacMurtry said. "Yeah, I like that word." He held up his rifle. "That's what I'm going to do to Smoke Jensen. I'm going to execute him, while you watch, then I'm going to execute both of you." He looked at Tamara with a leering expression on his face. "I'm told my brother made a woman of you. Is that right?"

Tamara didn't answer. Instead, she looked at the floor as tears began to track down her cheeks. They weren't tears of fear, they were tears of shame.

"I tell you what, before I kill you, I'll just have a little fun with you. That way, before you die, you'll at least know which of us was the better man."

MacMurtry laughed, maniacally, then jacking a round into his rifle, he walked outside to wait for his prey.

"Smoke won't have a chance if MacMurty shoots him with that rifle," Sally said.

"Maybe when we hear his horse coming, we can scream really loud, and warn him," Tamara suggested.

"If that is the only option we have left, that is what we will do," Sally said. "But I'm hoping we can do more."

"What else can we do?"

"First thing we can do is get out of these ropes. Then I'll come up with something."

"How are we going to get out of these ropes?"

"Smoke taught me a long time ago how to be bigger than I am while I'm getting tied. And he had me practice it many times until I could escape."

"Bigger than you are?"

"I was able to keep space between my wrists and, here you go." Sally smiled, then reached out before her with the loose rope dangling from her freed hands.

Sally untied her feet, then she freed Tamara.

"What do we do now?" Tamara asked.

"I'll come up with something," Sally promised. Moving to the front window, she looked out toward the creek and saw MacMurtry standing behind a tree in such a way as to have a good view of any approach to the cabin, even if Smoke attempted to come around to the back side.

Sally studied the terrain for a while, then she got an idea. "Tamara," she said. "I'm going to need your help."

Ten minutes later, both Sally and Tamara had escaped from the cabin. Sally had given Tamara specific instructions on the role she was to act as Sally put her own part into play. Holding a short length of rope in her hands, she moved quietly up the line of trees, behind MacMurtry. He didn't see her, but then he didn't expect to see her, as he believed she was still tied up in the canyon.

When Sally was in position, she held both hands up over her head, which was a signal to Tamara. She saw Tamara walking from the front of the cabin down to the creek, doing so as if she were just taking a stroll.

"What the hell?" MacMurtry growled. How the hell did she . . ."

That was as far as he got before Sally stepped up behind him, and with one end of the rope in her left hand, put that hand on MacMurtry's right shoulder. While MacMurtry was reacting to that unexpected move, Sally looped the rope around his neck and brought it back. Then, she crossed her hands behind him, pulling the loop tight against his neck. She dropped her head below his shoulder blades so that, as he slapped his hands back, there was nothing he could grab onto.

Sally was a strong woman, though it wasn't strength as much as it was technique, and she had learned from Smoke how to do this. She continued the pressure while, at the same time, squatting down slightly to push her knees into the back of MacMurtry's knees. As a result of that action, MacMurtry couldn't stand straight enough to give himself any purchase.

MacMurtry clawed ineffectively at the rope that was digging into his neck, completely cutting off his oxygen supply. He tried, but could make no sound; he struggled, but could get no air. His struggles grew weaker until they ceased altogether. As he started down, Sally put her shoulder against him, pushing forward, until he fell facedown on the ground. Putting her knee in the middle of his back she continued the pressure on the rope until she got tired, then she stood up and looked down at his prostrate form.

"Is he dead?"

Sally looked up and saw Tamara standing just a few feet away. She hadn't seen her until then.

"Yes, he's dead."

"I'm glad," Tamara said.

Sally held her arms out, and took Tamara into her embrace. That was when she saw Smoke approaching.

"It looks like I'm a little late to the party," Smoke said.

"Better late than never," Sally replied with a wan smile.

CHAPTER THIRTY-FIVE

Sally and Tamara rode double on the way back to town. Smoke led MacMurtry's horse with the outlaw belly down on the saddle. As they rode into town their arrival drew some attention. They stopped in front of the sheriff's office.

"Hatchett MacMurtry," Dalton said, with a quick examination of the body. "Yes, I remember him. What happened?"

Sally told the story of their capture and escape. "When I saw the opportunity to prevent him from being any further threat to us, I took it," she said, without going into specific detail.

"You sure it was MacMurtry?" Lanagan asked.

"It was him, all right," Slater said.

"Jensen?"

"Yeah," Slater said, "Jensen." The smile that appeared before he continued, could almost be described as demonic. "But it warn't the Jensen you think."

"What do you mean?"

"They're tellin' in town that it was Jensen's wife that done it. I went down to take a look at 'im, 'n to look at his neck, you would think he was hung."

"That's ridiculous, how would a woman be able to hang a man?"

"That had me puzzled too, but some as was talkin' about it said that, somehow she got a rope around his neck 'n just squeezed it 'til he died."

"I don't know how she coulda done nothin' like that."

"I'm just tellin' you what the folks in town is all tellin'. Why, they've near 'bout made her as big a hero as Jensen hisself."

Lanagan, who was sitting at the table drinking a cup of coffee, drummed his fingers for a moment before he replied.

"Tomorrow," he said.

"Tomorrow?"

"I got a message from Drury. The money is in the bank. We'll take it tomorrow, only this time we'll do more than huzzah the town."

"What do you mean, do more than huzzah the town?"

"We will shoot everyone we see." Lanagan laughed.

"Ever' one?" Joad asked. "Women 'n children too?"

"Everyone," Lanagan repeated. "That way, they will be so busy taking care of their dead and wounded, that they won't have time to come after us."

"One hundred thousand dollars," McCoy said. "How much would that be for each of us?"

"Well, now that MacMurtry is gone, that leaves me, you, Claymore, Slater, and Joad. Five of us, that will be twenty thousand dollars apiece."

"Whoo wee," McCoy said. "Twenty thousand? What would somebody do with so much money?"

"If you're smart, you'll leave Texas," Lanagan said. "I'm heading for California."

"New Orleans for me," Slater said.

"Hey, Clete, aren't you forgetting someone?" Claymore asked.

"Who?"

"This feller Drury, at the bank. Don't your cousin get a share?"

Lanagan's smile could have come from the devil himself. "He'll be the first one we kill."

Over lunch the group of outlaws began spending their money. McCoy said that he intended to go to Wyoming and buy a ranch.

"Not me," Slater said. "I'm goin' to buy me a whorehouse in New Orleans. I'll make a lot of money, 'n 'cause they'll be my whores, why, anytime I want one, they'll be right there for me.

Joad had been quiet for the whole meal, and even as the discussion continued, he got up to leave the table. Once outside he saddled his horse then led it away, quietly, until he was some distance from the cabin. Not until then did he climb into the saddle and urge his horse into a gallop.

What Joad did not realize was that Slater had stepped out to relieve himself, and was curious at seeing Joad walking away, leading his horse, as if wanting to leave without arousing attention. Slater saddled his horse and followed, staying far enough behind so as not to be noticed.

* * *

"Tamara has been through a lot," Dalton said. "She saw her mama and papa being murdered, then she was . . . she had to endure . . . unspeakable acts. And now to have been taken by force and held as a prisoner then see someone else killed, right in front of her eyes." Dalton stopped and glanced over at Smoke.

"Don't get me wrong, I mean, Miss Sally had no choice. If she hadn't killed Hatchett MacMurtry, he surely would have killed them."

"Tamara is a strong girl," Pearlie said. "And things like this make a strong person stronger."

"Pearlie's right," Smoke said. "I got to know Tamara very well during the time she was with us. She is a strong girl."

The conversation of the three men was interrupted when the door to the sheriff's office was pushed open and someone stepped inside. There was a harried look on his face.

"Can I help you?" Dalton asked.

"I don't know," the man answered. He looked directly at Smoke. "You're Smoke Jensen, aren't you?"

"Yes."

"Jensen, do you remember me? It was a couple of months ago, back in Ft. Worth. I braced you in a bar there . . . or at least, I tried to brace you. But you got the better of me pretty quick."

Studying the man before him, Smoke recalled the scene. "Your name is Joad, isn't it?"

"Yes sir, it is. Vernon Joad. Uh . . . what I'm goin' to tell you is goin' to get me in a lot of trouble but, even if I wind up goin' to jail, this is somethin' that I've got to say."

"We're listening," Dalton said.

"First, let me tell you what I done, so's that I can get that out o' the way. I'm pretty sure you know about the bank robbery that happened in Salcedo some few days back," Joad began.

"We know about it," Dalton said.

"I was there."

"You mean you saw it?"

"More 'n that. I done it. That is, I was with Lanagan, McCoy, 'n Slater when it was done. I held the horses outside. I found out later they was someone who was kilt inside, then, as we was leavin' we huzzahed the town. I didn't do nothin' but shoot my gun into the air, but found out later that they was a little girl kilt."

"That's true," Dalton said. "There was a young girl killed."

"Well sir, I want you to know that I didn't have nothin' to do with killin' either one of 'em. 'N when I found out later about the little girl bein' kilt, well I felt very bad about it."

"Have you come to give yourself up, Joad? Is that why you are here?"

"Give myself up?" Joad was quiet for a moment, then he nodded. "Well, now that you mention it, I reckon I am givin' myself up. Only, that ain't why I'm here. I'm here to warn you."

"Drury Metzger," Dalton said a few minutes later, after Joad had been put in a jail cell to await arraignment and trial. "I never did like that son of a bitch. And now we know that he's working with Lanagan."

"Sounded to me like he's more than just working with him. He's kin," Pearlie said.

"Though, according to Joad, that relationship doesn't mean all that much. Lanagan intends to kill him anyway."

"I'll alert the town," Dalton said. "Now that I have you two with me, it won't be all that hard to raise a posse. We'll be ready for them when they come into town, tomorrow."

"No," Smoke said. "We can't take a chance on that. Joad said the Lanagan gang plans to shoot everyone they see, women and children as well. I wouldn't want to see that happen here."

"But, what else can we do?"

"Joad told us where to find them," Smoke said. "Pearlie and I will take the fight to them."

"I'll go with you," Dalton offered.

"No. You've got Joad to take care of, and Drury Metzger."

"But there are four of them, and two of you."

Smoke smiled. "Yes, we don't often get the odds this far in our favor."

"The son of a bitch has turned on us," Slater said, when he returned to the outlaw camp. Lanagan, Claymore, and McCoy were attentive listeners to his report.

"Why would he do that, 'n turn his back on all that money?" McCoy asked.

"There are rewards on all of us," Lanagan said. "And if you was to add 'em all up, it would come to more 'n twenty thousand dollars. Plus he wouldn't have to take a chance on gettin' shot in the robbery."

"But hell, he was with us in Salcedo," McCoy said. "Won't he have to go to jail for that?"

"They'll more 'n likely drop that charge," Lanagan said. "Or else they'll give him a real light sentence 'n the reward money will still be there for him when he gets out."

"So, if he's gone into town and told what we was fixin' to do, what do we do now?" Claymore asked.

"There it is," Smoke said, pointing to the little cabin that was set back from the creek by about fifty yards.

"How are we going to take it?" Pearlie asked.

"We'll surround it."

"Surround it?" Pearlie chuckled. "Smoke, maybe you didn't notice, but there are only two of us."

"Well, we will do what is known in military tactics as the 'two man surround something' maneuver."

Pearlie chuckled again. "Military tactics, huh? They teach that in West Point, do they?"

"If they don't, they should," Smoke replied. "Work your way around back. Then send me a signal as soon as you are in position."

"How am I supposed to signal you?"

"Use your knife to catch the sun. I'll pick up the flash."

With a nod of agreement, Pearlie kept behind the tree line that bordered Turkey Creek, and hurried upstream until he found a way to move away from the stream until he was in a position that was even with the back of the cabin. A few more minutes of maneuvering put him about ten yards behind the building, with the advantage of a rock to provide both cover and concealment.

Smoke caught the flash from behind the cabin, and using his own knife, he returned the flash.

"What was that?" McCoy asked.

"What was what?" Lanagan replied.

"I seen a flash comin' from the crick."

"Sonofabitch! That fool deputy has raised hisself a posse!" Slater said.

"No, he ain't," Claymore said. He was looking through the window. "There's only one man out there."

"Are you sure there is only one man out there?" Lanagan asked.

"I'm absolutely sure there's only one."

"Who would be crazy enough to come out here by hisself?"

Lanagan answered his own question, matched by Slater who spoke at the same time.

"*Smoke Jensen.*"

"Do you see him?"

"Yeah, I seen 'im. He's under that elm tree there."

"All right, ever' one, aim at the base of the tree, 'n when I count to three, fire," Lanagan said.

The others pulled their pistols and aimed at the target Lanagan had pointed out to them.

"One, two, THREE!"

* * *

Four bullets whizzed by Smoke's head, concurrent with the sound of gunfire. Had he not repositioned himself a second after flashing the signal back to Pearlie, he would be dead by now. He was at least ten yards distant from where he had been when he sent the signal.

"All right, boys," Smoke said, quietly. "I was going to wait a bit longer before I opened the game, but you're on."

Smoke had snaked his Winchester .44-40 from the saddle sheath a moment earlier, and now, as another coordinated fusillade emanated from the house, he raised up to one knee, lifted the rifle to his shoulder and fired four times, jacking a new shell into the chamber before the echo of the prior shot had faded. Smoke also heard Pearlie joining into the fight from behind the cabin.

The little valley exploded in gunfire and black powder fumes. Back in the lean-to stable, horses screamed and bucked in fear. All the windows in front of the cabin were shot out, and there were bullet holes in the wood.

Then all shooting from inside the cabin stopped, and there were several seconds of quiet, before a rifle barrel was poked out through one of the broken windows. A white cloth hung from the end of the barrel.

"Jensen? This is Lanagan."

"What do you want, Lanagan?"

"I want to give up. The others is all dead. You done kilt ever'one but me."

"All right, come on out."

Still holding the rifle, Smoke walked out into a clearing so he could have a good view of the house.

A tall man with a prominent scar on his left cheek came through the door. Smoke knew that the description he had been given, that this was Lanagan, though this was the first time he had ever seen him.

Lanagan was holding the butt of his rifle on his hip, the barrel pointing up, with the white flag still attached. Smoke didn't like the fact that he was still holding the rifle, and, as he saw the slightest twitch of a grin, he knew that something was wrong.

"Now!" Lanagan called, and as he brought his rifle down to bear, three more armed men came rushing through the cabin door.

Smoke had to made a quick decision. If he used the rifle, he would have to jack the lever up and down between every shot. And to be honest, he wasn't certain how many bullets he had left.

Throwing the rifle aside, Smoke made a lightning grab of his pistol, and he was firing as quickly as the four men were. The sudden and intense battle lasted no more than five seconds and was over even before Pearlie, who came running to the front of the cabin with his own gun in hand, had been able to join the fight. When the noise and the gun smoke cleared, four men lay in front of the cabin, two of them already dead, two more dying from their wounds.

"Son of a bitch," Lanagan gasped. "Son of a bitch, how did you do that?"

EPILOGUE

From the *Audubon Eagle:*

<u>J</u>USTICE <u>H</u>AS <u>P</u>REVAILED.

Publius Horatius Cocles was an officer in the army of the ancient Roman Republic who stood alone at the Pons Sublicius defending the bridge from an attacking army.

In a feat that would pay homage to Horatio at the bridge, the gallant Smoke Jensen fought and single-handedly defeated the iniquitous outlaws Clete Lanagan, Dingus Claymore, Edward Slater, and Seth McCoy.

Having been told of the evil plans of the brigands by Vernon Joad, himself a recent member of the nefarious band of villains, Smoke Jensen knew where to find them, and in the ensuing engagement, made quick work of the four outlaws.

From this same source of information it was learned that Drury Metzger, a banker in our fair city, was in league with Lanagan and the others, with the intent of relieving the bank of the rather substantial amount of money recently entrusted to its keeping by the Texas and Pacific Railroad. Metzger will soon be sent to that infamous Huntsville residence to serve a term of imprisonment which, no doubt, will be greater than that of Vernon Joad, for whom all expect will be treated with lenience, due to his conversion from iniquity to altruism.

As a happy coda to the story, Dalton Conyers, but late a deputy sheriff here in Audubon, took as his bride Martha Jane Peabody in a gala wedding ceremony. Miss Tamara Conyers, who by recent adoption became Mr. Conyers' sister, acted as bridesmaid. Mr. Calvin Wood, of Smoke Jensen's entourage, stood in as best man.

As articles and stories of the deeds of derring-do by Smoke Jensen continue to enlarge his already larger-than-life persona, it is hoped that this editor's account of his heroics will but add another saga that can but increase his luster.

Turn the page for an exciting preview!

JOHNSTONE COUNTRY. PATRIOTS WELCOME.

In this thrilling frontier saga, bestselling authors
WILLIAM W. JOHNSTONE *and* J. A. JOHNSTONE *celebrate an*
unsung hero of the American West: a humble chuckwagon cook
searching for justice—and fighting for his life . . .

DIE BY THE GUN. LIVE BY THE GUN.

With one successful cattle drive under his belt, Dewey
"Mac" McKenzie is on a first-name basis with danger.
Marked for death for a crime he didn't commit and
eager to get far away from the territory, he's signed on as
cattle drive chuckwagon cook to save his own skin—and
learned how to serve up a tasty hot stew. Turns out Mac
has a talent for fixing good vittles. He's also pretty handy
with a gun. But Mac's enemy is hungry for more—and
he's hired a gang of ruthless killers to turn up the heat . . .

Mac knows he's a dead man. His only hope is to join
another cattle drive on the Goodnight-Loving Trail, deep
in New Mexico Territory. The journey ahead is even
deadlier than the hired guns behind him. His trail boss is
an ornery cuss. His crew mate is the owner's spoiled son.
And the route is overrun with kill-crazy rustlers and
bloodthirsty Comanche. To make matters worse,
Mac's would-be killers are closing in fast.
But when the cattle owner's owner's son is kidnapped,
the courageous young cook has no choice
but to jump out of the frying pan—and into the fire . . .

NATIONAL BESTSELLING AUTHORS
William W. Johnstone
and J. A. Johnstone

DIE BY THE GUN
A CHUCKWAGON TRAIL WESTERN

On sale now, wherever Pinnacle Books are sold.

CHAPTER ONE

Dewey Mackenzie spun away from the bar, the finger of whiskey in his shot glass sloshing as he avoided a body flying through the air. He winced as a gun discharged not five feet away from his head. He hastily knocked back what remained of his drink, tossed the glass over his shoulder to land with a clatter on the bar, and reached for the Smith & Wesson Model 3 he carried thrust into his belt.

A heavy hand gripped his shoulder with painful intensity. The bartender rasped, "Don't go pullin' that smoke wagon, boy. You do and things will get rough."

Mac tried to shrug off the apron's grip and couldn't. Powerful fingers crushed into his shoulder so hard that his right arm began to go numb. He looked across the barroom and wondered why the hell he had ever come to Fort Worth, much less venturing into Hell's Half Acre, where anything, no matter how immoral or unhealthy, could be bought for two bits or a lying promise.

Two different fights were going on in this saloon,

and they threatened to involve more than just the drunken cowboys swapping wild blows. The man with the six-gun in his hand continued to ventilate the ceiling with one bullet after another.

Blood spattered Mac's boots as one of the fistfights came tumbling in his direction. He lifted his left foot to keep it from getting stomped on by the brawlers. A steer had already done that a month earlier when he had been chuckwagon cook on a cattle drive from Waco up to Abilene.

He had taken his revenge on the annoying mountain of meat, singling it out for a week of meals for the Rolling J crew. Not only had the steer been clumsy where it stepped, it had been tough, and more than one cowboy had complained. Try as he might to tenderize the steaks, by beating, by marinating, by cursing, Mac had failed.

That hadn't been the only steer he had come to curse. The entire drive had been fraught with danger, and more than one of the crew had died.

"That's why," he said out loud.

"What's that?" The barkeep eased his grip and let Mac turn from the fight.

"After the drive, after the cattle got sold off and sent on their way to Chicago from the Abilene railroad yards, I decided to come back to Texas to pay tribute to a friend who died."

The bartender's expression said it all. He was in no mood to hear maudlin stories any more than he was to break up the fights or prevent a disgruntled cowboy from plugging a gambler he thought was cheating him at stud poker.

"Then you need another drink, in his memory." When Mac didn't argue the point, the barkeep poured an inch of rye in a new glass and made the two-bit coin Mac put down vanish. A nickel in change rolled across the bar.

"This is for you, Flagg. I just hope it's not too hot wherever you are." Mac lifted the glass and looked past it to the dirty mirror behind the bar. A medium-sized hombre with longish dark hair and a deeply tanned face gazed back at him. The man he saw reflected wasn't the boy who had been hired as a cook by a crusty old trail boss. He had Patrick Flagg to thank for making him grow up.

A quick toss emptied the glass.

The fiery liquor burned a path to his belly and kindled a blaze there. He belched and knew he had reached his limit. Mac had no idea why he had come to this particular gin mill, other than he was footloose and drifting after being paid off for the trail drive. The money burned a hole in his pocket, but Dewey Mackenzie had never been much of a spendthrift. Growing up on a farm in Missouri hadn't given him the chance to have two nickels to rub together, much less important money to waste.

With deft instinct, he stepped to the side as two brawling men crashed into the bar beside him, lost their footing, and sprawled on the sawdust-littered floor. Mac looked down at them, then let out a growl. He reached out and grabbed the man on top by the back of his coat. A hard heave lifted the fighter into the air until the fabric began to tear. Mac swung the man around, deposited him on his feet, and looked him squarely in the eye.

"What mess have you gotten yourself into now, Rattler?"

"Hey, as I live and breathe!" the cowboy exclaimed. "Howdy, Mac. Never thought our paths would cross again after Abilene."

Rattler ducked as his opponent surged to his feet and launched a wild swing. Mac leaned to one side, the bony fist passing harmlessly past his head. He batted the arm down to the bar and pounced on it, pinning the man.

"Whatever quarrel you've got with my friend, consider it settled," Mac told the man sternly.

"Ain't got a quarrel. I got a bone to pick!" The drunk wrenched free, reared back, and lost his balance, sitting hard amid the sawdust and vomit on the barroom floor.

"Come on, Rattler. Let's find somewhere else to do some drinking." Mac grabbed the front of the wiry man's vest and pulled him along into the street.

Mayhem filled Hell's Half Acre tonight. In either direction along Calhoun Street, saloons belched customers out to continue the battles that had begun inside. Others, done with their recreation outside, crowded to get back in for more liquor.

Mac brushed dirt off his threadbare clothes. Spending some of his pay on a new coat made sense. He whipped off his black, broad-brimmed hat and smacked it a couple times against his leg. Dust clouds rose. His hair had been plastered back by sweat. The lack of any wind down the Fort Worth street kept it glued down as if he had used bear grease. He wiped tears from his cat-green eyes and knew he had to get away from the dust and filth of the city. It was dangerous on the trail, tending a herd of cattle, but it was cleaner on the wide-open prairie. He might get stomped on by a steer but never had to worry about being shot in the back.

He knew better than to ask Rattler what the fight had been over. Likely, it had started for no reason other than to blow off steam.

"I thought you were going to find a gunsmith and get some work there," Mac said to his companion. "You're a better tinkerer than most of them in this town."

Mac touched the Model 3 in his belt. Rattler had worked on it from Waco to Abilene during the drive and had turned his pappy's old sidearm into a deadly weapon that shot straight and true every time the trigger was pulled. For that, Mac thanked Rattler.

For teaching him how to draw fast and aim straight, he gave another silent nod to Patrick Flagg. More than teaching him how to draw faster than just about anyone, Flagg had also taught him when not to draw at all.

Rattler said, "And I thought you was headin' back to New Orleans to woo that filly of yours. What was her name? Evie?"

"Evangeline," Mac said.

"Yeah, you went on and on, even callin' out her name in your sleep. With enough money, you shoulda been able to win her over."

Mac knew better. He loved Evangeline Holdstock, and she had loved him until Pierre Leclerc had set his cap for her. Leclerc's plans included taking over Evie's father's bank after marrying her—probably inheriting it when he murdered Micah Holdstock.

Being framed for Micah's murder had been enough to convince Mac to leave New Orleans. Worse, the frame had also convinced Evie to have nothing to do with him other than to scratch out his eyes if he got close enough to the only woman he had ever loved.

His only hope of ever winning her back was to prove Leclerc had murdered Holdstock. Somehow, his determination to do that had faded after Leclerc had sent killers after him to Waco.

Mac smiled ruefully. If he hadn't been dodging them, he never would have signed on with the Rolling J crew and found he had a knack for cooking and cattle herding. The smile melted away when he realized Evie was lost forever to him, and returning to New Orleans meant his death, either from Leclerc's killers or at the end of a hangman's rope.

"There's other fish in the sea. Thass what they say," Rattler went on, slurring his morsel of advice. He braced himself against a hitching post to point at a three-story hotel across the street. "The House of Love, they call it. They got gals fer ever' man's taste there. Or so I been told. Less go find ourselves fillies and spend the night, Mac. We owe it to ourselves after all we been through."

"That's a mighty attractive idea, Rattler, but I want to dip my beak in some more whiskey. You can go and dip your, uh, other beak. Don't let me hold you back."

"They got plenny of ladies there. Soiled doves." Rattler laughed. "They got plenny of them to last the livelong night, but I worry this town's gonna run outta popskull."

With an expansive sweep of his arm, he indicated the dozen saloons within sight along Calhoun Street. It was past midnight and the drinking was beginning in earnest now. Every cowboy in Texas seemed to have crowded in with a powerful thirst demanding to be slaked by gallons of bad liquor and bitter beer.

"Which watering hole appeals to you, Rattler?" Mac saw each had a different attraction. Some dance halls had half-naked women willing to share a dance, rubbing up close, for a dime or until the piano player keeled over, too drunk to keep going. Others featured exotic animals or claimed imported food and booze from the four corners of the world.

Mac had become cynical enough to believe the whiskey and brandy they served came from bottles filled like all the others, from kegs and tanks brought into Hell's Half Acre just after sunrise. That's when most customers were passed out or too blind drunk to know the fancy French cognac they paid ten dollars a glass for was no different from the ten-cent tumbler filled with the same liquor at the drinking emporium next door. It was referred to as poor man's whiskey.

"Don't much matter. That one's close enough so I don't stagger too much gettin' to it." The man put his arm around Mac's shoulders for support, turned on unsteady feet, and took a step. He stopped short and looked up to a tall, dark man dressed in black. "'Scuse us, mister. We got some mighty hard drinkin' to do, and you're blockin' the way."

"Dewey Mackenzie," the man said in a hoarse

whisper, almost drowned out by raucous music pouring from inside the saloon.

"Yeah, he's my friend," Rattler said, pulling away from Mac and stumbling to the side.

When he did so, he got in the way of the dark man's shot. Mac had never seen a man move faster. The Peacemaker cleared leather so swiftly the move was a blur. Fanning the hammer sent three slugs ripping out in a deadly rain that tore into Rattler's body. He threw up his arms, a look of surprise on his face as he collapsed backward into Mac's arms.

He died without saying another word.

"Damn it," the gunman growled, stepping to the side to get a better shot at Mac.

Shock disappeared as Mac realized he had to move or die. With a heave he lifted his dead friend up and tossed him into the shooter. The corpse knocked the gunman's aim off so his fourth bullet tore past Mac and sailed down Calhoun Street. Almost as an afterthought, someone farther away let out a yelp when the bullet found an unexpected target.

Mac had practiced for hours during the long cattle drive. His hand grabbed the wooden handles on the S&W. The pistol pulled free of his belt. He wasn't even aware of all he did, drawing back the hammer as he aimed, the pressure of the trigger against his finger, the recoil as the revolver barked out its single deadly reply.

The gunman caught the bullet smack in the middle of his chest. It staggered him. Propped against a hitching post, he looked down at a tiny red spot spreading on his gray-striped vest. His eyes came up and locked with Mac's.

"You shot me," he gasped. He used both hands to raise his six-gun. The barrel wobbled back and forth.

"Why'd you kill Rattler?" Mac held his gun in a curiously steady hand. The sights were lined on the gunman's heart.

He never got an answer. The man's pistol blasted another round, but this one tore into the ground between them. He let out a tiny gurgling sound and toppled straight forward, like an Army private at attention all the way down. A single twitch once he hit the ground was the only evidence of life fleeing.

"That's him!" a man shouted. "That's Mackenzie. He gunned down Jimmy!"

Another man said, "Willy's not gonna take kindly to this."

Mac looked up to see a pair of men pushing hurriedly through the saloon's batwing doors. It didn't take a genius to recognize the dead gunman's family. They might have been chiseled out of the same stone—broad shoulders, square heads, height within an inch of each other. Their coats were of the same fabric and color, and the Peacemakers slung at their hips might have been bought on the same day from the same gunsmith.

Even as they took in how the dead man had found the quarry Leclerc had put a bounty on, their hands went for their guns. Neither man was too quick on the draw, taking time to push away the long tails of their coats. This gave Mac the chance to swing his own gun around and get off a couple of shots.

Flying lead whined past both men and into the saloon they had just exited. Glass broke inside and men shouted angrily. Then all hell broke loose as the patrons became justifiably angry at being targeted. Several of them boiled out of the saloon with guns flashing and fists flying.

The two gunmen dodged Mac's slugs, but the rush of men from inside bowled them over, sending them stumbling out into the dusty street. Mac considered trying to dispatch them, then knew he had a tidal wave to hold back with only a couple of rounds.

"Sorry, Rattler," he said, taking a second to touch the brim of his hat in tribute to his trail companion. They had never been friends but had been friendly. That counted for something during a cattle drive.

He vaulted over Rattler's body, grabbed for the reins of a black stallion tethered to the side of the saloon, and jumped hard, landing in the saddle with a thud. The spirited animal tried to buck him off. Mac had learned how to handle even the proddiest cayuse in any remuda. He bent low, grabbed the horse around the neck, and hung on for dear life as the horse bolted into the street.

A new threat posed itself then—or one that had been delayed, anyway. Both of the dead gunman's partners—or brothers or whatever they were—opened fire on him. Mac stayed low, using the horse as a shield.

"Horse thief!" The strident cry came from one of the gunmen. This brought out cowboys from a half dozen more saloons. Getting beaten to a bloody pulp or even shot full of holes meant nothing to these men. But having a horse thief among them was a hanging offense.

"There he is!" Mac yelled as he sat up in the saddle

and pointed down the street. "The thieving bastard just rounded the corner. After him!"

The misdirection worked long enough for him to send the mob off on a wild-goose chase, but that still left two men intent on avenging their partner. Mac put his head down again, jerked the horse's reins, and let the horse gallop into a barroom, scattering the customers inside.

He looked around as he tried to control the horse in the middle of the sudden chaos he had created. Going back the way he came wouldn't be too smart. A quick glance in the mirror behind the bar showed both of the black-clad men crowding through the batwings and waving their guns around.

A savage roar caught his attention. In a corner crouched a black panther, snarling to reveal fierce fangs capable of ripping a man apart. No wonder the black stallion was going loco. He had to be able to smell the big cat.

The huge creature strained at a chain designed to hold a riverboat anchor. The clamor rose as the bartender shouted at Mac to get his horse out of the saloon. The apron-clad man reached under the bar and pulled out a sawed-off shotgun.

"Out, damn your eyes!" the bartender bellowed as he leveled the weapon.

Mac whirled around and began firing, not at the panther but at the wall holding the chain. The chain itself was too strong for a couple of bullets to break.

The wood splintered as Mac's revolver came up empty. When the panther lunged again, it pulled the chain staple free and dragged it into the room.

The customer nearest the cat screeched as heavy claws raked at him.

Then the bartender fired his shotgun and Mac yelped as rock salt burned his face and arm. Worse, the rock salt spooked the horse even more than the attacking panther.

The stallion exploded like a Fourth of July rocket. Mac did all he could do to hang on as the horse leaped through a plate-glass window. Glittering shards flew in all directions, but he was out of the saloon and once more in the street.

The sense of triumph faded fast when both gunmen who'd been pursuing him boiled out through the window he had just destroyed.

"That's him, Willy. Him's the one what killed Jimmy!"

Mac looked back at death stalking him. A tall, broad man with a square head and the same dark coat pushed back the tails to reveal a double-gun rig. Peacemakers holstered at either hip quickly jumped into the man's grip. Using both hands, the man started firing. And he was a damned good shot.

CHAPTER TWO

Dewey Mackenzie jerked to the side and almost fell from the horse as a bullet tore a chunk from the brim of his hat. He glanced up and got a quick look at the moon through the hole. The bullets sailing around him motivated him to put his heels to the horse's flanks.

Again the horse bolted through the open door of a saloon. This one's crowd stared at a half-naked woman on stage gyrating to bad piano music. They were too preoccupied to be aware of the havoc being unleashed outside. Even a man riding through the back of the crowd hardly pulled their attention away from the lurid display.

Mac slid from the saddle and tugged on the reins to get the horse out of the saloon. He had to shoulder men aside, which drew a few curses and surly looks, but people tended to get out of the way of a horse.

Finally he worked his way through the press of men who smelled of sweat and lust and beer. He emerged into the alley behind the gin mill. Walking slowly, forcing himself to regain his composure, he left the

Tivoli Saloon behind and went south on Throckmorton Street.

The city's layout was something of a mystery to him, but he remembered the wagon yard was between Main and Rusk, only a few streets over. He resisted the urge to mount and ride out of town. If he did that, the gang of cutthroats would be after him before dawn. His best chance of getting away was to fade into the woodwork and let the furor die down. Shooting his way out of Fort Worth was as unlikely to be successful as was galloping off.

Where would he go? He had a few dollars left in his pocket from his trail drive pay, but he knew no one, had no friends, no place to go to ground for a week or two. Mac decided being footloose was a benefit. Wherever he went would be fine, with the gunmen unable to track him because he sought friends' help. He had no friends in Fort Worth.

"Not going to get anybody else killed," he said bitterly, sorry for Rattler catching the lead intended for him.

He tugged on the stallion's reins and worked his way farther south along Rusk until he reached the wagon yard. He patted the horse's neck. It was a strong animal, one he would have loved to ride. But it was distinctive enough to draw attention he didn't need.

"Come on, partner," Mac told the stallion quietly. The horse neighed, tried to nuzzle him, and then trotted along into the wagon yard. A distant corral filled with a dozen horses began to come awake. By the time he reached the office, the hostler was pulling up his suspenders and rubbing sleep from his eyes.

He was a scarecrow of a man with a bald head and prominent Adam's apple.

"You're up early, mister," the man said. "Been on the trail? Need a place to stable your horse while you're whooping it up?"

"I'm real down on my luck, sir," Mac said sincerely. "What would you give me for the horse?"

"This one?" The liveryman came over and began examining the horse. He rested his hand on the saddle and looked hard at Mac. "The tack, too?"

"Why not? I need some money, but I also need another horse and gear. Swap this one for a less spirited horse, maybe? And a simple saddle?"

"This is mighty fine workmanship." The man ran his fingers over the curlicues cut into the saddle. "Looks to be fine Mexican leatherwork. That goes for top dollar in these parts."

"The horse, too. That's the best horse I ever did ride, but I got expenses. . . ." Mac let the sentence trail off. The liveryman would come to his own conclusions. Whatever they might be would throw the gunmen off Mac's trail, if they bothered to even come to the wagon yard.

He reckoned they would figure out which was his horse staked out back of the first saloon he had entered and wait for him to return for both the horse and his gear. Losing the few belongings he had rankled like a burr under his saddle, but he had tangled before with bounty hunters Pierre Leclerc had set on his trail. The man didn't hire stupid killers. Mac's best—his only—way to keep breathing was to leave Fort Worth fast and cut all ties with both people and belongings.

A deep sigh escaped his lips. Rattler was likely the only one he knew in town. That hurt, seeing the man cut down the way he had been, but somehow, leaving behind his mare, saddle, and the rest of his tack tormented him even more.

"I know a gent who'd be willing to pay top dollar for such a fine horse, but you got to sell the saddle, too. It's mighty fine. The work that went into it shows a master leather smith at his peak, yes, sir." The liveryman cocked his head to one side and studied Mac as if he were a bug crawling up the wall.

"Give me a few bucks, another horse and saddle, and I'll be on my way."

"Can't rightly do that till I see if I can sell the stallion. I'm runnin' a bit shy on cash. You wait here, let me take the horse and see if the price is right. I might get you as much as a hundred dollars."

"That much?" Mac felt his hackles rise. "That and another horse and tack?"

"Don't see horses this spirited come along too often. And that saddle?" The man shook his head. "Once in a lifetime."

"Do tell. So what's to keep you from taking the horse and riding away?"

"I own the yard. I got a reputation to uphold for honesty. Ask around. You go find yourself some breakfast. Might be, I can get you as much as a hundred and fifty dollars."

"And that's after you take your cut?"

"Right after," the man assured him.

Mac knew he lied through his teeth.

"Is there a good restaurant around here? Not that it matters since I don't have money for even a fried egg and a cup of water." He waited to see what the man offered. The response assured him he was right.

"Here, take five dollars. An advance against what I'll make selling the horse. That means I'll take it out of your share."

"Thanks," Mac said, taking the five crumpled greenbacks. He stuffed them into his vest pocket. "How long do you think you'll be?"

"Not long. Not more 'n a half hour. That'll give you plenty of time to chow down and drink a second cup of coffee. Maggie over at the Bendix House boils up a right fine cup."

"Bendix House? That's it over there? Much obliged." Mac touched the brim of his hat, making sure not to show the hole shot through and through. He let the man lead the horse away, then started for the restaurant.

Only when the liveryman was out of sight did Mac spin around and run back to the yard. A quick vault over the fence took him to the barn. Rooting around, he found a serviceable saddle, threadbare blanket, bridle, and saddlebags. He pressed his hand against them. Empty. Right now, he didn't have time to search for food or anything more to put in them. He needed a slicker and a change of clothing.

Most of all he needed to leave. Now.

Picking a decent-looking mare from the corral took only a few seconds. The one who trotted over to him was the one he stole. Less than a minute later, saddle and bridle hastily put on, he rode out.

As he came out on Rusk Street, he caught sight of a small posse galloping in his direction. He couldn't make out the riders' faces, but they all wore black coats that might as well have been a uniform. Putting his heels to his horse's flanks, he galloped away, cut behind the wagon yard's buildings, and then faced a dilemma. Going south took him past the railroad and onto the prairie.

The flat, barren prairie where he could be seen riding for miles.

Mac rode back past Houston Street and immediately dismounted, leading his horse to the side of the Comique Saloon. He had to vanish, and losing himself among the late-night—or early-morning now—imbibers was the best way to do it. The wagon yard owner would be hard-pressed to identify which horse was missing from a corral with a couple dozen animals in it. Mac cursed himself for not leaving the gate open so all the horses escaped.

"Confusion to my enemies," he muttered. Two quick turns of the bridle through an iron ring secured his mount. He circled the building and started to go into the saloon.

"Door's locked," came the warning from a man sitting in a chair on the far side of the door. He had his hat pulled down to shield his eyes from the rising sun and the chair tilted back on its hind legs.

"Do tell." Mac nervously looked around, expecting to see the posse on his trail closing in. He took the chair next to the man, duplicated his pose, and pulled his hat down, more to hide his face than to keep the sunlight from blinding him. "When do they open?"

"John Leer's got quite a place here. But he don't keep real hours. It's open when it's needed most. Otherwise, he closes up."

"Catches some shut-eye?"

The man laughed.

"Hardly. He's got a half dozen floozies in as many bawdy houses, or so the rumor goes. Servicing all of them takes up his spare time."

"You figuring on waiting long for him to get back?"

The man pushed his hat back and looked over at Mac. He spat on the boardwalk, repositioned himself precariously in the chair, and crossed his arms over his chest before answering.

"Depends. I'm hunting for cowboys. The boss man sends me out to recruit for a drive. I come here to find who's drunkest. They're usually the most likely to agree to the lousy wages and a trip long enough to guarantee saddle sores on your butt."

"You might come here and make such an appealing pitch, but I suspect you offer top dollar." Mac tensed when a rider galloped past. The man wore a plaid shirt and jeans. He relaxed. Not a bounty hunter.

"You're the type I'm looking for. Real smart fellow, you are. My trail boss wouldn't want a drunk working for him, and the boss man was a teetotaler. His wife's one of them temperance women. More 'n that, she's one of them suffer-ay-jets, they call 'em. Can't say I cotton much to going without a snort now and then, and giving women the vote like up in Wyoming's just wrong but—"

"But out on the trail nobody drinks. The cook keeps the whiskey, for medicinal purposes only."

"You been on a drive?"

"Along the Shawnee Trail." Mac's mind raced. Losing himself among a new crew driving cattle would solve most of his problems.

"That's not the way the Circle Arrow herd's headed. We're pushing west along the Goodnight-Loving Trail."

"Don't know it," Mac admitted.

"Don't matter. Mister Flowers has been along it enough times that he can ride it blindfolded."

"Flowers?"

"Hiram Flowers, the best damned trail boss in Texas. Or so I'm told, since I've only worked for a half dozen in my day." The man rocked forward and thrust out his hand. "My name's Cletus Grant. I do the chores Mister Flowers don't like."

"Finding trail hands is one of them?" Mac asked as he clasped the man's hand.

"He doesn't stray far from the Circle Arrow."

"What's that mean?" Mac shifted so his hand rested on his gun when another rider came down the street. He went cold inside when he remembered he hadn't reloaded. Truth to tell, all his spare ammunition was in his saddlebags, on his horse left somewhere behind another saloon in Hell's Half Acre.

When the rider rode on after seeing the Comique was shuttered, Mac tried to mask his move by shifting in the chair. He almost toppled over.

He covered by asking, "You said the Circle Arrow owner was a teetotaler. He fall off the wagon?"

"His missus wouldn't ever allow that, no, sir. He upped and died six months back, in spite of his missus telling him not to catch that fever. Old Zeke Sullivan should have listened that time. About the only time he didn't do as she told him." Cletus spat again, wiped his mouth, and asked, "You looking for a job?"

"I'm a piss-poor cowboy, but there's no better

chuckwagon cook in all of Texas. Or so I'm told, since I've only worked for the Rolling J in my day."

Cletus Grant's expression turned blank for a moment, then he laughed.

"You got a sharp wit about you, son. I don't know that Mister Flowers is looking for a cook, but he does need trail hands. Why don't me and you mosey on out to the Circle Arrow and palaver a mite about the chance you'd ride with us to Santa Fe?"

"That where the herd's destined?"

"Might be all the way to Denver. It depends on what the market's like over in New Mexico Territory."

"That's fair enough. I might be willing to go all the way to Denver since I've never been there, but heard good things about the town."

Cletus spat and shook his head sadly.

"Too damn many miners there looking to get rich by pulling skull-sized gold nuggets out the hills. The real money comes in selling them picks, shovels . . . and beeves."

"Which is what the Circle Arrow intends," Mac said. "That suits me." He thrust out his hand for another shake to seal the deal, but Cletus held back this time.

"I can't hire you. Mister Flowers is the one what has to do that." The man looked up and down the street, then rocked forward so all four legs hit the boardwalk. One was an inch shy of keeping the chair level. When Cletus stood, his limp matched the uneven chair. He leaned heavily on his right leg. "Let's get on out to the ranch so's he can talk with you. I don't see much in the way of promising recruits."

Mac mounted and trotted alongside Cletus. The man's horse was a fine-looking gelding, well kept and eager to run. From the way the horse under him responded, Mac thought it would die within a mile, trying to keep pace.

"Yup," Cletus said, noticing Mac's interest. "The Circle Arrow has the best damned horses. Mister Flowers says it pays off in the long run having the best. We don't lose as many cattle—or drovers."

"That's good counsel. There're too many ways of dying on the trail without worrying about your horse dying under you." Mac thought a moment, then asked, "What's the trail like? The Goodnight-Loving?"

"The parts that don't kill you will make you wish you were dead. Drought and desert, Injuns and horse thieves, disease and despair."

"But the pay's good," Mac said, knowing the man tested him. "And if I'm cooking, the food will be even better."

"You got a wit about you, son. Let's hope it's not just half a one." Cletus picked up the gait, forcing Mac to bring his horse to a canter.

As he did so, he looked behind and saw two of the black-coated riders slowly making their way down the street. One pointed in Mac's direction but the other shook his head and sent them down a cross street. Being with Cletus Grant might just have saved him. The bounty hunters thought he was alone. That had to be the answer to them not coming to question them about one of their gang getting shot down.

The thought made Mac touch his S&W again. Empty. He kept reminding himself of that. The saddle sheath lacked a rifle, too. If they caught up and a fight ensued, and he couldn't bite them, he was out of luck.

"You got a curious grin on your face," Cletus said. "What's so funny?"

"Drought and desert, Indians and—"

"I get the drift. And I wasn't joking about them. The trail's decent enough, but the dangers are real."

"Nothing like I'm leaving behind," Mac said. That got a frown from Cletus, but he didn't press the matter. That suited Mac. He didn't want to lie to the man.

Not yet. Not unless it became necessary to escape the killers Pierre Leclerc had set on his trail.

Connect with Us

Visit us online at
KensingtonBooks.com
to read more from your favorite authors, see books
by series, view reading group guides, and more.

for sneak peeks, chances to win books and prize packs,
and to share your thoughts with other readers.

**facebook.com/kensingtonpublishing
twitter.com/kensingtonbooks**

Tell us what you think!

To share your thoughts, submit a review,
or sign up for our eNewsletters, please visit:
KensingtonBooks.com/TellUs.